Once Upon a Time: Adapting and Writing Fairy Tales

Lucy Calkins, Shana Frazin, and Maggie Beattie Roberts

Photography by Peter Cunningham

HEINEMANN ◆ PORTSMOUTH, NH

This book is dedicated to my parents, who taught me the magic of imagination. —Maggie

This book is dedicated to Melanie Brown, for always believing. G'gunk. —Shana

This book is dedicated to Colleen Cruz, for being all one could hope for in a colleague. —Lucy

firsthand
An imprint of Heinemann
361 Hanover Street
Portsmouth, NH 03801–3912
www.heinemann.com

Offices and agents throughout the world

© 2013 by Lucy Calkins, Shana Frazin, and Maggie Beattie Roberts

The authors and publisher wish to thank those who have generously given permission to reprint borrowed material:

From *Prince Cinders* by Babette Cole, text and illustration copyright © 1987 by Babette Cole. Originally published by Hamish Hamilton, 1987. Used by permission of G.P. Putnam's Sons, a division of Penguin Group (USA) Inc. and by permission of Penguin Books Ltd.

From *Cinder-Elly* by Frances Minters, copyright © 1994 by Frances Minters. Used by permission of Viking Penguin, a division of Penguin Group (USA) Inc.

Excerpt from *Owen* by Kevin Henkes. Copyright © 1993 by Kevin Henkes. Used by permission of HarperCollins Publishers.

Excerpt from "The Real Princess" from *The Random House Book of Fairy Tales* adapted by Amy Ehrlich, copyright © 1985 by Amy Ehrlich. Used by permission of Random House Children's Books, a division of Random House, Inc. Any third party use of this material, outside of this publication, is prohibited. Interested parties must apply directly to Random House, Inc. for permission.

Cataloging-in-Publication data is on file with the Library of Congress.

ISBN-13: 978-0-325-04735-5
ISBN-10: 0-325-04735-9

Production: Elizabeth Valway, David Stirling, and Abigail Heim
Cover and interior designs: Jenny Jensen Greenleaf
Series includes photographs by Peter Cunningham, Nadine Baldasare, and Elizabeth Dunford
Composition: Publishers' Design and Production Services, Inc.
Manufacturing: Steve Bernier

Printed in the United States of America on acid-free paper
17 16 15 14 13 ML 1 2 3 4 5

Acknowledgments

I N FAIRY TALES, it always seems that magic happens not just because of a secret spell, but also because a cast of characters emerges from across the land, ready to stitch and sew, to search and build. You can picture the scene: all the many supporters bustling about, whistling a happy tune as they help to prepare for whatever the gala event might be.

That pretty much defines the process of working on this book. The three of us have a longstanding, deep love for fairy tales, fiction writing, and constructing curriculum. But this unit needed to be built for the expectations of the Common Core State Standards, shaped by the experience of teaching fiction to third-graders, structured upon the platform of the other books in the series that would undergird this teaching, influenced by a new commitment to self-assessment and to writing with increased volume and stamina, and molded by a deep commitment to higher levels of cognitive challenge (and of DOK). All of that meant that producing this book was no small effort! The good news is that people gathered from far and near to help us create something that we believe is as magical as the genre itself.

We couldn't be more proud of this unit—and especially, we are proud of its freshness and sparkle. We're proud not only of the unit, but also of the way that people came together to help make the magic happen. Colleen Cruz, senior lead staff developer at the Project and co-author of *The Arc of Fiction*, read the first draft of a unit plan and worked with us to revise that draft. Then Gita Steiner-Khamsi, an extraordinary graduate of the literacy specialist program at Teachers College and co-author with Sarah Weeks of an upcoming novel, joined us in piloting the unit and studying students' responses. Gita worked in Lisa Jaffe's amazing PS 11 classroom, with Lisa and her youngsters, and many of Lisa's ideas left an imprint on the unit. Lisa and Gita were able to do this work because of Bob Bender's leadership—and we could never thank

him enough. Rick Dedek, Leslie Lemieux, and Cindy Soule provided us with a second chance to pilot this unit and lent their enthusiasm and thoughtfulness to the unit. We thank Bernadette Fitzgerald, Julie Finn, and Pamela Coutain at PS 503, who welcomed us into their classrooms with open arms. Of course, these wonderful educators set the stage, but it was the children who actually taught us how to teach, and we're grateful to all who have helped, and especially to the third-graders at Woodside. Meanwhile, as we tried to capture all of that onto the page, Kathleen Tolan and Ali Marron joined us in a week-long writing retreat in the Adirondack Mountains and offered lots of sage advice and jolly company.

Then, too, there was the support team that helped us keep our spirits high even through a dozen rewrites. We thank Kate Roberts, Mary Ann Mustac, Kathleen Tolan, and Kate Montgomery for that sustenance.

But it was Zoe Ryder White, editor at Heinemann, who gave and gave and gave some more to the effort. Zoe helped us maintain the highest of standards throughout this project. When a write-up on small-group work was lackluster or less than graceful or when we couldn't figure out a way to orchestrate all the pieces that needed to come together, Zoe worked her magic—sewing, snipping, bridging, building. Best of all, she *did* whistle while she worked. Even when deadlines loomed and pressure mounted, Zoe maintained her grace, her delight in the project, and her energy. We cannot thank her enough.

The class described in this unit is a composite class, with children and partnerships of children gleaned from classrooms in very different contexts, then put together here. We wrote the units this way to bring you both a wide array of wonderful, quirky, various children and also to illustrate for you the predictable (and unpredictable) situations and responses this unit has created in classrooms across the nation and world.

Contents

BEND III Blazing Trails: Writing Original Fairy Tales

Welcome to the Unit

WHEN YOU WERE LITTLE, did you ever stomp about, calling, "Fee fi fo fum, I smell the blood of an Englishman"? Or did you ever stand at the door, calling, "Little pig, little pig, let me in"? What is it about fairy tales that makes them so participatory and so gleeful (even in their gruesomeness)? We are not sure of the answer to this, but we do know that your children, after months of writing information and opinion texts, will be enchanted by the invitation to write adaptations of fairy tales.

You'll be enchanted, too, once you see the ways your children's deep connection to fairy tales functions as a very beautiful scaffold, enabling them to write stories that are beyond anything they could have done otherwise. Years ago, Adriann Peetom, a Canadian literacy leader, told us, "Trust the books. Trust the books. Get out of their way and let them teach kids to write." Over all these years, we've repeatedly found that there is enormous truth in Adrian's advice. Texts themselves can teach writing. Fairy tales, in particular, can teach children to write with a story arc, to bring the resonance of a storyteller's voice onto the page, to create the world of a story, and to bring characters to life. In short, we believe that fairy tales can, in large part, help us to teach children to write fiction.

We originally developed this unit because the Common Core State Standards put a spotlight on the importance of folk and fairy tales in children's education. We soon found, however, that the unit had power beyond anything we could have imagined. Perhaps it is because fairy tales are by nature taut tales with clear story arcs, archetypes, and lessons. A group of innocent pigs face trouble with a dangerous wolf, and the trouble gets worse and worse with each house that falls. Then, too, in fairy tales, the unlikely hero often wins in the end. A young girl, constantly brushed aside by her not-so-loving family, wins the heart of a good prince in the end. Above all, we found these tales to be terrific models of the craft moves that youngsters can use in their own stories.

We also quickly discovered that the form of a fairy tale naturally led children to explore the writing qualities called for in the Common Core State Standards for Narrative Writing. This standard emphasizes a clear event sequence that unfolds naturally, the use of dialogue and description to develop the events, and language that signals event order (W.3). As we have taught and retaught this unit, it has become clear that this genre is a near-perfect vehicle for children to learn and practice this work. For example, as children read and think about phrases such as "Once upon a time," "Later at Grandma's house," and "Just then, along came a wolf," we realized that fairy tales are perfectly suited to teaching children how to use transitional phrases to glue the scenes of their own stories together (W.3.3c). And one trademark of fairy tales is the universal ending that provides closure for the characters and the problems they face with the simple phrase, "And they lived happily ever after." This form for ending helps children provide a sense of closure for their stories (W.3.3d). All of this made it clear to us that there could be great power in a unit on writing adapted and original fairy tales.

We also realized that since this unit is located at the end of the third-grade year, it's positioned to incorporate a few of the fourth-grade narrative writing components. You'll notice that this unit does not hit the brakes when writing moments arrive that are technically aligned to the fourth-grade standards. Instead, this unit embraces them, hoisting children up to try some of these writing moves on for size. For example, there is technically not a component in the third-grade narrative standard that highlights specific words and sensory details that help convey experiences. But the language of fairy tales is iconic, and we couldn't resist teaching children to embrace this language as their own when they wrote. So as we watch children become immersed in fairy tale language ("In the deep, dark woods" or "The big, bad wolf" or "Cinderella was the last to try on the shiny, glass slipper") and we help them name some of the ways authors use words with alliteration and sensory language to create effects, we begin to grasp the teaching power of this genre (W.3.4d).

Children move through three narrative writing cycles in this unit, writing two adaptations of fairy tales as well as their own original fairy tale. At the end of the unit, they pick one of these three stories to bring to publication. These multiple writing cycles allow children to practice many important writing lessons—structuring stories so that the reader can't turn the pages fast enough; finding the precise words and phrases to capture a moment, an image, an emotion; and, above all else, writing with a storyteller's voice. This unit design of multiple writing cycles will help your young writers see the value of hard work and become more willing to revise their writing, because each fairy tale draft improves upon the last. You'll end the year with a busy, buzzing colony of fairy tale writers!

OVERVIEW OF THE UNIT

This unit relies on your children having been steeped in at least a few fairy tales, so if your children have no background with "Cinderella," "Little Red Riding Hood," and "The Three Billy Goats Gruff," you'll want to do some reading aloud. You might tell children that actually, fairy tales are often shared by being told and retold, and then invite them to retell a tale or two to a partner. Then you will suggest that each writer in the room has the power to become this kind of writer—a fairy tale writer.

During the first bend in the unit, you'll rally each child to adapt a fairy tale that is one of two class favorites (we suggest children choose between either "Little Red Riding Hood" or "The Three Billy Goats Gruff"). If it seems odd to you that children aren't able to choose the fairy tale they want to adapt, know that in the second bend in the unit, they will be able to do this. The reason for channeling children toward these two stories early in the unit is that this allows for more scaffolding, which we find children need as they do this work for the first time. While children choose between "Little Red Riding Hood" and "The Three Billy Goats Gruff," you, meanwhile, might use the classic tale of "Cinderella" as the demonstration text for whole-class fairy tale adaptation work. This means that in your minilessons, you and the class

might write (co-write) an adaptation of "Cinderella" while the children work on their own adaptations of one of the two other stories. On the CD-ROM, you'll see examples of "Cinderella" adaptations.

Of course, once a writer has made the choice to adapt a particular tale, that writer will need to reread the classic version of that tale. At the start of the unit, then, children will take some time to reread and study and annotate "Little Red Riding Hood" or "The Three Billy Goats Gruff." In part, as they do this, the children will notice the storyline, and in part, they'll notice the qualities of fairy tale writing. Children will then plan their adaptations, thinking about which parts of the original tale they'll adapt. Will they change the setting from a countryside to a city? Will they change the characters from goats to kittens? Children will also learn to make significant changes that alter the course of the tale. For instance, maybe Cinderella should want something more significant than a handsome prince. Furthermore, children will learn that one change leads to another change, thereby affecting the course of their story. For example, if these are kittens instead of goats, they may not trip-trap across a bridge, and their destination may not be the soft green grass in the meadow.

At first, your children will be apt to write their stories in a "just the facts" sort of way. Their attention will be on getting the adaptations right and on reporting what happens first, next, and last. All of this will probably change midway through the first bend in the unit when you teach your children drama and storytelling as ways to rehearse and plan their fairy tale adaptations. Suddenly, in partnerships, children will use gestures, small actions, facial expressions, and dialogue to act out their adaptations. Their drama will bring their imagined stories to life—so much so that this work with drama will become one of the defining features of the unit.

Your children will be writing Small Moment stories, or scenes, but they'll quickly learn that a fairy tale requires more than one scene, one small moment. In this first bend, then, you will teach them that a narrator can function a bit like Jiminy Cricket once did in old-fashioned movies. Just as Jiminy Cricket would come onstage between scenes and tell viewers that time had passed, that the scene had changed, so too, youngsters will learn that they can use a narrator to stitch two or three of their small moments together.

In the second bend of the unit, your children will write their second adaptation of a fairy tale. This time, instead of being channeled to one of two tales that the class has studied, children can pick their own fairy tale to adapt, because the sky's the limit! You might have copies of *The Three Little Pigs* or *The Emperor's New Clothes* available for children who need to do a little shopping before they commit to their next tale. The theme of this bend is independence and transference. You'll teach a series of sessions that support students to apply what they learned in the previous bend to their second fairy tale adaptation. For example, children will use the anchor chart from the first bend to help them make writing plans for what they plan on trying in their second adaptation. During this portion of the unit you will need to address common pitfalls of third-grade narrative writing—drafts that are swamped with dialogue, sentences that lack sentence variety, and scenes that are summarized, rather than stretched out in detail.

Early in this second bend, you'll rally students to self-assess and to make goals that help them outgrow themselves as writers right from the get-go. This will set the stage for a message that will pervade this bend: push yourself. You can do more than you think. It will feel to you as if you're running alongside your children's writing like some people run along the sidelines of a soccer game. One of the important things to notice in this bend is that you'll help children to imagine far more dramatic revisions than anything they'd previously experienced. You'll let children know that they'll need to write a succession of entirely new drafts.

This bend wouldn't be complete without revision lessons that help children revise their fairy tales with an eye (and an ear) to their language. Specifically, you'll remind children of the power of using comparisons in their writing, including similes and metaphors. You'll highlight passages such as descriptions of the lamb whose "fleece was as white as snow." Children will also revise for the use of alliteration, as in "big, bad wolf," and for memorable word choice, as in "huff and puff and blow this house in."

After two rounds of writing adaptations, students will be ready to write their own original fairy tale. To celebrate their growth and to ensure continued growth, you will, in this bend, teach your students to write original fairy tales, applying all they've learned from Bends I and II to this final piece of writing. Like the previous bends, Bend III is fast-paced and rigorous. You will launch by teaching kids that writers of original fairy tales draw from the qualities of good stories—a character with traits and wants who encounters trouble, and then ta-da! there's a resolution—to generate story ideas. Once your writers have generated possible story ideas, they'll get right to the work of drafting and, more importantly, revising. The lessons in this bend lift the level of

previous revision lessons. This provides students with multiple opportunities to practice key revision lessons.

ASSESSMENT

Think back to the very first week of school, when you launched your writing workshop. You devoted a full writing workshop to assessment by asking your writers to produce an on-demand narrative. You then studied these narratives with your writers and most likely used the Narrative Writing Learning Progression, located in *Writing Pathways: Performance Assessments and Learning Progressions, K–5* to match the needs of your writers with your teaching. After such a long time away from narrative writing, you will want to assess by having your students write an on-demand narrative.

You might be wondering whether to assess your students by giving them a fairy tale on-demand task. Our experience has shown that when students produce a personal narrative on-demand, it showcases more fully all they know (and can do) in the narrative writing genre. We find that once you add the layer of fairy tales into the assessment, it clouds what the child can fully produce within the narrative writing genre. It might be helpful to think of it this way: imagine you had forty-five minutes to produce a narrative but first had to create fictional heroes and villains, elements of magic, and trouble your character faces all on the spot. And even if you could create all of this quickly, how likely would it be that you would do your best small moment writing? You might find it too tempting to draft a multi-scene fairy tale, filled to the brim with flashy fairy tale qualities, like magic, that overshadow the fundamental elements of strong narrative writing—elements such as showing, not telling, writing with detail, writing with voice, including a blend of dialogue and action, developing a setting, and so on. Remember, this is a moment to assess students on their knowledge base in narrative writing. It might prove to be easier to tell a story about your own life, allowing all of the attention and time you have in the on-demand sitting to let your knowledge of the elements of strong narrative writing shine.

With that in mind, you could decide to use the exact same prompt from the beginning of the school year. The advantage of this is you can compare apples to apples, their first on-demand with this recent one. You can find that prompt, of course, in the *Writing Pathways: Performance Assessments and Learning Progressions, K–5* book.

This on-demand task will give you vital information about students' current strengths in terms of their knowledge of narrative writing as a genre—its purpose, craft, and structure. You and your students will be able to assess these on-demand pieces against a checklist, or students can lay them out and describe to each other what they already know how to do as writers, which they'll carry into this unit. The Narrative Writing Learning Progression, located in *Writing Pathways: Performance Assessments and Learning Progressions, K–5,* can guide your assessment of this work. You can look at the rubric for third grade, noting which students meet grade level expectations (a level 3 on the rubric) and which students fall below (levels 2 and 1) or exceed (level 4) expectations.

Another form of assessment used in this unit is self-assessment, as used at the end of the first bend. Children return to the use of the Common Core State Standard–aligned narrative writing checklists used in the first narrative writing unit. Students reflectively assess their first drafts, take stock of what they've learned and what needs improvement, and set new, rigorous writing goals for the next two bends in the road. It is important to be sure to have these checklists printed and/or charted before the final session in this bend (see CD-ROM). You'll note that both the third-grade and fourth-grade narrative writing checklists are used, because children are on the cusp of ending their third-grade year and may move to more sophisticated writing goals.

One last note: there are moments in between drafts to informally assess your young writers. Students produce one draft at the end of each bend (sometimes more than one). Seize this time to cull the class's drafts and looks for trends. What is the majority of children struggling with in their writing? What is the majority of children succeeding in? Use these trends to inform the angle of your upcoming teaching. If you notice outliers, students that are soaring ahead of the class or students that are struggling to keep up, use this assessment to inform your small groups or conferences in the upcoming bend.

GETTING READY

Because this unit involves writing adapted and original fairy tales, you will want to invest time and energy collecting a stack of fairy tales. As you read your way through your stack, read as a reader and as a writer. As a reader, notice which versions of which tales are most engaging. Plan to read these aloud to your students. As a writer, read to notice which tales have a clear, replicable structure. (We found "Little Red Riding Hood" and "The Three Billy Goats Gruff" to be particularly well structured.) As a teacher of writing, you will also want to pay attention to which tales support the unit goals of crafting stories told in a storyteller's voice with rich and beautiful language. Mark up these texts with all the possible things you might teach your students, from structure to development to language conventions. Reference the bibliography of fairy tales on the CD-ROM if you'd like suggestions as you gather your fairy tales.

Next, it will be important for you to identify a mentor fairy tale adaptation. We chose *Prince Cinders* by Babette Cole because of its humor, its inclusive message (fairy tales aren't just for girls), and because it provides a strong example of narrative writing. A wide range of adapted and original fairy tales written by students can also be found on the CD-ROM.

As noted earlier, storytelling is at the heart of this unit. We aim to teach kids not only to write well-crafted tales, but to story-tell those tales with drama, precise action, and language that captures the hearts and minds of the listener. So you might spend some time watching video clips of storytellers, especially fairy tale storytellers, as a way to highlight excellent examples of storytelling to use when teaching.

Finally, give yourself a bit of time to begin planning your own fairy tale adaptation, a text that serves as your demonstration text. We chose to adapt "Cinderella," and you are welcome to do that too. You might even take yourself through the first sessions as a writer. Giving yourself the small gift of time can have big payoffs as you discover the writing road on which your students will travel in the unit. There are three different adaptations of "Cinderella" included on the CD-ROM for your reference.

Adapting Classic Tales

IN THIS SESSION, you'll teach students that writers create their own fairy tales by adapting classic ones. To gain inspiration and begin to write, writers study several versions of a classic fairy tale and then ask themselves, "Why might the author have made these versions?"

GETTING READY

✔ *Prince Cinders* by Babette Cole (see Minilesson and Active Engagement)

✔ Classic versions of *Cinderella, Little Red Riding Hood,* and *The Three Billy Goats Gruff,* which you will want to read aloud before today

✔ White paper folded into quarters to make a story-planning booklet, one piece for each student (see Connection)

✔ Your version of the story-planning booklet (see Connection)

✔ "Ways Authors Adapt Fairy Tales" chart (see Teaching and Active Engagement)

✔ Notebooks and pencils

✔ Your demonstration writer's notebook (see Teaching)

✔ Chart with phrases such as *Maybe . . . , Could it be . . . , My theory is . . .* (see Teaching and Active Engagement)

✔ Printed copies of *Cinderella,* enough for each student

✔ Printed copies of *Cinderella* adaptations, enough for students to be in groups of four with one copy per group

✔ Optional: A selected bibliography of some of our favorite classic fairy tales and adaptations

COMMON CORE STATE STANDARDS: W.3.5, W.3.7, W.3.8, RL.3.1, RL.3.2, RL.3.3, RL.3.5, RL.3.7, RL.3.10, RL.4.1, RL.4.3, RL.4.9, SL.3.1, SL.3.4, SL.3.6, L.3.1, L.3.3, L.3.6

S TARTING A NEW UNIT is like walking across an unbroken field of snow or writing on a blank page of notebook paper. It is beautiful thing—but it may also be daunting. Today will be especially highly charged because your children will be totally thrilled at the idea that they may now, at long last, write fiction. For many of them, the fact that this is not just a unit in fiction but in fairy tales will be even more exciting; they may bring giants and trolls, evil stepmothers, and talking mirrors into their stories!

It would be great if you could assume that all your children know what you mean when you tell them they will be writing fairy tales and that they understand your allusions to fairy tales. It would be great if your third-graders all understand, for example, that if you ask, "If I don't get it done by our deadline, will I turn into a pumpkin?" you are referring to Cinderella's rush to leave the ball before the clock strikes twelve and her carriage returns to its original shape. This unit would be easier if your children are all right there with you when you say, "It's real, honestly! Do I need to sleep on a pea to prove it?"

But the truth is, unless you have taught fairy tales yourself, some of your children may have only a hazy idea of what you mean by writing fairy tales. That's okay, too. One goal for the unit will be to immerse students into an intensive study in the essentials of fairy tales while they adapt and write their own. That is, your children will be learning on the job—which, after all, is what school should be about!

Although you needn't launch the unit with an intensive three-week unit on reading fairy tales, you will need to be sure that your children at least know the three fairy tales that will be especially central to this unit. If you follow the course set by this book, that will mean that before or on Day One of the unit, outside of the writing workshop, you'll read aloud at least the classic version of *Little Red Riding Hood, Cinderella,* and *The Three Billy Goats Gruff.* It would be ideal if you could read these more than once, and perhaps you also can assign children to listen to audio versions of these stories. If you don't have the books on tape or CD, you can digitally record yourself reading your favorite versions. Or even ask parents, the principal, beloved art teachers, and so on to record themselves reading the books.

We also include the old Norwegian version of *The Three Billy Goats Gruff*, the Grimm's version of *Little Red Riding Hood* (called *Little Red Cap*), and Charles Perrault's version of *Cinderella* on the accompanying CD-ROM. You may of course use a classic fairy tale version of your choice. "Wait," some of you may be thinking, "this is a book on fairy tale adaptations—isn't *The Three Billy Goats Gruff* a folktale?" Although *The Three Billy Goats Gruff* straddles both categories, the heart of our book is fiction writing, specifically writing well-structured stories. Both *Little Red Riding Hood* and *The Three Billy Goats Gruff*, with their clear, accessible structures, support our goal.

"We do well to pay conscious attention to filling our students' ears and minds with the rich sounds of this genre."

You will want your children to have the cadence and language of those three fairy tales in their bones. When Cynthia Rylant was asked, for example, "How do you teach children to write?" she answered:

> Read to them. . . . Take their breath away. Read with the same feeling in your throat as when you first see the ocean after driving hours and hours to get there. Close the final page of the book with the same reverence you feel when

you kiss your sleeping child at night. Be quiet. Don't talk the experience to death. . . . Teach your children to be moved and they will move others.

As you read and reread fairy tales to your students, as you remind yourself to be quiet and let kids feel and think, you are quietly building within them the capacity to emulate the language they are hearing—and of course, to innovate. Reading and writing are not simply visual processes. We do well to pay conscious attention to filling our students' ears and minds with the rich sounds of this genre.

If you can channel students to read fairy tales as well, perhaps collecting observations about how fairy tales usually go, that would be icing on the cake. If children have even just a bit of time to study fairy tales prior to this unit, this means they will be ready to ooh and ah over the prospect of writing tales in which trolls tackle the biggest goat and children outwit the evil witch. But the unit is designed so that it works beautifully if the only thing you've been able to do before it begins is to read aloud.

Today's session is a bit unusual because you channel children to read published fairy tale adaptations and do not suggest they spend today writing at all. They won't be able to adapt a tale until they understand what it means to do so, and to do this they need to compare and contrast several versions of a story and think about what the author was doing when he or she wrote a different version. Help children notice that adaptations are not arbitrary—the author is attempting to improve on the original tale: to make a character less stereotyped, to set more fairy stories in urban settings, to present girls in a less sexist fashion, to alter the moral of the story.

Adapting Classic Tales

CONNECTION

Support your students as storytellers of fairy tales, ensuring that classic tales are "in their bones" before they begin writing fairy tale adaptations.

"Writers, you know that today is the first official day of our fairy tale unit. You've probably noticed that I've been reading lots of different fairy tales to you lately. I've been doing that on purpose so that the stories—their language, their sounds—will be in your bones.

"Whenever I read a fairy tale, I think about the fact that before fairy tales were ever written down, they were told and retold, time and again, in different ways. They've been told and retold, passed from one person to another, because they work as stories. Fairy tales are our most beloved stories of all time."

Demonstrate storytelling a familiar fairy tale across four pages in a story-planning booklet.

"In a minute, you're going to practice getting either *Little Red Riding Hood* or *The Three Billy Goats Gruff*, whichever story you choose to work with first, into your bones. I gave you a piece of white paper as you came to the meeting area. Will you fold it into a little booklet? We'll call it a story-planning booklet, because that's what it will help us with." I folded my page in half once, then in half again, to show them. "Here's my booklet, and I am going to choose *Little Red Riding Hood*. Each of you decide on the story you'll tell—that will be the first story you adapt. Thumbs-up if you have that decided.

"My booklet has four pages, and I know yours does as well. I'm imagining that the first page will be the set-up speech, the second page will be the story of the first small moment—of what happens first—and the third page will tell the trouble. Then, on the last page, things are wrapped up.

"Think about your story, and think about how you will fit the whole story into just the pages of your story-planning booklet." I gave them a minute to think. "Touch each page, thinking what you'll tell on each page." They started thinking, and I added, as I flipped through my pages, "The background, the first scene, the trouble, the ending.

Just as texts have themes, and the start of a text hints at those themes, so too do units of study. This unit hints early on at the oral nature of fairy tales, emphasizing the way fairy tales have been told and retold over the ages, which sets students up for the work that will be especially important. Before long, students will be telling and retelling these beloved tales.

When children tell and write their stories, they often blend from one page to the next in a sort of cascading storyline. It helps them to have distinct boundaries between one page and the next, and to be clear about the job they'll do on each page. Describing the structure of fairy tales to children is tricky because all don't unfold in the exact same way. But using this booklet as a vessel for children's storytelling generally works to help clarify students' stories.

"I'll go first, then you try this." Touching the first page, I said in a dramatic storyteller's voice, "Once upon a time, there was a little girl who always wore a bright red hood, so everyone called her 'Little Red Riding Hood.' She was told never to talk to strangers—but she never remembered, because she was such a friendly little girl." I added, in an aside, "That's the backstory."

Then I turned the page, saying, "Now I'll tell the first small moment." I touched page 2 and said, "One day" [I interrupted myself to say as an aside, "Page 2 usually starts like that"]. Then I continued, "Little Red Riding Hood's mother said, 'Would you take a basket of lunch to your sick grandma? It will cheer her up.'"

Channel students to practice storytelling the tales they will adapt, touching each of the story-planning booklet's four pages as they go.

"Get together with your partner and will one of you do the same thing that I have done, only use all your own words? Remember to start with the backstory for the first page, then shift to your first small moment for the second page. That small moment should include dialogue and details—all of that you already know how to use in your writing."

As the meeting area erupted with storytelling, I moved among the students. The students didn't have time to finish telling one story, let alone to switch places, before I reconvened the class. "You know those classic fairy tales so well! I noticed that each story sounded a little bit different depending on who was telling it—you each gave it a little bit of your personality as you told it. That is so interesting because today, we are going to start thinking about—and studying—fairy tale adaptations."

Explain that writers often write adaptations of a classic story; suggest the class participate in an inquiry on how writers do this.

"Writers write adaptations all the time. They take a classic story and they write a different version of it. Writers call this kind of writing an 'adaptation.' And although writers adapt all sorts of stories, there is one kind of story that writers especially adapt—fairy tales.

"Today, instead of a regular workshop, you'll spend the time studying books, doing an inquiry. Tomorrow you'll each start working on an adaptation of one of the fairy tales you just told—and later in this unit, you will write your own original fairy tale. To do this work, we need to investigate a question that *all* of us have—myself included. We need to know how to go about writing fairy tale adaptations."

❧ **Name the question that will guide the inquiry.**

"The question we will be researching is: What does the author seem to be trying to do when he or she changes some things and not others?

"And most of all: How will a study of someone else's adaptations help me when I write my own?"

Notice that I start to tell my story as a small moment. I include the exact words that are said to the character, and I proceed along in a bit-by-bit fashion.

The predictable structure of a minilesson is meant to provide students with a lot of support. They can listen, knowing that within a minute from starting the unit, the teacher will crystallize the point of the minilesson in a teaching point that will later go onto anchor charts, or otherwise be remembered and referenced. Because that structure is meant to support students, it is helpful to let them know when we will deviate from the structure, thereby altering their expectations. You will notice that most of our units have at least one and often two inquiry sessions.

TEACHING AND ACTIVE ENGAGEMENT

Remind students that to inquire into the characteristics of any kind of writing, it is important to study an example of that kind of writing, asking, "What did the writer do to make this?"

"I do not know how authors go about adapting fairy tales, but I do know how to answer that question. When we want to figure out how to write a great poem, we find a few great poems and figure out what the writer probably did to produce them. We ask ourselves, 'What did the poet do to make this so beautiful?'

"So—are you thinking what I'm thinking? To get ready to write an adaptation of a fairy tale, we should probably . . ."

The children chimed in, "Study some!" and I agreed. "And we should try to figure out *how* the author made them."

Recruit kids to study a mentor text, noting what the author changes and why, keeping the guiding inquiry questions in mind.

"I know you have read or heard me read some of the many great adaptations there are of *Cinderella*. You've all heard the adaptation *Prince Cinders* by Babette Cole. By studying that adaptation and others, maybe we can figure out what authors do when they made adaptations. You'll all start by adapting either *Three Billy Goats Gruff* or *Little Red Riding Hood*, stories we've already gotten to know really well, and then later in this unit you'll be able to choose any fairy tale to adapt that you like.

"But let's study adaptations of *Cinderella* and let's think, when we look at each adaptation, 'When *this* author adapted the original story, what did she change? What did she keep the same?' Let's ask the harder questions, too: 'What does the author seem to be trying to do when he or she changed some things and not others?'

"I was thinking we could start by studying Babette Cole's adaptation," I said, and examined the cover of *Prince Cinders*, knowing the class was doing so as well. "What are you thinking?"

Charlie's hand shot up. "It's a boy!"

I nodded, "You are right. Babette Cole changed Cinderella from a girl to a boy. That's so cool. You already found one change—she changed the character. Let's keep reading to find as many changes as we can. No, wait—our job isn't just to *find* the changes, it's also to think about *why* the author might have made those changes and what her reasons might have been for doing so.

In minilessons, we often take some time to demonstrate in front of kids the work that we want them to do, trying to avoid the easiest possible path and leaving it instead for children to discover. In this instance, there was no way for us to talk about adaptations of this story without mentioning that Cinderella had become Prince Cinders, so we decided not to demonstrate coming to that realization but instead to invite kids to come to it themselves. Therefore, our demonstration is peppered with examples of students taking the lead, rather than us.

"Let's pause right here and think about why Babette Cole might've changed Cinderella from a girl to a boy. Hmm, . . . why *would* she do that? I am not really sure." (I then shrugged as if to say, "Oh well, I do not know the answer, so I might as well move on.") I added, "Too bad I can't call Babette on the phone and say, 'Hey, Babette, I have a question. Why is your Cinderella turned into Prince Cinders?'"

Coach writers to go out on the thin ice of conjecturing why authors may have chosen to make adaptations. Highlight that the authors' adaptations are consequential and purposeful.

"So class, we do not *know* what exactly was in Babette's mind when she turned Cinderella into a boy, so what do we do? Give up? Say, 'Oh well'?" I looked over the group and they clearly signaled that there was no way we should just give up. I agreed. "You are so right. When we aren't sure, when the answer is not right there on a platter for us to just reach out and grab, all that means is that we need to turn our thinking caps on high and we need to use phrases such as *Maybe it is because . . . , Could it be that she was thinking . . . , My theory is that. . . .*" I flipped over the chart paper to reveal those phrases.

> Maybe it is because . . .
> Could it be that she was thinking . . .
> My theory is that . . .

"Let's think together—Why *might* she have changed the main character to a boy? Turn and talk."

Chart the big picture of the class's thinking about how authors adapt fairy tales in consequential ways.

After a minute, I reconvened the class. "I overheard some of you saying something really interesting. You think maybe she made this change to the character because often people think that *Cinderella* is a girls' book, and Babette may have wanted to show kids that *Cinderella* is a for-everybody book. Fascinating idea—and that would be an important reason to make this adaptation, wouldn't it? I am going to start a list—'Ways Authors Adapt Fairy Tales.' I'll write *Changing the character* here, because that's one big thing that authors can change. I'll put *a girl to a boy* right below, because that's one example of how an author makes an important change to a character. Meanwhile, will you be thinking of other important ways—and reasons why—an author might make an adaptation?"

Ways Authors Adapt Fairy Tales

Changing the character:
- from a girl to a boy

Of course you will be playacting this a bit, and the kids will know it. You come to a hard question, ponder it for a moment, and then just give up. The kids are accustomed to you often demonstrating what not to do to make the point about what to do, so they probably will grasp that this is what you are doing; but if they don't, you tell them in a jiffy.

FIG. 1–1 It can be helpful to provide students with a few prompts to think about why authors make decisions.

To you, it may not seem all that interesting that Babette Cole made this gender switch, but we suggest you make a big deal of it. One of the big things you want to communicate today is that adaptations should be purposeful. When we have taught this unit, we've often found that children are apt to make changes that are utterly trivial—altering Goldilocks to Silverlocks, for example. Those changes have no consequences in the story, and they do not really alter the story in any important way. So we highlight the significance of authors' adaptations, even going a bit overboard.

Continue reading the adaptation you have chosen to share, channeling students to continue noticing adaptations and thinking about what could have prompted the author to make them.

"Let me read on, and this time will you make your own additions to our list in your notebook? After a bit we'll talk about the next adaptations you notice and the theories you develop."

I continued, reading the first few pages of the book. In the story, Prince Cinders is introduced as a "small, spotty, and scruffy" prince with three *hairy brothers* who are always zooming off to the disco and leaving him behind to clean. Instead of a fairy godmother appearing, a dirty fairy falls out of the chimney. Whenever I reached an adaptation, my voice signaled that I was seeing something really intriguing and I wondered if they were seeing it too, but I did not pause. At one point I looked up to say, "I have to do some jotting in my notebook before we read on—give me just a second?" Then I ducked my head and jotted like crazy, resisting the temptation to eye the class as if to say, "Are you doing this too?" I knew my absolute absorption in the task would be a more powerful nudge.

After a bit, I said, "Turn and tell the person beside you what you are thinking, and I'm going to be a researcher, recording what I hear you say. Oliver, you want to be a researcher too, and jot down what you hear people saying?"

Then Oliver and I listened in on conversations, and after two minutes or so I conferred with him to glean what he had heard.

List another adaptation you overheard children discussing and ask them to signal if they'd noticed that kind of adaptation as well.

Speaking to the whole group, I said, "I heard lots of you talking about the way Babette's fairy godmother is a dirty fairy. Will you put a thumb up if you and your partner noticed that very same thing?"

Ways Authors Adapt Fairy Tales

Changing the character:
- from a girl to a boy
- from a fancy godmother to a less fancy one (a dirty one)

This is, of course, a little spin on the traditional turn and talk. The reason we decided to do this is that after children generate some ideas by talking, we aren't planning to call on them to harvest what they generate. Instead, we plan to essentially report back what we heard them saying. We are doing this to be efficient so that kids will have more time to be deeply engaged in the work we are describing. We don't want to make the list of possible adaptations too all-encompassing because we want to leave space for children to see and name new adaptations later as they work on their own.

There are some much more obvious reasons why writers make adaptations, but later today students will have opportunities to do this on their own and generally we try not to name all the easier options. We often make a point of leaving the obvious choices for kids.

LINK

Channel students to spend today working with each other in small groups, going from table to table, reading other adaptations and adding to the chart.

"Writers, I am going to let you in on a secret. When you make a theory or two or three about why an author did this or that, even if you are not totally right, this helps your own writing. Because the theories you invent about how and why authors adapt fairy tales will fuel your own writing work. Be sure you are jotting those theories in your notebooks. You have your work cut out for you today! You know that to compare adaptations and get a sense for how they tend to go, you need to study more than one text. So . . . drumroll, please.

"At each of the tables in the room you will find a different adaptation of *Cinderella—Prince Cinders* and a couple of others. You will each have your own printout of the original story in your writing folders. I'm going to send two partnerships to each table, and after ten minutes at one table, I'm going to signal you that you need to switch to another table, whether or not you are done with the first story. When you arrive at a table, will you first set up your notebooks so you are ready to take notes and decide how four of you will study one text? I suggest one person reads it aloud, stopping after a chunk for you all to take notes and talk about the text, and then that person reads another chunk. But you may invent another system so long as it takes you no more than two minutes to get yourselves started.

"One more thing: It will be helpful, as you study these tales, to pay attention to the fact that a lot of things stay the same in the adaptation. The trouble is usually the same. For example, Prince Cinders *still* wants to go to the event where his brothers are and he *still* cannot go because he's home doing chores."

Teachers, we've designed this so that it puts the least burden possible on you. You'll see that we have grouped four children around a single copy of an adaptation of Cinderella and suggested they each also have a copy of the classic text, which you can print from the CD-ROM.

We do this not because it's perfect, but because we realize you have other subjects to teach and to provision and we do not want to be too greedy of your time or your budget. If you have the resources and wish to build your classroom collection of fairy tale adaptations, we recommend, in addition to Prince Cinders, *Susan Lowell and Jane Manning's* Cindy Ellen *and Frances Minters's* Cinder-Elly. *The best scenario would be to have duplicates of these books, which would allow each partnership to have a book; alternatively, you could have a small table with one lovely copy of the picture book and then give each writer a typed text of the words printed onto a sheet of paper that they may mark. Or, you could do both!*

Obviously, we are packing a lot into this lesson. First lessons are often like that—we provide lots of information and a variety of entry points, knowing that we'll follow up on them throughout the course of the unit. Don't expect your students to absorb everything you're telling them right away. You'll be able to better get a sense of what work you'll want to pull out and focus on as the unit progresses.

Using Notes as a Tool for Thinking

STUDENTS WILL BE ABLE TO KEEP THEMSELVES PRODUCTIVE and busy with very little assistance. You will still want to make sure that each group of students is organized so that everyone can see the text (either the original or a photocopy), has decided on a way to read the text together, and that each student has set herself up to record what she's noticing in her writer's notebook. If you feel like your students need more scaffolding, you might stop them after each step so they've followed the steps correctly the first time around.

Once you see that students are mostly engaged, you will want to get a sense of how this work is going to start determining what you'll need to teach. At right we've listed a few things that students often need help with as this unit begins; you'll notice other things as well.

It will be the last of these that you'll especially want to address, because chances are good that your children will need an extra nudge to dig deep enough to speculate about an author's reasons behind her adaptations. Jasmine, for example, was intent on listing every possible difference between *Prince Cinders* and the classic version of *Cinderella*. When I asked, "What are you working on as a writer?" she merely shoved her list toward me so that I could admire it (see Figure 1–2 on next page).

I said, "You are such a researcher, aren't you? It is impressive that you aren't just making these observations in your mind—you're recording them. I wonder, though, when you take notes like this, what do you *do* with them?" Jasmine looked a bit confused. "Show them to you? she asked. "Yes, and you did that," I confirmed. "But how do the notes you're taking help you? The reason I ask is that many writers take notes because once they have things on the page, they may *think* about them. And if I were you, after listing a bunch of ways in which the story changed, I'd want to *think* about those ways. Usually the author makes one big change and all the other changes sort of domino from that—they're connected. So I'd want to reread my list and star what I thought was the biggest change, or the first one. And I'd want to see if some of the other changes come from the first main change. Like, you wrote here that the author

If you see . . .	You could teach . . .
Students reading silently	"Fairy tales are a bit like poems in that they are meant to be read out loud. Piper, would you read this part like it's gold? And the rest of you, think about our questions: When *this* author adapted the original story, what changed and what stayed the same? What does the author seem to be trying to do when he or she changes one thing and not others?—so that as soon as Piper finishes you can begin talking about what changes and your theories about why."
Students recording adaptations they note without discussing them	"Whoa, writers, may I pause you before you move on? I see you discovered that Frances Minters changed the setting and you think she did this because it wasn't fair to city kids. Wow! But now you are already looking for more changes. I want to remind you to consider several possible reasons for the change by . . . [I let my voice fade and the kids fill in, saying 'Maybe . . . Or could it be . . . And, what about. . . .'].
Students pointing to what they see on the page, but not surmising why	"Why might the author have made this adaptation? You don't know for sure, none of us do, but we need to sort of wonder about possible reasons."

made the fairy godmother into a dirty fairy. But why? What else happens because she did that? How does it affect the rest of the story?"

Jasmine looked perplexed, so I nudged a bit more. "A perfect-looking, clean fairy godmother has perfect magic, right? How about this dirty fairy?" "She's always messing

MID-WORKSHOP TEACHING
Notes Capture Thinking, Not Just Facts

"Writers, look up for a minute. I want to tell you about the work Jasmine has just done as she records her thinking about the changes Babette Cole made in *Prince Cinders*. Jasmine showed me a *giant* list she had going in her notebook, and when I asked her to tell me what she noticed about the items on her list, she didn't have a lot to say."

Jasmine piped in, "I spent so much time making my list of changes that I never got to thinking about *why* she made those changes."

I nodded and added, "So Jasmine went back to her list and started thinking about *why* the author made each of the changes. Jasmine, can you tell us what you discovered?"

Jasmine continued, "I was just thinking that, you know how the fairy god-mother is a *dirty* fairy in this book? Well, I was noticing that she's this dirty fairy *and* she can't really do magic! So Prince Cinders has to figure his problems out on his own. Maybe that's why the fairy is a dirty fairy."

"Readers, do you see how Jasmine is really pushing herself to do more than just list adaptations she sees in the story? She even added another column to her notes so that she could record the *why* next to the changes she noticed. You might want to take a look at your notes and see if they are holding all of your deep thinking work, too. You don't need to organize your notes in the same way that Jasmine is doing, but you do need your notes to capture deep thinking about not only what you see, but also about *why* the author may have done that."

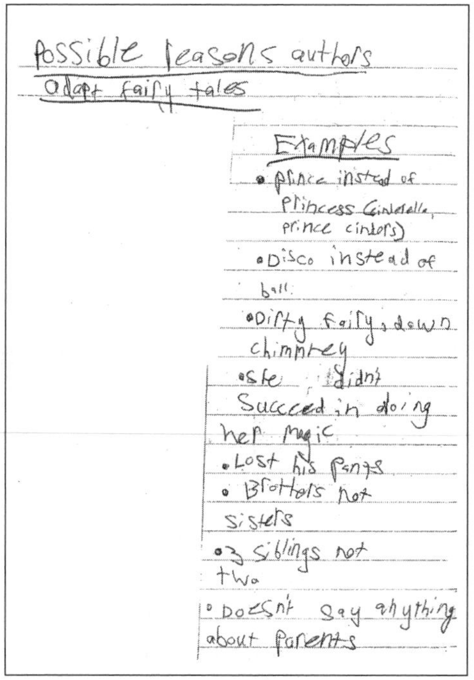

FIG. 1–2 Jasmine's notebook entry

Possible Reasons Authors Adapt Fairy Tales

Examples

- Prince instead of princess (Cinderella, Prince Cinders)
- Disco instead of ball
- Dirty fairy down chimney
- She didn't succeed in doing her magic.
- Lost his pants
- Brothers not sisters
- 3 siblings not two
- Doesn't say anything about parents

stuff up!" Jasmine said, her eyes starting to light up. "Aha! So the author is not just changing one detail about the fairy that doesn't affect anything—it affects everything! She can't even do magic! How does *that* affect what happens in the story?" "Well, it's like, the fairy messed everything up, so Prince Cinders doesn't go to the disco in a fancy car. It's like the opposite of *Cinderella*."

"What do you mean? Can you compare the two?" "In *Cinderella* the magic works and Cinderella just gets what she wants from the fairy godmother. She gets the coach and the fancy dress and stuff. But Prince Cinders doesn't get fancy stuff—he gets a toy car, and turns into a hairy gorilla! So . . . he kind of has to make the best of it and figure it out on his own. And he still ends up with the princess. Maybe Babette wanted him to have to figure it out on his own?"

"Ah. So a lot of big things are affected because Babette Cole changed the fairy god-mother into a dirty fairy who can't do magic! That is the kind of deep thinking writers do when studying adaptations like this—kind of like following the breadcrumbs of an idea, right? You follow the changes the author makes and discover some big ideas about why she chose to make those changes. I think you might need another column over here in your notes so you can write some of this stuff down!"

Pooling Knowledge Gleaned from Mentor Texts

Set students up to share what they've noticed about the *what* and *why* of adaptations, collecting the class's knowledge on the anchor chart.

I'd asked the students to bring their notebooks to the rug so that we could discuss what they'd noticed about the adaptations they'd been studying.

"Writers. You've now spent some time with several fairy tale adaptations, including *Prince Cinders*, which you're getting to know really well. This is a time for groups to share what you've noticed—not just about *which* adaptations authors have made, but *why* you think they've made them. We can pool our knowledge and collect it here on our chart. Take a moment to look through your notes, and let's hear from one writer in each group about one thing you noticed in one of the fairy tale adaptations you studied together. Don't forget to add the *why* when you tell us about it. Mariko, would you be our scribe and add on to the chart?

"Harry, you look ready—what's something you and your group noticed?" Harry scanned his notebook entry, which looked like this (see Figure 1–3):

changes to setting

olden → new

It might be easier to picture if new rather than old. For example, I can't picture Cinderella's village, but I can picture New York City.

changes to events

ball → basketball game

I think it changed to make it easier to understand.

"Well, when we were studying *Cinder-Elly*, we noticed that she isn't going to a ball, she's going to a basketball game!"

> Ways Authors adapt
> fairy tails
> changes to
> setting   olden → New
>
> it might be easier
> to picture if new
> rather old. for eggsample
> I cant picture cinder-
> ellas village but I can
> picture newyork city
>
> changes to events
> ball → basket ball Game
>
> I think
> it changed to make it
> easier to under stand

FIG. 1–3   Harry's notebook entry

"Ah, okay, interesting. That's not really a change to a character, is it, it's a change to the story's events. I think we need another section—Mariko, leave some space, and then write a heading, *Changing the events*. Harry, what did your group think might be the read on *why* Frances Minters decided to make that change?"

"Well we were thinking that it kind of makes the story more modern, like it could happen now. I mean, like we go to basketball games too, now. It's like Cinder-Elly could be anyone."

"Whoa, that's a big one! Changing from something old-fashioned to something modern. Mariko, would you add that to our list? Did any other groups notice adaptations that made the story more modern? Turn and tell someone who wasn't in your group what you noticed. That way you're working to spread what you learned all around the room."

Ways Authors Adapt Fairy Tales

Changing the character:
- from a girl to a boy
- from a fancy godmother to a less fancy one (a dirty one)

Changing the events:
- from something old-fashioned to something modern

Channel your students to consider which fairy tale they might choose to adapt.

"This list is growing into a really helpful collection of your knowledge! It's going to be a great tool for you to use as you work on your very own adaptations. Tomorrow is a really exciting day—you're going to actually start working on your very first fairy tale adaptations! And everything you've noticed about these published adaptations will be so helpful as you start planning and writing. I mentioned that for this unit's first story, you are going to get to choose between two tales, *Little Red Riding Hood* and *The Three Billy Goats Gruff*. We've been reading these tales together, so I know that you all know the classic versions really well. You may even have been doing some thinking already about which tale you'll choose. I want to give you a couple of minutes right now to think and start coming to a decision about which tale that will be. I can't wait to get started with this tomorrow, and to hear all of the interesting and meaningful ways you start adapting these stories! It's going to be so cool—we'll start with just two classic tales, and after tomorrow, there will be the beginnings of twenty-six totally different adaptations of them in the room!"

This teaching share is about collecting more ideas about how writers make consequential adaptations of fairy tales, but it is also an opportunity to highlight the importance of students sharing what they have learned with each other—promoting independence, ownership of the material, and a sense of writing community.

Teachers, your class's list will look different from this one; this lesson is a student-driven inquiry, so while you will be guiding students and pushing them to think deeply—especially about the why part of the changes they notice—the content of the list will depend on not only the selection of fairy tale adaptations your students are using, but also on the things your students notice. More important than the actual changes they notice is the idea that writers who adapt fairy tales do so in meaningful ways, for reasons that are larger than "just because it's cool," for reasons that are connected to big-picture ideas.

Writing Story Adaptations that Hold Together

IN THIS SESSION, you'll teach students that writers adapt fairy tales in meaningful ways. When changes are made, they must be consequential changes that affect other elements of the story, rippling throughout.

GETTING READY

✔ Students' writers notebooks (see Link)

✔ "How to Write a Fairy Tale Adaptation" chart (see Connection)

✔ "Ways Authors Adapt Fairy Tales" list (see Connection)

✔ Chart paper and markers (see Small-Group Work and Conferring)

THE CHALLENGE WHEN TEACHING is not finding topics one could teach, but selecting from the many possibilities to make the biggest difference for children. As you embark on this unit, your mind will brim with observations about the genre that you could share with your children. Do children know things generally come in threes in a fairy tale? Do they understand these stories were written to teach life lessons—that *Little Red Riding Hood* is a cautionary tale, warning children against talking to strangers? Do they know that in fairy tales, there is often a villain in the shape of a troll, a giant, an ogre, a mean stepmother? One could easily imagine an inquiry lesson that channels students to talk about what they notice in this genre.

That lesson will come in this unit, but we postpone it until the start of the third bend. At that point, children have lived inside fairy tales for a few weeks, so they'll be able to draw on a close knowledge of fairy tales to make those observations. They'll also need at that point to be conscious of the characteristics of the genre because they'll be embarking on the project of writing their own original fairy tale.

For now, we immerse students in the genre and provide them with opportunities to work inside the supportive scaffolds of a familiar fairy tale; we don't overwhelm them with too many specifics about the particular genre. This is a deliberate decision, made because our priority is that students use fairy tales as a vehicle for understanding story and writing fiction. We want them to see the structure of a short story that undergirds all fairy tales, and for now it is less important that they learn the unique features of fairy tales.

Of course, it is not a small challenge for children to learn traditional story structure. Within that general topic, this unit spotlights helping children learn the plotting work that a short-story writer does. It is essential that children learn that in a story the main character usually wants something and encounters a bit of trouble along the way. That's the focus of this session.

As the children work with fairy tale adaptations today, help them to grasp that the parts of a story are interconnected. As you read aloud an adaptation or two of one story, show

COMMON CORE STATE STANDARDS: W.3.3.a, W.3.5, W.3.10, W.4.3.a, RL.3.1, RL.3.2, RL.3.3, RL.3.5, RL.3.10, RL.4.2, SL.3.1, SL.3.4, SL.3.6, SL.4.4, L.3.1, L.3.3, L.3.6

children how any adaptation, any change in plot, may lead to a cascade of subsequent changes. This domino effect is an important pillar of this session.

"We want students to use fairy tales as a vehicle for understanding story and for writing fiction."

You'll especially encourage children to take note of the types of changes authors make to traditional tales as they adapt them. Authors of adaptations may aim to make a tale more modern, more inclusive, or more socially just. You'll lead children to resist making cosmetic or surface changes, such as simply changing the name of a character. Instead, you'll rally your class of writers to make purposeful changes, ones that improve the original tale or make it more modern.

As children think about the adaptations that other authors have made, they will also think about their own. In this session, children will write plans for their stories, not only planning how they will adapt a traditional fairy tale, but how they will tell a good story. This session is filled to the brim with reminders of the work of strong fiction writing—rehearsing plotlines, creating character traits, imagining story setting. At the end of workshop today, children will move from writing story plans to planning and storytelling scenes. Scenes may feel new to your children but you'll show them how one scene is like one small moment, a familiar structure children learned in the beginning of the year. This unit allows children to come full circle, ending the year with a unit that recycles and elevates the narrative writing with which they began their third-grade year.

Writing Story Adaptations that Hold Together

CONNECTION

Channel students to think about the underlying ideas about adaptations that they'd discussed in the previous session, especially highlighting the way one adaptation creates a cascade of others.

"Let's start today by thinking about yesterday's realizations. When writers adapt fairy tales, what do they change? And more importantly, Why do they make those changes? We noticed two big changes authors tend to make—they change the characters and they change the events. Hmm, . . . will you look over your notes, and think to yourself about why the author made the adaptations he or she made?" I turned to my notes and began rereading them with rapt attention, knowing that my doing so would channel students to do likewise.

After a moment, I said, "Turn and tell your partner some of the reasons why you think an author might alter an original fairy tale, making an adaptation of it. Go."

As children talked, I listened to one, then another. Realizing that children weren't drawing on the chart from the preceding day, I called out, "Writers, the charts in our room are meant to be references. When you need something to jog your memory, check a chart."

After a minute, I reconvened the class. "Writers, many of you are talking about the fact that when a writer makes one change—say, changing Cinderella from a girl to a boy—that one change changes other things, right? What were some examples, I'm trying to remember?"

Jasmine said, "Yes, 'cause changing the Cinderella losing her glass slipper to Prince Cinders losing his pants made a whole lot of other changes!" Soon the class recalled that this one change, changing a glass slipper to pants, meant that the princess would write a proclamation to find the man with the lost trousers, which would lead every prince trying to fit the trousers, which would lead to Prince Cinders finally trying on and fitting into the pair of pants.

"So, am I right that you are saying the first big change the author makes—say, turning Cinderella into a boy—is like a domino that falls over and pushes other things to change?" I asked, adding, "So, what if we decided that too often the main characters in fairy tales are farm animals, and for children everywhere to enjoy fairy tales it would be better

Your goal today will be to channel students to make their own adaptations of a fairy tale; your hope is that these will be consequential and purposeful. Across the length of the unit, you will want children to realize that authors alter fairy tales for reasons— perhaps an author thinks too many tales are set in pastoral setting, are sexist or old-fashioned, or aren't centered on positive values. That is, you are hoping to make the project of writing an adaptation as consequential as possible.

If you know that some of your students still haven't internalized the two original tales they are choosing between, you might orchestrate having these children in writing partnerships where both children are adapting the same tale, to provide an additional layer of support.

I'm not sure that all of the children have a grasp of what it means for things to fall like a row of dominoes, so I used my hands to illustrate this important concept.

if the characters were household pets that city kids as well as farm kids might know about? How might that affect a story like *The Three Little Pigs*?"

Charlie announced, "It could be the three little . . . um . . . hamsters?"

I nodded. "So if the pigs were hamsters, would they still build houses, would it still be a big, bad wolf that terrorized them? With your partner, think about the changes that might result if you changed the pigs to hamsters."

As the children talked, I listened in and after a minute I called the class back. "My goodness, I am so impressed with the 'domino thinking' that I heard. Some of you were saying that it would be a big, bad cat that was after the hamsters! And the cat wouldn't say, 'I'll huff and I'll puff,' he would say, 'I'll hiss and I'll scratch.' The hamsters wouldn't reply, 'Not by the hair on my chinny, chin, chin,' but . . . but . . . well, no one figured out that part yet.

"So, writers, this leads me to the idea for what I want to teach you today."

❧ Name the teaching point.

"Today I want to teach you that when writers plan how an adaptation of a story will go, they do two things. First, they decide on a change that they think will improve the story, and second, they make sure that the change leads to other changes so the whole story fits together. Often the one big adaptation cascades like a row of dominoes through the writer's adaptation of the fairy tale."

> #### How to Write a Fairy Tale Adaptation
>
> - Know the classic story and tell it often.
> - Decide on a change to improve the story.
> - Make the change lead to other changes so the whole story fits together.

TEACHING

Recruit children to join you in thinking about a purposeful adaptation of a fairy tale and how that one change could lead to a domino effect, creating the need for other changes.

"I know yesterday you did some thinking and talking about which fairy tale—*Little Red Riding Hood* or *The Three Billy Goats Gruff*—you'll choose to adapt. If you haven't chosen your tale yet, take a minute now to decide." I paused.

"Thumbs up if you have decided." I scanned the room, making sure most thumbs were up. "I'm going to be writing an adaptation of *Cinderella*—and hoping you help with that."

You will want to emphasize imagining the implications of any one of those decisions. You could, of course, go an entirely different way than thinking about hamsters. If one child suggests they all explore the possibility of The Three Little Pigs *being renamed* The Three Little Dogs, *then you will want to help students wonder whether the villain should still be a hungry wolf. Might it be an eager dog catcher? Would the story still be set in the country, or might it be in a city? If the children decided that their adaptation of* The Three Billy Goats Gruff *involved turning the goats into raccoons, will the raccoons trip-trap over a bridge to get to the meadow? Will they skitter across the bridge? Or will the author invent a different route to their destination? If their destination is a brimful garbage can in the alley, are the raccoons crossing a porch instead of a bridge?*

The reason that we ask children to get their story in mind is that this means they may listen to the work with Cinderella *while beginning to do similar work adapting their own story. You'll notice fairly often throughout the series that we shoehorn topic choice into the connection of a minilesson for just this reason.*

"Before a person can think about a possible adaptation, it helps to have the original well in mind. So I'm going to list in my mind the main things that happen in *Cinderella*; will you meanwhile do the same for your story?" I was quiet in front of the class, touching one finger, then another, as I silently recalled the main events in *Cinderella*.

Then I resumed talking to the class. "Now comes the hard part. We need to think—what is an important way in which we could change the elements of this story to make it better? I usually start by thinking, 'Is there a part or an aspect of the story that I don't really agree with, the way it is now? Is there a reason to change the story?' Will you join me in doing this work first with *Cinderella*, because it is hard work and I'd love your help, and then with your fairy tale? Okay, let's recall the main events in *Cinderella* and as we do, think, 'Is there a reason that we don't love the message in this story, or the way it goes?' Let's review the plot of the story." Then, referring to my fingers as I proceeded through the plot outline, I said:

◆ Cinderella is mistreated by her stepmother and her stepsisters. She has to do all the work.

◆ An invitation comes to a ball at the palace; they tell Cinderella she has to get them ready for the ball and then to stay home, cleaning the ashes out of the fireplace.

◆ A fairy godmother gives Cinderella a fancy dress and a fancy pumpkin carriage so she looks like a fancy princess. The magic will go away at midnight.

◆ Cinderella goes to the ball and dances with the prince.

◆ At the stroke of midnight, she runs out, leaving a glass slipper, which the prince finds.

◆ The prince searches for the owner, finds Cinderella. They get married and live happily ever after.

"So let's think about a big reason to change this story. Hmm, . . . what do you think?" I left a long stretch of silence while I thought. Musing to myself I said, quietly, "It's about this girl, who wants the fancy dress and fancy car so she can get the fancy prince. . . ."

"Tell the person beside you what might not be so great about this story, what you might change."

After listening as the children talked, I reconvened the class. "You have really got me thinking. I agree that it isn't that great to have a story where the one and only thing the girl wants is to go to the ball and marry the right man. She isn't really the sort of powerful girl that many of us want in our stories—all she does is goes to a dance and look fancy."

Sam was on his knees with excitement. "And who cares if she has the fanciest dress or goes in the fanciest car, I mean, the fanciest pumpkin? The story is like teaching bad values, it is practically saying 'go spend money,' 'go get stuff,' and that's not right."

Take some time to do this. Giving children spaces within a minilesson and asking them to think about something in those intervals is very important. As long as you are talking, your voice fills the minds of the listeners. When you stop talking, you leave space for them to do their own thinking.

You needn't muse, "It is about a girl who wants the fancy dress . . ." if you do not think your children need this scaffold. Your job is to modulate the amount of scaffolding you provide so that students are left to do some important and challenging work. This last bit of thinking aloud may provide too much scaffolding for your students. Be conscious when you provide support that lowers the cognitive demands you place on kids, but also realize that it takes a lot of depth-of-knowledge level 1 work for students to be able to handle depth-of-knowledge level 4 work.

In this instance, chances are good that you were the first one to object to the materialistic bent to the story. But you needn't tell that to the kids. Resist the instinct to say, "I thought of that first," and instead, if a child says this, support this idea!

"So, . . . are we all saying that we want to change what Cinderella wants, what she wishes for? Maybe instead of wishing to go to the ball and marry the handsome prince, maybe she wants . . . hmm, . . . what? We'll have to think what better or a bigger goal we'd want to give her. Maybe she wants something that will make the world a better place, not just to marry the right guy. Like she wants to save the dolphins. . . ."

"Or to open a library!"

"Or give homes to the homeless!"

I nodded. "And if we decided, for example, that the invitation would be to go to a meeting to plan a new library, not a ball, then we'd need to decide if Cinderella's job was to get the mean stepsisters ready for that meeting about the library, or maybe they wouldn't even want to go. And we'd need to decide if she needed a fancy car and dress—what do you think?" Children called out that maybe she'd just need a bike.

Debrief in ways that highlight the fact that the class is making a significant change in the fairy tale and a change that will cascade like dominoes throughout the story, affecting a lot of other things.

"So, do you see that first you think about a way to improve the original story? Someone could decide to change a fairy tale because they thought that the fairy tales too often are set in the country, so they might decide to write a city version. Or . . . what else?"

Children suggested that a person might decide that authors might change something in a story from being really rich and fancy to something more regular, that everyone could relate to—like our Cinderella's bike! Sierra mentioned that for our class adaptation of *Cinderella*, we wanted to change it so Cinderella didn't just want fancy things and riches (for example, money and power), she wanted to do something good in the world. I highlighted the idea that another *big* thing that authors change is motivations, doing so in such a way that Sierra thought she'd had the idea herself. I asked Harry to add that as another category before the bullet. Our list, "Ways Authors Adapt Fairy Tales," now looked like this:

Ways Authors Adapt Fairy Tales

Changing the character:
- from a girl to a boy
- from a fancy godmother to a less fancy one (a dirty one)

Changing the events:
- from something old-fashioned to something modern
- from something rich and fancy to something more people can relate to

Changing the motivations:
- from wanting more money and power to wanting to do good in the world

Let children chime in. You want their thinking. If they don't seem to be activating their brains in moments like this, you may need to signal to kids that they need to be thinking with you and to have something to share.

Don't worry about resolving the whole story with all its details. Writers don't proceed in that way. This is planning. If you do resolve the story, however, be sure you look ahead to what we do with the story in the upcoming sessions, deciding whether you want that to influence you. There is no reason that your adaptation needs to mirror ours.

Then I said, "The other thing you realized is that one change makes other changes, right? The fact that Cinderella is going to a meeting, not a ball, changes what the fairy godmother will give her, right? The one change—turning her from a girl who wants to marry the right guy and needs a fancy dress to a girl who wants to help work on a new library for the town—ends up meaning that the story has other changes too."

ACTIVE ENGAGEMENT

Channel students to go through the same process, this time thinking about their intended adaptations.

"So think about your story with your partner and ask those important and hard questions. What don't you love about your fairy tale, if anything? How might you change it? You probably will come to different ideas. Turn and talk."

As children worked, I crouched alongside one group after another. I tried to steer children toward more consequential adaptations, noticing that many were making inconsequential changes at first. For example, Sam was saying he hated trolls and goats, so he planned to make his version of *The Three Billy Goats Gruff* about a parrot and a dirty pony. "Why a dirty pony?" I questioned, nudging for meaning or purpose. Sam shrugged, "I dunno. Well, a rhino then," he said.

"Hmm, . . ." I said, realizing that Sam and his partners might be making random changes instead of ones for bigger reasons. "Remember, Sam, and all of you—it's really important to make sure the changes you make are meaningful ones that lead to other important changes. One way is to keep story elements in mind as you're thinking about what changes to make. For instance, what does the parrot *want*? What's in its way? Answering these questions might help." After some thinking out loud, Sam decided that his parrot lives in a zoo and wants his freedom—so the troll became the security guard that stood in his way—a more consequential change that would lead to other consequential changes in the story.

LINK

Channel students to get started writing plans for their own adaptation of a story. Remind them that the change should be significant, making it a better story.

"Writers, may I stop you? Oh my gosh, I am floored. You are not coming up with silly little adaptations like changing the wolf to a tiger, but with big ones. Shelly wants to make the story more current and changes the goats into people, and the bridge will be a busy, city bridge with cars and trains going over it. The poor troll has a lot to deal with! And Simone changed the goats to moles—which means the setting is totally different and the problems are totally different, because they live underground—can you guess what she changed the troll into? A hedgehog!

The active engagement is a time to assess how the strategy is working in action, a time to get your fingers on the pulse of your entire classroom. It's okay if you stumble across a partnership that is struggling, not yet grasping the essence of the strategy. Embrace this struggle as a teachable moment, giving students a tad more coaching so that they will feel supported in trying the strategy successfully. This is an important collaborative moment before they move into the independent part of the workshop.

When you send kids off to work, it is best if you have a clear idea of the range of options that you have in mind for what they'll be doing. Usually your minilessons cumulate options and you end the minilesson by reminding kids of all the choices before them. But right now, you are trying to move all to start drafting and revising adaptations of a fairy tale. So for this session, you are expecting them all to write a page or so in their notebooks, and to be detailing how their proposed story could go. You'll expect them to try more than one option, to especially think about the opening scene (you'll teach into that later).

"So, here is my suggestion for today. Get your plans down in your writer's notebook. Don't write plans as a story—don't start it, 'Once upon a time . . .' and try to tell everything in a bit-by-bit story way, but do write a lot of the details for how things will go, and write in paragraphs. It might sound like this, 'In my story, there will still be a character named . . . and like in the classic story, she will still . . . When the story starts I am thinking she will be. . . .'

"My other suggestion is to be hard on yourself. After you write a bit, pull back and think over your plan, draw a line, and try a different plan until you get one that feels great."

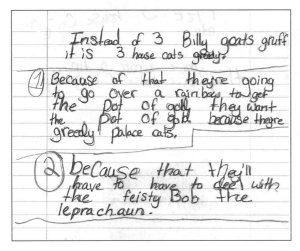

FIG. 2–1   Ella's notebook entry

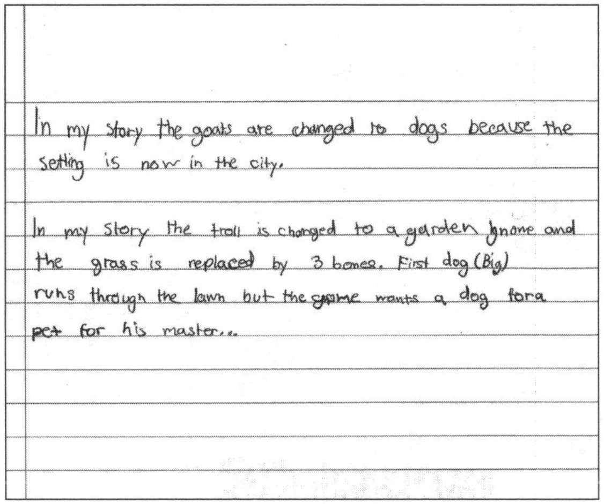

Instead of 3 Billy goats gruff it is 3 house cats greedy.

① Because of that theyre going to go over a rainbow to get the pot of goll they want the pot of gold because theyre greedy palace cats.

② beCause that they'll have to have to deel with the feisty Bob the leprachaun.

FIG. 2–2   Jackson's notebook entry

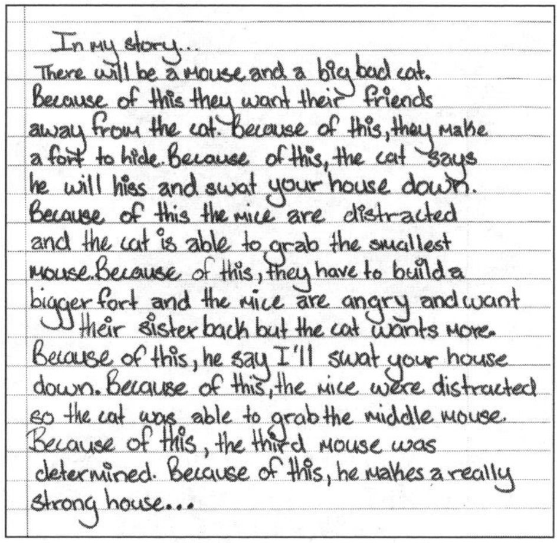

In my story the goats are changed to dogs because the setting is now in the city.

In my story the troll is changed to a garden gnome and the grass is replaced by 3 bones. First dog (Big) runs through the lawn but the gnome wants a dog for a pet for his master...

FIG. 2–3   Cora's notebook entry

In my story...
There will be a mouse and a big bad cat. Because of this they want their friends away from the cat. Because of this, they make a fort to hide. Because of this, the cat says he will hiss and swat your house down. Because of this the mice are distracted and the cat is able to grab the smallest mouse. Because of this, they have to build a bigger fort and the mice are angry and want their sister back but the cat wants more. Because of this, he say I'll swat your house down. Because of this, the mice were distracted so the cat was able to grab the middle mouse. Because of this, the third mouse was determined. Because of this, he makes a really strong house...

Wrestling with Cohesion and Story Structure

D URING THE FIRST FEW DAYS OF THE UNIT, you'll want to touch base with a majority of your writers, making sure that they are really thinking through their adaptations and not just changing the story at the surface level. You may find that some writers become overwhelmed by all of the possibilities for change and have a hard time focusing in on making changes that are consequential. If you find that a group of students is in this boat, you might reel them in with some guided practice using a mentor text (in this case, *The Three Billy Goats Gruff*) and a simple flowchart that might look something like this:

Character → Setting → Motivation/Trouble → Resolution

You might explain the logic behind the flowchart by saying something like, "If I change something about the character, then other changes will follow—just like one domino knocking into the next. For example, if we change the billy goats to house cats, then the setting will change as well; they'll probably live in a house." Pointing to the chart as you go, you might continue, "and they'll probably want big, juicy mice instead of sweet, tender grass. And probably the humans will get in their way! The resolution would need to change, too. Let's try another version: If the billy goats become wolves, then they might live in a deep, dark forest in Alaska, and they might want rabbits to eat, and a hunter might stand in their way."

You might ask students to use the chart, with your support, to come up with other potential adaptations for *The Three Billy Goats Gruff*, making sure to guide them toward changes that will cascade across the whole story. You'll find, as I did, that understanding this crucial element of writing fairy tale adaptations will increase students' motivation exponentially. In fact, after this small-group work, Sam asked, "Can we take our notebooks home tonight to write?"

MID-WORKSHOP TEACHING   Checking Adaptation Plans

"Writers, may I stop all of you? Tomorrow you will begin actually writing the story, so I want to remind you to check that the adaptation you're planning is a consequential one that will improve on the story in big ways. Let's say that someone was adapting *Cinderella* and they decided to give her a magic leprechaun instead of a fairy godmother, and he *hopped* in instead of *flew* in. Would that change be consequential? To answer that, think if it would affect a bunch of other things in the story and think whether it seems to be a significant, important change or a sort of silly—trivial—one. What do you think?"

The students, in unison, chimed in that it would be trivial.

"Let's say someone was changing *Cinderella* and they decided that too many fairy tales are about brothers and sisters who are jealous of each other, and that in real life it is more usual for classmates to be jealous of each other. If the writer decided to change this to a story of competing classmates who wanted not a royal prince but something that they might get at school, would that be a change that changed other things—like changed the setting, changed the people, changed the actions?"

The students agreed that yes, that would be a significant, consequential change.

"So will you tell your partner the adaptations you are thinking of making, and help each other think whether those adaptations are significant, and if they are not, help each other come up with a different plan?"

After children did this, I said to them, "Writers, I have one more tip that I want to tell you. When you write your story tomorrow, you need to make sure that your adaptation doesn't miss some of the super important parts of a good story. So right now, will you get in your mind how your adaptation is probably going to go? List, across your fingers, your plan for how your adapted fairy tale will go, and then I'm going to ask you something." I gave them a minute to do this.

"Now, here comes the thing you need to consider. Remember, good stories include a character who wants something—do you have that in your story? Thumbs up if you do, thumbs down if that is not yet clear.

"Good stories have a character who runs into trouble, who has a problem. Does your story have that?" I motioned with a thumbs up and thumbs down to signal I was expecting a response.

After children talked for a bit, I said, "You have a few more minutes to think through and write about your plan for your story in your writers' notebooks. If you've got the plot all figured out, you might take some time to jot down character traits for your characters. Perhaps you'll do some writing about the type of person or animal your main character is, how he responds to other characters, or the troubles he faces. I've put this on our "How to Write a Fairy Tale Adaptation" chart so you can remember the work you can be doing today."

> • Make a character with traits and wants who runs into trouble.

FIG. 2–4   A chart like this with moveable Post-Its supports students in understanding the concept of changes that cascade across the story.

You may encounter other students who need support reconstructing a coherent story line after their adaptations essentially deconstruct the original plot. We've found that sometimes it helps a child to try to summarize his story by using this thinking template:

> Once upon a time there was ___. Every day, ___. One day ___.
> Because of that, ___. Because of that, ___. Until finally ___.

For example, Jackson's consequential changes to his story led him to follow so many tangents that he lost his story line. He used the template to come up with this plan: "*Once upon a time* there were three dogs who lived in the city. *Every day*, they loved eating bones. *One day* there was a mean garden gnome blocking their way. He wanted to take them as pets to his master. *Because of that*, they couldn't get to the bones. *Because of that*, the two biggest ones made excuses to get by and the little one tricked him. *Until finally* all three dogs got the bones."

As you work with children, keep in mind that the goal of this unit is not so much that they learn all about the genre of fairy tales, but that their work with fairy tales helps them grasp the extremely powerful concept that stories often follow a predictable structure. This means that in your conferences and small-group work, you'll want to be assessing which of your children seem to be aware of the fundamentals of story and which still need help with that. You will probably need to explicitly point out to some students that in all fairy tales, and indeed in any story, there is a character who has wants, who has motivations, and who runs into trouble meeting those wants. This is not a new concept for your children, but actually applying this idea to a new adaptation of a fairy tale may be challenging. Again, there is a thought template that may help remind children that they may use the key words to help them construct a story line.

> Somebody wants something because . . . but . . . so . . .

Organize Notes to Plan Scenes

Teach children to organize their story-planning notes into a few scenes, or Small Moment stories.

"Writers, may I stop you? It's going to be time to get started on your first scene soon. So I want to help you a bit with that right now.

"Before you can write anything, you need to realize that a short story—and a fairy tale is a short story—is actually made up of two or three Small Moment stories. So we can look back at our plans for our *Cinderella* adaptation and we can think about the two or three Small Moment stories, or scenes, we'll use to carry the whole of the plot. During today's minilesson, you helped me think about the plot for the class *Cinderella* adaptation. Here are some notes that detail one plan for this story." I showed a sheet of paper with my jotted notes.

- Cinderella is still the stepsister who is treated like a servant. She loves reading.
- A letter comes inviting them all to a fund-raiser to save the town library.
- The stepmother and stepsisters throw the letter away because they hate the library.
- Cinderella cries and her fairy godmother arrives.
- The fairy godmother grants Cinderella's wishes so Cinderella may go to the fund-raiser.
- Cinderella saves the library.

"Will you and your partner look at that plan and see if you can box off two or three scenes we can write that would allow us to capture the whole story? You'll see some of these points on the timeline can all be smushed into one flowing scene, and that is often the case."

Rally children to plan with you the first scene of the class text.

Soon I asked, "What will our first scene, our first Small Moment story be?" The children agreed that *Cinderella* would be doing some kind of work and then an invitation would come in the mail about the event to save the library. I said, "So you are saying we can write that whole part of the story like it is one scene? Then we will jump ahead to a scene that comes later in the story—and we haven't figured that one out yet. We'll work on that more later."

Ask students to plan the first scenes of their own fairy tale adaptations and to practice storytelling that scene by writing in the air, making sure to get into the action.

"Right now, will you think of what the first scene, or Small Moment story, in *your* fairy tale will be? Doing this remembering you only get to write about two or three scenes, so the first scene usually needs to be right where a lot of action is happening." I left a pool of silence. "Give me a thumbs up if you have thought of what the first Small Moment story, the first scene, might be.

"In a fairy tale, that scene usually starts, 'One . . . ,' and then there is a time, like 'one day, one morning, one evening.' Then the main character usually does or says something important. These stories are short so they don't waste a lot of time about things that don't relate to the story. Partner 2, turn and try to write in the air how your story will start. Begin with, 'One' . . . Go!"

His finger swirling elaborately in the air, Sam said, "One day, the parrot was resting in the zoo and the security guard was pacing up and down. The parrot began to peck at the door with his red beak. . . ."

Jackson shared, "One afternoon, Little Green Cleats was heading to soccer practice. He took a shortcut through the woods so that he would be first on the field."

"Remember that the beginning of a story sets the stage for what's to come. It should get right into the action because fairy tales are short—no words are wasted! Tonight, as you plan possible opening scenes, ask yourself, 'Is there enough action? Does my main character do or say something important right away—something that sets the story rolling?' I'll add this to our chart."

How to Write a Fairy Tale Adaptation

- Know the classic story and tell it often.
- Decide on a change to improve the story.
- Make the change lead to other changes so the whole story fits together.
- Make a character with traits and wants who runs into trouble.
- Tell the story in two or three scenes (Small Moment stories).

Storytelling, Planning, and Drafting Adaptations of Fairy Tales

IN THIS SESSION, you'll teach students that writers story-tell or act out their stories to help as they plan their drafts and as they write their drafts.

GETTING READY

✔ Writers' notebooks and writing folders stocked with several sheets of lined paper

✔ "How to Write a Fairy Tale Adaptation" chart (see Connection)

✔ Your demonstration writer's notebook (see Teaching)

✔ Blank paper to make scene-planning booklets for homework, several sheets per student (see Share)

COMMON CORE STATE STANDARDS: W.3.3.b, W.3.4, W.3.5, W.3.10, W.4.3.b,d; RL.3.1, RL.3.2, RL.3.3, RL.3.5, SL.3.1, SL.3.2, SL.3.4, SL.3.6, L.3.1, L.3.3, L.3.6

TODAY YOUR CHILDREN will start writing their stories. What we have found is that they are apt to pick up their pens, start writing, and write on and on and on, not making deliberate choices or crafting anything, but still writing up a storm with great pleasure. When they come up for air, they are totally committed to their story. "I already have four pages!" they'll tell you. "I *love* my story," they'll say. Their intensity and absorption will be a beautiful thing, but their writing will probably be less beautiful. There is truth to the saying that fiction is the genre that kids want worst to write—and write the worst!

The answer here is that you mustn't be afraid to teach. Your children will need you to teach with decisive clarity. And frankly, front-end revision is going to be much more efficient and satisfying than back-end revision.

Remember that the goal of the unit is not so much for kids to learn to write fairy tales but for them to learn to write fiction, and to learn through their work with fiction, to write more effectively in every genre. Eudora Welty once said, in *One Writer's Beginnings*, "Poetry is the school I went to in order to learn to write prose" (1984). In this unit, fairy tales will be the school that children go to in order to learn to write fiction—and to learn to write well, in general. Your clarity about the purpose of the unit should help you spotlight the qualities and processes of good writing that are applicable across all stories.

This means that whereas the first two sessions focused on the unique challenges of adapting fairy tales, this session probably should focus on processes that would be equally important had this been a unit on writing realistic fiction or short fantasy or historical fiction or mysteries. We've taught all those genres many times, and found that until children have had a huge amount of experience writing narratives—and specifically, fiction—the biggest challenge for them, hands down, will be that they tend to summarize instead of storytell. Children stride in big steps across the plot of the tale, overviewing the events and reactions to the events instead of writing in such a way that readers can climb into the shoes of the character and *live* the events. In *The Stuff of Fiction* (1972), Gerald Brice writes, "It's not enough for a writer to tell a reader about a person or a place, he must help readers be the person . . . the basic failure of most writing is a failure of the writer's imagination . . . he is not trying hard enough to live moment to moment in the shoes of his character."

John Gardner, in *On Becoming a Novelist* (1999, 71), adds to that advice: "Write as if you were a movie camera. Get exactly what is there—the trick is to bring it out . . . getting down what you the writer really noticed."

"There is little that matters more to a fledgling fiction writer than learning to step into the shoes of the characters, to live the story, to reenact while writing."

These are big guns to bring out in preparation for a little lesson that aims to teach third-graders how to tell a story, but we hope these quotes fill you with resolve to teach this session as if it were one of the most important lessons you will ever teach, because we think that for narrative writers, it is. There is little that matters more to a fledgling fiction writer than learning to step into the shoes of the characters, to live the story, to reenact while writing.

Specifically, this session teaches children the importance of rehearsal. Children will first recall what they have learned about rehearsal and then, through guided practice, you will set them up to story-tell as a way to try out different ways their stories might go. The focus today will be on bringing stories to life through acting, so you will want to encourage children to first embellish their story scenes with enough detail so that they may then bring heightened drama and emotion to their acting. This use of storytelling and acting is not only an essential tool for planning stories, it honors the rich tradition of oral storytelling that accompanies fairy tales and spans many cultures. You may choose to weave in examples from famous children's storytellers from different cultures and backgrounds.

You'll encourage children to craft their enactments, pausing to consider whether they have gotten a character's tone of voice, gesture, or posture just right. Of course, by teaching students to pause and to reconsider, you are also teaching them to revise their writing, even before a word is written. Writers revise as they plan; they are revising when they reconsider where, in the sequence of events, they'll start the story—wanting to start it close to the main action—and when they think, "What exactly will the main character be doing or saying when the story starts?" Writers are revising when they pause after they've written a portion of the story and ask, "How could I do this even better?"

Storytelling, Planning, and Drafting Adaptations of Fairy Tales

CONNECTION

◆ COACHING

Celebrate the volume of work children have produced and ask them to share their progress with a partner.

"Writers, can you believe all that we've done in just two days? Quickly tour your partner through your writer's notebook, showing your partner how much writing work you have done in just two days."

After a moment, I interceded, "Okay. It is great you have already gotten into the swing of doing a lot of work because today you are going to do even more in one day than you did in that last two days!"

Point out that writers need to rehearse; recruit children to list ways they know to rehearse for writing.

"By now, writers, you are experienced enough that you should be able to tell *me*, not the other way around, what you need to do first to get started writing your actual stories. I'm pretty sure you already know that you need to rehearse. But will you think about the ways that you know writers of stories, of narratives, use to rehearse? Go ahead and call out ways writers rehearse!" From throughout the group, voices called out, "Story-tell to each other!" "Sketch or act out what happens." "Think what is first, next, next!" "Timeline." "Try different leads."

❖ **Name the teaching point.**

"Today I want to remind you that the real goal when you rehearse for writing a story is not to come up with something to say, but to make the story you will write much stronger. If you story-tell and act out your story, your rehearsal brings your story to life." I referenced our chart where I had added this new bullet.

If your writers haven't gotten a lot of writing done, you won't start this way. The point is to create a little buzz at the start of the minilesson. The other goal is to make this part of the minilesson extremely brief, as the middle section is very long and includes several cycles of guided practice.

How to Write a Fairy Tale Adaptation

- Know the classic story and tell it often.
- Decide on a change to improve the story.
- Make the change lead to other changes so the whole story fits together.
- Make a character with traits and wants who runs into trouble.
- Tell the story in two or three scenes (Small Moment stories).
- Story-tell or act out the first scene, filling in lifelike details.

TEACHING

Help students recall and then embellish the steps of the Small Moment story that they'll be telling.

"Let's use storytelling and acting as a way to rehearse the first scene in our *Cinderella* adaptation, and while doing that I think I can give you some tips that will help you do the same work with your own fairy tale adaptation. Before we can story-tell or act out the adaptation, we probably want to story-tell at least the start of the classic story. Then we need to get clear about the facts of our adaptation, right? We're going to use the same blank booklets we've used to story-tell and plan an entire story, but we're going to use them differently. This time, when I use the booklet, I'm going to use it to tell just one scene.

"So—next we need to think about our first scene. We have figured out Cinderella will be doing some kind of work for her mean stepsisters and then a letter arrives about a meeting to plan a way to save the town library.

"Okay, right now, across your fingers, list what is going to happen in this first scene—in detail. You know Cinderella is working, but what is she doing, exactly? Is she sitting? Standing? Who is near her? Who says what? Plan what happens first, then next, then next . . . across your fingers. Go."

I pulled in to listen for a minute and heard Caleb suggesting a reasonable plan, so I called out to the class, "May I have your attention? Listen to Caleb's plan and then let's all work off that one plan for now. Caleb—lay out the plan."

Caleb began talking, touching his fingers as he proceeded through the plot outline: "Cinderella is doing a job, like laundry, and then someone comes with the invitation to the library thing, and third, the sisters throw it away, and fourth, Cinderella says she wants to go, and fifth, they laugh at her."

Channel one partner to story-tell to the other partner the scene the class just planned, reminding them to include specific actions and dialogue. Then harvest a class lead for the story.

"Okay, let's work off Caleb's plan. Partner 1, you are going to start storytelling Caleb's version of this. Story-tell in ways that show what Cinderella is doing, and then who says or does what. Go!"

After a minute, I intervened. "Many of you are storytelling with so many details that I can picture it exactly! Marco's story starts like this":

> One sunny afternoon Cinderella was folding her stepsisters' gowns. She had a whole mountain of more laundry to fold. Then all of a sudden the doorbell rang.

"Notice how Marco filled in details. It's no longer just a line drawing—he's colored in the story with details. Who has figured out what people say after the doorbell rings? And what have you added to show that the stepsisters are mean

In this session, you'll be using the method of guided practice because this lesson has several parts. You'll take children through multiple cycles of rehearsal, beginning with the rehearsal of the class story. Then, you'll coach them to rehearse their adaptations one way, then another way. You'll coach into their talk, lifting their level of work. You wouldn't want to demonstrate this all in one sitting, having children stare for long periods of time without opportunities to practice. Therefore, you'll break it down into small steps, demonstrating for a bit and then coaching them to give it a try in bite-sized steps.

Calling on the child will only work if you have a student who is ready and able to lay out a clear plan. Otherwise say the plan yourself. This plan needs to be clear and stable.

Watch the pace of this minilesson. You need to plan on being very quick. You need to channel writers to do whatever it is you have in mind with forcefulness and urgency, and to interrupt their work in short order so as to progress to the next step. Otherwise this minilesson will lag on. You may quickly jot the story as you go, using the method you're most comfortable with. You might choose to jot notes to yourself that you'll write up on chart paper later or you might choose to write on an overhead projector, Smart Board, or document camera if you have the access and inclination.

to Cinderella? Let's take Marco's story as our class version and embellish it," I said, and repeated Marco's story. Soon the class had added:

> One sunny afternoon Cinderella was folding her stepsisters' gowns. She had a whole mountain of more laundry to fold. Then all of a sudden the doorbell rang.
>
> "You lazy girl," the mean stepsister said to Cinderella. "Go get the mail. Hurry. Don't waste time."
>
> Cinderella went to the door.

Channel the children to retell and extend the story, building off of the lead you helped the class produce, this time encouraging them to highlight certain character traits and to enhance the storytelling.

"I'll retell what we have so far, then Partner 2, repeat what I say, only try to make it even better and then add on. Partner 2, remember Cinderella is slaving away, and the stepsisters treat her horribly. Make sure that those big things shine through in your version. After you retell, keep going in the story, remembering to include specific actions and specific things people say. You ready? I'll start us off. You repeat what I say and keep going, but jazz things up. What sorts of looks are the mean stepsisters giving Cinderella? What does Cinderella look like, do, think about? Like Marco, fill in more details." Again the children storytold to partners for just a minute or so.

I reconvened the writers. "I heard one of you say that the stepsister growled at Cinderella and shot angry looks at her! No wonder Robert Munsch says that before he writes a story, he story-tells it a hundred times."

Repeat the cycle, this time supporting children to reenact the same scene, adding small actions, gestures, and interactions.

"So, now we're going to make our storytelling even more powerful. Remember the main parts of our *Cinderella* scene—starting with her folding the mountain of laundry. This time, Partner 1, you are going to *be* Cinderella—acting her out. This is pretty similar to the amazing storytelling you just did, but you're going to add in a little bit of movement—some gestures, some of the small actions that happen as the first scene begins. Do you see the pile of laundry in front of you?

"Partner 2, you are one of the mean stepsisters. While you are sitting right there in your seats, assume your roles. Cinderella, get started. I'll be the doorbell. Go!"

A minute later I called out over the bustle, "Writers, storytellers, freeze. You have got to see what Sam and Simone were doing as actors in that scene, watch." For a moment the class watched their classmates' reenactment, complete with gestures. "Take lessons from Sam and Simone and add little actions when the character speaks, like twirling a strand of hair, or chewing a piece of gum. Or think about *how* the character talks. Change your character's voice. Partner 1, you are Cinderella again, and Partner 2, you are the stepsister, hounding her while she does the laundry. Action!"

A minute into the drama, I called out "Ding dong," and the plot moved forward. A minute later, I called, "Bring the scene to an ending, we're stopping in a sec."

The process of collaboratively writing a text—whereby one child's suggested text becomes foundational for a text that each child continues to author—is one that your students will have already experienced in the previous units. There is something intense and fast-paced about this way of channeling students into producing a flash-draft. We think it is a very effective way to give them a sense for a genre.

You'll be tempted to open the floor for a whole-class conversation, but the minilesson is already very long. Keep the pace quick.

When I got the class's attention, I said, "I hope you can see how storytelling and drama can help you bring a story to life. Now our job would be to take all that good storytelling and acting and put it onto the page, onto drafting paper. I'd probably start writing something like this. . . ."

I reread the notes I'd jotted, and then I told the next part of the story, incorporating the students' ideas. I'd made sure to jot notes to myself in my own notebook, knowing I'd go back later and rewrite the story for students to see.

> One afternoon Cinderella was folding her stepsisters' laundry. She had a whole mountain of more laundry to fold. Then all of a sudden the doorbell rang.
>
> "You lazy girl," one stepsister said to Cinderella. "Go get the door. Hurry. Don't waste time."
>
> Cinderella went to the door. When she opened it, no one was there. She looked left, right, and then down. There on the doorstep was a letter.
>
> "Well," said her stepsister. "Who's there and what do they want?"
>
> Cinderella picked up the letter and handed it to her stepsister. "It's an invitation. From the town's mayor! It says 'Save the library' on the envelope."
>
> Her stepsister looked at Cinderella and smirked, "I don't know what you're getting excited about. You're not going anywhere dressed in rags and dirt. And besides, who cares about a library?" She ripped the invitation in two and threw it in the trash. "A library? How ridiculous."
>
> Cinderella returned to folding her mountain of laundry. "It's not ridiculous," Cinderella thought. Taking a deep breath, Cinderella said, "May I go?"

ACTIVE ENGAGEMENT

Set members of the class up to use the class's work with storytelling and drama as a model for their own storytelling.

"Try this with your own story. Start by retelling the beginning of the classic tale, using a booklet to help you do so." I gave them a minute to do this. "Next, make sure you get the facts straight about what will happen in your opening scene, your first Small Moment story. Who is doing what, exactly? Remember, we had Cinderella *doing* something, and then something is said, or something happens—for us it was the stepsister getting mad at Cinderella, and then the doorbell.

"Right now, think in your mind about who is doing what and saying what in your opening scene, in your first small moment. Be specific—we had to decide exactly what kind of work Cinderella was doing, and you will need to make decisions like that too. Think about that for a second." I left enough silence that I could see kids turning their minds to the job of making those decisions.

When you do this, draw your adaptation from your own class. But you'll probably want to follow a storyline something like this, or that echoes this. Be sure that your character has wants and trouble getting those wants fulfilled. That's the crux of any traditional story, and fairy tales fall into that category. We recommend, too, that the part of the story you tell all occur within one small moment, one scene. This will become more important as you move deeper into the unit.

Channel one partner to story-tell or act his or her opening scene to their partner, reminding them to include specific actions and dialogue.

"Your tale will probably begin 'One day . . .' or 'One early morning. . . .' Think of your way to begin and think of the words you say when you story-tell, storytelling in your mind right now." I left another pool of silence.

"Partner 1, you are going to start at the beginning and story-tell or reenact to your partner. Show and tell what your character is doing and who says what, exactly, in his or her words. Partner 1, on your mark, get set, turn and story-tell or act with your partner."

Coach with lean prompts that raise the level of what individuals do during the partner talk. Then convene the class and share.

As I listened, I coached using brief verbal and also many nonverbal cues. When one partner in a partnership storytold her opening scene, I pointed to my eyes to show that she needed to tell about what she saw. I mimed people talking and made quote marks with my hands to channel another child to add more dialogue. When one writer was speeding through her scene, I made an impromptu stop sign with my right hand, holding it up like a traffic guard.

As I silently prompted beside him, Jackson storytold to his partner Shane, "'I don't care if it's dangerous,' said the big German shepherd. So the big dog ran across the field. But the gnome caught him and in a wicked voice said, 'You will make a great gift for my master.' 'Wait for the middle-sized dog,' said the German shepherd. 'He will prove to be a much better pet.'"

LINK

Channel the students' acting energy toward writing.

"Class, I am impressed with how you slowed the scene down, acting out what the characters were actually saying through dialogue and storytelling exactly what the characters saw. I can't wait to see that appear in your writing! Writers, we are on the brink of writing time! Pull a sheet a clean paper from your writing folder." I paused as the students readied their materials. "Partner 1s, you have your opening scene fresh in your mind from storytelling and acting. Will you return to your seats right away and get started drafting that scene? Remember to add in all the details, actions, and dialogue you just discovered while rehearsing. Partner 2s, stay behind here at the rug for a moment. We are going to rehearse our opening scenes too."

"Okay, Partner 2s, it's your turn to story-tell! Remember all that we've worked on today—slowing down, adding dialogue, including actions—and think of your opening scene. Get with a new partner and when I say 'Go!,' story-tell or act out your opening scene. On your mark. Get set. Go!" As children rehearsed, I coached using the same brief verbal and nonverbal cues as I did with the Partner 1s. After a minute or two, I stopped them and sent them off to join the others and draft. A few remained to tell the start of their story to me.

This type of nonverbal cue is helpful when giving children quick, direct feedback, while not derailing their opportunity to practice. You might, another time, coach partners to use visual clues to give each other similar sorts of feedback.

Send half of the class off to write and keep others for a little more coaching. Half of the partnerships have not had a moment to rehearse their story ideas, so it's important to provide them a small amount of time to story-tell in their minds before they draft.

Coaching Children to Use Drama for Writing

Because it is early in the unit and many children will need help, you are going to need to balance your time between one-to-one work and small-group work. When going to individuals, your first instinct might be to support your strugglers, and surely you need to do all you can to get them up and going in this work. But you also need to work with some children who can provide examples that other children can follow.

Piper was one of the first children to get started writing and she wrote with ease, quickly filling her page. I glanced at what she'd written, and noticed a disparity between the dramatic work she'd just done and her draft. It was as if Piper was plowing through the storyline, trying to cover the basics of the plot. I knew that she wasn't alone with this, and knew that I'd need to spend a lot of time supporting children to move from summarizing to storytelling.

I took a seat next to her and interrupted her writing for moment. "Piper," I said. She looked up, clearly slightly annoyed to be interrupted as she plowed headlong through her storyline. Knowing that she was, in fact, probably feeling pretty successful—she was zooming through her first sheet of draft paper, after all—I wanted to make sure to honor her efforts—not simply because she actually was writing with great stamina, but because I knew she'd get onboard with the conference more quickly if I called out this observed strength of hers first.

I complimented, "You know, I saw you from all the way across the room—I could tell from the quiet and serious look on your face that you were *really* focused, and I could tell from the way your hand was zooming down the page that you were writing fast and furiously, getting your ideas down, with a whole lot of stamina. That's great!" She beamed. "But . . . I actually want to switch gears for a minute and talk with you about that talent you have for storytelling—and acting! Are you aware that you have a real knack for bringing people to life when you story-tell? When I watched you during the minilesson, it seemed like you'd become your characters—your hands weren't

MID-WORKSHOP TEACHING   Storytelling Not Summarizing

"Writers, I want to stop you and first say how impressed I am with the amount of writing you are doing. I love that you have been writing fast and furiously.

"I want to caution you that *some* of you are slip-sliding into the next scene of your story. I bet you don't even know that you had stopped writing about one small moment, one scene, and slid into another. Chances are you'll find that you were writing bit by bit for a while, letting the story happen slowly, and then all of a sudden you speeded up and *vroom*. You were out of that small moment.

"Think of it like this—you are in a car, driving down the street. Think of each small moment, each scene, as a stretch of road in between two red lights. If you step on the gas too fast, you run past the red lights! That's against the law—not just the police law, but the law of writing.

"Will you reread your story, and see if you are still writing within the first small moment—or did you step on the gas and go *vrooming* to other parts of the story? If you went past the opening small moment of your story, will you draw a line on your draft paper at the place where the first small moment ends, and see if for now you can go back to that small moment and revise it, improve what you've written?"

As Students Continue Working . . .

"If you really want to move on to a second Small Moment story, I want to first meet with you and give you another lesson, another tip. But your first scene should be something like a page in length, not a few sentences. If it is four or five sentences, start it all over on a new sheet of paper."

yours any more, they were your characters'. Your voice, your posture—it was as if you became someone else."

Piper blushed and also lit up, becoming the characters all over again as we talked. Moving on to teach, I said, "I'm telling you this because when you started writing this story, it felt like you forgot that you have a special talent for making a story come to life when you story-tell it and act it out, and you forgot that the world needs you to bring that talent to your work. And in this instance, to your writing. Right now, it looks like your draft is zooming along through the story without including *any* of that lively action and dialogue that I saw coming out of you earlier. Do you mind me saying to you that I think you can do much, *much* better at this, and that you really should start over again?"

A huge sigh from Piper, and a rueful glance down at her full page of writing. We may be tempted, in situations like this one, to not push. She had, after all, been producing lots of writing. What a bummer to have to start all over again! But in actuality, it's not a bummer at all—it's an opportunity to not only help Piper get started on the right foot, incorporating the richness of her dramatization into her draft, but also to teach her that revision sometimes means beginning again—and again, and again—and that this is not at all a bummer, but a wonderful and necessary way to enrich writing.

Getting specific now, I said, "I think you should just fold this draft up, and get a new sheet of paper and write *Draft 2* on the top of your page. And this time, before you start writing, relive the scene, exactly. Think, 'Who am I in this scene?' Only, you need to switch from being one character to being another . . . to be all the players. And as you start your new draft, make sure that you're putting all of that great stuff in—what the characters do, feel, say. . . . Right now, may I give you a moment to think about this and get started, and then I'll come back in a bit?"

On the flip side, there was Simone, who was always one to get swept into the drama of an event. I'd seen her out of the corner of my eye, dramatically marching around her desk, waving her arms, and then sitting down to write. At first glance, what could be better? She was certainly feeling the story in her bones! But when I sat down next to

her to read her draft, it seemed that the acting may have carried her away. In her draft of the first scene in her story about the three moles, it became clear that there were so many changes being made that it was becoming less like an adaptation of *The Three Billy Goats Gruff* by the minute.

"What are you working on, Simone?"

"Well, I added this change where the humans are digging the soil up so the moles are having a hard time. Every time they try to get somewhere, a shovel comes down and stops them!"

She was clearly thrilled with this, and full of energy for writing. But the work at hand was writing adaptations—and to write an adaptation, the bones of the original story need to be strong.

"Simone," I said, after skimming the rest of her draft and confirming that she could use some reining in, "you're really diving in here and making some creative changes to your story. But, you know, when writers are adapting a story, they have to make sure not only that the changes they are making are meaningful, but that they don't change the original story so much it's unrecognizable. Think about the adaptations we've been reading. Big changes are made in *Prince Cinders*, right? But we never doubt that we're reading a version of *Cinderella*. I think that your readers are not going to know, at this point, that you're adapting *The Three Billy Goats Gruff*."

Simone added, "The humans and the shovels are cool though."

"Totally. But you know what, you just put your finger on the part that doesn't need to be in this adaptation. It doesn't mean it's not great—it just doesn't fit with this adaptation. Tell you what—why don't you save it for another story? Maybe you can write the moles' continuing adventures sometime! But right now, dig back into this first scene, and reread it. Think about what changes belong in this story, and which ones are too much. You might want to start a second draft if you find that there are so many changes that you can't see the original story at all."

Using Story-Planning Booklets as Scene-Planning Booklets

Recruit writers to listen to one student's work, noticing what he has done well.

"Writers, you've each written the first scene or small moment in your fairy tale adaptation. Let's study Sam's opening scene and see if we can notice specific things Sam does to story-tell this scene in ways that allow us to picture the unfolding story. Ready to listen to the start of Sam's story? List across your fingers three things you hear him doing to bring this to life." I read aloud Sam's piece, making sure my voice came to a slow stop as I neared the last few lines (see Figure 3–1):

> One sunny Wednesday, Gruff the parrot was resting when the zoo guard walked by. He was a bad person because he was smoking. He twirled his keys. Gruff did not like the zoo but he really hated the zookeeper. Gruff was pacing up and down in his cage. Also he was making a bunch of weird noises and said to himself, "I've got to get out of here! I wish I could fly free in the air."
>
> He was about to cry but then he came up with a plan.

"Turn and tell your partner what Sam has done that you admire." After a second, I reconvened the group and heard a few of the things they especially admired.

Set up children to plan upcoming scenes by using scene-planning booklets.

Then I switched the subject a bit. "Tomorrow you'll move on to later scenes, or Small Moment stories. Instead of trying to write your way to that next Small Moment story, for now I'm going to suggest you make yourself another scene-planning booklet. Sketch really quickly the timeline of the next scene in your story—and it is probably the second of three scenes—and then story-tell out loud, as you learned to do earlier this year, making sure that on each page of the booklet you tell what happened first, next, and last in the scene. You can do that by yourself, in your mind, as you sit with each page of the scene-planning booklet in front of you.

"And the cool thing is, writers often try out lots of possible ways that they could tell a scene, so make more than one scene-planning booklet and try telling the next scene in a bunch of different ways." I passed out multiple sheets of blank paper to each child. "So tonight for homework you'll make a few booklets, quickly sketching out different possibilities for the next scene in your story. Remember, you'll want to story-tell each page just like we worked on today because tomorrow we are drafting these next scenes!"

> One sunny Wednesday, Gruff the parrot was resting when the zoo guard walked by. He was a bad person because he was smoking. He twirled his keys. Gruff did not like the zoo but he really hated the zookeeper. Gruff was pacing up and down his cage. Also he was making a bunch of weird noises and said to himself, "I've got to get out of here! I wish I could fly free in the air.
>
> He was about to cry but then he came up with a plan.

FIG. 3–1   Sam's first draft of scene 1

Writers Can Story-Tell and Act Out as They Draft

IN THIS SESSION, you'll teach students that writers can rehearse for writing by storytelling or acting out each scene.

GETTING READY

✔ Students' scene-planning booklet homework (see Connection)

✔ Class adaptation of *Cinderella* from Session 3 (see Connection)

✔ "How to Write a Fairy Tale Adaptation" chart from previous sessions

✔ Students' writing folders containing their drafts (see Link)

✔ *Prince Cinders* by Babette Cole (see Small-Group Work and Conferring)

COMMON CORE STATE STANDARDS: W.3.3.b,d; W.3.4, W.3.5, W.3.10, W.4.3.b,e; RL.3.1, RL.3.2, RL.3.3, RL.3.5, SL.3.1, SL.3.4, SL.3.6, L.3.1, L.3.2, L.3.3, L.3.6

TODAY YOUR STUDENTS will be drafting their fairy tales in earnest. The goal is for their drafts to be as informed and as full of the qualities of good fiction writing as possible from the beginning—knowing full well that a draft is a draft, and that the story will evolve through revision.

Part of what you need to teach early on in this unit is that there is no way that a six-page booklet can contain a whole novel or a whole TV series-like saga. What your children will be writing are *short* stories or picture books, not epic sagas. You may find that some of your students get carried away by the fun of fiction writing and, despite what you have said to them, the text they produce resembles the kind of epic saga that spans a character's lifetime. You will want to channel those students toward writing a more focused story from the beginning. To do so, we recommend telling students that their stories will be apt to involve two, maybe three characters, and two or at the most three "scenes," as writers say, or "small moments" as your children say.

Once children realize that their fairy tales will be written as a series of scenes—Small Moment stories—they are free to tap into their skills and experience as writers of small moment narratives. You may need to explicitly remind children to draw on all that they already know. Because prior instruction in small moment, personal narrative storywriting will need to be front and center to the new challenges they are now undertaking, you'll definitely want the anchor charts from the *Crafting True Stories* unit to be prominently displayed. Be prepared to remind students that there is great value in rehearsing along the way as they flesh out their plans into scenes, and remind them that their Small Moment stories need to include action and dialogue. Students used the folded blank booklets to plan scenes as opposed to an entire story for the previous session's homework. They will be chomping at the bit to get started. Those who eked out words during earlier units will write with new volume, new stamina, new engagement, their scrawl filling one page, another, another as the unit taps into a great energy source. You'll set them up to have a great start and then get out of their way.

Writers Can Story-Tell and Act Out as They Draft

CONNECTION

Channel partners to share their writing with each other and to talk about what might happen next in their fairy tales.

"Writers, meet me at the rug and bring both your writer's notebooks and your scene-planning booklets that you worked on last night for homework!" As children began settling on the rug, I encouraged them to take a moment to reread their writing to their partners and to talk about what will happen in their next Small Moment story.

"Writers," I interrupted, "like you, I am thinking about what will happen next. Our class story needs to jump ahead now, probably to the part when the fairy godmother comes. For homework, you worked on figuring out what you might jump to next in your story. You thought, 'What's the next scene, the next small moment, that I need to storytell?'"

Work together to plan the start of the next scene of the shared class fairy tale adaptation.

"Let's do this work with our class story. We know it will be that the fairy godmother comes, but where does she come, and how? And when she comes, is Cinderella still folding laundry in the same place, or has the scene changed?" Then I added, "I know in the original story, Cinderella is by the hearth, cleaning up the ashes . . . hmm. . . ."

Charlie said, "Maybe the fairy godmother comes down the chimney, like Santa, and stands beside the washing machine."

I thanked Charlie and started jotting notes about the class story on a white board. Pausing, I said to the class, "Do you see how you're helping me to think through the plan for the next scene? Will you do the same planning with your own story, making sure you ask, 'What will happen next? How might the scene go?' You may use your scene-planning booklets from last night's homework to help you." I added, "While you jot your plans, I'm going to do the same for our class story."

Record plans for the class story on a chart while children jot plans for their own stories and share them with a partner.

On the easel I jotted:

Notice that we are reining the kids in a bit, trying to be sure they write in scenes rather than just blasting through the whole story. Their progress will be less scaffolded and less controlled during the next portion of the unit.

Teachers, later we will teach the students how to glue their scenes together, but for now we are focusing students on planning their scenes and getting those scenes drafted.

I'm hoping you notice that "my" story is also the class's story. There are times when I demonstrate with this text, and other times when I recruit children to join me in doing some work, with lots of support, on that text.

- Cinderella, in her bedroom/in the basement laundry room? Crying.
- Her fairy godmother comes down the chimney?
- Cinderella wants a bike and clean clothes to get to the fundraiser—gets them.

❖ **Name the teaching point.**

"Today I want to teach you that when you are writing, you can rehearse in the middle of writing as well as at the start of it. And specifically, when writing a fiction story that contains several small moments or scenes, it helps to story-tell or to act out each small moment before writing it—or at least to do this *while* writing it. I'm going to add that to our chart."

How to Write a Fairy Tale Adaptation

- Know the classic story and tell it often.
- Decide on a change to improve the story.
- Make the change lead to other changes so the whole story fits together.
- Make a character with traits and wants who runs into trouble.
- Tell the story in two or three scenes (Small Moment stories).
- Story-tell or act out a scene, filling in lifelike details. Then write the scenes.

TEACHING

Give children tips that will bring their characters and stories to life.

"Because you all are storytelling, or acting your story to get ready for writing it, I'm going to give you a few acting tips. The first tip is that when you act, you need to not only show what the character *says*, but also what the character *does*. Even little tiny actions may make a big difference.

"The second tip is this. When you are acting or writing a story, you not only bring some *characters* to life—say, a girl and a wolf—you also bring a *place* to life. Always make sure you know where, exactly, your character is, what the things are that are nearby, and what the place feels like."

Perform the new, second scene of the class story in a flat, motionless way. Ask children to coach you to improve your performance to better help your writing.

"So let's try doing some acting with our *Cinderella* story, first, and then you may try with your own stories. Remember—you are working on the second scene of your stories! I'll play the part of several characters, and you may watch, and then after I act out the scene, coach me. Okay, here goes."

As you will recall, there are a few common methods used in the teaching component of minilessons. This minilesson uses a rather unusual method—the teacher is telling the students and showing an example. In a moment, this will switch.

When trying to make a point in a minilesson, I tend to exaggerate. There is no advantage to being subtle. You want to drive home your point as forcefully as possible.

Standing stock still, I said, "Stop crying, Cinderella. I am your fairy godmother and I am here to grant your wish."

Switching places so that I became the second character in the story—Cinderella—I said, "Wh . . . at? Who are you?" I meanwhile stood motionless.

Hopping back to the place where the first character—the godmother—had spoken, I stood still and said to Cinderella, "You want to go the fund-raiser for the library, and I have the magic to make that happen. Let's see, you'll need. . . ."

I stopped. "Any suggestions for how my acting could be improved?" I asked. "Remember, acting helps me bring the characters and place to life." The kids jumped to point out that I had forgotten all about adding actions, and added that I also forgot all about adding in the place. "I need to think what objects we might be holding. And also I need to feel what the place might feel like . . . hmm, . . . let me try it again. I want to think about what action could show that I just came down the chimney."

Perform the scene again, incorporating their ideas.

I spun around as if I were a top, stopped as if I'd just landed, and then looked at an imaginary Cinderella. I raised my wand, twirling it in the air a bit, as if releasing a cloud of fairy dust. "Stop crying, Cinderella," I said, pointing my wand toward the girl. "I am your fairy godmother and I am here to grant your wish."

As Cinderella, I then gaped up at the magical woman, taking a few steps back in awe.

Set up half the class to play one part in the scene, while you play the other. Ask the other half of the class to watch, noting any suggestions.

"Okay, Partner 1s, you'll take over the scene! Partner 1s, you will be Cinderella and talk back to me," I said. "Act like her and bring her to life—remembering she has a whole pile of laundry in front of her." Then I repeated my fairy godmother lines.

The kids tended to fall backward in amazement, open mouthed, saying something like, "Wh . . . at? Who are you?"

Approaching the whole class full of Cinderellas, I continued my lines, "You want to go the fund-raiser for the library, and," touching my chest, "I have the magic to make that happen. Let's see, you'll need. . . . " I let them respond to me, to their partners.

Demonstrate how acting out the scene improves the quality of writing.

"Writers, or should I say actors, the acting we just did together helped us discover different ways to bring the characters and place to life. We stumbled across little, tiny actions that make a big difference once we add them to our writing, like the twirling of a magic wand or Cinderella falling back in amazement. Let's add these tiny details we discovered through acting to our class story."

When contrasting two versions of the same thing, it is important to make sure the two versions are the same in every way except the one dimension that is meant to be different.

ACTIVE ENGAGEMENT

Channel children to act out their own scenes with a partner. As they do, listen and coach in as needed.

"Okay, time to try this in your own scenes. Partner 2, will you tell your partner what's going to happen in *your* next scene, and then will the two of you try acting that out? You can use your scene-planning booklet and the notes you jotted earlier to remind you. Get started."

I listened to Sam sharing his scene with his partner Shelly. He said, "Gruff, the parrot, was resting. He was thinking about how bored he was. He didn't want to be there anymore."

Caught up in the excitement of acting, Shelly and Sam immediately began to act out the scene, each imitating a parrot resting.

I coached, "Remember, you want to use acting to bring your characters and place to life! This will improve your writing. Hmmmmm, where could Gruff be resting?"

Shelly exclaimed, "On a tree!"

"Yeah, but he's in the zoo. He lives in a cage. That's why he's bored!" Sam clarified.

"Oh, let's act that!" I nudged. "Who can be the bars of a cage? Who can be the bird? Remember, bring the characters and place to life with your acting."

Sam threw up his arms to represent bars of a cage, while Shelly leaned back and forth as if she were on a swing with eyes heavy and a fallen face.

"So, Sam, how could your writing improve now that you and Shelly have acted out this little part?"

Sam began again, "One sunny afternoon Gruff, the parrot, was resting on a branch in his cage at the zoo." Sam looked up at Shelly as if to ask, "Is that better?" and got a thumbs up.

LINK

Ask children to revisit the start of the scene they just acted, clarifying a character's words and actions, and then to start writing the scene.

"I know you've only had a chance to act out one partner's scene, but that is okay because usually when a person writes, she *acts in her mind the story she is going to write*. That is, when *you* write, it helps to be acting the story out with your body or in your mind as you rush to get it onto the page. So right now, go back to the start of this scene in your writing. Picture what you just acted out. Or picture what you could act out. Who is saying what? What is that person doing? Picture what that person is holding, where he or she is. You got it in your mind?" I gave the children a little bit of silence. "Start writing, right here, right now. Go!"

Don't let yourself become convinced that there always needs to be a time for sharing after the partner work in an active engagement. That is an option, but if minilessons are taking too much time or kids aren't getting enough writing done, you need to be economical. Reporting back or even just debriefing after partner work may become a luxury you can't afford.

Sometimes, it may be particularly powerful to get started writing as a whole community while still in the meeting area. This is what we are suggesting for today. As soon as you see that a writer has a good, strong start, say, four or five lines of writing, you might whisper, "Off you go."

Teaching the Balance of Narration, Description, and Dialogue

AFTER THE PREVIOUS SESSION, I'd read through the work of children who sat at one table and I'd made notes about some of the conferring and small-group work I would need to do in this session. I'd noticed, for example, that Sam had zipped through the first scene hardly adding anything to the initial story he'd told a day or so earlier. It read, *The parrot was resting, and the guard was pacing up and down. Then the parrot began to peck at the door with his red beak.* Sam had already moved on to other scenes, and those other scenes felt equally underdeveloped.

In contrast, Leroy's draft brimmed with dialogue and description. His story was stretching longer and longer and nothing had happened in it yet. He seemed to have overdone the emphasis on telling the story bit by bit.

I decided to gather both Sam and Leroy for a small group. Although they were coming at the challenge of writing a story from different angles, I thought the fact that they had opposite issues and opposite strengths might allow them to help each other.

Once we were settled together on the rug, I said, "I want to help you work a bit on the first scene in each of your stories. Would you reread each other's first scenes so that we can all talk about all the texts?"

After they read, I asked, "So, what did you notice?"

Leroy said, "Sam's is really short. Like, it's a *really* small moment. The parrot is just sitting there and the guard guy is just pacing."

"Yes," I agreed. "Sam has really zoomed in. There's some good things about that, and sometimes some hard things about it too, right? Sam, what did you notice about Leroy's draft?"

(continues)

MID-WORKSHOP TEACHING
Being a Spelling Fairy Godmother

"Writers, may I interrupt you? As I move about the room, going from writer to writer, I see you carrying all that you've learned across these past few days into your drafts. I am going to read our chart, and if you have done or are doing one of the items on the chart, give a thumbs up.

"It feels good to hold yourselves accountable to the things you know how to do, doesn't it? What I am wondering, and you are probably wondering as well, is are you holding yourself to all that you've learned across this year, to the things that writers remember to do always? I specifically want to remind you of the important work you have learned to do as spellers, because I see some of you acting like a fairy godmother is going to come along and with a magic wand make your spelling look like the work of an almost-fourth-grader. Guess what—*you* need to be your own spelling fairy godmother. And the magic dust is actually elbow grease.

"So here are three things you need to remember to do as spellers."

◆ Try a word a few different ways.

◆ Check the word wall.

◆ Circle the word and come back later.

"Writers, take a moment right now to become your own spelling fairy godmother. Reread a part of your draft looking for words that don't look quite right and remember you can try the word a few different ways in the margin, check the word wall, or circle it, reminding yourself to figure it out later."

"He's got a lot of dialogue. They are talking the whole time!"

"Yep. Again, dialogue—like zooming in—is an important thing that Small Moment writers do. But Leroy, I get the sense that you're suggesting Sam's draft may be too focused, and Sam, that Leroy's might have too much talk, and I think you both are on to something. I think that sometimes writers tend to do one thing in a really big way—something the writer is good at—and sometimes that one thing gets almost overdone, with other things being ignored. You two are good at different things, but both of your pieces are somewhat out of balance because you each do one thing really well, and forget some other work.

"For example, may I tell you one thing that I think both of you could work on? Neither of you have got much action yet in your drafts. Will you look over your draft and see if you agree?"

The children looked, and agreed that yes, that was sort of true. "Let's see if I can help you work on that one aspect of your writing, okay?" I said. "Will you think about your Small Moment story as a scene in a play? Will you think about what the action is that happens up on stage?"

"I could add the thinking, like what the parrot was thinking about," Sam said.

"Sam, I think you need some action as well. Are you sure you have figured out what actually happens in the story, because making those decisions may help you put more action in. May I leave you two to help each other think about the actions that characters are making, and about how you put those into your draft? I'm pretty sure you are

going to need to start a new draft, this time telling not only what people are thinking and saying, but also what they are doing." As I left the boys to their revising, I thought to myself that later I might suggest that children study the way that *Prince Cinders* provides a balance of action, description, dialogue, and narration.

Sam, meanwhile, began a new draft, this time writing (see Figure 4–1).

Assured that both kids were poised to not only make meaningful revisions of their first scenes but to carry their Small Moment story knowledge into drafting the rest of their scenes, I moved on.

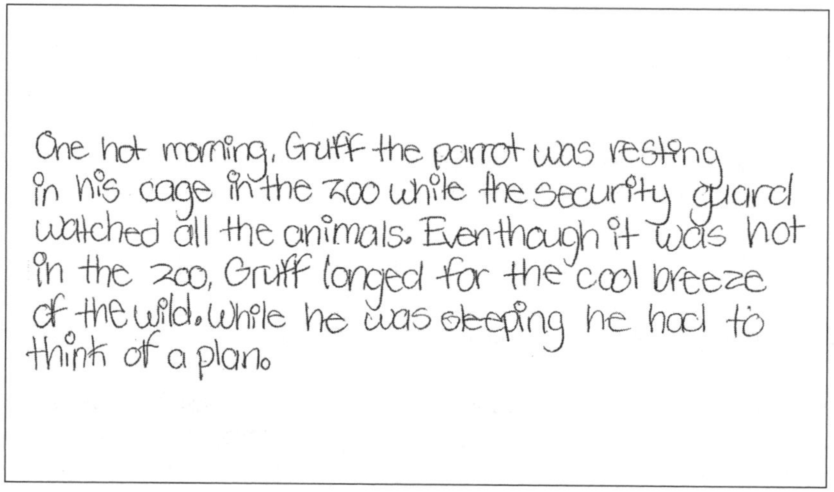

One hot morning, Gruff the parrot was resting in his cage in the zoo while the security guard watched all the animals. Eventhough it was hot in the zoo, Gruff longed for the cool breeze of the wild. While he was sleeping he had to think of a plan.

FIG. 4–1   Sam's revised draft of scene

Ending Stories

Ask students to discuss what they know about writing strong endings, and then highlight a few for the class.

"Writers, gather the scene-planning booklets you've been using and meet me on the rug." I gave them a moment and then said, "You've put so much time and care into rehearsing and storytelling the first and second scenes of your fairy tale adaptations. Many of you will be ready to start drafting your final scenes, or endings, tomorrow." I held up a booklet and pointed to the final page. "Let's make sure you end these books with a bang! Before we close for the day, let's think about how endings to stories usually go and then try out a few ways our story could end.

"You already know a lot about writing effective endings to a story," I said. "Turn and talk to your partner about one thing that you think makes an effective ending." I stopped them after just a few moments.

"I am impressed, writers! Some of you were talking about using important actions or important dialogue, others remembered that many books end with rich images. The truth is, sometimes a writer uses all of these things to create

FIG. 4–2   Jackson's scene-planning booklet

an end. I also heard a few of you say—and I think you're right about this—that an effective ending makes you feel like the story is *over*. And that, writers, happens when all of the problems that your character faced at the beginning of the story are solved."

Ask students to identify what happens at the ending of a classic tale.

"Could we try something together, writers? Could you think with me about the classic *Cinderella* story we all know and see if we can, together, figure out how the ending of the classic story solves Cinderella's problems and helps us feel the story is over?

"The first thing I'm going to do is list for myself what happens at the end." I retold plot events across my fingers using the story's ending language. "Now that the ending is fresh in our minds, turn and talk with your partner. What happens at the end that solves Cinderella's problems?" I gave the class just a moment to do this, then summarized their talk, highlighting the process.

"I heard many of you saying that the ending fixes Cinderella's problems by letting her marry a prince because at the beginning she is so lonely. Some of you are saying that the ending solves Cinderella's problems because the evil step-mother and stepsisters get sent away—those wicked girls were her real problem all along! Both of these problems do get solved in the classic tale! But writers, do you know what I noticed? I noticed that when you want to figure out what is an effective ending for a story, you have to ask yourself, 'What were the big problems at the beginning?'"

Challenge children to find the central problems of the main character in the class adaptation.

"So writers, now I have a challenge for you, and this is the kind of writing that I know some students are doing even in the seventh grade! Do you think you are ready for it?" The students chorused "Yes!"

"Okay, this is it—to write an effective ending for our story, we not only need to write an ending that's different from what happens in the classic story, but also we need to write an ending that solves the big problems that we have created for *our* story, *our* Cinderella." I added a new item to our chart.

"So writers, let's stir up some ideas for our ending! I want you to think about this silently first, just to yourself—what were our Cinderella's problems at the beginning? Thumbs up when you have an idea." I waited until thumbs are up across the rug. "Okay, now take this idea and try rehearsing an ending with your partner. Partner 2, as you listen, make sure you are thinking, 'How does this ending solve our Cinderella's problem?'

"Right here at the rug, think about how you might tie up the loose ends of your story, and—I know it's a lot—keep all that you know about strong endings in mind as you do that." I gave them a moment to think and then said, "Now, what could be *another* way that you end your story?" After another quick moment of thinking time I said, "Work with your partner and story-tell or act out a possible ending or two to your fairy tale. Use what you've learned about great story-telling and acting to make the final scene, the ending, come alive for your partner! You might want to jot yourself a few notes in your scene-planning booklet, too, so that you remember what you've planned for tomorrow's writing time."

How to Write a Fairy Tale Adaptation

- Know the classic story and tell it often.
- Decide on a change to improve the story.
- Make the change lead to other changes so the whole story fits together.
- Make a character with traits and wants who runs into trouble.
- Tell the story in two or three scenes (Small Moment stories).
- Story-tell or act out the first scene, filling in lifelike details. Then write the scenes.
- Figure out an ending that solves the character's big problem.

Session 5

Weaving Narration
through Stories

I N CRAFTING TRUE STORIES as well as many other narrative writing units, we have focused on the importance of showing, not telling, and that skill continues to be important in this unit. It is important for readers to be brought into a story and for the story to unfold right in front of the readers' eyes. Still, as important as showing is, *telling* also has a role in narrative craft. Gail Carson Levine, author of *Ella Enchanted* (1997), suggests that when the author *shows* readers something, the author allows the reader to live on the ground of a story, to get traction. Readers are in the shoes of characters. On the other hand, when the author *tells* instead of showing something to readers, this allows readers to see the story as if looking out from the window of an airplane. The world rushes by so quickly that only the largest landmarks—lakes, mountains, a sprawling city—stand out.

Levine argues that as writers, we need to both the show *and* tell. Writers *show* when they want to slow the story the down, inviting the reader into a scene, entering the world of a character and catching an important part of the tale. Writers *tell* when they want to cover a lot of ground quickly, laying out the most important parts of the story and then moving on.

This technique of telling in fairy tales is often embodied by an anonymous narrator who stands outside the tale. Remember how many Disney fairy tales open? An illustrated olden-days book opens under the light of a candle and a soothing voice begins, "Once upon a time. . . ." In *Pinocchio*, Jiminy Cricket, an animated cricket, played the role of this narrator. He was the first character the audience met, a formally dressed fellow who sat outside of the storybook—in fact, on top of it—just like a narrator stands outside the red curtain at the opening of a play. He spoke directly to us, the audience, narrating the beginning of the story and giving us important context: "One night a *long* time ago, my travels took me to a quaint little village. It was a beautiful night, stars shining like diamonds." Jiminy Cricket invited both young and old into the world of an old tale.

In this session, you'll explain the concept of a narrator who functions like Jiminy Cricket, providing context and stitching the story together meaningfully. You'll highlight the difference between telling and showing, teaching children that it is powerful and effective to use both techniques.

IN THIS SESSION, you'll teach students that writers often weave narration through fairy tales as a way to establish background, tie together scenes, and teach a moral or end a story.

GETTING READY

✔ *Prince Cinders* by Babette Cole or other fairy tale adaptations (see Connection)

✔ Fairy tale excerpts you plan to read, copied onto chart paper (optional)

✔ "How to Write a Fairy Tale Adaptation" chart from previous sessions

✔ "The Power of Narration" chart (see Teaching)

✔ Class adaptation of *Cinderella*, Scene 1 and the start of Scene 2 (see Active Engagement)

✔ Students' writing folders (see Active Engagement and Link)

COMMON CORE STATE STANDARDS: W.3.3.a,b,c,d; W.3.4, W.3.5, W.3.10, W.4.3.a,b,c,d,e; RL.3.2, RL.3.3, RL.3.4, RL.3.6, RL.3.10, SL.3.1, SL.3.4, SL.3.6, L.3.3.a

Weaving Narration through Stories

CONNECTION

Introduce the concept of a narrator by telling children about the role Jiminy Cricket played in the movie *Pinocchio* long ago. Explain that fairy tales often rely on narrators and cite a few.

"When I was little, when I watched the movie *Pinocchio*, there was a little cricket guy named Jiminy Cricket who came on screen, wearing a top hat and coat and carrying a cane, at various times in the story, and he would talk right to those of us watching the movie. He'd say things like, 'One night, a long time ago, my travels took me to . . . ,' or he'd say, 'Of course, I'm just a cricket singing my way from hearth to hearth, but let me tell you what made me change my mind. . . .'

"Now, as a grown-up, I know that the fancy word for that little cricket guy is *narrator*. You all know about narrators because when you and your partner, during reading time, decide to take parts and read aloud in the role of characters, and there are some words that none of the obvious characters say; that's usually the narrator's part.

"I'm telling you this because if you read a ton of fairy tales, you quickly realize that many of them have a Jiminy Cricket character in them—a narrator who comes out on stage and makes a little speech to readers. Listen to the start of these stories, and you'll hear the narrator, and then you'll hear when the actual story gets started. Listen to this part of *Prince Cinders* by Babette Cole":

> *Prince Cinders was not much of a prince.*
> *He was small, spotty, scruffy and skinny.*
> *He had three big, hairy brothers who were*
> *always teasing him about his looks.*

"Then the narrator stops saying his lines, and the Small Moment story takes over":

One Saturday night, *when he was washing the socks, a dirty fairy fell down the chimney.*

◆ COACHING

Of course, this is one of those places where showing a bit of a video would be a terrific addition. We have found several useful clips on YouTube. If you find others that feature Jiminy Cricket or other narrators and if that footage helps your children grasp the important concept you are teaching, send us word and we'll include the reference in future editions.

The italics are ours. When you read the bits from fairy tales in this session, make sure that your voice accentuates the transition between telling and showing, between the narrator talking, and the narrator standing back to let the scene resume, the characters carrying the story.

"Or here is another, from *Cinder-Elly* by Frances Minters":

> *Once upon a time,*
> *Or so they tell me,*
> *There was a girl*
> *Called Cinder-Elly.*
> *Elly was good*
> *And she was pretty.*
> *She lived with her folks*
> *In New York City.*

"And again, the narrator's part ends and the story starts":

> *But then* one day
> *El got a note.*
> *So did her sisters.*
> *Somebody wrote . . .*

✤ Name the teaching point.

"Today I want to teach you that writers of fairy tales use narration, or *telling*, in some important ways: to introduce the story, to stitch one scene to the next, and to end the story."

TEACHING

Set up your teaching by telling students you'll be giving them a lot of new information in the form of a little lecture, just like in a college class.

"Today is going to be a course about the narrator's job. I'll teach you a bit, then we'll practice together on the class fairy tale, and then I'll give you some time to practice on your own fairy tale adaptation. You're going to get a taste of what it's like to be in a lecture class in college, where you hear a bunch of new information all at once, and you have to be really alert and awake to catch all of the kernels of information. So, shake your hands, stretch your necks, take a deep breath, and get ready! After I give you a little talk about the narrator's role, I'm going to ask you to say back what you have learned to your partner."

Explain some of the different ways in which narration is used in stories. Start by discussing the jobs that narrators do at the start of fairy tales, providing examples, then spotlighting transitions.

"The first place where writers of fairy tales use the power of telling is at the beginning of the story. Fairy tale writers often start by almost coming out on stage, talking to readers, filling them in on the background to the story. For example, the classic *Cinderella* tale does *not* begin in the ways you've learned to begin a story, with a small moment and a character who is saying or doing something. Cinderella isn't even out on stage at the start of the classic version.

It will help later in the minilesson if you have a chance to write these excerpts on chart paper. Later, you'll ask students to write narration for the class adaptation of Cinderella, *and having model texts in front of them will help. But it is not crucial.*

When you need to give a little bit of content up front, it may be helpful to use the metaphor of a college class because you set your students up to learn a bunch of new content quickly. If you recall, there are four kinds of teaching that one draws upon in the teaching component of minilessons. Usually you are demonstrating, sometimes teaching through guided practice, as in the previous lesson. This minilesson uses another unusual method; you are teaching by explaining and showing an example.

Of course, you'll read the first few lines of the classic Cinderella *version you choose to use with your class here.*

Instead, it is as if a narrator comes out on stage and gives the readers a little speech, explaining some of the background to the story. The narrator tells the readers, 'There once was a man whose wife died and so he took another. The new wife was proud and haughty, and had two daughters who were just like her in every way. But the man also had a daughter, and she was sweet and gentle and good as gold.' Did you hear how the narrator pops in like Jiminy Cricket and gets the story going?

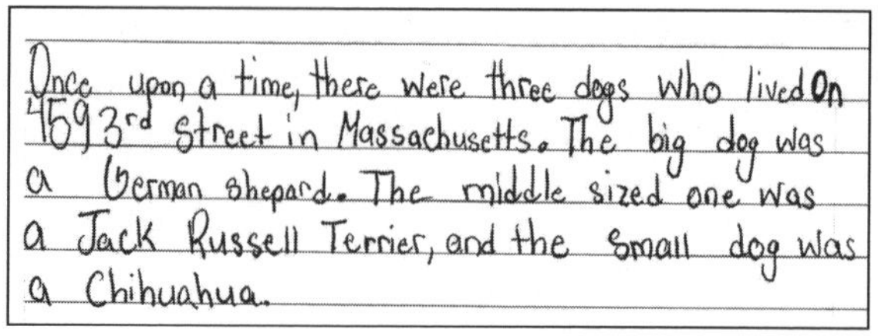

"And that's not the only place that writers use narration. The narrator is also used to stitch the scenes, the small moments, of a story together. Usually, there is a jump-in time and place between one Small Moment story and another, and the narrator of the story—the Jiminy Cricket—comes out on stage and talks directly to readers, saying, 'After this, a bunch of time went by. Then one day, in this other place,' and then readers are back into a second Small Moment story.

"In fairy tales the narrator often uses fancier words to stitch scenes together, like they might say, 'After some months had passed, the king's son gave a ball for all the stylish people in the countryside' and 'For two days the sisters could hardly eat for excitement' and 'At last the evening of the ball came.' But the important thing for you to know is that another powerful way to use narration is to stitch together Small Moment stories so that readers understand how they fit together."

Debrief by asking students to recap what they've heard, while you chart your main points.

While partners did a quick recap of what they'd heard to a partner, I quickly jotted on chart paper two ways narration is powerful.

The Power of Narration

- Provides backstory at the beginning of a story
- Stitches together Small Moment stories

ACTIVE ENGAGEMENT

Ask students to practice, in partnerships, the two types of narration you've discussed in the context of the class fairy tale.

"Let's try using these two kinds of narration in our class adaptation of *Cinderella*. We haven't finished drafting all of our scenes yet, but I think we have enough of a start to practice. Partner 1, quickly jot on a clean sheet of paper from your folder what narration you might add at the start of our *Cinderella* story to provide readers with some backstory. Remember, this doesn't need to be a long, drawn-out overview of the characters or the place; you can cover a lot of ground in just a few sentences.

Once upon a time, there were three dogs who lived on 4593rd street in Massachusetts. The big dog was a German shepard. The middle sized one was a Jack Russell Terrier, and the small dog was a Chihuahua.

FIG. 5–1   Jackson's narration at the start of his story

"Partner 2, you're going to think about and jot a way that you could use the narrator to stitch together Scene 1—it is written up here—and Scene 2—the start of it is written here. Keep in mind that readers might be confused about how Cinderella gets from the laundry to her attic, and might not have any idea what time it is. Write quickly—the exact words you suggest we stick into the story. We'll share ideas in a minute." As students wrote or thought, I circulated, prompting students to keep the narration succinct, to use some of the exemplar text that I'd cited earlier. I kept my ears open for some child's narration that I thought would especially add to the class tale.

Share some strong examples of narration.

"Okay, partners, let's wrap it up. Quickly, exchange papers, and read what each other has written." As the children did this, I continued searching for some good examples. Before the children even had time to finish reading each other's work, I asked for their attention. "May I stop you? I think our story is going to hang together with a lot more power because of the narration you just came up with. We could use the work any one of you just did. Let's take Sierra's idea for now. She said the beginning could go something like:

> Once long ago, in a land far away, there lived a girl named Cinderella. Cinderella tried to be cheerful, but it was kind of hard. She lived with her evil stepmother and two mean stepsisters. They made Cinderella work all the time. All she wanted to do was read.

"And José thought that in between Scenes 1 and 2, the narration might go something like:

> Later that night, as she sat in her room, Cinderella . . .

Debrief. Name what students have just practiced and plan to add new narration to class text later.

"Did you notice how, in just a couple of sentences, we used the power of narration to give readers backstory at the beginning and to stitch together two scenes? We'll have to add those narrated parts to our class story later."

LINK

Remind students of the ways that narration may be used in fairy tales; set them up to try it out on their own pieces.

"Today you'll have time to do some of this work, and all the rest of the work you need to do, in your own fairy tale adaptations! You've got your drafts in hand. Before you leave the rug, take a minute to look quickly through them to get your minds going, thinking about ways you might add narration at the beginning or to stitch together your Small Moment stories. This is really, really important work. When you add the voice of the narrator your story becomes a *story* rather than just a collection of wonderful scenes. Where would Pinocchio be without Jiminy Cricket to keep his story together?

"Get started, right here and now on the rug. It probably makes sense to start with trying out narration at the beginning of your story—but do what makes the most sense to you. I'll come tap you when it looks like you've got yourself set up to be really productive today. When you go off, you'll want to be pushing ahead with rehearsing and drafting remaining scenes as well. Some of you might even finish drafting today!"

How to Write a Fairy Tale Adaptation

- Know the classic story and tell it often.
- Decide on a change to improve the story.
- Make the change lead to other changes so the whole story fits together.
- Make a character with traits and wants who runs into trouble.
- Tell the story in two or three scenes (Small Moment stories).
- Story-tell or act out the first scene, filling in lifelike details. Then write the scenes.
- Figure out an ending that solves the character's big problem.
- With narration, give a backstory at the start and stitch scenes together.

Encouraging Students to Take on Challenging Work

IT MAY BE TEMPTING—REALLY TEMPTING—to spend much of our conferring and small-group time working with those students who so obviously and desperately need our help. And it may indeed be fine to tilt the balance in favor of spending more time with those students who clearly need more support. But, we think it's incredibly important to make conscious plans for working with students who are sailing ahead. Not only do all writers have things to learn, but sometimes it is especially students who excel who benefit from the idea that continuing to develop richness in our lives as writers and as learners means not resting on our laurels. You may have writers who are able, seemingly effortlessly, to incorporate your minilesson work into their writing. It would be easy to walk by and give a supportive nod here and there and know that those students are meeting expectations for the unit and for the year. But if we do that, we miss the opportunity to teach them what it feels like to stretch, to be challenged, to push. That is a huge opportunity that may affect children's writing lives not only for the time they spend in their classrooms, but forever. When we teach all students that taking on challenges is immensely satisfying and important work, we prepare them for those times that will occur in the lives of all learners when they genuinely are challenged by something, genuinely stumped, genuinely unprepared. We prepare them to take on issues in their own learning rather than sticking to a comfort zone, to what's always worked in the past. A valuable lesson for writing, and for life.

In the situation below, I decided to push Simone, one of the strongest and most natural writers in the class, to build on the absolutely adequate bit of narration with which she'd begun her story. After approaching Simone, I read over her shoulder (see Figure 5–3):

> There were three moles who lived underneath the ground of a field of grass and eventually the humans took over. That caused the moles' home to be destroyed. The moles got very upset.

MID-WORKSHOP TEACHING
Using Narration to Wrap Up a Story

"Look up for a minute, writers. I know that some of you are in the middle of drafting your very last scenes. Even if you're not, listen carefully, because you will be soon. There is *another* way that writers use narration—it may be used at the end of a story, to wrap up the loose ends and sort of send the reader on her way. Listen to the ending of the classic *Cinderella*—you'll see what I mean."

> *Cinderella was taken before the prince. He was overwhelmed with love for her and some time later they were married. Cinderella, who was as good as she was beautiful, gave her two sisters a home in the palace, and that very same day they were married to two lords of the court.*

"It's kind of like Jiminy Cricket coming back onstage one last time to tell us a few things we need to know about how everything fits together in the end. When you all draft your endings today, try this out. We can add this third kind of narration power to our chart, too."

The Power of Narration

- Provides backstory at the beginning of a story
- Stitches together Small Moment stories
- Wraps the story up at the end

After noticing out loud Simone's excellent work setting up her story by adding the narration, the telling, I said, "Simone, you are so strong with this kind of work. I wonder if you might be up for taking on something a little trickier, something a little more sophisticated. I think this is a great beginning—and you did exactly what we talked about Jiminy

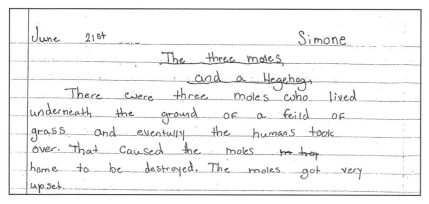

FIG. 5–3 Simone's narration at the start of her story

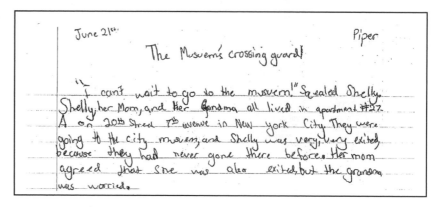

FIG. 5–4 Piper's narration at the start of her story

Cricket doing with his narration—you set the scene, and you gave us the backstory we need to understand what's happening when we get into your first scene. Sometimes, though, writers are a little more flexible about where they put in that beginning narration. Sometimes, writers actually do start with the characters saying something, or details about the setting or the weather, and *then* tuck the narration in. That may make readers even more curious about what will happen. Do you think you might want to try something like that?"

Simone was slightly put out that I was asking her to revise a perfectly good beginning, but she was willing to try another way too. She thought it might be interesting to have the moles talking to each other at the beginning and then to have the narration come in.

I decided to ask Simone to share her work with Piper, another strong writer in the class who I thought could benefit from the same tip. I set this small group up so that Simone would really take ownership of the strategy and basically teach it to Piper herself. I was there to guide and offer tips, but Simone was able to share what she'd done with

Piper in a way that set Piper up to replicate that strategy in her own work. Piper's story beginning soon read (see Figure 5–4):

"I can't wait to go to the museum!" squealed Shelly. Shelly, her mom, and her grandma all lived in apartment 27A on 20th Street, 7th Avenue in New York City. They were going to the city museum, and Shelly was very, very excited, because they had never gone there before. Her mom agreed that she was also excited, but her grandma was worried.

If you have other students who you think are ready for this kind of sophisticated work, you could invite them into the small group as well. And you will know your students well enough to determine if the work done within the small group will be best launched by you, or if you might choose to encourage a student who has tried the strategy successfully to run the group, with or without your support.

Giving Each Other Feedback

Invite students to the meeting area to share the endings of their tales.

"Writers," I called, "take a moment to jot a plan for what you'll do next and meet me at the rug." Within a minute, most of the writers had gathered on the rug, folders in hand. "Yesterday we experimented with endings. Today many of you drafted your ending one way then another way, solving the characters' big problems and let the reader know the story was *over*. It helps to share endings with a friend or a partner, reading it out loud and getting a reaction. So today read your ending to your partner. And partners, your job is to let your partner know if the ending is doing its job."

I pulled up alongside Simone as she read aloud her ending to Sam (see Figure 5–5).

Sam clarified, "So the mole's big problem was the hedgehog?" Simone nodded. "And it's clear the story is over." Simone nodded again. Sam put his fist out and Simone, smiling, bumped it with her fist.

I moved on to Piper and Jackson. Piper read (see Figure 5–6). Jackson put up one thumb, then the other. "Two thumbs up," he said.

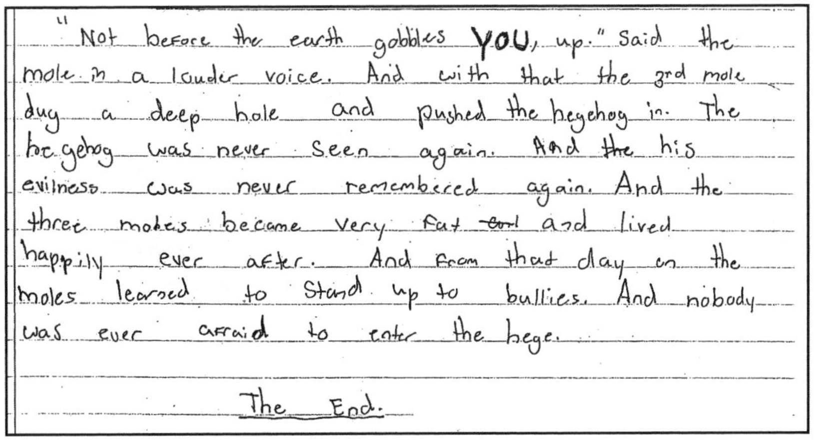

> "Not before the earth gobbles **YOU**, up." said the mole in a louder voice. And with that the 3rd mole dug a deep hole and pushed the hegehog in. The hegehog was never seen again. And the his evilness was never remembered again. And the three moles became very fat and lived happily ever after. And from that day on the moles learned to stand up to bullies. And nobody was ever afraid to enter the hege.
>
> The End.

FIG. 5–5   Simone's ending

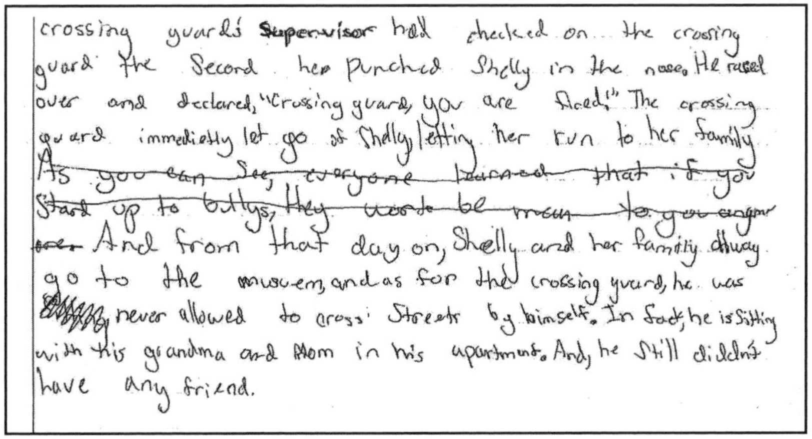

> crossing guard's supervisor hall checked on the crossing guard the second hea punched Shelly in the nose. He ruced over and declared, "Crossing guard you are fierd!" The crossing guard immediatly let go of Shelly letting her run to her family As you can see, everyone learned that if you start up to bullys, they would be mean to you anymor. And from that day on, Shelly and her family always go to the musuem, and as for the crossing guard, he was never allowed to cross streets by himself. In fact, he is sitting with his grandma and Mom in his apartment. And, he still didn't have any friend.

FIG. 5–6   Piper's ending

Session 6

Mirror, Mirror on the Wall
Assessment Using Self-Reflection

IN THIS SESSION, you'll teach students that writers check their work and plan for future projects.

GETTING READY

✔ Students' writing folders containing their drafts

✔ Pens or pencils

✔ Narrative Writing Checklists, Grades 3 and 4, one copy per student (see Active Engagement)

✔ Optional: Printouts of fairy tales for students to take home

THIS LAST SESSION IN BEND I is critical in several ways. Your students will have finished drafts of their very first fairy tale adaptations ever. It is worth taking a moment to pause and celebrate the fact that in just over a week, they've immersed themselves in an unfamiliar genre and have produced something brand new. The share becomes the foundation for Bend II, setting students up to write new and stronger adaptations of the fairy tale of their choice.

During the start of the minilesson, you'll support writers as they assess their work, reminding them that although they may be thinking of what they've been writing as specifically fairy tales, they are actually stories—narratives. This means that students can bring in all that they already know about narrative writing as they self-assess; you can encourage them to weigh their fairy tale adaptations in relation to the qualities of narrative writing that were front and center during the *Crafting True Stories* unit earlier in the year. The work of self-assessing provides an opportunity for goal setting, and you'll see that this session's mid-workshop teaching supports students to develop clear goals and plans that can then influence their upcoming work.

You've now taught several minilessons like this one. In every unit, you've brought out a checklist that captures qualities of strong writing in that unit's genre, and you've asked writers to self-assess. We have suggested that in this session you champion the fact that some of your students have initiated this process of self-reflection on their own. You might be skeptical, thinking, "It is not likely that my students would do that." But the truth is that you can do the engineering to pull this off. On the day before today's session, leave a narrative checklist where writers can easily see it, and if necessary suggest that writers self-assess. Later, convene students and describe the writing work that you witnessed.

This lesson, then, functions as a pivot point between the two bends—celebrating students' first, best efforts at writing fairy tale adaptations, rallying them to thoughtfully examine and assess what they've done in the context of narrative writing, and setting them up so that they jump into the next bend with greater independence.

Common Core State Standards: W.3.3,b,c,d; W.3.4, W.3.5, W.3.10, W.4.3.a,b,c,d,e; RL.3.1, RL.3.2, SL.3.1a, SL.3.2, L.3.1, L.3.2, L.3.3, L.3.4, L.3.5a, L.3.6

Mirror, Mirror on the Wall

Assessment Using Self-Reflection

CONNECTION

♦ COACHING

Celebrate students' completion of their first fairy tale adaptations, and then, using the example of a student who did so, rally students to independently use available tools to assess their writing and set goals.

"This is an important day, writers. Last night as I was getting ready for today's writing workshop lesson, knowing that you will all be finishing your very first fairy tale adaptations today, I was thinking about how much you've grown into yourselves as writers since the beginning of the year. I remember lots of times, early this year, when some of you would creep up next to me during writing time and ask, 'Is this good?' or 'What should I do now?' This still happens sometimes, but more and more I see writers who are asking *themselves* those questions, and finding ways to answer them. Listen to this—yesterday I was watching Edwin during writing time, and I noticed that he wasn't actually writing—he was instead poring over some kind of paper. So, I sidled over to him and peeked over his shoulder at the paper. And guess what? Edwin wasn't a bit off task. In fact, he had pulled the Narrative Writing Checklist from his folder of work from the first unit in the year, *Crafting True Stories*, and was reading the checklist over, then glancing at his fairy tale adaptation. When he saw me behind him, he said, 'Just checking!'

"So, writers. We need to celebrate what Edwin was doing—totally on his own. Edwin has discovered that writers spend a fair amount of their writing time not actually writing, but *preparing* to write and *reflecting* on their writing. A really superb writer does what Edwin has done and picks up checklists, even when no one suggests it, and rereads the writing, thinking, 'Does this piece of writing match the items on this checklist, and my hopes for it?' Another wonderful thing that Edwin and I noticed as he used the checklist is that he was feeling much more ready for those more grown-up, fourth-grade goals than he was earlier in the year. I bet a lot of you will notice the same thing!"

❖ **Name the teaching point.**

"Today I want to teach you that writers know that their writing gets better not only from what they do *on the page*, with their pen, but also from what they do *off the page*. And no work is more powerful than being a really tough critic of one's own draft, rereading one's writing and judging it against goals in such a way that the writer comes away with goals to live by, stars to steer by."

Notice in this instance that we are using the Small Moment narrative structure ourselves to write a little story to use at the start of the minilesson. You'll find that most of your minilessons are actually a composite of small moments, essays, and how-to texts! You'll also notice that we've caught Edwin in the act of using the checklist independently, although it's easy to orchestrate this situation if you don't see it happening naturally. At this point in the year, students will be more ready for the fourth-grade checklist than they were earlier in the year when they first used it. You can use this as an opportunity to celebrate their growth!

TEACHING

Demonstrate using a checklist in a superficial way.

"Let me show you what I mean. When I watched Edwin using his checklist yesterday, one thing I noticed is that he didn't just read it without thinking. It can be easy to just skim through like this." I got out my own narrative checklist and slumped in my chair with it with a big sigh. Pointing to the top item on the list, I muttered to myself, "Sure, I do that, kind of," and then checked it off. Moving on to the next item, I continued, "Yep, I think I sort of do that too." With another big sigh, I stared off into space.

Looking up at the class, I asked, "Do you think that kind of work is going to help me get better as a writer?" I looked into a sea of shaking heads.

Contrast superficial assessment and decision making with an explanation of thoughtful assessment and decision making.

"All of you know what it feels like to be deeply engaged in assessment and you also know what it feels like to shrug and say, 'It's fine,' like I was doing earlier. And to become stronger writers, it's important for you to try the deeply engaged way of assessing. As you are doing this work with your own stories, you are not only thinking deeply about those particular stories, you are thinking about the stories you will be working on next, starting in the very next writer's workshop session. You will be asking yourself, 'What kinds of things do I want to rally my energies around as I begin new drafts? Are there things that I find particularly challenging?' And you might decide to focus particularly on those things as you start your new stories tomorrow."

ACTIVE ENGAGEMENT

Encourage students to use their narrative checklists thoughtfully as they begin assessing their drafts and setting writing goals.

"So, writers, pull out your drafts and your Narrative Writing Checklists, Grades 3 and 4, right here on the rug. As you read back and forth between the first few items on your checklist and your draft, don't just read with that 'eh' kind of energy and focus, but read with a deeply engaged kind of focus. And make sure you're also taking a deeper look at those goals on the fourth-grade side. Get started!"

As the class got to work, I circulated, celebrating any time when I noticed writers looking back at their writing to ask, "Did I do that? Let me check."

"Writers," I called out. "Thalia was just reading the goal about using paragraphs and I heard her say, 'Well, I sort of did that but I can work on it to make it much stronger.' She's really thinking deeply about this, for sure!"

Of course, you might come up with an example. You might compare choosing what kind of breakfast cereal you'll have with choosing the perfect birthday dinner. Or deciding what to do on a regular Saturday morning and deciding what to do on the Saturday after your grandparents arrive from far away. There are many apt metaphors for this situation, but if you choose to use the one we've included, your students will ride along on the way it resonates for you. Your enthusiasm and engagement is the key to theirs.

And then in a moment, I called out again, "You know, writers, you can all make a mark alongside anything on the checklist that you want to work on in particular."

LINK

Remind students that as they continue assessing their drafts, they are also creating a list of writing goals for their next stories.

"Writers, this is a long checklist, and it will be really important that you don't just *read the checklist* but also *reread your writing* to check on whether you really, truly tried to do each of these items in a super-duper way. It would be really cool if some of you labeled places in your draft where you did the things on the checklist. But the most important thing of all is that you come from this work with a list of goals for the work you want to do when you get a chance to write *another* fairy tale adaptation. Writers get better by assessing their own writing and setting goals. Off you go to do this!"

Narrative Writing Checklist

	Grade 3	NOT YET	STARTING TO	YES!	Grade 4	NOT YET	STARTING TO	YES!
	Structure				**Structure**			
Overall	I told the story bit by bit.	☐	☐	☐	I wrote the important part of an event bit by bit and took out unimportant parts.	☐	☐	☐
Lead	I wrote a beginning in which I helped readers know who the characters were and what the setting was in my story.	☐	☐	☐	I wrote a beginning in which I showed what was happening and where, getting readers into the world of the story.	☐	☐	☐
Transitions	I told my story in order by using phrases such as *a little later* and *after that.*	☐	☐	☐	I showed how much time went by with words and phrases that mark time such as *just then* and *suddenly* (to show when things happened quickly) or *after a while* and *a little later* (to show when a little time passed).	☐	☐	☐
Ending	I chose the action, talk, or feeling that would make a good ending and worked to write it well.	☐	☐	☐	I wrote an ending that connected to the beginning or the middle of the story.	☐	☐	☐
		☐	☐	☐	I used action, dialogue, or feeling to bring my story to a close.	☐	☐	☐
Organization	I used paragraphs and skipped lines to separate what happened first from what happened later (and finally) in my story.	☐	☐	☐	I used paragraphs to separate the different parts or times of the story or to show when a new character was speaking.	☐	☐	☐
	Development				**Development**			
Elaboration	I worked to show what happened to (and in) my characters.	☐	☐	☐	I added more to the heart of my story, including not only actions and dialogue but also thought and feelings.	☐	☐	☐

Helping Writers Set Personal Goals

THIS SESSION PROVIDES ANOTHER OPPORTUNITY for you to encourage children to set high goals for themselves and to get genuine pleasure out of saying, "I can work harder on that!" You can also think of this time as an opportunity to show children that sometimes they'll want to take on goals that are not on the checklist but are important in their own particular writing process. For example, you might help individual children know that any one of these goals might be added to their checklist:

◆ Write longer, aiming to produce a four- or five-page story.

◆ Work harder, making sure that the story always makes sense to someone who doesn't know the backstory. This means putting on the hat of being a reader, reading the story over, and asking "Huh?" at the confusing parts.

◆ Make the story sound more like a fairy tale, using more literary language and longer, fancier sentences.

◆ Intersperse more action with the dialogue so the whole story doesn't seem like a script of a play with no one acting.

◆ Study published stories more often, noticing more cool things that the author does to try doing as well.

Setting outside goals allows each student to bring a personalized workload into their writing experience. Writers have different needs and their goals should reflect that diversity. Use the goals included here to inspire students to create additional learning goals that complement the checklist.

Also, use this time to help children think toward the next fairy tale adaptation they plan to write, getting a head start on the orienting conferences that every child is going to urgently need at the start of the next session. Start asking children now if they have thought of what fairy tale they want to adapt next time around. Set some children up to carry home a book or a page printout of the fairy tale that child is considering adapting.

MID-WORKSHOP TEACHING
Studying Other Writers' Drafts to Add to Writing Goals

"Writers, I want to stop you. The room is full of such deeply engaged, wedding-dress kind of assessment right now! Here's what we're going to do next. You've each started a quick list for yourselves of things you want to work on, moving forward in your new adaptations and in your writing lives in general. In a moment, you are going to leave your drafts on your tables and you are going to move to another table in the room, settle down to read someone else's draft, and admire that writer's work. Hopefully there will be time for you to read a few other people's work as well. Each of your drafts, each of you as writers, has something to teach the rest of the class—so we're going to devote some time to learning from each other now. As you admire each other's drafts, add on to your list of things you want to work on in your next stories—things you love about your classmates' writing that you aspire to incorporate into your own writing next time around. I'm going to collect some of these things that you admire in each other's work so that we can display them on a bulletin board, which can be a resource to you all as you begin work on another fairy tale tomorrow."

It will be important for you to call on all your skills to provide some children with the scaffolding they need. For example, a child who struggles might benefit from writing an adaptation of the two texts that have already been in circulation in your class. If he wrote about *Little Red Riding Hood* the first time around, perhaps this time he wants to write about *The Three Billy Goats Gruff*. We selected those two texts as a starter set because they each contain a very clean storyline, and we thought adaptations would be easier for those texts than for some others. But the adaptations will be even easier now because there are possibilities in the air of the classroom. Or you can provide support simply by making sure that a child works with a text that matches the one her partner is using.

Preparing to Write Adaptations that Teach a Lesson

Celebrate students' thoughtful assessment and goal setting, and set them up to plan for new fairy tale adaptations that teach a lesson.

Gathering the class, I said, "It was so exciting to see you studying your drafts of your very first fairy tale adaptations just now. You used your checklists—and you used the great resource of each other's writing—to set some important writing goals. I've told you that you'll be starting new fairy tale adaptations tomorrow. But here's what I haven't told you: This time, you are in charge. *You* will choose the tale, and *you* will be the ones who make changes in it. I know you're ready! And I know you are ready to keep one new thing in mind as you prepare: *Some fairy tales are written to teach people a life lesson.*

"Have you ever done something less than perfect and something bad happens to you? For instance, you pull a toy away from your brother and it smashes in your face—and a grown-up says, 'That'll teach you!' Well in fairy tales, when a character gets into trouble, and sometimes it is bad trouble, like the character falls into a deep, dark slumber, sometimes there's a little voice in the story saying, 'That'll teach you!'

"For example, some people say the fairy tale *Little Red Riding Hood* teaches kids not to talk to strangers because of all the trouble Little Red Riding Hood gets into when she talks to the strange wolf. As a new fairy tale writer, you might completely agree with these life lessons! You might want to write your own adaptations that teach similar life lessons. You could think, 'How else could a character learn not to talk to strangers? Or what other story could teach that beauty is on the inside, not just on the outside?'

"But what's also fun is to think about a fairy tale that teaches a life lesson that you don't agree with one hundred percent. For example, you might not totally agree with the idea that Jack gets rewarded for stealing all the giant's stuff in *Jack and the Beanstalk*. You might be thinking to yourself, 'How could I teach my readers a different life lesson through my own adaptation?' Starting right now, and continuing tonight, each of you will be thinking about how you might adapt a fairy tale that you know really well, using all that you know about planning adaptations. You might choose a fairy tale that has a life lesson you agree with, so you'll adapt the tale to teach a similar life lesson. Or the fairy tale you choose to adapt might teach a life lesson that you don't agree with one hundred percent. If that's the case, you might decide what different life lesson you could teach your readers through your own adaptation."

To further ensure that your students come prepared to the next session, you may want to make this work be homework, and ask students to choose a tale and begin brainstorming potential adaptations.

Share an example of a way you might adapt a fairy tale so that it teaches a lesson.

"I've been thinking that I might write an adaptation of *Goldilocks and the Three Bears*. I've always loved that story. Goldilocks makes mistakes, but she's got spunk! The reason I'm thinking of adapting that story is because I've always wanted the ending to be different. Somehow it seems wrong that when the bears come and she's broken their stuff, she just runs away. I mean, why doesn't she stand up and say, 'I did it! I'm sorry!' I think I'll change the ending, give it a twist, and have her take responsibility for everything she did. If I end the adaptation this way, I'll teach readers that it's important to take responsibility for one's actions. That's a good life lesson, right? I can give a famous fairy tale a twist, like having Goldilocks taking responsibility for her actions, to teach a new life lesson to my readers."

Encourage students to keep the idea of teaching a lesson in mind as they plan their next adaptations.

"So you can be thinking about the life lesson you want to teach in the fairy tale *you* choose to adapt. Think carefully. Is there a fairy tale that teaches a life lesson that you really agree with? And if so, how might you adapt the tale to teach a similar lesson? Or is there a fairy tale that teaches a life lesson that you don't totally agree with? For instance, does anyone here not really like the way the Billy Goats Gruff all tell the troll to eat their brother? Or does anyone think it is wrong that a princess is so soft-skinned that she gets bruised from just sleeping on a pea?

"Turn and talk to your partner about the ideas you have for the adaptation you might write next, keeping in mind the life lesson your tale might teach. Tonight for homework, as you think about this, you might even start envisioning some Small Moment stories that will be scenes in your fairy tale!"

Goals and Plans Are a Big Deal

IN THIS SESSION, you'll teach students that writers rely on each other and themselves to independently plan not only their stories but their writing process.

GETTING READY

✔ Students' writer's notebooks and pens

✔ Planning chart template, a version of the "How to Write a Fairy Tale Adaptation" chart with a deadline column, one copy per student (see Teaching)

✔ Your demonstration writer's notebook (see Active Engagement)

✔ Optional: A chart highlighting the writing process (see Active Engagement)

✔ Blank paper folded into fourths to make story-planning booklets (see Mid-Workshop Teaching Point)

✔ Optional: Post-it notes for students to record writing plans and place them visibly, enabling you to quickly take stock (see Conferring and Small-Group Work)

✔ "Ways Authors Adapt Fairy Tales" chart (see Share)

COMMON CORE STATE STANDARDS: W.3.3, W.3.4, W.3.5, W.3.10, W.4.3, W.4.4, RL.3.1, RL.3.2, RL.3.3, RL.3.5, RL.3.6, SL.3.1, SL.3.4, SL.3.6, L.3.1, L.3.2, L.3.3a, L.4.3.a

OVER MY DESK, I have pinned a few quotes. One, from Jerry Harste, reads, "Our job is to provide kids with the kind of richly literate world we believe in and then to invite them to role-play their way into being the readers, writers, learners we want them to be."

To me, it has always been the case that my richest learning experiences come from the times when I step into a role and take on a challenge that feels utterly beyond my reach. For a while, I flounder, feeling like an imposter, but somehow or other I fake my way until lo and behold I am actually somewhat accomplished and comfortable with the role. That's what it was like for me when I first taught. I was just out of college, and felt like I had no business calling myself a teacher—I was still a student. But I put on my teacher outfit, and took my place at the front of the classroom. It felt like an absurd stretch. I was sure that anyone would be able to tell that I was a fraud, dressed up in a teacher's role.

This is how human beings learn. Babies join into conversations, assuming a role in the dialogue, before they have a clue what the interchange is about. Toddlers pick up a broom and join in sweeping the kitchen floor before they grasp the point of the activity. This same sequence is the essential philosophy that undergirds writing workshop instruction.

This session, then, reissues the invitation that underlies all good writing workshop instruction. "You can write like professional authors," you say, and you define that by emphasizing that writers work with independence, developing and using a process that works for them toward the goal of producing good writing—and strong growth in writing.

Your goal is to inspire your students to write with enormous resolve, to reach deep inside themselves for reserves of determination and zeal. Begin the session by telling them about MacDowell and other colonies for writers. And continue to lead from behind, this time subtly coaching students to plan the adaptations of a second fairy tale by drawing on all they have learned to do.

Goals and Plans Are a Big Deal

CONNECTION

Suggest that because their fairy tale work is very professional, the classroom might become more like a writing colony—a place where writers are supported with their independent work.

"Writers, I know that since you finished your first fairy tale adaptations, you've each been thinking about another fairy tale that you know really well and about a way you might want to adapt it. Right now, will you share some of the fairy tales you're considering adapting? Just call them out, and I'll jot them up here on chart paper."

I wrote as fast as I could while the students called out, "*Goldilocks and the Three Bears*!" "*The Three Little Pigs*!" "*The Emperor's New Clothes*!"

"Writers, I need to tell you that it doesn't feel like you are writing papers for third grade so much as writing literature for the library. There is something very professional about your work lately. So I have been reading a bit about how real, professional writers get their writing done, thinking this may give us some ideas for how our writing workshop may support the very professional work you are doing.

"This is what I found. There are places that writers go to that are called writing colonies, where each writer is given a little woodsy cabin to live in, with just a desk, a bed, a chair—and a porch, for looking out at the horizon, dreaming. The writers tack bits of inspiration onto their walls—goals, words to live by. They wake up in those little cabins, reread their drafts, decide what the next thing is they need to do, and work for hours without someone telling them what to do. The place just leaves a picnic lunch outside each writer's doorstep at lunchtime so as to not disturb the writers at work.

"*But* there are places to go for help. There is a library of books—and people mark up the books with notes, so one book might contain the note, *I love the description of this character*! There are seminars, too, as the writers call them. They are little courses on a topic, a bit like our minilessons, and there might be two in a day. If a writer is on fire with his or her work, the writer might just say, 'I need extra writing time,' and not go to a seminar—that is okay. There also is a place called the meeting space where people go to get help from each other.

"But the most important thing is that the writing colonies are places where people plan and then do their writing. They usually have a deadline—the writing usually gets planned and done in a week.

◆ COACHING

The process of helping each child settle on a fairy tale should not take long as you've asked students to give it some thought beforehand. It's nice to collect a list, though, so that students may remind each other of tales they might not have thought of. When you listen to the titles that students call out, you might want to lend special weight to the tales that are simpler in design, as they are easier to adapt. Jack and the Beanstalk *and* The Twelve Princesses, *for example, are both quite complicated stories with plot and subplots, whereas* The Three Little Pigs *is more straightforward. You may especially want to watch your more struggling writers, steering them subtly toward a fairy tale with a very straightforward plot.*

"I'm telling you this because I've been thinking that because you are doing such professional writing work during this unit of study, maybe there are ways in which our writing workshop could be more like those writing colonies. I can't build each of you a cabin with a porch or bring you a picnic lunch so you may write straight through every day, but I think we could bring the spirit of those writing colonies to our classroom."

Clarify the expectations for the upcoming bend in the unit, embedding them in invigorating talk about the classroom becoming a writing colony.

"It would mean that you take on the job of writing a new fairy tale adaptation, from start to finish, this week, and that you plan the work you do each day so that your writing is done by that deadline. You'd need to set your desks up like writing cabins—maybe giving yourself some inspirational sayings or goals—and you'd need to figure out where we could make a fairy tale library and a meeting space. Talk among yourselves and see what you think about the idea."

Ask for and use children's input, so they help to coauthor an environment in the classroom that supports investment in writing.

"Maybe I'm being sort of crazy, I mean—you are only what, eight, nine years old? It's a wild idea, but . . . turn and talk with whomever about your thoughts." I wasn't surprised to hear lots of rising energy and suggestions. I noted ideas that we'd be able to fly with, and when I convened the students, I especially drew out those suggestions. Soon some volunteers had agreed to set up a library area filled with published fairy tales and the kids' own work from earlier in the unit, several corners of the classroom had been designed as meeting spaces for conferring, and every child had resolved to set up his or her own writing spot, complete with photos or words of wisdom for writing advice.

❖ **Name the teaching point.**

"Today I want to teach you that all good things are made twice. Once in the creator's imagination, and once in reality. Writers plan not only their writing, but also their process for making a piece of writing."

TEACHING

Convey again that students will be working independently, and suggest they think of the anchor chart as the basis for a work plan, adding interim due dates for different items on it.

"What many pros do when they get ready to write is that they have a sense of what they want to make and of how their writing process needs to go; they also have a calendar. Using all this—their image of what they are making, their understanding of the process they'll be using, and the calendar, pro writers make work plans for themselves. Like they might take the anchor chart from the first adaptation, and write *Monday* beside two items on that chart, signaling those will be done on Monday, and *Tuesday* beside another item on the chart. I've got the template for a planning chart if you decide to use it, or you could come up with a different way to plan the way you'll progress through the week."

Although the quote at the start of the prelude from Jerry Harste suggests that it is the teacher who creates an environment that supports writing and only then are kids invited to role-play their way into being avid readers and writers within that space, the truth is that when we say to kids, "How should we set up our mentor texts so that you may all study them?" and "What else do you need so you may do your best work?," the kids coauthor the literate environment, and in doing so, they coauthor their identities.

How to Write a Fairy Tale Adaptation	Due By . . .
Know the classic story and tell it often.	
Decide on a change to improve the story.	
Make the change lead to other changes so the whole story fits together.	
Make a character with traits and wants who runs into trouble.	
Tell the story in two or three scenes (Small Moment stories).	
Story-tell or act out the first scene, filling in lifelike details. Then write the scenes.	
Figure out an ending that solves the character's big problem.	
With narration, give a backstory at the start and stitch scenes together.	

The "How to Write a Fairy Tale Adaptation" planning chart may be found on the CD-ROM.

Remind writers that each item on the work plan is an activity that may be done especially well if the writer aspires to improve on what he or she did previously.

"The other thing that writers do is set goals not only for *what* the work will be for each day, but also for *how* they'll do that work. And to do this, writers think, 'How did I do that work before? How might I do things even better?'

"And here is the thing. The way that a writer gets to be a pro is by always asking, 'How might I do things better this time than I did them before now? How might I do a better job planning my writing? How might I do a better job using my partner to help me? How might I do a better job organizing my writing? How might I do a better job . . . at *everything*?' The writer doesn't always know the answer to that question—to how to do things better than ever—but true pros work to figure out how they might do things even better. Many pros write notes to themselves about those goals. Like beside a writer's anchor chart, on which she jotted, say, that planning would be done on Monday, she might write: *Make sure to plan the end of the story not just the start* or *Make sure to reread the classic tale a bunch of times and to keep it near as I write.*"

ACTIVE ENGAGEMENT

Recruit children to consider the question, "How might I do better at planning the next fairy tale adaptation?"

"I'm assuming you all will be working today on planning your next fairy tale adaptation, so maybe you can help each other ask, 'How might our work, planning the next fairy tale adaptation, go even better than before?'

"Because a lot of the writing you'll be doing this week will be on your own—in your own writing cabin—why don't you think about ways to improve your planned adaptations on your own, instead of talking about it with a partner? The goal is to think, 'How might the plans I make for this next adaptation be even better than they were last time?' Just think quietly—or if you want, you may write in your notebook. Some of you may want to look back on your last story to think about this.

In the book Happiness: A Guide to Developing Life's Most Important Skill, *by Matthieu Ricard and Daniel Coleman (2007), the authors cite research that suggests that people tend to improve at an activity for a while and then level off. The heart surgeon improves over his first five years doing heart surgery, but the surgeon with twenty years of experience may be no more skilled than the one with five years of experience. The reason for this is that apparently people do not get better just by practice. Instead, it is deliberate, mindful practice that makes a person more skillful, practice where the person is consciously working to improve upon prior performances. Your goal is to rally kids to engage in that deliberate, mindful practice.*

"I know you have a fairy tale in mind, and probably the start to an adaptation as well. Will you give your adaptation the test—think, 'Is it consequential?' Remember, if it is, then the change that you make will end up dominoing into other changes. Think whether the story you have in mind fits together—that one change does need to alter other things." I left some silence. "Think whether the story you have in mind actually is a story—is there a character who wants something and runs into trouble? Your planning chart may help you do this work."

"Now will you think about what you noticed about your last adaptation when you were done? You set some goals for yourself—does your adaptation get you started addressing those goals?"

After another minute, I said, "Why don't you form small circles of about four to six kids and talk about what you will do today to make sure that you plan not only your adaptation, but also your writing process and your goals?"

I listened in as the children talked. Andrew started, "I am not sure what my next adaptation will be. I am deciding between *The Emperor's New Clothes* and *Jack and the Beanstalk*. But I know what I need to do better. I need to write scenes that don't slide into each other."

The other writers nodded at Andrew and then, uncomfortable with the silence, began to giggle. Cora looked at the planning chart. "I think I did okay with writing scenes," she said. "But I want to make sure that I story-tell and act out every scene, not just the first. My first scene is *so* much better than the others. I want my whole piece to be as good as the first scene."

Eliza chimed in, "That makes me think about my ending. I definitely want to write a better ending this time around."

After a bit, I reconvened the group. "As I listen in to your talk, it is obvious to me that you have big plans for your pieces and your process!" I continued by retelling some highlights from the students' conversations, then added, "There are some blank rows at the bottom of the planning chart where you can add the goals that will make your writing even more magical."

LINK

Offer lots of alternatives, emphasizing that those who choose to plan adaptations need to draw on all that was taught at the start of the unit.

"I know that today, some of you will get started on your plans for what work you will do each day of this week," I said as I held up the planning chart. "Others of you will be working alone in your writing cabin, your writing spot, planning your new fairy tale adaptation, in which case I know you'll remember," I listed across my fingers, "first, to make sure you use a fairy tale you know well, second, that the changes are consequential, and third, that you think through whether the story you plan has the elements of a good story. I'm hoping you will also have time to think about making your writing spot into a good place to work. If you need any help from me, talk to me about that. And perhaps a few of you will want to work on building a library of fairy tale resources that writers may draw on anytime."

I modeled opening my writer's notebook. I wanted to show children the importance of returning to the notebook as we returned to the beginning of the writing process.

It's helpful to have a writing process chart posted clearly where students can refer to it during this bend. As children plan and write their own adaptations, it's helpful for them to have access to tools that foster their independence, such as following the writing process chart.

Keep Doing . . .
- describing objects in detail
- including character thoughts and feelings

Also remember to . . .
- add periods
- let the reader know where the character is

FIG. 7–1 Cora's writing goals and plans

Using Your Input to Encourage Student Ownership

TODAY IS THE FIRST DAY IN A NEW CYCLE, making it again a very important time for you to listen to children's plans and ratchet them up. Your input in a child's writing process early on has much more leverage than input later on. So, for example, if a child has chosen to write an adaptation of a complicated story such as *Jack and the Beanstalk*—with the early story about the boy exchanging the family cow for a bag full of beans and the later story about climbing the beanstalk and finding the giant, the harp, and the hen with the golden eggs—and if that child is floundering, it is vastly more efficient to teach that child now rather than to do so later on.

This means, then, that you can approach today knowing from the start that you have a few challenges on your hands. You will want to give forceful, clear, and fast-paced help to lots of children, and yet children are now in charge of their writing process. It is often cumbersome to help children with plans because those plans are often not written down at all, making it impossible to scan through them. You might decide, therefore, to ask kids to jot their plans down as a way of clarifying what they intend to do, thereby allowing you to quickly grasp the state of the class. This also will allow you to imagine the small groups you might convene around some of the more popular fairy tales. You'll want to think about how many students are adapting which tales, and whether the collection of children working with a specific tale seems to you to be a workable support group.

One of the ways to shape what kids do without being too heavy-handed is to simply use compliments to affect the work that every child does. For example, if you see a child who has listed six to eight possible adaptations for one tale and seems to be going through a process of weighing all those different possibilities, you'd want to celebrate that child. I often highlight the good aspects of a child's work by creating an imagined alternative. "Rachel didn't just come up with one possible idea for adapting *The Three Little Pigs*—no way. She came up with about a half a dozen possible ideas, and now she is combing each idea through the story, thinking, 'How would the story go if I did that?' It is like she is testing out about ten ideas to settle on a really good one. What smart work she is doing! I'm dying to see if any of the rest of you are doing

MID-WORKSHOP TEACHING
Planning Adaptations with Collaborators' Help

"Writers who get a chance to write in a writers' colony often get their books published afterwards. And inside the front cover of those books, they often say, 'This book would never have been written except for the time I spent at MacDowell Writers Colony.' Then they add some of the specifics. Here's the thing. They never say, 'I'm grateful for the cheese sandwiches that were in my picnic lunches.' They rarely even say, 'I'm grateful for the little seminars that were taught during my stay at the writing colony.' Instead, what they almost always say is, 'At the writing colony, I was given the greatest gift that a writer could ever have—I was given the gift of other writers—people who listened to my drafts and my ideas, who gave me honest feedback, and who helped me figure out what I needed to do to make this the book of my dreams.'

"Mariko just suggested to me that maybe, for today, those of you who are adapting the same story might like to share ideas. How might that go, Mariko? Might this sharing space," I said, pointing to one corner of the classroom, "be for those who are working on adaptations of, say, *The Three Little Pigs*, and this other sharing space be for . . . what are the other popular stories?" Soon small groups had formed of children who were working with the same story, with another group or two of children who were willing to talk about assorted fairy tales. I encouraged each group to begin by storytelling the classic tale, with great feeling, while touching the four pages of a story-planning booklet. I celebrated aloud to the class one child who used page 1 as the backstory, page 2 for the first Small Moment story, page 3 for the rising, repeating trouble, and the final page for resolution.

As children storytold the classic tales that they planned to adapt soon, I pointed out to them that each of their stories unfolded in a somewhat similar way. "First, on page 1 of the booklet, a narrator tells the background—who these people are, where they lived, what the setting was like.

(continues)

"Then on page 2 of a booklet, there are the starting actions and the dialogue, and during that small moment story, one sees what the main character is like, what he or she wants, and what the problems are."

"Then on page 3, trouble starts . . ." and I pointed out that this is generally the place where things get worse and worse, as one thing after another happens. The first goat goes across the bridge, the next one, the next one. The wolf threatens one little pig, the next, the next. The little train tries to go over the mountain, tries again, tries again. Cinderella is told she has to stay home, then she's told the magic spell only lasts until midnight.

I suggested that children might think of that page as being divided into three or four parts, because usually there is a list of times when things go badly—once, twice, three times. "Then, on page 4, things are resolved.

"Once you've told the classic story a few times and fit it onto your story-planning booklet, I'm thinking some of you might want to talk about how your adaptations might go—and even try telling your ideas for an adaptation on the booklet."

that sort of experimentation early on in your writing process. It's definitely going to yield a much better story."

Another way you might guide children in a way that gives them a sense of ownership of their work is to set them up to teach one another in small groups. You might pull together a group of children who have in fact been productive in different kinds of ways, and suggest that they swap ideas, taking turns to instruct one another about the work they've done to push their writing. Perhaps one child has focused extensively on crafting more compelling beginnings or endings while another has challenged herself to consider a more drastic adaptation of the original fairy tale she selected. Chances are your children are trying out—and finding success in—different things in their work, and that they will benefit from this sort of exchange of ideas.

Additionally, you might also compliment the students who are using the planning chart template. It is likely that your students will embrace the easier work of setting deadlines and skip over the harder and more significant work of planning how they will do that work better. If you notice this, you might even decide to gather a group of writers who share this need in one of the meeting spaces, compliment them on setting deadlines, and then teach them quickly how to reread a bit of their draft and to ask, "What could I do to make this work even stronger my second time around?"

Making Meaningful Changes to Characters, Events, and Motivations

Remind students of previous work they did making meaningful changes as they adapt fairy tales, referring to and adding on to the chart you created earlier in the unit.

As the students gathered on the rug with their notebooks full of notes, I said, "I'm hearing that some of you are changing your character, in ways that we talked about earlier and also in new ways. Just take a moment to read through your notes now, and share them with your partner if you haven't already. Then let's add a few things to our chart."

I listened in and read over students' shoulders as they talked. See Andrew's notebook (Figure 7–2).

Instead of the emperor, it will be a president

because of that the palace will become a white house

Instead of the emperor it would be governor Lepage

because of that the palace would be a government

Instead of the Emperor it would be a principal

Because of that the palace would be a school.

The trouble is going to be the shop is all out of desks.

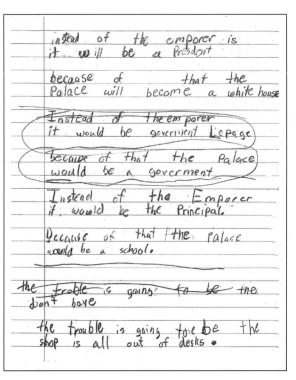

FIG. 7–2   Andrew's notebook entry

And see Maggie's notebook (Figure 7–3).

I pointed to the chart from early in the unit, "Ways Authors Adapt Fairy Tales," as I read off the ways children had previously changed their *character*, and then added another way that I'd overheard them doing that today. "Some of you are changing *events* in the story"—and again I read off the reasons they'd already changed the events, and added another few reasons that I'd overheard. "And most importantly, some of you are changing *motivations*— what the characters want." Again, I added some new items to the list, based on what I'd overheard the children saying.

Remind students that in addition to making changes in their stories that are important and meaningful, those changes should appear not in isolation but should affect the rest of the story as well.

"Writers, these changes you're making as you write your second fairy tale adaptations are really meaningful ones—not just changing the color of someone's hair, or their outfit, or what they eat for breakfast—but really important changes. As you keep working, make sure that you're thinking about how those changes domino," I said, and reminded the students what I meant by domino with a gesture, "into other changes; anything you change is going to sort of bump through the rest of the story and affect everything else, right? Keep that in mind as you work tomorrow."

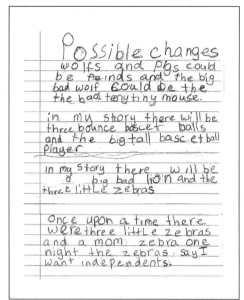

FIG. 7–3   Maggie's notebook entry

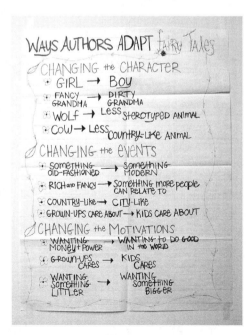

FIG. 7–4   Ways Authors Adapt Fairy Tales

Possible changes

Wolfs and pigs could be friends and the big bad wolf would be the bad teeny, tiny mouse.

In my story there will be three bounce basket balls and the big tall basketball player.

In my story there will be a big, bad lion and the three little zebras.

Once upon a time there were three little zebras and a mom zebra. One night the zebras say, I want independence.

Telling Stories that Make Readers Shiver

I N THE PREVIOUS SESSION you rallied your students to think of the classroom as a writing colony, complete with meeting spaces, a library of resources, and optional seminars geared to help the writers with their writing. In this session, you'll continue the theme, finding added ways to invite children to join into the work of co-constructing a place for writing within the classroom.

I take very seriously the job of inviting kids to construct a place for writing, writing lives, and above all, writing identities. If I were to think back over the turning points in my own trajectory toward becoming a writer, one of the most important moments occurred after I left a writing conference with Donald Murray, the man known now as the "father of writing process approach," and drove to a lumberyard where I bought myself a wooden door which I then proceeded to lay between two file cabinets, making myself a writer's desk. My identity was sealed when a few days later I received a letter in the mail from the great man, and the address on the outside of the envelope, written in Murray's small scrawl: Writer Lucy Calkins, 128 Riggs Street, Middlefield, CT. I remember staring hungrily at that title: *Writer* Lucy Calkins. Then I sat down at my desk.

Looking back now, I realize that Murray was being kind. He was employing a teaching technique. He didn't really regard me, a twenty-three-year-old fledgling teacher, as some great author. But—his technique worked. Let's borrow it now for our students!

We had thought, at one point, about having this session be an optional one for children, in the interest of following up on the independence you've been urging them toward. We learned, however, through testing it in a variety of contexts, that this session proved to be one of the most beloved. Students *loved* adding refrains. And the refrains they added truly made their stories stronger. The challenge in this session, then, is to not just suggest that students plop in a cool-sounding refrain, but to genuinely lift the level of their stories and their storytelling by tapping into the oral tradition of the fairy tale genre. The minilesson encourages writers to write in such a way that when their story is told, it will sweep the listeners up, pull them close, keep them spellbound, and make their hearts race. This genre is tailor-made for such a lesson. After all, fairy tales have been passed from grandfather

IN THIS SESSION, you'll teach students that writers make fairy tales sound like fairy tales by using special language—in this case, by adding refrains.

GETTING READY

✔ Strips of paper with classic fairy tale refrains, folded and placed in a hat (see Connection)

✔ A baton for conducting the Fairy Tale Symphony (optional)

✔ Students' story-planning booklets (see Active Engagement)

✔ Class scene from *Cinderella* for reference (see Link)

✔ "How to Write a Fairy Tale Adaptation" chart (see Link) 🔗

✔ Students' copies of planning chart template from Session 7 (see Mid-Workshop Teaching)

✔ Your demonstration writer's notebook (see Share)

✔ Optional: Video clip of student storyteller to show as an example 🔗

COMMON CORE STATE STANDARDS: W.3.3, W.3.4, W.3.5, W.3.10, W.4.3.d, RL.3.3 RL.3.5, SL.3.1, SL.3.6, L.3.1, L.3.2, L.3.3a, L.3.6, L.4.3.a to grandson, mother to child, across generations, and they have endured in large part because they are such fun to tell. The stories are part of an oral tradition, written to be told and retold. The stories are written for children who are just waiting to squeal with fright at the troll under the bridge or the giant thundering through his house in the sky.

"That's the lesson of this session. No writer can always have an audience on hand but all of us can have an imaginary audience in mind. Writers write for that person."

The advice to write to an audience is absolutely crucial for writers of any age, in any genre. This was a big part of what children learned to do in the *Changing the World* unit when they wrote petitions, persuasive letters, and speeches meant to rally listeners to care about a cause. This session extends the emphasis of that unit on writing for readers. And it teaches a concept that is profoundly important to any writer. Brenda Ueland, a famous journalist, editor, and teacher of writing, once said in *If You Want to Write: A Book about Art, Independence, and Spirit* (1997):

> Once I was playing the piano and a musician, overhearing it, said to me, "It isn't going anywhere. You must always play to someone—it may be to the river, or God, or to someone who is dead, or to someone in the room, but it must go somewhere." This is why it helps, often, to have an imaginary listener to whom you are writing, or telling a story. A listener helps to shape and create a story. Say you are telling the story to children. You instinctively tell it, change it, adapt it, cut it, expand it, all under their large listening eyes, so they will be held by it throughout.

That's the lesson of this session. No writer can always have an audience on hand but all of us can have an imaginary audience in mind. Writers write for that person. "Come close," the writer says, "I have a story: Once, long, long ago, in a little village by the sea, there lived. . . ."

Telling Stories that Make Readers Shiver

CONNECTION

Recruit writers to join you in reciting and reenacting the most popular refrains from familiar fairy tales.

"Writers, I'm going to say a few words from a fairy tale—and if you remember those words, will you say them along with me? Here's one: 'Fee, fi . . .'" and the children joined in, saying at least part of the refrain with me, "'fo fum, I smell the blood of an Englishman. If he's alive or if he's dead, I'll use his bones to grind my bread.'

"How about this one: 'Little pig, little pig, let. . . .'"

Again the children joined, saying, "'me in,'" and the retort, "'Not by the hair of my chinny, chin, chin.'"

Followed by, "'Then I'll huff and I'll puff and I'll blow your house down!'"

I tried another: "'Trip, trap, trip-trap. . . . Who's that walking on *my* bridge?'" and the response, "'It is I, the littlest billy goat gruff.'"

And "'Mirror mirror on the wall, who's the loveliest of all?'"

Or, "'Run, run, as fast as you can. You can't catch me, I'm the gingerbread man, I am, I am. I've run away from the little old woman, I've run away from the little old man. . . .'"

Also, "'Grandma, what big ears you have! The better to see you with, my dear. . . . What big ears you have! The better to hear you with. . . . What big teeth you have! The better to eat you with, my dear.'"

Explain that people know the refrains of fairy tales by heart because these texts were written to be said aloud. Help children savor the language by getting involved in some storytelling work.

"Many people know those refrains by heart. That phrase, *knowing them by heart*, is a good one because we don't just *know* those words, we *love* them. It's fun to tromp through the house calling, 'Fee fi fo fum!' and it's fun to tell someone who is cowering under the blanket or the sofa cushion, hoping not to be sent to bed, 'Then I'll huff and I'll puff and I'll blow your house down!' I remember when my nephews were little, whenever they were about to cross one particular

We are putting third-graders through the school of fairy tale writing to help them learn fiction. But fiction, itself, is not the goal. The goal is narrative craft. And it is important for you to realize that students will progress through an entire spiral curriculum on narrative writing. No one unit can or should attempt to teach everything about narrative craft. So this is a long-winded way of saying that you want to approach this session with a clear sense of your goals. For us, one of the real priorities is to help kids begin to have a story—story structure and story language—in their bones. You'll see, then, repeated attention to the language of fairy tales and to storytelling and dramatizing of fairy tales. This session is part of that.

There are a few life messages that we glean from all of these books. One, surely, is valuing hard work. Another is appreciating literacy. Every day, teachers need to show the value of rich literacy and to make it so appealing and so inviting that there won't be one child in the class who isn't eager to participate.

little bridge, I'd race ahead of them, hide low in the bush so that as they walked across the bridge I could rise up from underneath, and in my best troll voice, growl, 'Who's that walking over *my* bridge?' while the kids scampered as fast as their little legs could carry them to the safety of the other side of the bridge.

"It is *still* fun for me to playact fairy tales. Let me show you what I mean. I've got some fairy tale refrains in this hat," I said, pulling out a baseball hat, "and I'm going to pass the hat around for you to draw one of these out. When you pull out your refrain, don't show it to anyone but read it to yourself, *silently*, with lots of expression. Then, in a minute, we're going to have a Fairy Tale Symphony. I'll be the conductor, and when I tip my baton at you, instead of playing your clarinet or your bassoon, say your refrain, with all the expression in the world. You won't all have a chance, so afterward I'll say the start of a refrain, and hope that you'll join in if it is a refrain that is on your paper or that you know."

I tipped my baton toward one child, another, another, until I'd done so with about half the class, and then started saying a string of familiar refrains, with children singing along with me. After a few minutes I stopped, got serious, and leaned close to the kids.

❖ **Name the teaching point.**

"Today I want to teach you that fairy tales are written to be read aloud, or storytold, in ways that make listeners squeal and shiver. At the exciting parts, there are often repeated refrains that add to the tension. And throughout, the story is written so that listeners will feel what the writer wants them to feel, to see what the writer wants them to see."

TEACHING

Tell children about a storytelling course in which people were taught that the storyteller needs to see and feel what he or she wants listeners to see and feel.

"Once upon a time, long ago, the world-famous storyteller Mem Fox—the author of *Koala Lou*, one of your favorites!—taught a storytelling class to about thirty teachers, and a friend of mine was one of them. My friend told me afterward that Mem taught them a few really important tips. She said that when you tell a story, you are always desperate for your listener to see what you see, to feel what you feel. And the best way to get your listeners to do that is for *you* to be seeing and feeling what you want your listener to see and feel."

"Mem Fox said to the teachers in that class, 'If you are writing about those three Billy Goats Gruff who brave that scary bridge to get to the meadow with its sweet grass, *you* need to see that meadow.' Then she said, 'See it, right now.' And she added, 'Is it sprinkled with dandelions? Is the grass that sweet green color of soft new grass?' Mem added, 'If *you* don't see that meadow, full of grass, with your eyes, how will your listeners, your readers, see it with their eyes?'

It would be interesting to trace the numbers of times in which children are engaged in a symphony share, across all these books—and the variety to those times. We think it is really helpful to return to rituals and practices, using them in new ways, for new effects. Each time one returns to a familiar technique, things are smoother because of the children's increased familiarity with that technique.

Mem Fox also taught that you should always learn the start of your story by heart so that as you start the tale, your eyes can sweep the room, making contact with all those who have gathered around you. She said, "It is as if you are saying, 'Welcome, pull close'."

Mem also had the students in a class—it was an advanced section at one of the Teachers College Reading and Writing Project's institutes—recite a single poem perhaps five times. The poem, "Sampan," by Tao Lang Pee, contained the description "down the long green river" and she told people to see that long river, and to say "long" in a way that showed the length of that river: "down the lonnnnng green river." Another part of the poem included the phrase, "branches brush" and Mem coached participants to say "brushed" as if the word were a branch, brushing lightly.

"She went on to say that when that giant troll rises up from under the bridge, we—the storyteller—need to feel our knees shake, we need to tremble as we stutter, 'Don't eat me! My brother's coming soon and he's much bigger. Eat my brother!' When writers create refrains, they aren't just any old repeated words—they are descriptive and important enough that they add to the story every time they appear."

ACTIVE ENGAGEMENT

Recruit children to story-tell a favorite part of the classic-tale version of their fairy tale adaptation, working to make listeners see and feel what they want them to experience.

"So let's practice storytelling in ways that really pull listeners in. Will you think of a favorite part of the classic tale your adaptation is built on? Don't go to the adaptation yet. Go to the page 3 of your story-planning booklet, to the part where tension builds, where something big happens. Story-tell that tension-building part in your mind, silently, where things get worse and worse." I gave children a pool of silence in which to do this, and sat before them, silently doing this for my own story in ways that I knew would channel them to do the same. After two minutes, I said, "Once you've told the story one time in your mind, tell it again, only better. Jazz it up. And make sure that you are seeing what the character sees, feeling what the character feels. You might want to try coming up with a refrain that captures this."

I left more silence, while again I modeled doing this with rapt attention with my own story-planning booklet. Then I said, "Partner 1, will you tell your story—your classic fairy tale—to Partner 2? But here's the thing. As you tell it, be really aware what you want your listener to see, and to feel. Try to tell the story so that you create that effect."

Now channel students to story-tell their adaptation of the classic tale, again trying to get listeners to see what they see, feel what they feel. Use voiceovers to coach into their work.

After children did this for a few minutes, I intervened. "Even if you are not finished with that version, can you stop because I'm going to make the challenge much harder. Will you do the same thing—story-tell your fairy tale in ways that make listeners see what you want them to see, feel what you want them to feel? Only this time you'll be storytelling *your* adaptation of the story. You probably won't be exactly clear how the story goes—fudge it a bit as you go—but the goal is to make it up as you go, not stopping, no matter what. And see if you might come up with a refrain that really helps create the world of the story for your readers."

After children did this for a bit, I again intervened. "Storytellers, will you do that again—go back and story-tell your adaptation to each other, but *this* time, act out the story as you story-tell it. You'll be acting while sitting in your place in the meeting area so it won't be a perfect sort of acting, but add little gestures and expressions. And when you switch from one person talking to another, use the storyteller's technique of shifting from looking in one direction to looking in another to show the change in point of view." I showed them how a shift in posture could convey a different speaker.

Be aware that kids often paint an entire story with one feeling. So they're apt to say that they want listeners of Jack and the Beanstalk *to feel fear. But any good story will put listeners through a whole progression of feelings.* Jack and the Beanstalk *is a story that inspires absolute awe at times. Imagine waking up to see that your beans, discarded by your mom, were magic after all, and that a beanstalk has grown in your very own yard. Crane your neck, following that beanstalk with your gaze . . . up, up, up. Surely you feel awe, amazement. Later, when you first arrive in that house in the sky, don't you feel goosebumps as you tread carefully through that empty house? Then, oh yes, then there will be those footsteps that shake the floor, and the booming voice that sends you racing to find a hiding spot, anywhere, quickly, fast, oh my gosh! Teaching kids to tell a story so that it makes the listeners feel what you want them to feel—that is a tall order indeed. And it is worth caring about.*

The truth is, anything you teach should feel absolutely critically important. Always remember that you are keeping writers from their writing when you sit at the front of the meeting area and talk to them. Your words better be important because you are pulling writers from their writing.

As children reenacted and storytold their stories, I voiced over, saying, "Don't forget that in the problem part of your story, things will get worse and worse. This is the time when the wolf comes to one pig's door, another pig's door, another. This is the time when the train tries, tries, and tries to get over the mountain. Make things get worse and worse."

Another time, as they storytold, I said, "When you can tell your story is getting through to listeners, soup things up. Fan the flames. What bit of language might you make into a refrain that can keep coming up?"

Debrief in ways that cull from this activity the points you hope learners will carry with them.

After a bit, I intervened one more time., this time asking for everyone's full attention. "Writers, do you see how storytelling and acting out your story—both the classic version and your different adaptation—can help you create a story that will reach listeners, getting them to see what you want them to see and to feel what you want them to feel? Whenever you're rehearsing for a new story—whether it's a fairy tale or some other kind of story—keep this in mind. And here is the real secret to success in narrative writing: As you write—which you'll be doing in a second—story-tell in your mind to an imaginary audience."

LINK

Set students up to rehearse through storytelling, supporting those students who need more scaffolding before working independently.

"Those of you who have told your story to your partner, off you go to your writing spot. I expect you'll be touching the pages of your story-planning booklet and storytelling your adaptation a number of times before you actually start writing your first scene on draft paper—which is probably page 2 of your story-planning booklet. I'll post our first scene of *Cinderella* for you to use as a mentor text as you start your scene.

"Meanwhile, those of you who haven't yet had a chance to storytell your story, stay here on the rug and help each other do the storytelling you need to do so you are ready to get started writing soon too.

"And writers, as a reminder, I'm going to add the idea of refrains to our chart as you head off."

If you go online, you'll find a zillion sites about storytelling. Peruse them and you'll find lists of tips. We have also included a video on the accompanying CD-ROM that gives a wonderful example of a student storytelling a fairy tale with expression and gusto. You might want to show this to your students at some point during or after this session. One tip that seems to make its way into every list is this: Tell the whole story through, without stopping, even when you have no clue, really, what you plan to say.

How to Write a Fairy Tale Adaptation

- Know the classic story and tell it often.
- Decide on a change to improve the story.
- Make the change lead to other changes so the whole story fits together.
- Make a character with traits and wants who runs into trouble.
- Tell the story in two or three scenes (Small Moment stories).
- Story-tell or act out the first scene, filling in lifelike details. Then write the scenes.
- Figure out an ending that solves the character's big problem.
- With narration, give a backstory at the start and stitch scenes together.
- Make your readers remember by adding a refrain.

Supporting the Transition from Rehearsal to Writing

I T IS PREDICTABLE that when the day comes for writers to actually go from prewriting to writing, there will be resistance. If some children complain that they are stuck, you might tell them that the author Katie Wood Ray has told us she's learned two of the most important writing lessons from her dogs: Sit and stay. Ultimately the job of a writer is to write, and we often accomplish this by putting in "fanny" time—sitting, pen in hand, staying in "our writing cabins," capturing our stories on paper.

Even still, some children may benefit from a sprinkle of inspiration to boost themselves from storytelling to drafting. You may decide to share video or audio clips from the top young storytellers in the country. The National Youth Storytelling Showcase (NYSS) or National Youth Storytelling Olympics offer excellent examples of youth performances that both demonstrate the power of storytelling and show how storytelling, as a planning tool, can lead to vivid writing. Perhaps your students will watch the video provided on the accompanying CD-ROMs.

You may decide that a few children may need more structure to work out their first scene. Perhaps they'll benefit from creating a quick timeline of the big parts of the scene. Once they know the sequence of microevents, you can help them retell the plot line, this time adding in setting. When Mem Fox encourages storytellers to see the meadow in *The Three Billy Goats Gruff*, to fill in the color and smell of the grass, the flowers, she is suggesting a popular writing strategy. A child who is writing an adaptation of *The Princess and the Pea* might think about what, exactly, the biggest, most comfortable bed looks and feels like.

Often young writers have a tendency to include too few or inconsequential details. Guide your writers to focus on adding details to descriptions of characters, scenes, and elements that are key to the drama of the story. If something is especially alluring in a story, children can ask themselves how they might describe that thing—the meadow or apple or forest—so that it is irresistible not only to the characters but also to the writer or reader herself. When something scary happens—when a reader gets that "uh-oh" feeling—what, exactly, makes it scary? What details and words can the writer use to bring out that reaction?

MID-WORKSHOP TEACHING
Keeping Deadlines and Plans in Mind

"Writers, may I interrupt you? I'm so glad that you all are moving yourselves along through your plans. I just want to remind you that most of you planned that you'd do the sixth item on your planning chart today," I said, pointing to the line that read, *Story-tell or act out the first scene, filling in the lifelike details. Then write the scenes.*

"It has been totally impressive to see so many of you pushing yourself to make that switch from planning to writing, doing this without me having to say, 'Boys and girls, now you need to do this, now you need to do that.' And you are wise to remember that it is all too easy to get lost in the world of storytelling and acting, and to lose sight of the fact that a writer's most important job is to write!

"The other thing that has impressed me is that most of you remember that you are writing a Small Moment story. You all might want to look back at the start of what you have written and ask, 'Does it start with dialogue? Do I show what the main character is doing and saying—exactly?' I know you'll be deciding on the work you are doing right now. I just wanted you to know that I'm admiring the way you are keeping your deadlines in mind."

Even your students who are "getting" today's work will benefit from this sort of small-group work, as it will push them to write with even more exact and sensory detail. Writing in a way that pulls a reader in, inspires chills or goose bumps, or gets the heart racing is a tall order. The more concrete examples of this you can provide, whether auditory or visual or in writing, will increase your children's understanding of how to do this themselves.

Reflect Progress as a Writing Community

Using the class's writing colony metaphor, encourage students to assess progress and next steps.

"Writers," I interrupted, "meet me in the meeting area, bringing your story-planning booklets, notebooks, and folders." As I waited for the writers to settle in, I suggested that they review their planning sheets, taking note of their progress. When most of the writers had gathered, I began. "Writers, I've been thinking about the ways the classroom is becoming a writing colony and I thought we might end today's writing workshop with whole-class conversation about our prog- ress and our next steps. Let's first remind ourselves of the features of a writing colony and then let's assess ourselves to see how we are doing on the goal of transforming our writing workshop into a writing colony. Go ahead and call out some of the things we'd planned and then we'll talk about whether we are meeting those plans."

"Library of fairy tales," said Gio. "Those fancy lessons that are like minilessons for college," added Leroy. "You mean seminars," said Sarah. Alejandro continued, "We have meeting spaces and writing cabins."

"Great!" I said. "Okay, let's take a moment and study our list." I waited. "Give me a thumbs up when you have thoughts on ways to make the most of our writing colony." When I noticed six or eight thumbs up, I nodded to Wendy as a signal to begin.

"I think we need to think about ways to use the fairy tale library. We have all the books in a basket, but we're not doing anything with them." I nodded and recorded her idea in my notebook. "Hey," said Jackson, "That could be a seminar! You could teach us how to use the fairy tale library."

FIG. 8–1   Shane's story planning booklet

Encourage students to take ownership of their writing community to meet their goals independently.

A few other students shared their thoughts and I recorded. "I am wondering what you can do to help make the classroom be the writing community you all want it to be. Turn and discuss this with your partner."

I reconvened students and resumed the whole-class conversation. "So what ideas do you have about the ways you can make our writing colony all that you want it to be?" The conversation continued with different students volunteering to do a variety of tasks, from making a suggestion box for seminars to the formation of a library committee. "Writers, this is so important—you are taking charge of your writing colony and your writing lives. Beautiful!"

FIG. 8–2   Zander's story planning booklet

Revising Early and Often

IN THIS SESSION, you'll teach students that writers make significant revisions as they draft, using other authors' writing as mentor texts.

GETTING READY

✔ Chart paper to record ideas for a writing colony motto (see Connection)

✔ Strong writing work by one or two students (see Active Engagement)

✔ Writing folders, drafts, and pens (see Active Engagement and Share)

✔ Excerpt of the class adaptation of *Cinderella* (see Active Engagement)

✔ "If . . . Then . . ." chart (see Conferring and Small-Group Work)

✔ "A Storyteller's Voice Shows, Not Tells. It . . ." chart from Unit 1 *Crafting True Stories* (see Mid-Workshop Teaching Point)

✔ Strips of paper with classic fairy tale refrains, folded and placed in a hat as used in Session 8 (see Share)

I WILL NOT FORGET THE DAY the first copy of *The Art of Teaching Reading* arrived at Teachers College. I held the book in my hands, felt its heft, and was so glad it was finally done. I couldn't resist telling someone—anyone—that my new book had arrived, so I turned to a nearby teacher and said, "My new book is here."

The teacher asked to hold the new book—the perfect request—and then she joined me in admiring its heft. At one point, she said, "Imagine—you wrote this many words!"

I smiled faintly, and didn't say anything, but in my mind I thought: "What are you talking about? I wrote twenty times this many words! One doesn't write a manuscript and then publish it—one writes, discards, writes, discards . . . !"

We recently had some construction on our kitchen and the contractor parked a giant, bedroom-sized refuse trailer outside the house. Looking at that trash trailer, I thought, "I need one of those any time I write a book." Always, so much gets cut.

This session, then, is a celebration of revision. The goal is to intercede before kids get totally committed to their (sometimes awful) drafts. We've found that when kids are writing fiction, front-end revision is much more practical than back-end revision. Catching them now, and reminding them to write in small moments, to write with details, to show not tell, to include thoughts as well as actions . . . all of that can mean that the writing kids do on upcoming days will be more apt to reflect this knowledge.

COMMON CORE STATE STANDARDS: W.3.3, W.3.4, W.3.5., W.3.10, W.4.3.d, RL.3.2, SL.3.1, SL.3.6, L.3.1, L.3.2, L.3.3, L.4.3

Revising Early and Often

CONNECTION

Return to the theme of the class co-creating a writing community by talking up the possibility of a class motto.

"Writers, you know how different companies have mottos? Like Nike, their motto is *Just do it.* Or Burger King, their motto is *Have it your way.* Last night, I was thinking that this writing colony should have a motto, some words to live by. I tried out some of the fairy tale refrains that we love, but somehow I don't think our motto could be, *Don't eat me, eat my brother!* I thought of *Whistle while you work;* have you heard that song?" and I sang it to students for effect. Breaking into another Disney rendition, I then sang, "'Hi ho, hi ho, it's off to work we go!'

"I'm pretty sure you could think of something better. It doesn't need to come from fairy tales—it could come from a song or a TV show that you guys know that I don't even know. Will you turn and talk and see if you come up with ideas for a motto, or a saying, for this writing colony? Turn and talk."

Soon we'd started a brainstorm list on a piece of chart paper, and kids agreed they'd record other suggestions when they came to mind. "Writers, before you 'hi ho, hi ho and off to work you go,' I want to teach you a writing secret."

❖ **Name the teaching point.**

"Some students think you draft your *whole* piece, then you revise your *whole* piece. The truth is that serious writers, sophisticated writers, revise early and use those early revisions to lift the level of what they have yet to write."

TEACHING

Convey that writers may decide *when* to do a second draft, but it is nonnegotiable that they do one. Meanwhile, suggest that front-end revisions are more economical and powerful than back-end revisions.

"Writers, I know that this week you are each deciding on your own writing plans. Some of you may ignore the advice of this minilesson, and that is okay. I'm going to encourage you to revise early—to draw a line in the draft, wherever you are in it, and to say, 'I'm going to stop, reread, rethink, and start my second draft right now.'

◆ COACHING

When writing the books for this series, a group of coauthors joined me for a writing retreat in an Adirondack camp. We worked fifteen-hour days, but that work was punctuated by joviality. There was no time to take a fifteen-minute drive to the grocery store, so when the napkins and paper towel supply ran dry, we carefully folded strips of toilet paper so they looked like napkins, and set the silverware out on the toilet paper. That created lots of laughter—and that laughter spurred on our writing. Writing requires the writer to put himself, herself, on the page. That is not easy to do. It is impossible to overemphasize the value of creating a supportive community. So does this little interlude of talk about a class motto really matter? Not really—and yes, really!

"But you are the boss of your writing, and you may decide not to do that. By Friday, you do need to show me two almost entirely different drafts; but you may finish this draft and *then* stop, reread, rethink, rewrite, or you may do that now. You are in charge.

"I want to tell you two things. First, stopping now has a few advantages. You haven't written that much yet, so rewriting the start to a draft is less writing than rewriting the whole draft. Also, if you rewrite now, your revision work will lift the rest of the story. But this is your decision."

Convey also that to revise, a writer first makes himself or herself smarter, and to do that it helps to reread great writing and to think, "How did the author do that?"

"The other thing I want to teach you is that whenever it is that you do revise, the first thing you have to do is become a smarter, better person. Put on a professor's glasses and make yourself be really smart. Then—still acting as that genius-type person—reread your writing, thinking, 'Hmm, . . . how could this story be made better?' This is important because if you just go from writing to rereading your piece, without becoming a new person, you'll think, 'This seems just about right to me,'" I said, shrugging for effect. "It is only if you make yourself into a super-smart, genius-type person before you reread your writing that you'll be able to imagine how your writing could be so much better.

"So, all that I need to do is to tell you how to become a super-smart genius-type person, and the good news is that this is a fairy tale unit of study, so here's what you do. You say, 'hocus pocus' and spin around three times.

"I'm joking, of course. The truth is that writers have a very practical way to become smarter. You know what this method is—writers find a text they wish they'd written, study it to find passages they love, and then ask, 'What did this author do that I could try?' Then they sort of become like that writer. I know you have studied the work of many published writers—Karen Hesse, for example, and Babette Cole—and letting their writing rub off on you is a super-smart thing to do. You might do that today. What you may not realize, though, is that when you work within a writing colony, you also may study the work that your friends have written. Your friends may not be famous writers, but some of their writings are amazing. If you could write like the best parts of the writing of everyone in this room—*look out*!

"So find those parts, and then ask, 'What did the writer do that I could try?' And if the writer is a living, breathing member of your very own writing colony, get that writer to help you."

ACTIVE ENGAGEMENT

Rally kids to try rereading a classmate's writing to become smarter, then bring their new stance to the job of rereading and revising their own writing.

"Last night, I wanted to revise my draft of our *Cinderella* story, so I reread through some of your work. Reading Piper's draft was like taking a course in character development, and it definitely gave me new eyes to see our *Cinderella* story differently. Listen as I read you a bit of what Piper wrote in her adaptation of *The Three Billy Goats Gruff*, and see if just listening to this can make you smarter. Watch how she has the grandmother, the mother, and the daughter each doing

When we say to kids, "You are in charge of your own writing," we don't mean we pull out from supporting students. We just want to give them the space to make decisions. You'll see lots of ways in which we continue to lead from behind.

I am, of course, somewhat tongue-in-cheek as I say all this. Enjoy your teaching.

the same thing—crossing the street—and see if Piper's writing gives *you* a course in character development that will change how you reread *your* writing." (See Figure 9–1.)

"I can't wait to go to the museum!" said Shelley.

"You're not going anywhere until I punch you in the nose," [SAID THE CROSSING GUARD].

"Oh, please don't! My daughter is way more punchable than me," pleaded Grandma. "Okay, fine. Off you go, old lady." And with that Grandma gratefully hobbled across the street.

Next it was Mom's turn. She started to walk across the street. As soon as she had taken only a few steps on the pavement, the crossing guard thundered, "Who's that crossing over my street?"

"It's me! Mom! I've come to look at the museum across the street!"

"You'll do none of that sort until you get punched in the nose!"

"Oh, please don't! My daughter is way more punchable than me."

"Oh, all right." And with that, Mom ran across the street to join Grandma.

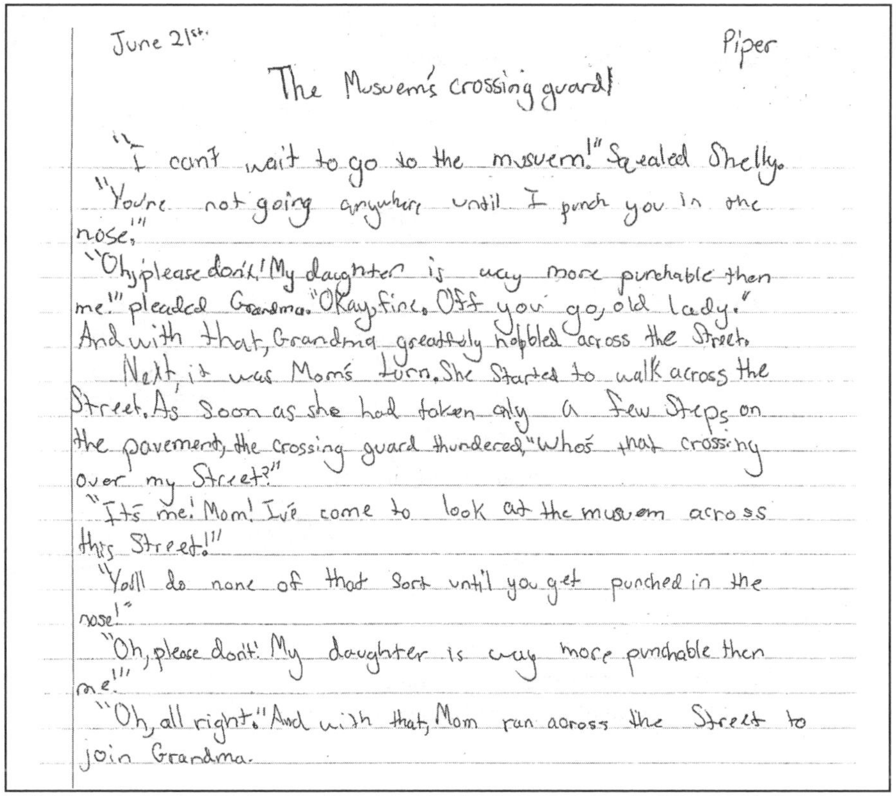

FIG. 9–1   Piper's draft showing character development

"Notice how the grandma talks and moves one way and the daughter talks and moves another way. I admire that and I want to revise the *Cinderella* story—I haven't had time to work on a second adaptation!—to make it good like Piper's. I'm learning so much about good writing, it is like the fairy godmother just came and threw fairy dust on me! Do you all think you could reread your stories and notice ways you could revise your characters' actions? Get out your story and see if you can find a place where Piper's writing helps you get ideas for how to make your writing better. While you do that, I'm going to be thinking about this part of *Cinderella*. If any of you want to help me with this story, you may."

While the children reread their own drafts, I reread a part of our adaptation of *Cinderella*, saying to myself, "I want to check whether we've made each of our characters act and talk in their own way, like Piper did with hers." I reread this section of our writing:

Cinderella entered the library. It was big and beautiful. And so empty it echoed. "Where are all of the books?" Cinderella wondered aloud.

"We ran out of money," said the mayor, walking toward her and holding out his hand. "I'm Donald, the mayor."

Debrief to name the work the students have just done and to channel their rereading and rethinking toward revisions.

After a minute or two, I said to the children, "May I have your focus back here?" Once I had their attention, I said, "Give me a thumbs-up if Piper's piece made you smart enough that you could imagine fixing up a part of your draft." Many children held their thumbs up in agreement. "Would you jot some marginal notes about what you'd change?" I said.

In the margins of the Cinderella draft I jotted, "Make Cinderella move and sound like Cinderella. Make Donald move and sound like Donald." I whisper-read my jottings making my revisions audible to all. Then I added, "Write exactly what Cinderella saw as she walked into the library."

LINK

Invite children to read the work of many classmates, letting that work spark new ideas and plans for revision.

Then I said, "So writers, the important thing for you to know is that you can read some other people's writing, too, and their writing can give you yet more ideas. For example, you might read the refrain Jackson has written, playing off of *Goldilocks and the Three Bears*." (See Figure 9–2.)

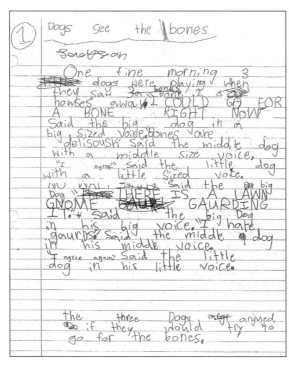

FIG. 9–2 Jackson's draft showing use of refrains

With a deep voice, I read, "'I could go for a bone right now,' said the *big dog* in a *big*-sized voice."

With a less deep voice, I read: "'Bones are delicious,' said the middle dog in a middle-sized voice."

With a voice like Baby Bear's, I read, "'I agree,' said the little dog in a little-sized voice."

"After reading Jackson's work, you might say, 'Why didn't I use repetition like he did—fairy tales are full of repetition.' Or you might say, 'Dang it all. Both Jackson and Piper have each character doing an action differently to show they are different. I definitely can do that.'"

Channel children to go from rereading and aspiring to writing. Talk up the value of writing entirely new drafts.

"And then . . . then, you write. Sure, you could just use little carets to stick a few small changes in between your lines. But what writers do is that after they fill themselves up with ideas for how to improve their writing, they go back to the start. They story-tell it all over again, and they get out a blank sheet of paper, label it *draft two*, and get started.

"But you'll decide. And I can't wait to admire what you do." I started humming "Hi ho, hi ho, it's off to work we go!" and signaled with my hands for students to get to work.

You may want to add in a ritual where kids reread their own work, identify parts of it they believe are especially well written, and label what it is they have done well, making it easier for others to know what sections of the work merit further study.

We strongly believe that entirely new drafts are vastly more effective than little alterations stuck in between the lines of a draft. Rally kids to have the chutzpah to write whole new drafts. Don't let their whining get to you. Your job is to teach, not to always be loved. And they'll thank you later when the new draft is light years better than the old one.

Supporting Children in Writing New Drafts

DURING THE MINILESSON, you dropped a bit of a bombshell when you said, "By Friday, you need two almost entirely different drafts." Because today's conferring and small-group work needs to heave everyone into a whole new draft, the conferring tips are in the form of an "If . . . Then . . ." chart (at right).

MID-WORKSHOP TEACHING
Using Available Tools to Support Revision Work

"Writers, may I interrupt you? As I move around the room, our writing colony, I see many of you taking on this work of revising early in your drafts. Some of you are trying out the strategies we learned from Piper and Jackson. Others are gathering with other writers to read aloud your drafts. And a few of you are even dipping into the fairy tale library. Fabulous!" Now I held up the storytelling chart from the *Crafting True Stories* unit. "Remember this chart?"

A Storyteller's Voice Shows, Not Tells. It . . .

- describes actions that took place.
- uses dialogue.
- describes what we saw, smelled, tasted, or felt.
- describes images around the storyteller.

"Right now, take a moment to reread the 'Storyteller's Voice' chart with your partner, thinking especially about the strategies that worked well for you in the past. Choose one section, one part of your draft, and reread looking for one thing—say, describing actions—then reread that same part looking for a different thing, like describing images around the character, and so on. Try this now."

If . . .	Then . . .
Writers are continuing to work on their same draft	You might check in with these writers to see what they are doing to lift the level of what they have yet to write. Keep in mind the list of strategies that you've taught, such as studying mentor text and including tiny actions, to name a few. In these types of exchanges with kids, it's important to push past their words, what they say they are doing, and push into their drafts so you can see whether their writing matches their intentions.
Writers are writing a second draft that is very close to the first draft	You might place the two drafts side by side and suggest that you study them together to notice the big, significant ways that they are different. Since they won't be significantly different, you might teach that when writers begin a new draft they do it the way people begin a new year—by making New Year's resolutions. Students might write their resolutions on the top of each sheet of draft paper: *In this draft, I resolve to . . .*
Writers are rising to the challenge of a new, improved draft	Do a happy dance! You might research by asking, "What troubles are you encountering in this new draft?" Peter Johnston, in his book *Choice Words* (2004) teaches that talking openly and matter-of-factly about trouble normalizes it, makes it something all writers, and all people, experience. For example, when I asked this question of Shelly, she let me know that she was having trouble weaving those tiny actions into her scenes.

Celebrating Adapted Fairy Tale Refrains

Immerse students in the sound of fairy tales by encouraging them to chorally chant back individuals' adapted fairy tale refrains.

I held up the baseball cap with the strips of fairy tale refrains I had prepared. "Writers, remember how a few days ago we sang out some of our favorite refrains from classic fairy tales? Well, today I thought we might end workshop in a similar way." My suggestion was met with shared smiles.

"With one small twist," I continued. "Instead of singing out classic refrains from classic fairy tales, let's sing out any *adapted* refrains from your adapted fairy tales. I thought you could do this is in a call-and-response kind of way, where one writer calls out his or her repeated refrain and we all respond by singing the refrain back to the writer. In this way, we'll be immersing ourselves in the sound of fairy tales. Who can get us started?"

After a moment of awkward silence, Ella read from a crumpled sheet of draft paper (see Figure 9–3): "'Who's that swish, swashing across my rainbow?' roared Feisty Bob the Leprechaun."

"Cool," commented Jackson. "You're adapting *The Three Billy Goats Gruff*." Ella grinned and nodded.

I led the class in a call-and-response. "Everyone, let's sing back Ella's refrain. All together now! "'Who's that swish, swashing across my rainbow?' roared Feisty Bob the Leprechaun.'"

"'I'll claw and I'll tear, and I'll rip your house apart!'" read Maggie, then continued, "I'm writing *The Three Little Zebras*, a version of the *Three Little Pigs*," she explained. (See Figure 9–4.) The class echoed Maggie's refrain.

Zander took a deep breath, "Mine is an adaptation of *The Emperor's New Clothes* called *Usher's New Outfit*." Zander cleared his throat, "'I must be cool. I must be hip. I need a new outfit.'" (See Figure 9–5.) The refrain boomed throughout the classroom.

"These are awesome!" I beamed. "Your refrains are catchy and clever. Your readers are definitely going to want to read your tales over and over again."

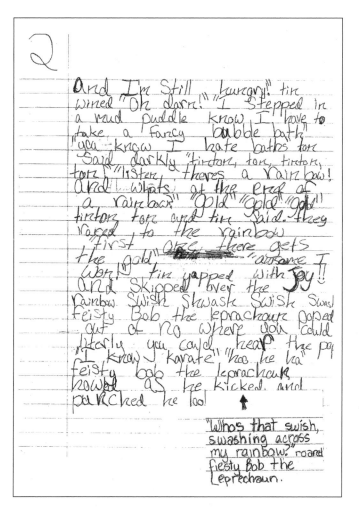

FIG. 9–3   Ella's refrain on a Post-it, bottom right

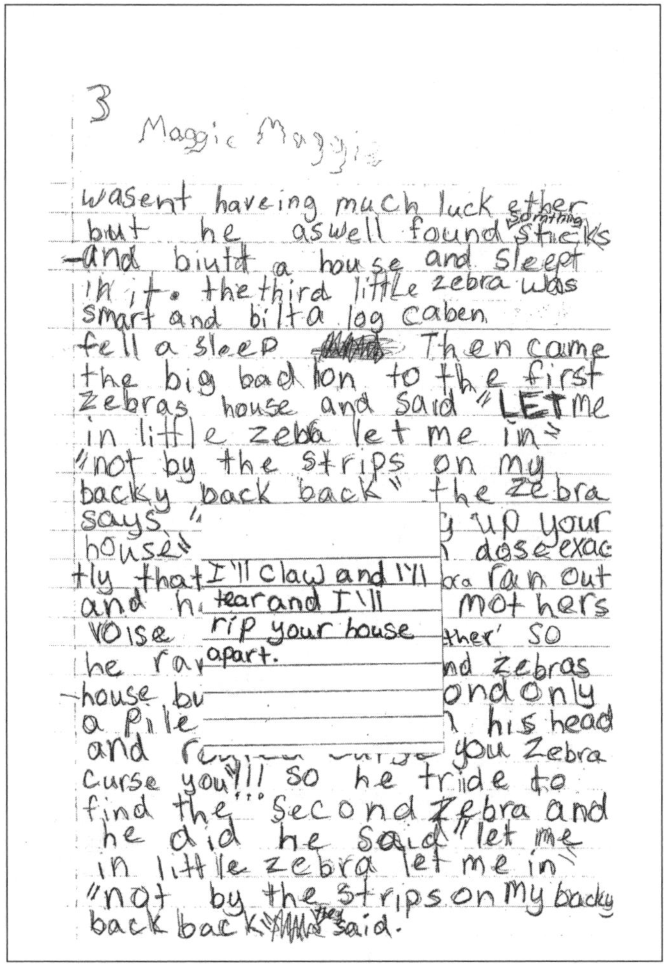

3

Maggie Maggie

wasent haveing much luck either
but he aswell found sticks _something_
and biutt a house and sleept
in it. the third little zebra was
smart and bilt a log caben
fell asleep ~~XXX~~ Then came
the big bad lion to the first
zebras house and said "LET me
in little zebra let me in"
"not by the strips on my
backy back back" the zebra
says, "_____ up your
house I dose exac
tly that | I'll claw and I'll | ran out
and hi | tear and I'll | mothers
voise | rip your house | ther' so
he ra | apart. | nd zebras
house bu | _____ | ond only
a pile | _____ | his head
and r~~XXX~~ you Zebra
curse you"!! so he tride to
find the "Second zebra and
he did he said "let me
in little zebra let me in"
"not by the strips on My backy
back back" ~~XXX~~ he said.

FIG. 9–4 Maggie's refrain on a Post-it in the center of her draft

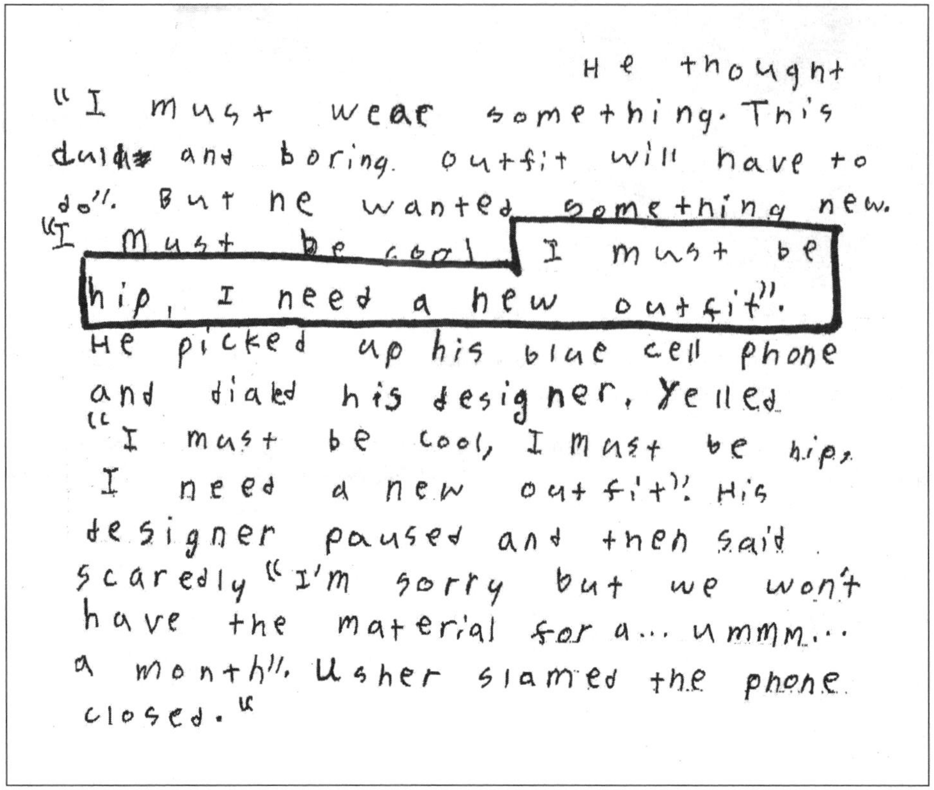

He thought
"I must wear something. This
duld# and boring. outfit will have to
do". But he wanted something new.
"I must be cool. I must be
hip, I need a new outfit".
He picked up his blue cell phone
and dialed his designer. Yelled
"I must be cool, I must be hip.
I need a new outfit". His
designer paused and then said.
scaredly "I'm sorry but we won't
have the material for a... ummm...
a month". Usher slamed the phone
closed. "

FIG. 9–5 Zander's refrain, outlined

Session 10

When Dialogue Swamps Your Draft, Add Actions

W̲E DEVISED THIS MINILESSON out of a feeling that the kids do not need us to throw yet more lists of "qualities of good writing" at them. They already have all too many lists to juggle. What they need, instead, is for us to help them with some of the problems that persist. Although we do not know your students and haven't studied their work, we do know that if you are doing many things right in this unit, the result could very well be drafts that are swamped with dialogue. We've seen it so often. As soon as kids truly buy into the idea that writing a narrative is not all that different from drama, as soon as they actually begin to write stories by making movies in the mind and writing the unfolding story of those movies, it will happen that their drafts become swamped with talk. Try it. Imagine a scene between two people, say a mother and her daughter. The mother is explaining that no, the daughter can't go to the party. So start by thinking of the exact words the mother says . . . then keep going with the imagined story.

Chances are good that your story unfolds in a she said–he said sort of way. Chances are good you never have the mother push the daughters' bangs behind her ear, or pull her collar out from under her sweater, smoothing it so it lies flat. You probably never have the mother glance at the clock, or finger her wedding ring. This is work that writers of story will be aware of and will continue to work on not just in third grade but also in fourth grade when they tackle realistic fiction and throughout their story-writing careers.

The point of this lesson is that those small actions are not small. This is a lesson that will help you with your writing, and will surely help your kids as well. Best of all, it should be fun. It also does not put special demands on students. It doesn't force them to set aside whatever agendas were already important to them so as to pursue this one thing. So you can end the session by inviting kids to do the work they need to do: "Go to it," you can say, and this time, you mean it.

IN THIS SESSION, you'll teach students that writers balance their dialogue by adding accompanying actions.

GETTING READY

✔ Loose-leaf paper, two sheets per student (see Teaching and Active Engagement)

✔ "How to Write a Fairy Tale Adaptation" chart (see Link)

✔ Class adaptation of *Cinderella* (see Conferring and Small-Group Work)

✔ *Prince Cinders* by Babette Cole (see Mid-Workshop Teaching Point)

COMMON CORE STATE STANDARDS: W.3.3.b,d; W.3.4, W.3.5, W.3.10, W.4.3.b,d; RL.3.2, RL.3.4, SL.3.1, SL.3.6, L.3.1, L.3.2, L.3.2c, L.3.3, L.4.3

When Dialogue Swamps Your Draft, Add Actions

CONNECTION

Tell students that you read their drafts, spotted a widely shared problem, and plan to address it in today's minilesson. Name the problem: Dialogue swamps everything in the draft.

"Writers, thanks for leaving your drafts on your desk for me to study while you were at gym. I got so involved reading your work that I didn't even take a second to get a cup of coffee. I just sat here, reading and reading and reading. As I read, I thought hard about what the most important thing is that I can say to you. What can I teach you that will take your writing from here," I asked, and gestured to indicate waist height, "to here," this time gesturing over my head. "The totally cool thing is that I have found a source of trouble and I have a solution for that trouble.

"The trouble that I am seeing is this. There are many times when your writing reads like the soundtrack, without the visuals, in a television show. It is like watching TV when there's no picture on the screen. One person talks, the next, the next . . . but we do not see who is doing what, where."

Explain that adults struggle with this too, and tell about a writing teacher who taught adults that when writing about a conversation, it helps if the characters are making a salad. Illuminate that comment.

"Grown-up writers struggle with this as well. Let's say my story includes a conversation between two people: He said . . . then she said . . . then he said . . . then she said. . . . Perhaps the people are just sitting there, talking, so there aren't any actions to speak of. When my writing included conversations like that, the Pulitzer-Prize–winning writing teacher, Donald Murray, told me, 'If your characters are talking or thinking about something, be sure they are making a salad together.'

"I looked at him like he was nuts. I thought, 'A salad? To write well, characters need to be making a salad?' Somehow I couldn't see Little Red Riding Hood stopping in the woods to peel a cucumber, or the three little pigs washing their lettuce as the wolf huffs and puffs outside the door. When I pressed him to learn more, Murray said, 'I don't mean that *literally* they need to be making a salad! But if characters are going to be talk, talk, talk, or think, think, think, then you need that conversation to be supported with some actions. Instead of making a salad, they could be sweeping or walking in the woods or washing the dishes.'"

Don't you love: "The totally cool thing is that I have found a source of trouble in your writing." What a message regarding the real work that we are all about—the project of getting better as writers. I'm hoping that you teach in a place where the same sort of comment could be said about your teaching. The totally cool thing is that someone helped you to see not only a source of trouble with your teaching but also a solution for that trouble. We should all thank our lucky stars if we live and work in communities that value revision, not just on the page but in life.

The truth is that Don Murray then illustrated by pretending he was writing about a woman who was furious with her husband. "'Dang him,' she thinks, and grabs a head of lettuce, smashing it down onto the granite countertop, she then rips out the heart of the lettuce. 'He's always late,' she says, and grabs a cleaver, a cutting board" . . . I'll leave the rest to your imagination, but enough to say that it has been twenty years since Murray taught me that lesson and I still remember it. We can hope that your kids will remember today's session as well.

❖ **Name the teaching point.**

"So that is my teaching point. If characters are having a conversation, it helps if they are making a salad—or doing some other accompanying action. Those actions can say as much as the dialogue."

TEACHING AND ACTIVE ENGAGEMENT

Demonstrate in ways that contrast what a conversation is like with no actions punctuating it, and what it is like with small actions bringing home the content.

"Instead of me trying to explain why, let me show you. I'm handing out two sheets of paper. You are going to need these for our next activity. When you get them, put one sheet aside." Once each student had the pages, I said, "Okay, I'm going to tell a story and I'm going to tell it like you guys often write, with just dialogue. Then I am going to retell it a second time, and each of you will be the main character, adding actions that I'll help you with."

I stepped into the role being a character—still unclear to my audience—and began talking in a string of thoughts and comments from the point of view of that character. Writing-in-the-air, I said:

> *I'm so mad at my brother. He comes to me with these lists of things. I'm supposed to do this, this, this. I just put it out of sight and ignore it. But he comes back at me with his list of demands. I feel like taking his list—actually, taking him, and squashing him, I get so mad. I feel like putting him right out of my life.*

"Don Murray's point is that when you are writing a string of thoughts or of dialogue, like that, the writing will be stronger if the speaker is doing some accompanying action. It needn't be making a salad. For now, you're going to be the character, acting out whatever I say, while sitting in your place. And the one prop you have is your sheet of paper. I'll be doing this too." I started once again to chronicle my thoughts, this time, using my page of paper as a prop, and leaving spaces in the script so the kids could assume the role too, and act it out, in unison, but each in his or her own way.

I'm so mad at my brother. He comes to me with this list of demands.

I'm supposed to do this, this, this.

I just put it out of sight and ignore it.

But he comes back at me with his list of demands.

Set kids up to supply the actions themselves, using just a sheet of notebook paper as the one prop. That one page, however, can be flung to the side, crushed, torn, all to accentuate a point.

Then I said to the kids: "You are on your own from now on. I'm just saying the thoughts and you do the actions." And I began, "But he comes back at me with his list of demands." I paused. "I feel like taking his list—actually, taking him, and squashing him, I get so mad." As I said that, I looked out to see many children taking the sheet of notebook paper and squashing it. "I feel like telling him he can't come in my bedroom again." I watched to see if the kids would act

Of course it would have been easy to say this differently, so the emphasis was not on making a salad, but on some more general thing like "engaged in a repetitive action." But a good teaching point, especially, and a good minilesson, in general, is above all memorable. The salad is what makes this memorable.

When you say this, no one will understand. That's okay. Press on. They'll get it soon enough.

as if they were locking him out. "I feel like tearing him apart," I finished. I waited to see if the kids were ripping paper, and then I joined them.

"Writers, what I hope you are grasping is that Murray could have said, "If you are having a conversation or thinking a bunch of thoughts in your story, make sure you are holding a piece of paper—and that you use it to accentuate what you say and think. Now the story would sound like this: "I'm so mad at my brother. He comes at me with this list of demands," I said, and angrily shook a page of writing. "I'm supposed to do this, this, and this." As I spoke, I jabbed at the items on my brother's list of demands.

"Writers, instead of holding a piece of paper, a character could be holding onto an old pocket watch, clutching it in his pocket, taking it out to give it a stolen glance, only to return it to his pocket quickly."

LINK

Recap the lesson, but remind students of the bigger goals for today, letting today's lesson be an offering, not a demand.

"So writers, I know you've been writing and revising your drafts of your story. I'm hoping today's lesson will remind you that if your story reads like a soundtrack without any visuals, you'll want to revise it to add actions. Give your character something to hold, something to do, and let the story go *action, dialogue, action, dialogue.*

"But this is just one of many ways in which you can work to make your story the best that it can be. Will you think, for a minute, of five things you know you can do to make this the best story ever? Turn and talk."

The children talked, and I listened in. "I heard you saying that you can be sure to write a few Small Moment stories, and not let one Small Moment story blend into the next. I heard you saying that you can make a movie in your mind, and show what the character is doing and saying. And that you can think about how to make your different characters act differently, in ways that give them each their own traits. I heard you say that you can think about how stories go—is there a problem, do things get worse and worse?

"That's a long list—and I know you also have deadlines to meet. So 'Hi ho, hi ho, it's off to work you go . . . !'"

If you don't like the violent overtones, know that we also imagined doing this with the notebook paper essentially standing in for a puppy: "I so want a puppy that I can hold tight. If I got a puppy and he wandered off, when I called, he'd come. He'd sit at my side. Any little thing could become a toy for him. . . ." The kids will prefer the take on "Don't eat me, eat my brother." Too much immersion in this fairy tale world and you find yourself being a bit crude!

Supporting Students Who Struggle with Adding Action

IF YOU FIND THAT SOME CHILDREN NEED SUPPORT with the concept you taught in the minilesson, you might convene a small group to join you in transferring the lesson first to the class's rendition of *Cinderella*, then to students' own work. For example, I noticed that Lainie, Eliza, and Sam either had not attempted to add actions to their stories yet or had done so in a disconnected-feeling way that took away from the story rather than added to it, or simply seemed stumped about how to translate what they were acting out into words. I gathered them together on the rug with the class text in front of us.

"Writers, I need help with something. I was rereading our class story about Cinderella, and I was thinking that we've missed some great opportunities to add in the kinds of small actions that I talked about in today's session. I'm hoping that you can help me, and that helping me will help you practice trying this out in your own stories. Game?"

As the kids nodded, I continued, "So, I am thinking about the first scene in our *Cinderella* adaptation. She's already doing something, remember? She's folding laundry. But we haven't pictured or acted out *exactly* what she's *doing* with the laundry in a way

MID-WORKSHOP TEACHING Stitching Scenes Together

"Writers, may I interrupt you? Many of you are using your planning sheet to move yourselves through the process of writing your adaptation. You remember that writers don't wait for others to tell them what to do—you are your own job captains. This means that many of you have drafted your first scenes and are well into drafting the rising action scenes of your adaptations. It may be time soon for you to think about ways to stitch your scenes together. You already know one way to do this— remember Jiminy Cricket?—add in narration. However, narration isn't the only way to stitch scenes together. Let's take a quick look at *Prince Cinders* to see if we can figure out how Babette Cole stitched her scenes together. I'll read the end of one scene and the beginning of the next. Give me a thumbs up when you hear the word or words that connect one scene to another.

"Writers, I am on page 14, end of the dirty fairy scene. 'Prince Cinders didn't know he was a big, hairy monkey, because that's the kind of spell it was. He thought he looked pretty good. Soooo, off he went to the disco.' Did you hear it? How did Babette stitch these two scenes together? Let me reread because it happened so fast."

I reread and some thumbs tentatively went up. I put my hand to my ear to signal it's okay to call out. I heard a few hesitant "Soooos."

"That's it. I think of these words as ant-sized—they're small like ants but also they do heavy lifting like ants; they do the work of connecting one scene to the next! Let's practice one more time."

I turned the page and began, "New scene. Listen. 'So off he went to the disco. The car was too small to drive but he made the best of it.' I turned the page, showing the change of scene from traveling to the disco to arriving at the disco. "'Buuuut when he arrived at the Rock 'n Royal Bash . . . he was too big to fit through the door!'" I put my hands to my ear and heard a chorus of "Buuuts." I said, "Awesome, writers, you now know two ways to stitch together your scenes—Jiminy Cricket narration and ant-sized words like *so* and *but*. You may also use flow phrases like *one morning*, *just then*, or *when suddenly* to keep the scenes flowing and to stitch together your scenes."

that shows what she's thinking or feeling. Watch as I give it a try, and then I'll need some help from you! Let's see, how can I get started on this . . . hmm, . . . I think it makes sense to read the piece out loud, to act out tiny actions as I go, and to add them to the draft. Watch me and see if these tiny actions bring more life to the story, and to my writing in general."

I began, "One sunny afternoon, Cinderella was folding her stepsisters' gowns." I pretended to fold a gown, my shoulders heaving with a big sigh. "She had a whole mountain of more laundry to fold." I wiped my brow and stared off into space with another sigh. "Then all of a sudden the doorbell rang." Dropping my imaginary gown, I threw up my hands in surprise.

"Did you see that? What I did with my body may tell me exactly what actions to write. When I did this [folding the gown and sighing again], I could write, *Cinderella tucked the gown's sleeves in expertly, shoulders rising and falling in a big sigh.* When I did this [wiping my brow again], I could write, *Cinderella wiped her brow with the back of her hand and sighed again.* Something like that. So now, let's keep going. Join in, writers; let's try a bit more of this together."

I continued, "'You lazy girl,' one stepsister said to Cinderella. 'Go get the door. Hurry. Don't waste time.'" I pushed back from the laundry and stood up. Jasmine followed my lead, throwing up her hands and rolling her eyes.

Smiling at and gathering the writers, I asked them each to say out loud what they might write to describe what they'd just acted out. "Just say exactly what you did with your body," I prompted. After each student had put their actions into words, I asked them to find a place in their own writing where they might try the same thing. I got them started physically acting out those bits, and moved among them offering tips about how to put those actions into words—"Notice what you're doing with your arms, Toby. You've got to write that down!"

Ensuring Endings Fit the Story

Giving examples, remind writers that strong endings provide a sense of closure.

"Writers, you know from movies and television shows and books, especially from reading books, that endings matter. That's part of what makes fairy tales so satisfying. You close the book, you hold it to your chest and say, 'That was good!' One thing that makes for a strong ending is a sense of closure. You know exactly what happens and why. You feel like, yep, that's exactly how that was supposed to go. Take *Little Red Riding Hood*, for example. The woodsman comes. He saves both Little Red Riding Hood and her grandmother. He fills the wolf's belly with stones. The wolf dies. That ending provides a sense of closure."

Encourage writers to make sure their endings are connected to the rest of their stories.

"Another thing that makes for a strong ending, however, is not the ending itself but rather the way the ending connects to the main events of the story. Let me try and explain this another way. Imagine you're making a delicious, chocolaty layer cake. You take the cake out of the oven and let it cool—it's almost done. All you have to do is frost it . . . with . . . *spaghetti sauce*!"

I paused to leave time for the giggles and "eew!"s that of course erupted across the room after this ridiculous suggestion.

"What?" I asked, incredulously. "Spaghetti sauce doesn't go with chocolate cake?"

"No way!" "Gross!" "That would taste terrible!" the children said.

"Of course it doesn't," I smiled. "You wouldn't frost a chocolate cake with spaghetti sauce—you could frost it in lots of different ways, but you'd want to choose frosting that goes with the flavor of the cake. It might be chocolate, it might be vanilla, it might have sprinkles, it might have flowers—totally up to you—but to make a delicious cake, you need to choose frosting that tastes good with the cake. It's the same with stories. You wouldn't want to add an ending that doesn't fit with the rest of the story—it wouldn't make any sense! There are lots of different ways to end your stories—and you are the one in charge of making decisions about that. But to write a strong story, you need to choose an ending that fits.

"I want you to be thinking about this because tomorrow many of you will be onto drafting your endings and revising your pieces and we want to make sure that we don't have any spaghetti sauce on the cakes of our adaptations."

Painting a Picture with Words
Revising for Language

IN THIS SESSION, you'll teach students that writers of fairy tales use figurative language, "painting a picture" in their readers' minds.

GETTING READY

✔ "Painting Pictures with Language" chart (see Connection and Mid-Workshop Teaching)

✔ Chart paper with two or three sentences from classic fairy tales that make comparisons (see Teaching)

✔ Chart paper with two or three bare-bones sentences from the class adaptation of *Cinderella* (see Active Engagement)

✔ "How to Write a Fairy Tale Adaptation" chart (see Link)

✔ *Prince Cinders* by Babette Cole and other mentor fairy tales (see Conferring and Small-Group Work)

✔ List of the five or so most commonly misspelled words in students' drafts (see Share)

✔ Writers' notebooks and pens (see Share)

COMMON CORE STATE STANDARDS: W.3.3.b, W.3.5, W.4.3.b,d; RL.3.4, SL.3.1, SL.3.6, L.3.1.i, L.3.2.3f, L.3.5, L.3.6, L.4.5, L.4.6

A WRITER SHOULD WRITE WITH HIS EYES," Gertrude Stein said in a 1946 interview with Robert Haas in *What Are Masterpieces* (1970). Both the artist and the writer paint pictures, one with paint, the other with words. Writers envision the world of the story and find words to match. You'll encourage your third-grade writers to "write with their eyes" during this session, to explore various ways to use language to paint pictures in the minds of their readers. The session begins by revisiting classic poetry writing strategies that students will remember from their work as poets in second grade, techniques such as using comparisons to create a more vivid picture. Relying on past learning helps you to encourage children to apply and transfer what they've learned when writing something new.

Bringing forth past knowledge and applying it in new ways helps students deepen their understanding of content. Depth of Knowledge (DOK), developed by Norman Webb, a senior research scientist at the Wisconsin Center for Education Research, helps teachers assess the depth of their curriculum and the activities children experience in school. When students apply prior knowledge to new contexts, Webb's DOK categorizes that as *strategic thinking* (level 3). This session rallies children to tackle this level of work in fun and inviting ways.

In this session, you'll also teach writers to make choices around language as they revise, dipping into mentor texts and making personal, genre-specific word walls to use as reference. Children will expand their repertoire of writing moves by learning other examples of figurative language, such as alliteration. All of this work helps students access the fifth Common Core Learning Language Standard that encourages students to "Demonstrate understanding of figurative language, word relationships, and nuances in word meanings" (CCSS L.3.5). Children don't just learn a list of figurative language terms in this session, but instead live as writers: studying, experimenting, and making choices about the language they use. After all, an artist doesn't just know the names of her paintbrushes; she uses them as she paints!

Painting a Picture with Words

Revising for Language

CONNECTION

Using the example of a second-grade class, remind students of their previous work with figurative language as second-grade poets.

"Writers, I was eating lunch with some other teachers today and one of the second-grade teachers brought in a stack of poems his students wrote. With a huge smile on his face, he passed out the poems for us to read. Do you know what I noticed as I read? The poems weren't fairy tales, but the words *did* paint rich, beautiful pictures—something that writers of fairy tales do as well.

"When I asked the teacher how he inspired his students to write with such beautiful language, he jotted me a list of all the cool things he was teaching in poetry. I have a feeling you're going to recognize lots of the things that are on it!" I revealed a chart:

Language Paints a Beautiful Picture

- Use describing words.
- Reach for exact, precise words.
- Use opposites to show differences.
- Use repetition of sounds, words, and lines.
- Make a comparison, like He walked like a penguin.

Ask writers to turn and talk about the figurative language techniques they remember, and tell them that they can use all that they already know to add in figurative language as they revise their fairy tales.

A buzz filled the room. This chart definitely jogged children's memories. I responded, "Does some of this sound familiar? Turn and talk to your partner about what on this chart feels familiar, like an old friend." After a brief moment, I reconvened the students. "Writers, you already know a ton about how to make your language paint beautiful pictures. In fairy tale writing, we want to do the same kind of work, right? I bet we can use some of these same tools when revising our fairy tales to make them even more beautiful."

This chart cycles back to teaching in the Second-Grade Poetry Unit of Study, Poetry: Big Thoughts in Small Packages. *You can develop your own version of this chart based on the language work students were taught previously.*

FIG. 11–1

❖ Name the teaching point.

"Writers revise their fairy tales by using what they know about language to paint pictures in the minds of their readers."

TEACHING

Refer back to familiar strategies and demonstrate their use in a new genre.

I pointed to the "Language Paints a Beautiful Picture" chart. "Many of the tips on this chart may be helpful reminders to you when you revise your fairy tales. You might look at one of the tips and think, 'Oh, yeah! I remember that from poetry!' and you'll try it again as you revise.

"But let's take a closer look at this chart. There are two tips I want to focus on today because they are used so often in fairy tales. First, let's revisit comparisons. Remember, in the poetry unit, you learned about making comparisons to help your readers paint a picture in their minds? Here's an example: *The sky is blue as the ocean.*"

Using sample fairy tale sentences, have students first notice comparisons and then revise their work by generating them.

"Comparisons are used in lots of different kinds of writing besides poems. Have you noticed that fairy tales are chock-full of them?" I turned a page of chart paper over and revealed three sentences I'd previously written. (These could also be written up on sentence strips.)

> Cinderella was sweet and gentle and good as gold.
> At once she arose and fled, nimble as a deer.
> The glass slipper went on at once, as easily as if it had been made of wax.

"Turn and tell your partner what the comparisons are in these sentences. What is the author comparing Cinderella to? What is the author comparing the slipper to?" After a moment, I continued, "Adding comparisons is one way writers revise fairy tales to make sure they paint pictures in the minds of their readers. Remember how to write a comparison? You can take something ordinary, like a shoe or a tree, and compare it to something that's similar in some way."

I added a sentence strip to the chart:

> Little Red Riding Hood wore a cape as red as . . .

"Let's try one together. Hmm, . . . the cape was red and not a pale red or a pinkish red but a strong, vivid red. We have to think of something else that has a similar kind of red . . . something that's a strong red. The cape was as red as . . . or red like a. . . ." As comparisons were not new to the children, their ideas came forth quickly: "Red as your cheeks when you're embarrassed!" "Red like the sign for the number two trains!" "Red as drops of blood." "Red as a heart when it loves something!"

We hope that these techniques will be familiar ones for students at this grade level. If you know that your students will need a more in-depth reminder about figurative language techniques, you may decide to just choose one technique from the list to highlight in your lesson so that you can spend more time on it.

Teaching children comparisons—metaphor and simile—is not just about putting two unrelated things together using the words like *or* as. *Nor is it about comparing things that are so similar or so often used that they become less surprising. Metaphor opens windows in our minds; a strong metaphor, or comparison, helps us to see resonance in the world in a new way. So we want not simply to tell students to compare any old thing. We want to teach them the thought process behind comparing two things. To write strong comparison, the objects must have a similar nature. Modeling a writer's thought process is one way to help teach this.*

"Awesome, writers! I'm already seeing vivid pictures in my mind with this comparison work!"

Using fairy tale examples, draw students' attention to the use of describing words to paint a picture in readers' minds.

"Okay, let me give you one more tip." I pointed back to the chart. "Let's also revisit using describing words. We focused on this a lot during poetry! We made sure to use describing words that really painted a picture for the reader. We used describing words like *red*, *tiny*, *grimy*!

"Well, in fairy tales, describing words are often used to describe characters. Describing words help us picture the characters living in these fairy tales. For instance, we don't just call her 'Riding Hood,' we call her. . . ." We all said together, "*Little, Red* Riding Hood." I continued, "And in *The Three Little Pigs*, we don't just call him 'The Wolf,' we call him . . . 'The *Big, Bad* Wolf'!" I added these examples to sentence strips and attached them to the chart. "You can revise your writing by finding the names of characters in your fairy tales and imagining different words to describe them, like '*Little, Red* Riding Hood.'"

Debrief, reminding students that they can use the techniques you've just studied as they revise their fairy tales.

"Writers, did you see how we can remind ourselves of writing tips we learned in the past and use them again in different ways? This practice helps us become better and stronger writers. Writing comparisons and using describing words help paint beautiful pictures for our readers."

Comparisons and describing words are two critical components of fairy tale writing, but you'll want to tailor this lesson to mirror your students' prior figurative language work. This session does not solely serve as reminder of past work, rather it encourages students to transfer and apply past learning on new learning. This focus paves a solid path toward independence.

ACTIVE ENGAGEMENT

Use a piece of demonstration writing to practice revising fairy tales with figurative language in mind.

"Writers, let's give this a try. Would you help me revise this fairy tale by adding comparisons or describing words, or anything else from the chart, to paint a vivid picture?" I put up a small piece of demonstration writing and read it aloud:

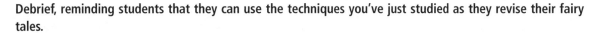

Cinderella sat in the attic on her cot. A tear slid down her cheek.

"Turn and talk." The class erupted into conversation, excited by the idea of bringing their knowledge of poetry into fairy tales. I picked up the pen. "Help me out," I encouraged.

"The attic is dark and dusty," said Shane. "Yeah," piped in Ella, "and the cot is raggedy and old."

I inserted the words onto the chart.

Some students will make comparisons that are general and universal. That's a fine place to start. But use this time to push children toward writing comparisons that aren't so predictable, but still spot-on. This creates a surprise for the reader and helps create meaning.

"Ready to try again? This time push yourselves to make the sentence more poetic, more beautiful by including a comparison." Revealing a second sentence, I read:

The smoke cleared, revealing a fairy.

I listened in as partners talked. Lainie and Cora described the smoke as thick and thunderous.

"What could we compare the fairy to?" I prompted.

"Fireworks?" giggled Cora.

Lainie added, "Yeah, 'a fairy as bright as fireworks on the Fourth of July.'"

Ask partnerships to choose one figurative language technique to use as they revise.

"Quickly, with your partner, choose a technique off the chart to try out as you revise your own writing. It's totally up to you!" I gave them a moment to choose and continued. "Turn and write in the air with your partner. How might you revise your fairy tale so that your writing paints vivid pictures in a reader's mind?"

I ducked into different partnerships and coached. One partnership was coming up with good, but standard, metaphors. "Writers, you are on the right track! Green as grass is a comparison. Sometimes writers try comparisons that take a little thinking and aren't the first idea that comes to mind. Yes, grass is green but what else is green?" I thought aloud. "Hmm, . . . a fresh dollar bill out of the ATM is green. Or wait, a banana that's not yet ripe is green. What else might be green? What will help you decide which comparison to make?"

LINK

Encourage writers to use tips from the "How to Write a Fairy Tale Adaptation" chart when revising their writing.

Gathering the class, I pointed to the "How to Write a Fairy Tale Adaptation" chart one last time. "Remember, writers, there are lots of tips you can try out when you revise your writing. Right now, make a quick writing plan with your partner. What tips might you use when you revise and make your language beautiful and vivid for your readers? It would be great to see what tips you end up using from the chart. As you write today, if there is a tip that you use a bunch in your writing and you think it would be cool to bring other writers' attention to it, come on up and grab a sentence strip. Write an example on the sentence strip that matches one of the tips just like we did in today's minilesson. That way, we can have other fairy tale examples of these tips to help as we revise. I'm going to add *paint pictures with language* to our chart as you go off."

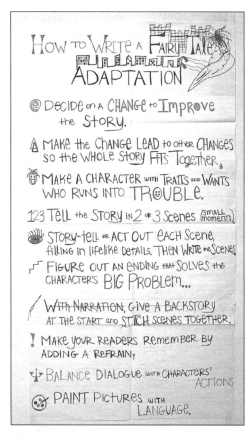

FIG. 11–2

Revising for Specific Vocabulary

AS YOU WADE INTO THE SEA OF WRITERS TODAY, many of them will be revising, as that's the rallying cry of the minilesson. However, they'll be revising in a variety of ways. It's helpful to anticipate different categories of help the writers might need today.

First, in the spirit of a language study, you will want to have several copies of a mentor text tucked under your arm as you approach students. Flag the text for a multitude of things that would be helpful to show students as examples of why they might be trying out. In this unit, flag classic fairy tale language, such as *happily ever after* or *a dream is a wish your heart makes*, as some children might need to revise and amplify the genre-specific words and phrases of fairy tales.

Creating personal word walls can also be an exceptionally helpful and rewarding instruction. You may find yourself having conferences like this one:

I pulled up alongside Andrew. "How's it going?" "Okay," he replied, "I am writing an adaptation of *The Emperor's New Clothes* but mine is about a governor and his new desk." I took a quick look at Andrew's draft and saw that he was struggling with the vocabulary that went with his story about a governor.

"Andrew, one of things I am noticing as I look at your draft is that you seem to be struggling to find the exact words to match your story. Like here," I said, pointing to a sentence in his first scene. "You've written *lady*, but I am guessing you meant *assistant*." Andrew nodded, "Uh-huh, you know, the person who makes the governor's . . . tells the governor when he does what."

I nodded. "And there, I think you mean *appointments*, right? Andrew," I continued, "you know how we have word wall in our classroom for math and science and social studies?" Andrew looked up and pointed to the math word wall. "Well, some writers have personal word walls. Word walls that are just for them, that use the exact words

---

"Writers, may I have your eyes?" I paused briefly. "Let's admire the additions to the 'Language Paints a Beautiful Picture' chart and read some aloud. Listen to how Ella describes the field behind the house of her *Three House Cats Greedy*: 'The field had fresh, green grass that swayed in the wind.' And listen to how Shane uses repetition: 'The magic wings were whispering in his ear, "Jack, you only have three wishes. You only have three wishes. You only have three wishes."' So many of you have added language like this to your fairy tales, language that paints pictures in readers' minds. And you've also become the kind of writers who know that your first words are never your best words and that's why you . . ." I let my voice fade as the kids joined in, "Revise, revise, revise!"

"You know, there's another tip we can revise our writing for." The kids looked puzzled. "Listen to this." I read the words *Little Red Riding Hood* and *Big Bad Wolf* and then continued, "Red, Riding, Big, Bad. Do you hear how those word pairs start with the same sound? That's called *alliteration*—you might have studied alliteration before when writing or reading poetry. Alliteration creates a nice sound when you read it aloud and it also helps writers describe things in their writing. We should add that tip to the chart; that's another way to paint a picture with language.

"As you revise your fairy tales, continuing to make them sound magical, one thing you may try is writing word pairs that start with the same sound, like *Once upon a time, in the* deep, dark *forest* . . ."

---

that match their story." I pulled a blank A-to-Z grid from my conferring folder. "I was thinking that you and I and maybe your writing partner, Zander, might spend a few minutes creating a personal word wall for a story about a governor."

I suggested that Andrew's writing partner, Zander, join the conference because I wanted to reinforce that this is work they could continue with each other. I also included Zander so that all the vocabulary would not come from me.

"Okay gentlemen, what words will Andrew need to write a story about a governor? Let's think about character words and setting words." As Andrew and Zander brainstormed words—*mansion, capitol, assistant, appointment, office*—I jotted the words onto Andrew's word wall. Not only would this word wall help Andrew spell those words, it would push him to use more specific vocabulary as he wrote.

The Common Core State Standards can provide a helpful lens to use when conferring with students about revising for more specific vocabulary use, as I did with Andrew. Third-graders are encouraged to learn different "shades" or meanings for words that mean something similar. That is to say, children might match their word choice for how the character is feeling. How did the character sound? Did she holler, bellow, or scream)? Third-graders are also encouraged to unpack words like *friendly* and *helpful*, clearly describing the actions that show a character's friendliness, for example.

My "just-for-me, only-for-me, especially-for-me" Word Wall by *Andrew*					
Aa assistant appointment	**Bb**	**Cc** capitol	**Dd**	**Ee**	**Ff**
Gg governor	**Hh**	**Ii**	**Jj**	**Kk**	**Ll**
Mm mansion	**Nn**	**Oo** office	**Pp**	**Qq**	**Rr**
Ss	**Tt**	**Uu**	**Vv**	**Ww**	**Xx Yy Zz**

FIG. 11–3 Andrew's personal word wall

Spelling Words Correctly

Remind students that writers use conventional spellings so that readers can read their work.

"Writers," I called, "Come to a stopping place and meet me at the rug. Bring your notebook and a pencil." I waited for most of the writers to settle onto the rug. "Writers, there is such precise language in our room right now. I noticed so many of you painting pictures with your words. Like Cora; when she was describing the kitchen in her story, she wrote that it was *messy like a doghouse.*

"Here's the thing. When painters paint, they generally have universally agreed upon colors for the objects in their paintings. Think with me for a moment. If an artist wanted to paint a poisonous apple from *Snow White*, she would most likely use . . ."

"Red!" "And if a painter wanted to paint the beanstalk from *Jack and the Beanstalk*, he would probably use. . . ." "Green!"

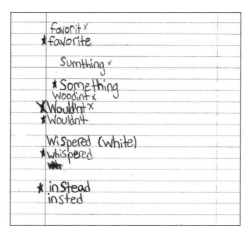

FIG. 11–3   Andrew's spelling work

Using the five most commonly misspelled words you've just collected, ask students to practice their spelling.

"Agreed. When painters paint, they generally use agreed upon colors for things. They do this because they want their viewer, their reader, to understand their painting. It's no different with writers; they want their readers to understand their pieces, but rather than agreed upon colors, they have agreed upon spellings." I nodded to add emphasis to my point. "Today as you were writing I was collecting the five most frequently misspelled words in our drafts. They are . . . drumroll, please . . . *favorite, something, wouldn't, whispered,* and *instead.* Open your notebook to a clean page. I am going to say each word, and you can use any of your spelling strategies—try it three ways, use a word you know to figure out a word you don't know, use the word wall, ask a partner—to work on the agreed upon, that is, the correct spelling."

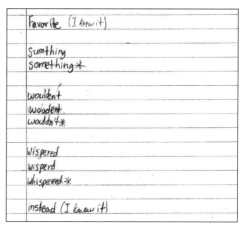

FIG. 11–4   Ella's spelling work   FIG. 11–5   Sophia's spelling work

The Long and Short of It
Editing for Sentence Variety

IN THIS SESSION, you'll teach students that writers read their stories aloud, identifying choppy or abrupt sentences and smoothing them out by simplifying long-winded ones or complicating simplistic ones.

GETTING READY

✔ Chart paper and markers (see Teaching)

✔ Chart with a few choppy sentences about *Little Red Riding Hood* (see Active Engagement)

✔ *Prince Cinders* by Babette Cole (see Conferring and Small-Group Work)

✔ Writer's notebooks (see Share)

✔ Pad of brightly colored Post-it notes (see Share)

*U*LYSSES BY JAMES JOYCE CONTAINS A SENTENCE of 4,391 words. One of the shortest sentences one can write is the declaration, "I am." This could be fun English trivia—and certainly we don't suggest that students try to break those records, in either direction—but we can certainly begin teaching them that the lengths of sentences is an important consideration for writers. The point of this session is not to shower children in technical grammatical terms that are unlikely to be meaningful to them at this stage—we don't aim to teach them to identify types of clauses—but rather to suggest that strong writers make use of a variety of sentence lengths and structures, and to provide some examples for how students might begin to think about this and try it out.

In this session, students will be offered lots of inviting ways to attemp more complicated and fancy sentences: the use of drama and mentor texts. The engine behind this session is a love for the craft of writing, which is echoed in the Common Core State Standards. These standards, one of them being "Produce simple, compound and complex sentences" (CCSS L3.1.i.), lay out possibilities for children to edit their writing.

So far we have taught children to use ant-sized words such as *so* and *but* or flow phrases such as *one morning*, *just then*, or *then suddenly* to stitch scenes together. This session adds complexity by layering on the use of subordinating conjunctions such as *when* (CCSS L3.1.h.). Students have also already begun working to intersperse action in ways that balance dialogue (CCSS W3.3.b).

More importantly, this session encourages us to teach children to write in the storyteller voice that is so essential to a fairy tale, for example, by varying their sentences. Learning how to pace will be especially important for third-graders who rely on either awkward, choppy sentences, or long-winded run-ons to pace their tales, indicating that they are ready to explore ways to vary the length and structure of their sentences. In this session, you'll encourage them to do that.

COMMON CORE STATE STANDARDS: W.3.3.b, W.3.5, W.4.3.b, RL.3.1, RFS.3.4, SL.3.1, SL.3.6, L.3.1.h,i; L.3.2, L.4.1.f

The Long and Short of It

Editing for Sentence Variety

CONNECTION

Using an example from life that will resonate for your students, remind them that writers follow certain rules and conventions to help readers read their writing.

"When I say editing, what comes to mind?" The children's hands shot up in the air. "Fix your capitals!" "Add periods!" "Make sure you spell all your words right!"

I continued, "Yes, absolutely, when you edit your writing, you make sure you are following the rules of writing—capitals, punctuation, spelling. Rules are important, right? When you go to gym and play a game of basketball, you make sure you follow the rules of the game; in basketball, you can't just run with the ball, you have to dribble down the court. Following the rules allows everyone to play the game smoothly."

I segued to writing. "Writing has rules, too. The rules are like a code that all writers agree on, like when to capitalize certain words or how to indent at the beginning of new paragraphs. And when writers edit their work, they go back and check to see if they've followed the rules so their readers can read the writing with ease and without being confused."

If you want another example, you could reference the rules of the road. What if cars didn't stop at stop signs and just plowed on through them? The rules of the road let us know what to expect, just like punctuation and grammar rules do.

Tell students that editing is about more than following rules—it's also about creating a particular style.

"But editing is not just about following the rules perfectly or mechanically, like a robot. During editing, writers can be artistic and can show their personality and style! Let's return to basketball. Some of the greatest basketball players— Michael Jordan, Dr. J, LeBron James, Larry Bird—are not just known for following the rules of basketball. They are known for the personality and style they bring to the game! A great basketball player does both—follows the rules and brings his or her own style—and a great writer does the same.

"When writers are editing, they think about following the rules of writing. But they also use the editing process to add personality and style to their writing. It's actually really fun and provides ways to think creatively about how writing sounds when it's read."

If you use the rules-of-the-road analogy, you could make the parallel between the way people add personality and style to their cars using bumper stickers, fancy tire rims, or rearview mirror decorations. Or perhaps the way different driving styles—some slow and steady, others fast and zippy—reveal the person.

✤ **Name the teaching point.**

"Today I want to teach you that one way to create your own writing style is to experiment with different types of sentences when editing. This means that in addition keeping an editing eye out for writing rules, writers edit to smooth out short or choppy sentences. Writers turn those sentences into smoother, more precise, and well-paced sentences."

TEACHING

Let students know that sometimes when writers edit for sentence variety it's hard to find a place to start. Suggest children start by reading aloud to locate short or choppy sentences.

"But what does that mean? Where do you start? Let me give you an example. I know sometimes when I reread my writing during editing, I have to read some parts twice because during the first go-through, I stumble. I might have put things in an awkward order. Sometimes I don't stumble, but the sentences sound boring—they might sound short and choppy, making the whole piece sound like it is lurching between stop and go, stop and go. For example, it might sound like this," I said, accentuating the choppy sentences by reading them robotically:

> Little Red Riding Hood left. She was happy. She walked. She had a basket. She was in the woods. A wolf came. She told the wolf where she was going.

"See what I mean? Thumbs up, writers, if you notice the choppiness of these sentences! Reading your writing out loud can be a really helpful way to find sentences like these. Once you've found short or choppy sentences in your own drafts, you can edit them and make them smoother and fancier."

Demonstrate the contrast between using choppy sentences and smooth sentences to describe a student volunteer's actions.

"Let me show you what I mean. Wendy has volunteered to help us with this. She's going to act something out, and I'll show the difference between short, choppy sentences and longer, smoother ones.

"Wendy, go outside the classroom and walk back in. Head over to the meeting area." Before Wendy left, I leaned over and whispered for her to have emotion as she walked into the room, to be excited, smiling, with a hop in her step. "Writers, watch very closely as Wendy enters the room. Try to notice all the different things about her, like how she is walking and what she looks like."

Wendy opened the door and walked to her place on the rug, beaming, skipping a little. I said, "One way to write about what Wendy just did could be something like this," and I jotted on chart paper:

> Wendy walked in. She came to the rug. She looked happy.

The text is written to be over-the-top choppy. Minilessons aren't a time to be subtle. During this demonstration, I overemphasized the choppiness as I read aloud, making the trouble very clear to the children. This is important because the lesson is not just about learning about sentence variety, it's a lesson on finding places to edit.

"Those are perfectly fine sentences. But do you hear how I wrote a bunch of short and choppy sentences in a row? Let me show you how I might edit these sentences to make them smoother and fancier. First, I can add some information *at the beginning* of my sentence. I can add more details about *how* Wendy walked into class. For example, I could write":

> With a smile on her face and a skip in her step, Wendy walked in.

"Or," I continued, "I could add more details about the setting."

> With morning light streaming through the windows, Wendy walked in.

"Do you see how adding a little information to the beginning of the sentence makes the sentence sound smoother and fancier, and the meaning clearer?

"I can also add information *at the end* of my short or choppy sentences to make them fancier. I might say a little more about the last word in the sentence, like this":

> Wendy walked in, the heavy classroom door slamming behind her.

Debrief the demonstration in a way that names all the parts of the strategy.

"Here's what I just did—and what you'll have a chance to try doing in a second. First, I reread my writing aloud to find the short or choppy sentences. Then, I experimented with making those choppy sentences smoother and fancier. I did that by adding information in the beginning and ending of a sentence. When you are editing your stories, you'll make a decision about whether you want to add more information into a short choppy sentence, and if so, whether you want to add information to the start of the sentence, or to the end of the sentence."

ACTIVE ENGAGEMENT

Using sample lines you've created from a familiar fairy tale, ask students to try making choppy sentences smoother by adding on.

"So, let's give this a try. Here are the choppy sentences from *Little Red Riding Hood* that I read to you at the beginning of the lesson." I flipped over the chart paper, revealing the sentences I'd prewritten, and I underlined the sentence *She walked*.

> Little Red Riding Hood left. She was happy. <u>She walked.</u> She had a basket. She was in the woods. A wolf came. She told the wolf where she was going.

Notice that to compare one method with another, everything is kept the same save for the one change that I am trying to highlight.

Informal language charts such as the one you create by simply jotting down the contrasting types of sentences above are helpful resources for children to use when learning a new strategy. You may know the power of word walls and the importance of publicly posting new words children learn so they can use them again and again in their writing correctly. Posting examples of language follows the same concept and can be just as helpful to young writers.

"With your partner, experiment with making the sentence I've underlined smoother, longer, and fancier. You could try adding information to the beginning or endings of it, too."

As children began practicing, I listened into several partnerships. Charlie said, "She walked into the woods, the deep dark woods." I voiced over, "Way to go, Charlie. You not only made the sentence fancier, but you gave me chills! That's creating the mood of your story. Keep it up!"

In a moment, I gathered the class. "I heard many of you adding information at the beginning of the sentence, and some of you tackled adding information at the end. That is a great way to edit choppy sentences to make them smoother and fancier.

"I noticed something else really cool as I was listening in—as you said your new sentences out loud, I noticed that you often put little tiny pauses in between the new part of the sentence and the original part. That means you were sort of automatically adding in a comma; when you edit choppy sentences by adding on, adding a comma will tell readers to do the same little pause in between the parts of the sentence."

LINK

Encourage students to use editing strategies they know as needed, and ask them to share writing plans with their partners before heading off.

"Writers, when you're rereading your writing today before getting started, you might want to try reading it out loud. And if you notice a bunch of short, choppy sentences in a row, you might want to think about editing some of them to make them sound smoother and fancier, like you just practiced doing with the *Little Red Riding Hood* sentences. But you know many other rules for writing, so some of you might realize that you need to use this editing strategy today, and others might put this tool in your editing toolbox and take it out when you need it.

"Before you head off, can you tell your partner two or three things you plan to edit your writing for today during writing time? What rules are you trying to follow as an editor today? You might even jot down what your partner tells you to ask about later."

I gave the children a chance to meet briefly, nudging them to take notes on their conversations before they headed off to write.

Formally naming the use of the comma toward the end of the session is intentional. Now that children have been exposed to many visual examples and verbal examples, the use of the comma is tangible and relevant. Students won't always need to add a comma when they add on to a sentence, but it is helpful to mention to them that they often may add one.

Helping Writers Construct Complex Sentences

THIS IS A TIME THAT YOU'LL BE CIRCULATING, looking for trends that emerge that reveal the editing tips kids need. You may continue the theme of the minilesson and focus on the ways to clean up sentences, making them clearer and better paced.

For starters, a short sentence does not necessarily make a bad sentence. The main thing we want students to be exposed to in this session is the idea that writers vary the length and structure of their sentences to suit their purposes. There is a lot of power in a solid simple sentence. Some children rely heavily on simple sentences, but the simple sentences are redundant or incomplete, such as *It was hot. She left. She went home*. Honor their attempts at simple sentences, and teach them a way to round them out, making them pack a bigger punch. For instance, teach them to add a bit more information to the sentence. *It was hot* outside. Or perhaps *She left* the park. Or even *She went home* in a hurry.

Although there is a place for simple sentences, children can rely on them so exclusively that their sentences are homogenous. If you peer over the shoulder of a student and notice that she tends to start the beginning of each sentence with a pronoun, like *she* or *he*, as in, *She left her house. She went into the woods. She met a wolf. She was scared*, you might decide to springboard off the work of the minilesson and teach that child to experiment with different ways to start a sentence. For example, starting a sentence with action will probably pay off: *Grabbing her basket and cape, she left the house*. Or *Pulling the basket closer to her, she went into the woods*.

Additionally, there are other ways to complicate sentences, making them read with more energy. You might bring along a copy of *Prince Cinders* and highlight even more examples of interesting sentences, like *When his work was done, he would sit by the fire and wish he was big and hairy like his brothers*. Using ant-sized words like *and*, *so*, and *but* are accessible ways to tack on more information to short or choppy sentences.

(continues)

MID-WORKSHOP TEACHING
Finding Examples of Types of Sentences

"Writers, I have to tell you about something that I saw Oliver and Mariko doing just now. They brought a couple of fairy tales to their table and they were studying them. When I asked what they were doing, they told me they were on the hunt for interesting sentences. That's so smart because there are lots of ways to write interesting sentences! Some fancy sentences they found were from *Prince Cinders*. Take a look at this sentence":

> One Saturday night, when he was washing the socks, a dirty fairy fell down the chimney.

"Do you see how the information adding at the beginning of the sentence describes where the story is happening? That's beginning a sentence with the time and place. That could be a cool thing to try! Or how about this one":

> When his work was done, he would sit by the fire and wish he was big and hairy like his brothers.

"You could try that, too! Use the word *when* to start off your sentence":

> When Little Red Riding Hood walked into the woods, the wolf came up to her.

"Class, we call these *echo sentences*. Echo sentences are sentences that we find in mentor texts, and we want to be just like them! Writers echo these sentences to write their own sentence. Writers copy the structure, the *way* they're written, but add in their own story. Feel free to use any of the sentences on the chart as echo sentences or find your own in a mentor text!"

Don't be dismayed if you stumble across writing that is overusing a structure or word, such as *and*, leading to the opposite problem: long-winded run-ons. Donald Bear points out that when kids try their hands at spelling patterns or grammar techniques and mess them up, the fact that they are "using and confusing" something is a sign that they are especially ripe for instruction. Incorporating question or exclamation marks in between sentences, or even commas or dashes to show moments of pause, is a great way to outgrow the use of *and* and helps break up long-winded sentences.

When working with Shane, for example, I noticed that he was using *and* to connect each and every thought on the page. "Hey Shane," I said. "May I give you a quick tip?" He nodded. "I'm noticing that you are using the ant-sized word *and* to do a lot of work in your draft." I pointed and began to count. "Look at these first five lines—you wrote *and* four times in five lines of writing. That makes for some *long* sentences, doesn't it?" Shane nodded. I continued, "Here's the tip: You could try replacing *and* with ending punctuation in this part. Reread your draft, and when you come to *and*, decide whether you want to replace it with ending punctuation."

Shane read (see Figure 12–1), "'Once upon a time there was a boy named Jack and his mom didn't have a name so I guess it was just mom.'" Shane stopped, "There's an *and*. I could put a period. . . ." He crossed out the *and* and replaced it with a period and then read, "'Once upon a time there was a boy named Jack. His mom didn't have a name so I guess it was just mom.'"

> Once upon a time there was a boy named Jack. His mom didn't have a name so I guess it was just mom.

"Great! When you notice that you're using lots of *ands*, you might want to try adding punctuation. Sometimes you're going to want long sentences, but if you realize that lots of your sentences go on and on and on and use lots of *ands*, this is a good trick to try!"

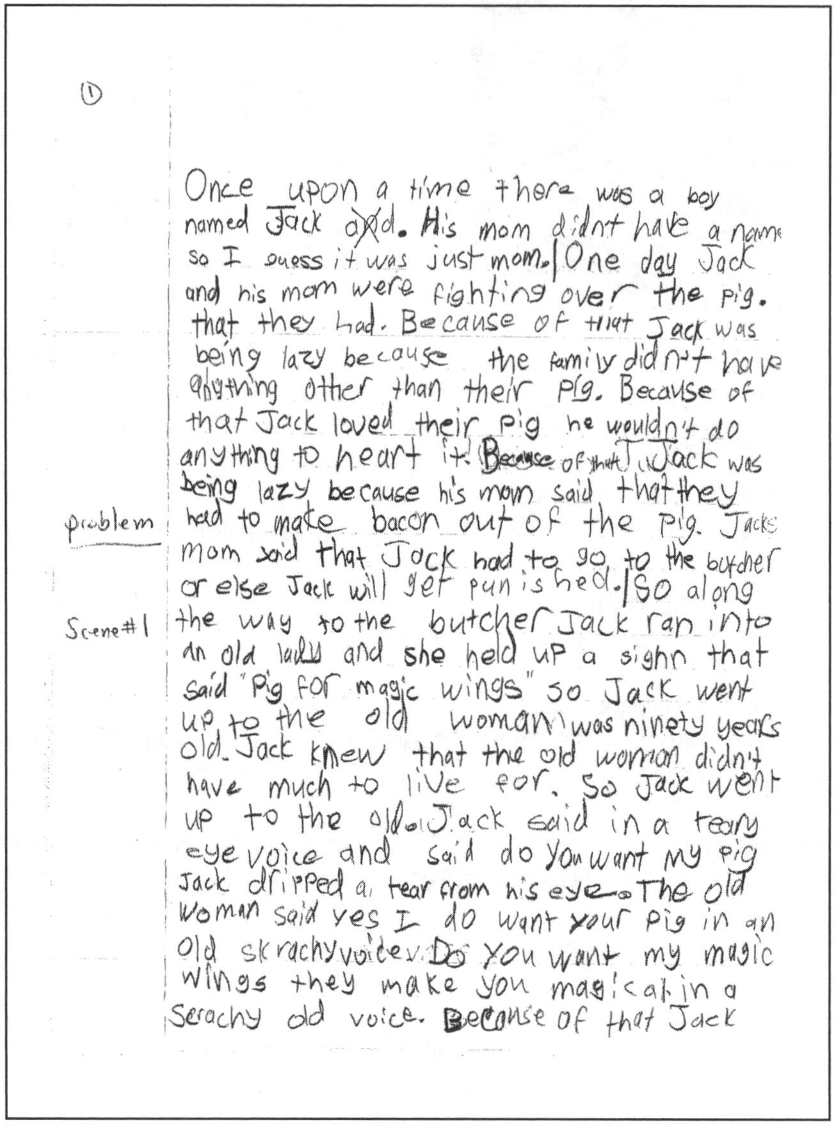
1

Once upon a time there was a boy
named Jack ~~and~~. His mom didn't have a name
so I guess it was just mom. | One day Jack
and his mom were fighting over the pig.
that they had. Because of that Jack was
being lazy because the family didn't have
anything other than their pig. Because of
that Jack loved their pig he wouldn't do
anything to heart it! Because of that Jack was
being lazy because his mom said that they
problem had to make bacon out of the pig. Jacks
mom said that Jack had to go to the butcher
or else Jack will get punished. | So along
Scene#1 the way to the butcher Jack ran into
an old lady and she held up a sighn that
said "Pig for magic wings" so Jack went
up to the old woman was ninety years
old. Jack knew that the old woman didn't
have much to live for. So Jack went
up to the old. Jack said in a teary
eye voice and said do you want my pig
Jack dripped a tear from his eye. The old
woman said yes I do want your pig in an
old skrachy voice. Do you want my magic
wings they make you magical in a
serachy old voice. Because of that Jack

FIG. 12–1 Shane's draft

Sharing and Celebrating Powerful Editing

Encourage students to share edits they are proud of. In this case, ask students to teach each other what they know about editing.

"You have so much to teach each other about following the rules of writing." I paused, inviting kids to muse with me. "What if . . ." I looked around the room. "What if . . ." I said, picking up a pad of brightly colored Post-it notes. "What if each of you found a place in your drafts where you edited with power, and what if you marked that place with a Post-it that reminds all the writers in the room of that thing? Like if you found a place where you used an interrobang, you might remind everyone that interrobangs add excitement to a question. Remember," I continued, "an interrobang is a special character we make by putting a question mark and an exclamation point together." I quickly jotted an arrow on my Post-it and wrote, *Use an ‽ to add oomph to a question.*

"Yeah," Ella called out. "Then we could walk around the room and learn from all the other kids in the room."

"What a great idea! Maybe half of you could stay at your desks to explain your edits, while the other half walks around with your notebooks. That way you could take notes on the editing you want to try in your own writing. And then you can switch!"

You may choose to have students simply leave their Post-it noted drafts at their tables and all walk around at the same time with their notebooks, sort of like a museum share. Or you may decide to close the session with a symphony share, inviting children to read aloud their favorite edit from the day's work. Perhaps you will want to scribe the exact and descriptive language kids share, creating a class chart of the powerful language children edit for across their writing.

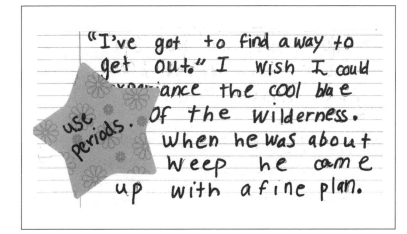

FIG. 12–2   Sam's powerful edits

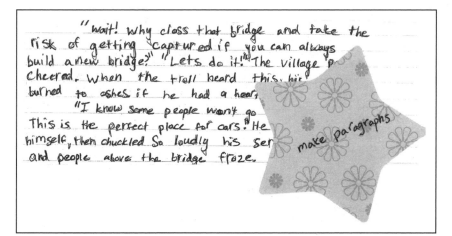

FIG. 12–3   Shelly's powerful edits

Collecting Ideas for Original Fairy Tales

IN THIS SESSION, you'll teach students that writers write original tales by using elements of strong narratives: specific characters, motivations, troubles, and resolutions.

GETTING READY

✔ Students' notebooks and pens (see Active Engagement and Share)

T HIS SESSION IS A BIG ONE FOR MANY REASONS, not least because it launches the last bend in the unit's road. In fairy tales, unlikely people are able to accomplish wondrous things: a small boy climbs a beanstalk and defeats a giant, a young woman in rags is transformed into a beautiful princess and wins the prince's heart, two young children find their way out of a witch's trap, through the woods and back home. In fairy tales, children use wits and ingenuity and courage to do what most people might think is beyond their reach. The content of fairy tales can become part of your effort to rally kids to do the work you've challenged them to do. Your message might well be that if Hansel and Gretel can figure out how to escape from the cage in which they were imprisoned, if each of those three little pigs can outwit the wolf at their door, then each one of your students can surely solve the challenge of figuring out his or her own *original* fairy tale!

This session rallies kids to embark on their third cycle of writing fairy tales. During the first two bends, they were supported by the structure of writing *adaptations* of fairy tales, and now they will use all that they've learned, and all that you're about to teach them, to create their own, original, from-scratch tales. This means, then, that a bit more instruction in the essential elements of a fairy tale is in order. You'll see that we suggest in this session that when a writer starts out intending to create a fairy tale, she generates possible story ideas, each of which needs to reflect the basic elements of a story. John Gardner, the man reputed to be America's greatest storyteller, describes those basic elements this way in *On Becoming a Novelist* (1999, 54): "In nearly all good fiction, the basic—all but inescapable—plot form is this: A central character wants something, goes after it despite opposition (perhaps including his own doubts), and so arrives at a win, lose, or draw."

COMMON CORE STATE STANDARDS: W.3.3, W.3.5, W.3.10, W.4.3, RL.3.1, RL.3.3, SL.3.1, L.3.1, L.3.2

Collecting Ideas for Original Fairy Tales

CONNECTION

Rally your students around the challenge of the upcoming and final bend in the unit: writing an original fairy tale.

"In fairy tales, people accomplish amazing things. Hansel and Gretel trick the witch and escape. Jack manages to save his family from the poorhouse by bringing home a hen that lays golden eggs. The three little pigs roast the wolf in a pot on their fire. Cinderella, who usually cleans the cinders from the hearth, is the belle of the ball and marries the prince.

"Writers, we have just one more bend in our fairy tale unit. You have a little more than a week to not just *adapt* someone else's fairy tale, but to *write your own*. I am so excited to see these brand-new fairy tales taking shape!"

❖ **Name the teaching point.**

"What I want to teach you is that when trying to write fairy tales, hard work matters, but hard work *alone* won't produce a beautiful fairy tale. What you need, above all, is the magic formula. The formula includes a character with traits and wants, and then a dose of trouble, then more trouble, and more. And then somehow, ta-da!—that's the magic part—there's a resolution."

TEACHING

Suggest that fairy tales might emerge first as a sparse but complete story idea, one that is structured like a story.

"When you write your own fairy tale, you could start by surrounding yourself with charts and lists and marching orders and To Do lists. You could probably list ten things that you know you need to remember to do just to get a good lead. You know stories begin with a narrator who gives the backstory and that the first scene usually begins with someone doing or saying something . . . and the list goes on.

"And in the long run, you *will* want to remember those things and check for them. But the thing about a fairy tale is this: It needs to include each ingredient in the magic formula *from the very beginning*. From the very beginning, a fairy tale writer thinks about the whole story. Let's quickly review the ingredients in the magic formula for a story. First, there

◆ COACHING

You will be accustomed to the fact that mini-lessons often use stories from outside the writing workshop as metaphor to teach something about the writing process. The source of those stories is not inconsequential. Although there are advantages to drawing on youth culture, on topics that are especially child-centered, there are also advantages to drawing on stories that come from the literary life. In a fifth-grade unit on Westward expansion, for example, some stories come from history. In a unit on research reports, some stories come from the lives of journalists. Throughout this unit, the content of fairy tales helps to engineer the teaching.

is *a character who wants something.*" I looked around the room, hoping the children were thinking with me of what comes next. "Next," I said, sticking out a second finger, "*There's trouble, more trouble, and possibly even more trouble.*" I whipped out a third finger as I said, "And. . . ."

"Ta-da!" called several writers.

"Then there's *resolution*," I concluded. "You can plan your whole story using this magic formula in your mind or on your fingers. *Or* you can use a storyboard, where you sketch out three boxes, one for the beginning, one for the middle, and one for the end."

ACTIVE ENGAGEMENT

Channel students to think of and jot into their notebooks a story idea for an original fairy tale.

"So try it. Think to yourself about the three ingredients in the magic formula: Who will your story be about? What does he or she want? What's the trouble? How will it be resolved?" I sat at the front of the room and thought of possible story ideas for a fairy tale I would write—quietly—knowing that my engagement in this would nudge children to do the same mind work.

"I'm not going to ask you to share," I said. "I know your idea will probably change a bunch of times over the next half hour. What I do want to suggest is that you open up a page of your writer's notebook and get one possible story idea onto the page."

LINK

Explain that writers generate a bunch of story ideas and use collaborators to help. Then send them off to work.

"Writers, once you have thought of one of these, think of another. You'll want to generate half a dozen story ideas, probably, or versions of a story idea. Once you have an idea in mind, you can think in more detail about what your scenes will be. Think, before you get started, about whether there are ways that our writing colony can support you, or whether there are questions you have for me," I said. "Turn and talk about that."

After a bit, I said, "Jasmine asked if her story could be sort of an adaptation, and that was a terrific question because really, almost every story in the world is an adaptation of a fairy tale. So absolutely, you can choose a fairy tale as the basis for your plan. I also heard Alejandro tell Leroy that after collecting a few story ideas, he hoped they could work together in the meeting space to story-tell their ideas. Thumbs up if this is a way that you'll be using some of your writing time today.

"Thumbs up if you know what to do today." Most children signaled that they did, and they were off and running. I began humming "Hi ho, hi ho . . . ," and off to work they went.

Notice that in this minilesson, as in many minilessons, there really is more than one point that you want to convey. But the points unfurl in the fullness of time. You'll want to think carefully about that age-old baking advice, "Add flour slowly, stirring all the while," whenever you teach children.

Helping Writers Develop Ideas into Plans Through Conversation

IT IS CRITICAL THAT YOU PACE THIS BEND so that each child in your class makes steady progress. So while you just invited kids to make decisions about how to plan their writing time, the truth is that you'll need to create a sense of urgency around settling on a story idea. Once children have settled on the kernel of an idea, they still have a lot of work to do before they can write that story.

You may want to show children the value of talking together to grow their ideas into story plans. I recently convened a small group of children, Sophia, Maggie, Caleb, and Eliza, who had developed a few ideas, and I suggested they try talking through those ideas. I asked one child to read her idea to the group, and suggested that the other children join me in listening to the idea and offering suggestions. This may seem

(continues)

MID-WORKSHOP TEACHING   **Adding to the Magic Story Formula: *Villains!***

"Writers, eyes up here," I said. "We talked earlier about the magic formula for stories, and how that formula can really help you plan the gist of your story. How many of you have a story in mind?" Many children signaled that they did.

"May we hear a few of your ideas?" I asked.

Sierra said, "I don't know that much about mine, but I think a girl has moved to a new school and she wants to look right, to fit in, and she doesn't have the money or anything. I am not sure what gets worse and worse. And then a fairy godmother gives her the right clothes."

Cora said, "My fairy tale is about this really sporty girl who wants a magical swimsuit so that she can wins races against her big sister."

"Those are great ideas . . . but there is still a ways to go, isn't there, between the seed of an idea and the story. I'm pretty sure that like me, you have been wracking your minds over what's missing in your story plans. And I thought of a missing ingredient that is found in most fairy tales. That missing ingredient is a *villain*. Right now, will you list the fairy tales you know best and see how many of them have an evil character? Talk to each other."

I listened in and said, "I heard you say that yes, in many stories there is a villain of some kind—what fairy tale villains do you know?" Students called out:

- the evil stepmothers (there are a lot of them!)
- the troll under the bridge
- the big, bad wolf
- the giant
- the gross little guy with the gold

"So here is the challenge. But the trick is that the bad guy has to *somehow* belong to the original story, which means you will need to change things around. You remember that so far, she wants a dog, so she asks her family members and one is allergic, another had another excuse, and they all say no. Think about how a villain could get in the way of the girl getting or keeping a dog. This is hard work, so help each other."

As the room buzzed, I listened in. After a minute, I said, "Great ideas. Maybe everyone in the family says yes, not no, except an evil someone—maybe stepmother—who says no. Or maybe she gets herself a dog from the dog pound, and then there is an evil dog catcher who comes and scoops the dog up. Maybe she goes and gets another and again the evil dog catcher comes.

"Of course, that's Sophie's story, and each of you will need to decide what you want to do in your story."

---

simple—and it is—but the simple act of gathering students to listen and respond to each other's work can provide an important kind of both support and motivation at this stage.

Sophia read, "This fairy tale is about a girl who really wants a dog. She asks her mom and her mom says no. She asks her dad and her dad says no. She asks her brother and he says no. Then something magic happens and she gets a dog. Ta-da!"

Maggie started, "I think you need to say *why* each person says no. Like the mom says no because she got bit once when she was a kid. And. . . ."

Caleb piped in, "And the dad says no because he's allergic. The brother probably says no because he doesn't want to help take care of the dog."

Sophia nodded. "Okay, let me try it again." She revised in her head and told her new, improved story idea to the group. "This fairy tale is about a girl who really wants a dog. She asks her mom and her mom, who is afraid of dogs, says no. She asks her dad and her dad, who is allergic to dogs, says no. She asks her big brother who isn't afraid or allergic, he's just lazy, so he says no. Then one day something magic happens and ta-da! A dog appears."

Eliza followed, "My fairy tale is about a girl who loves soccer and dreams of winning the championship. She gets injured in the finals, then ta-da! the magic soccer fairy comes and heals her broken leg so she can play in the championship game."

After listening in for a moment and offering prompts when necessary, I suggested that the group continue helping each other grow their ideas, and also suggested that in the end they might each disperse and collaborate with a different group to do that work.

Helping One Another Work Hard

Using the fairy tale metaphor of a magic mirror, rally your students to be mirrors for each other and help each other make writing plans.

"Writers, join me on the rug. Since we've been reading and writing lots of fairy tales, I started to wish that I had a magical mirror like the evil stepmother in *Snow White*. You see, whenever I am beginning a piece of writing, I find that I have a lot of questions. Sometimes they are little questions like, 'What's a good name for this place or that character?' And sometimes they are big questions like, 'What's the lesson or the message of this story?' I want a magic mirror to answer my questions!"

I mimed picking up a mirror. "Then I could just look at the mirror and say, 'Mirror, mirror, on the wall . . . what's a clever and catchy refrain?' Or, 'mirror, mirror, on the wall . . . how should my story end?' And then the magical mirror would give me the magical answer! Thumbs up if you'd like such a mirror in your writing life." Several students put their thumbs up and others were nodding.

"Then I realized you already have magic like this in your writing lives—your writing partners! Your partner can be a kind of mirror, helping you think about the questions you have and helping you with your plans to work hard. So take a moment right now and think about the big writing questions you have." I paused. "Give a thumbs up when you are ready to talk to your writing partner. You can even begin with 'Partner, partner on the rug . . . ,'" I said with a wink. I popped out of my chair, eager to listen in.

Leroy turned to Gio, "Partner, partner on the rug . . . ," he said with a bit of a smirk. "I am not sure which fairy tale idea to choose. I've written a bunch. . . ." Leroy opened his notebook and began talking Gio through his different fairy tale ideas.

From "This Is a Fairy Tale about" to "Once upon a Time"

ear Teachers,

Some might say that teaching is the art of taking stock. So, as you reflect on Session 13 and head into Session 14, you'll take stock. Our sense is that you'll agree that your writers will need strong teaching to move now from a story idea kind of writing, *This is a fairy tale about . . .* into a storytelling kind of writing, into *Once upon a time in a land far away. . . .* However, the truth is that your writers are already chock-full of planning and rehearsal strategies, so adding yet another strategy may not provide the next step your writers need. So what do they need?

In her book *When Kids Can't Read: What Teachers Can Do: A Guide for Teachers 6–12,* Kylene Beers (2002) writes that the difference between readers who read above grade level and readers who read below is *not* struggle. All readers struggle with text. The difference is repertoire and persistence. That is, strong readers are strong because they have a toolkit of strategies *and* because they persist. When one strategy doesn't work, they try another, then another until they make meaning. We think this is also true of writers. Strong writers have a toolkit of strategies and they persist in trying one thing, then another and another until the words on the page match the meaning they are trying to make. This is what you will aim to teach in this session: Writers draw on a repertoire and decide how they'll work. As they do so, they audit their work, making new plans when necessary.

That is, in a way, this session's message: Students need to draw on all they have already learned, to being willing to study what works, and to try something different when need be. It's not a session that dumps a whole lot of new strategies onto kids—after all, think how much teaching you've already done that lifts the level of students' rehearsal. Mostly your message is to *use what you know*.

COMMON CORE STATE STANDARDS: W.3.3, W.3.4, W.3.5, W.3.10, RL.3.3, SL.3.1, L.3.1, L.3.2

MINILESSON

You might gather your students and say something like, "I know many of you are really chomping at the bit to be able to write today—and you're right to feel that way! After all, you have ideas you're really excited about, and you've spent lots of time rehearsing, storytelling, planning—getting ready to write up a storm. Before I turn you loose, though, I want to remind you about something that might help you get organized as you begin.

"Writers, today I want to remind you that writers learn from their own writing. Writers look back over previous pieces they've written, especially those in a similar genre, noting the processes and strategies they used to write those pieces. They ask, 'What worked that I should do again?' 'What didn't work that I could rethink this time?'"

You might teach writers that it helps to study the work they did earlier, thinking not so much about the specific story that they wrote, but instead thinking about the strategies they used and could have used but didn't, thinking, "What worked for me?" "What could I do differently?" For example, a writer might look between two drafts that she made during an earlier unit of study, and might realize that although the writer produced two drafts, each labeled *draft one* and *draft two*, in fact the two drafts are mostly the same as each other. The writer could resolve then to make sure her revisions are significant, that they make her story better in obvious ways. She might use the tools available in the room—the Narrative Writing Checklist, the "How to Write a Fairy Tale Adaptation" chart—to choose specific lenses to look through as she revises.

You might offer students clean copies of the "How to Write a Fairy Tale Adaptation" planning chart that they used in Session 7, altering it slightly to account for the fact that they are now writing original stories. You might suggest they make notes to themselves right on their copies, for example, adding in "Make sure there is a villain" or other important tidbits they want to work on.

Your minilesson might end with you suggesting writers need to give themselves a self-assignment for the day. You might send them from the meeting area by asking, "Which of you will be making yourself a story-planning booklet and storytelling, trying to make the first page by backstory, the next page the first Small Moment story? Off you go. Which of you will be. . . ." In that way, you channel children toward the activities that you hope most of them will be doing today as they progress from talking about a story plan to actually writing the story.

CONFERRING AND SMALL-GROUP WORK

The beauty of small-group instruction is its efficiency. A quick "Here's why I gathered you . . . " coupled with explicit teaching provides lots of time to coach, coach, coach. One tool that makes planning small-group instruction even more efficient is an "If . . . Then . . ." chart. These charts are teaching gold. They prepare you for the predictable scenarios you might encounter in a given unit, session, or stage of the writing process. This tool's power is amplified exponentially when you create it in collaboration with your colleagues. You might come across situations like the ones below as you confer with your students today.

If you notice . . .	Then you might teach . . .
Writers are writing underdeveloped story ideas	Somebody . . . wanted . . . because . . . but . . . so . . .
	Once upon a time there was ___. Every day, ___. One day ___. Because of that, ___. Because of that, ___. Until finally ___.
	Character with traits who wants something; there's trouble, trouble, trouble and ta-da! resolution
	Villain, Magic, Refrains
Writers' story ideas are lacking in tension	Add motivation—why does the character want this?
	Raise the stakes—make the trouble worse and worse.
	Raise the stakes—create a deadline.
Writers are summarizing scenes rather than storytelling those scenes	(*Teachers, you know lots of different ways to teach storytelling. Add those ways to this chart.*)

MID-WORKSHOP TEACHING

You might think of the mid-workshop teaching point as the little black dress of workshop teaching. That is, the mid-workshop teaching point is highly versatile and always in fashion. If you were to scan back through this unit reading only the mid-workshop teaching points, you would find that we've used them to improve the quality of the work by sharing out one student's work, to provide guidance to stay on track by giving a bad example and a good example. We also encouraged writers to try addressing a predictable pitfall by placing a "speed bump" or a "yield" sign. We highlighted previous teachings and also added to current instruction and goals on anchor charts, such as the "How to Write a Fairy Tale Adaptation" chart and the Narrative Writing Checklist, and provided some independent practice.

Because your goal, in this one precious session, is to move writers from story idea to drafting first scenes, you'll want to focus on that and to provide some mix of information and, above all, inspiration and pressure. For example, "Writers, today you've reread your old work, made lists of goals and plans, clarified your expectations for yourself. What I want to tell you now is that there is a way in which all of that is like the throat clearing that the famous singer does before taking the mike, stepping forward on the stage, and letting it rip.

"Most writers absolutely *do* need to ready ourselves. Some sharpen pencils. Some houseclean. Some reread the existing draft aloud. Some make *Do Not Disturb* signs for the door. Most do as you do and think, 'This time I gotta remember to. . . .' Some put signs up or tie yarn around their finger as reminders.

"But in the end, all of that needs to be behind us. We say the opening words of our story, 'Once upon a time . . .' and suddenly we, ourselves, are going into that rabbit hole of imagination. We are living in another place. We hear, we feel, we think, we talk, we notice, we remember, we want to say, we bite our lips, we clear our throats. And yes, we sing out." You could end with the charge: "Go for it!"

SHARE

After gathering your writers on the rug, you might suggest that part of making plans for writing is checking in to see how those plans have worked. Point out that most writers don't have teachers who read over their writing, writing marginal *awkward* and *good* and *check again* comments. But that doesn't mean that no one reads the writing to check it. Instead, writers do that.

Just as a potter making a pot pulls in to work on the pot and then pulls back to ask, "How does it look?," writers are always shifting among planning, making, checking.

When writers check their writing, they know there are some things to check first—and later. Early on, writers check for structure. To check for structure, writers look at a text as if they are in an airplane, flying above it, looking at the chunks, thinking about how big each chunk is, how many parts it contains, how the chunks go together. Writers ask, "What kind of text am I making?" "How should this be structured?" "How *is* it structured?" "What's working, what's not working?"

Writers of a particular genre check their texts to make sure they have used their knowledge of the genre. Storywriters, for example, ask themselves, "Have I created the world of the story?" "Can people picture my setting?" "Is it real—does it act on people?" Writers think about their plot: "Is there a problem?" "Is there rising tension as things get worse or the wanting gets greater?" "Is there a resolution that comes out of the story and doesn't seem to fly in from outer space?" As part of this work, writers might return to the Narrative Writing Checklist. They might ask themselves such questions as, "Does my beginning show what is happening and where? Does it set up the main problem or tension?" You might ask your writers to begin this work now, on the rug.

Enjoy,

Lucy, Shana, and Maggie

Tethering Objects to Characters

IN THIS SESSION, you'll teach students that to make scenes even more meaningful, writers not only include a character's actions but also objects important to the character.

GETTING READY

✔ A few favorite picture books, such as *Owen* by Kevin Henkes and *Those Shoes* by Maribeth Boelts (see Connection and throughout session)

✔ Chart paper and markers (see Share)

COMMON CORE STATE STANDARDS: W.3.3.b, W.3.4, W.3.5, W.4.3.b, RL.3.1, RL.3.2, RFS.3.4, RL.4.2, SL.3.1, SL.3.4, SL.3.6, L.3.2.c

Y OU PROBABLY WILL SEE TWO EXTREMES AS STUDENTS are beginning to draft their original fairy tales. The first extreme you may notice is that there is little to no dialogue in the writing. The opening scenes children are drafting might still be closer to summary writing rather than storytelling. For instance, children's writing might look more like *The girl wants a dog and her mom said no.*

On the other hand, the second extreme you may notice is the writing is swamped with dialogue! The opening scene could be swimming in chit-chat between characters. In this example, children's writing might look more like, *"May I have a dog, Mom?" "No, Sophie, I told you no yesterday and I mean it." "C'mon, pleeeeeease?" "No means no. We can't get a dog."*

As you know, the best way to address the first extreme is to return to the basics of good storytelling. That is, if children are still defaulting to summaries, not storytelling, you'll remind them of the power of making a movie in their mind, showing, not telling, the story. But, if you notice the second extreme, where the opening scenes are swamped with dialogue, this is a sign of growth. As children learn new moves in their writing, like making movies in the mind, storytelling, and using dialogue, they can fall into the trap of overusing dialogue, in a fashion that feels a bit inflexible. The resulting text may seem like the soundtrack of a movie without the visuals.

In this session, you build on the work you did in Session 10 to encourage students to balance a dialogue-heavy story with the inclusion of small actions. You'll remember that children were previously taught that writers can add small actions to their characters' conversations as a way to balance their writing. You taught the importance of characters "making a salad" together as they spoke. This session teaches a more sophisticated version of that work: Invite children to think about objects that are near and dear to their characters. Whereas in an earlier session, the object that we suggested children use was utterly disposable—a sheet of paper—in this session, we suggest that the objects in fiction often aren't just any ole' object, rather they are important to the character and the storyline. Just think of some of your children's favorite stories. Perhaps *Those Shoes* by Maribeth Boelts, where Jeremy is obsessed with a special pair of shoes. Or *Owen* by Kevin Henkes, where young Owen loves his childhood blankie so much that he carries it everywhere he goes. Just like in life, characters in stories have objects that are important to them. As writing teachers, we can teach young writers to not only create but involve the story around these special objects.

One reason to give the character an important object is that this gives the character something to fiddle with during the conversation. It truly could be anything—a pocket watch, a basket of goodies, a special compass. But objects take on significance in stories and often function as symbols. It's unlikely that third-graders will grasp symbolism, although some might, yet this session nudges children to consider the meaning behind the objects given to the character. That is to say, instead of children randomly assigning their characters objects that seem out of the blue, you'll teach them how a character's small actions with important objects make writing better. Perhaps the object gives insight into the character's deeper self. Or the small actions with an object show a character's true feelings or even help predict future events. Circling back to the concept that writers make choices with a sense of meaning will support more sophisticated craftsmanship as well as continue to help children story-tell without being swamped by dialogue.

> *"Invite children to think about objects that are near and dear to their characters . . . But objects take on significance in stories and often function as symbols."*

Tethering Objects to Characters

CONNECTION

Link students' strong work writing fairy tales with strong work in familiar and beloved mentor texts.

"We've been living in a world of fairy tales over the past few weeks. Sometimes when I walk through the doors of our classroom in the morning, it almost feels as if I'm stepping into the pages of a storybook. As I turn on the lights and get ready for the day, I can almost hear three little pigs scurrying around and Little Red Riding Hood skipping off to see Grandma! We are totally living as fairy tale writers and I can barely wait to read your original tales.

"As I was tidying up our class library this morning, I was reminded of some of our favorite stories we've read this year and how the things we love about those stories match up with things you are working on, or can start working on, in your fairy tales." I pulled out several picture books. "Remember Jeremy and *Those Shoes*? How about *Owen* by Kevin Henkes?"

Using examples from familiar mentor texts, draw students' attention to the fact that writers of narratives often tie small actions to objects that are important to their characters.

"To be honest, I sat down on the couch and began rereading these favorite stories. I couldn't help myself! And you know, I noticed a lot of things that make these stories so wonderful—things that you are doing in your fairy tales, too. And then I noticed something important that Jeremy and Owen had in common." I let my voice drift off for a moment. "I noticed that both characters have a special something that they love and carry around with them."

Before I could finish, Sam spoke up, "Shoes! Jeremy loves his shoes." "Yeah, and Owen loves that blanket!" Piper continued.

"Bingo," I said. "Both characters carry important objects with them. And often the things those characters *do* are tied to those important objects, right? So I got to thinking—this is a common situation in lots of stories, and since we are living in the world of fairy tales I wondered if this might happen in fairy tales too. Let's test this theory out. I'll call out a character from one of our favorite fairy tales and you see if they have a favorite object. Ready? Set?

"The evil queen from *Snow White*?" I called out. "The mirror on the wall!" a few voices replied. "Okay, let's see, how about Little Red Riding Hood. What is she always carrying on the way to Grandma's house?" There was a slight pause before Marco called out, "Her basket of goodies!"

In this connection with mentor texts, you'll recall not just the fairy tales that children know well but also the stories that they know and love. This is important to do because you are teaching fairy tales as a way to teach fiction. You want children to grasp that when you talk about stories involving a character who wants something, you are not referencing only fairy tales.

By using familiar stories to teach kids about emblematic, treasured objects, you let the story itself do half your work. All you need to do is to recall the story, to conjure up the way in which the story did whatever you are now trying to show.

"I think you are onto something, writers. I'm thinking that since many famous authors do this in their stories—give their characters a special object—that you could give this a try too."

❧ Name the teaching point.

"Today I want to teach you that writers sometimes focus characters' actions around an object that's important to the character, which makes those actions more meaningful."

TEACHING

Pretend that you are a famous author who is well known to your students, and deliver the lesson as that author.

"I was thinking that instead of *me* teaching this lesson, we could invite one of our favorite authors, Kevin Henkes, into the room to teach." An anticipatory quiet settled over the class.

I changed my posture a bit and lowered my voice a register. "Hello, third grade," I said quietly, attempting my best Kevin Henkes impression. Giggles spread throughout the room. "I heard you were interested in learning more about how to make your characters' actions really meaningful." The class nodded, caught up in the fun and silliness. I continued, "Sometimes when we writers imagine our characters' actions—things they are doing—it helps to imagine things that they might be doing with a particular object that's important to them. When we have our characters interacting with an object that's important to them or meaningful in some way, the actions become more meaningful and revealing, too."

Encourage students to begin by imagining an object that is meaningful to the character—not just any old object—and then to imagine and act out what the character might *do* with that object.

"Well, first things first, ask yourself what object might be really special to your particular character. In my story, *Owen*, I knew that it would be about Owen growing up from a baby into a little boy. I thought that Owen might hold onto an object he really loved when he was a baby. Like how kids sometimes have a hard time letting go of old toys even if they've really outgrown them. I decided that a blanket was the perfect thing to hold onto and carry around throughout the story!

"Next, I didn't start writing. Instead, I imagined holding onto the object myself. I pretended that I was Owen and I pictured holding onto the blanket. I spent time with the object in my mind, acting out different things my character could do with it." I held up a pretend blanket. "I imagined dragging it behind me." I mimed dragging it behind. "I imagined cuddling next to it while playing with blocks." I gestured at the children, inviting them to pretend along with me.

Describe how authors move from imagining and acting out to drafting, keeping in mind what they learned about what actions might fit with the character's special object. Share an example.

"Last, as it was fresh in my mind, I put Owen in a scene and starting writing! I thought about what trouble Owen might run into. Then, I rehearsed what he might say and how he might interact with his blanket in a way that's important to him in that moment. You want to see how it turned out?"

You might feel a bit silly, at first, assuming the role of another author. But I encourage you to give it a try. We are deep inside this unit of study and it may be a fun change of pace to give the illusion of another writer, a real writer in the world, teaching the demonstration of a lesson! It also could reignite engagement and create a sense of wonder deep in the midst of the unit.

Notice that I'm beginning to lay out steps to implement the strategy. It's important to model the strategy in a step-by-step action. This way, children have a recipe to follow when trying the strategy on their own or practicing it with a partner.

I opened the pages of *Owen*. "In this part of the story, Owen's parents are trying to convince Owen to get rid of his baby blanket, a fuzzy yellow blanket named Fuzzy. But Owen wants no part of that! He continues to hold onto Fuzzy and play with it all the time!" I read a bit:

> *"Fuzzy's dirty," said Owen's mother. "Fuzzy's torn and ratty," said Owen's father.*
>
> *"No!" said Owen. "Fuzzy's perfect," and Fuzzy was.*
>
> *Fuzzy played [the game] Captain Plunger with Owen. "To the rescue!"*
>
> *Fuzzy helped Owen become invisible. "Bet you can't see me!"*
>
> *Fuzzy was essential to nail clippings, and haircuts, and trips to the dentist.*

"Do you see how when Owen was having a conversation with his mom and dad, he held onto and played with his super-important object? Owen didn't let Fuzzy go when his parents wanted him to let it go. In fact, he continued playing with it as he talked!

"Writers, I have to go now, but it's been great working with you. I can't wait to see how you might try this move with your partners! See you next time!" I waved good-bye to the class as I shifted my posture back to normal.

Return to your regular teacher persona, and summarize how an author goes about including small actions based around an important object.

Speaking in my normal voice, I said, "Whoa! How cool was that? Kevin Henkes gave us a great strategy to try in our writing as we draft. I was taking notes as he was teaching and it seems like he gave us a couple of steps to try. First, we ask ourselves, 'What object could be important to my character?' Then, we imagine and even act out what the character might *do* with the object. Last, we continue drafting our scenes, making sure to include some actions the character makes with the object as they talk or think."

ACTIVE ENGAGEMENT

Channel students to try out adding small actions that are tied to an important object in the context of a familiar fairy tale.

"Who's ready to give Kevin Henkes's tip a try?" Hands shot up.

"Okay, let's practice with Little Red Riding Hood. Marco reminded us at the beginning of class today that Little Red Riding Hood is always carrying that basket of goodies to take to her grandma's house. That's important to her, right? The basket of goodies is probably important to her because. . . ." I let my voice drift off. "Turn and talk with your partners. Why do you think the author created this basket of goodies for Little Red Riding Hood to hold? Why might that be important to this character?"

The illustrations are chock-full of actions at this part of the story. You might use the illustrations during this demonstration and story-tell or act out Owen playing with his special object, his blanket, as he talks with his parents and talks during playtime.

Incorporating an object into a child's writing could happen many more places than just during dialogue. But remember the goal of this session—to invite kids to move beyond just writing a stream of dialogue, and to diversify their writing with other craft moves.

I listened in to kids' talk. Lee said, "She's taking the stuff to her Grandma to make her feel better. I mean, that's why she's going. She wouldn't be in the woods to meet the wolf if she didn't have the basket."

Tanya added, "Yeah, I mean, that's the whole reason the story happens. If she didn't have to take some treats to Granny, she might not have gone at all!"

Ask writers to act out what the character in the familiar tale might do with her important object.

"Yeah, that basket is really important, isn't it? Okay, next, let's pretend. Picture a basket of goodies in your minds. Go on, lift your arms out to hold it. Is it heavy? Is it made of wood? Straw? How would you carry it on your way to Grandma's? Why don't you act it out with your partner?" Some children closed their eyes to pretend by themselves, while other children talked about the pretend baskets in their hand with their partners.

"Last step! What if the wolf were to walk up to you right now? Here you are on your way to Grandma's with this heavy basket of goodies. Partner 1s, you're Little Red Riding Hood. Partner 2s, you're the wolf. You all know this story! What happens when they meet? What do they say to each other? Partner 1s, keep thinking about what you might do with the basket as this is happening. Act it out!"

Coach into students' dramatizations, encouraging them to act out characters' use of the important object.

I took a moment to watch the students try the strategy. I found a partnership that was role-playing with dialogue but had forgotten about the special object. I coached, "Ah, I love how the wolf says, 'Where are you headed to, Little One?' and Red Riding Hood responds, 'Off to see my grandma!' But remember the basket! What could she be doing with the basket?" I passed it back to the partnership and watched as they reenacted the scene. This time, Partner 1 clutched the basket close to her body, shaking it as she shook with fear. "Nice!" I affirmed.

LINK

Send students off, encouraging them to revise their drafts to include small actions based on characters' important objects.

"Writers, many of you started drafting your opening scenes yesterday and will decide to redraft that opening scene using Kevin Henkes's tip today! Of course, you may continue to draft forward, moving into your middle scenes, writing forward with this tip in mind. Either way, I bet many of you won't be able to get Kevin's great tip out of your minds! I imagine you'll reread your opening scene, taking note of all the dialogue you're using to tell your story. But you'll hear Kevin's voice in your mind. You'll want to think of an object that is near and dear to your character, pretend to hold it, and then redraft the opening scene, making sure to have the character both talk and fiddle with their object. This is a helpful way to show what the character is really feeling and what's truly important to him or her."

Other coaching prompts could be "How does she hold the basket?" or "What does she do with the basket as the wolf comes near?" or simply "Remember the basket!"

Teach How Small Objects Affect the Story in Big Ways

A S IS OFTEN THE CASE when we introduce something new, students respond in a variety of ways. This is to be expected. It may be helpful to be on the lookout for certain to-be-expected responses. We've collected a list of common conferences, shown in the table on the following page.

Some teachers refer to these "If you see . . . You could teach . . ." charts as *conferring cheat sheets*. Thinking ahead to predictable troubles and possible solutions means entering your conferences and small groups with a plan. Planning in this way ensures more efficient and effective instruction during independent writing time.

MID-WORKSHOP TEACHING
Creating Unity with Recurring Objects

"Writers, eyes up here. Many of you have rewritten the opening scene of your original tales and are motoring on to your middle scenes. You'll remember I taught you a few different ways to stitch scenes together: You could use a Jiminy Cricket narrator's voice, some ant-sized transition words like *but* or *so*, or flow-phrases like *one morning*, *just then*, or *then suddenly* to transition from scene to scene. Those are still important ways to stitch scenes together. But your scenes may be stitched even more tightly when you make sure your object comes back in the next scene. Cora, for example, made sure that the picture of the swimsuit she finds in her first scene stays with her character when she goes to talk to her mom, her dad, and her sister.

"Many of you have been pointing out to me that characters carry their objects across scenes. Owen wouldn't all of sudden forget about his blanket in the middle of the story! Vicky pointed out to me that Little Red Riding Hood carries the basket in three scenes: from her house, through the woods, and into Grandma's house. Doing that—making an object thread its way through your book, or at least across two scenes—is another way to stitch your scenes together. Of course, things change in a story, and it may be that the character's interactions with the object change, so you might ask yourself, 'How does my character change the way he or she interacts with the important object in the beginning, middle, and end of the story?'"

If you see . . .	You could teach . . .	If you see . . .	You could teach . . .
Students writing small actions about objects that seem unrelated to the story's plot	"Think about the objects in fairy tales you know well. They aren't just sort of tacked on—they are often the thing that gets the whole story, the whole plot, up and running. Think about the beans in *Jack and the Beanstalk*. There wouldn't even be a story without those beans. Or the magic mirror in *Snow White and the Seven Dwarves*. Or the pea in *The Princess and the Pea*—that pea is so important to the plot that it's even in the title! When you are adding in actions based on objects, make sure it's not just any old object—it should be important to the story's plot."	Students who have tried writing characters' actions based on important objects in one part of a draft and are ready for a step up	Highlight that, for example, in *Little Red Riding Hood*, the basket appears in multiple scenes across the story, creating a cohesive through-line: "Just like the basket appears in each scene in *Little Red Riding Hood*, you can think about ways that your character's important object makes an appearance in each scene. This is another important way to make all of the scenes in your story fit together."
Students who struggle with integrating small actions and dialogue naturally, so that their writing comes across as stilted and mechanical	"Acting out your scenes with your objects can be a powerful way to mix action and dialogue naturally. The trick to doing this well is to pay close attention not only to what your characters say, but also to what they do with the object *while* they are talking. Then pause after a tiny bit of action and dialogue and write it 'in the air,' exactly how you want it to sound on the page."	Students whose stamina and productivity suffer because they get bogged down in adding lots of tiny details	"One of the great things about fairy tales is that a few small details make a big splash. Fairy tale writers don't have to crowd their writing with lots and lots of tiny details; rather they concentrate a few small details and repeat them along the way. For example, Little Red Riding Hood's red coat is one small detail that makes a big splash because it pops up over and over again. This means, instead of getting stuck thinking of tons of tiny details, you can focus on one or two and try to repeat them throughout the story."

Using Summary to Balance Drafts

Ask students to share ways they've learned to keep their drafts balanced.

"So, we've been making sure our drafts are balanced and not just a bunch of dialogue. We don't just want to write soundtracks of people talking; we want to write vivid, action-packed scenes that help readers get lost in our fairy tales. What are some ways you've tried to help make sure that your writing isn't swamped with dialogue?"

I listened in and then named out. "Ella remembered that we can make sure our characters are doing something as they talk—remember we talked about that earlier in the unit, the idea of how a conversation gets more interesting when characters are making a salad together? That's about including small bits of actions as characters talk together. Edwin reminded us that we can have our characters interact with important objects; that kind of action balances out the dialogue as well, and is really meaningful because it's happening with a meaningful object."

Explain that one more technique writers sometimes use to keep their drafts balanced is to include small bits of summary. Demonstrate this in the context of a willing student's draft.

"So I think you're ready to learn one more way that writers balance their drafts: they include tiny bits of summary." I waited for the class to look confused. "Yes, I know, I know. We always talk about storytelling, not summarizing, don't we? Well, I want to tell you a secret." I leaned forward to whisper: "Sometimes writers use summary writing to speed through a dialogue that's taking forever to write and isn't very interesting. That is, summary may be a fast and helpful way to move the story forward. You could think of it as another place to add a bit of narration—another place that Jiminy Cricket might come along and give us some quick bits of information that moves the story along. Let me show you what I mean.

"Remember Sophia's story? The tale about the girl who really wants a dog? Sophia has a place in her writing where she realized the dialogue was kind of dragging on and wasn't that interesting. It's a perfect place to give summarizing a go." (See Figure 15–1.)

"Hmm, . . . if Sophia wants to try this strategy, she needs to think about what parts of this she could summarize instead of using dialogue. Anyone have ideas?"

"Well, it seems like the girl just keeps on begging—you know, with the 'pretty please'? Maybe that could change to summary," Leroy said.

> "Can I have a dog, please?" she asked her mom.
>
> "I'm sorry, but no," said the mom.
>
> "Pretty please." she asked.
>
> "I said no," the mom said.
>
> "Pretty pretty please," she asked.
>
> "No and that's it," said the mom.

FIG. 15–1   Sophia's draft

"Okay, let's give it a go. Sophia, will you read out your first two lines of dialogue, please?" Sophia read:

> "Can I have a dog, please?" she asked her mom. "I'm sorry, but no," said the mom.

After a quick conversation, the class suggested that Sophia add:

> She begged and begged but her mom said no.

"Sophia will of course decide what she wants to do with her story—but do you see how just a little bit of summary can move the story along? Keep this strategy in your bag of tricks as you're thinking about ways to balance out your drafts."

Remind students that they've learned ways to incorporate other moves in their writing besides dialogue. You may want to quickly jot a chart that holds this thinking and encourages students to keep the dialogue grounded and balanced in their stories, for example:

Writing Balanced Drafts

- Add small actions.
- Add important objects.
- Add small bits of summary.

Using Descriptive Language While Drafting

IN THIS SESSION, you'll teach students that writers balance out *telling sentences* with *showing sentences*.

GETTING READY

✔ Two sentences from *The Real Princess* and from *Jack and the Beanstalk* (or from fairy tales of your choice) written on chart paper (see Teaching)

✔ Writing folders containing all drafts, current and previous (see Active Engagement and Share)

COMMON CORE STATE STANDARDS: W.3.3.b, W.3.5, W.3.10, W.4.3.b,d; RL.3.1, RL.3.3, SL.3.1, L.3.1.i, L.3.2.c, L.3.3a, L.3.5, L.4.5

I REMEMBER WHEN I WAS A STUDENT in one of my first writing classes ever. My teacher had taught us a strategy for collecting narrative entries, and for a few minutes I struggled to write an entry about two brothers I'd known when I was in middle school.

> The doorbell rang. "I'll get it," I called as I walked out of the kitchen. I opened the door and there was Dr. Parr, his wife, and their two sons, Howard and Stuart. "Come in," I said. "Everyone is in the backyard. I hope you brought your suits." I led the way to the pool, quickly glancing back at the two brothers.

"May I interrupt?" my teacher asked, breaking my focus. "What I want to tell you is this," she continued. "There are some quick and easy ways to make your writing better *immediately*." She then taught us that adding even a tiny bit of descriptive language—perhaps some lines to describe the setting or the characters or an object—can have powerful effects. I stared down at my entry, and thought, "I might as well try it." In a moment, my entry went to this:

> The doorbell rang. "I'll get it," I called as I walked out of the kitchen. I opened the door and there was Dr. Parr, his wife, and their two sons, Howard and Stuart. "Everyone is in the backyard," I said. "I hope you brought your suits." Then I followed the two brothers toward the pool, my eyes only on Howard, the older of the two brothers.

> To understand Howard Parr, you needed to understand Stuart. Stuart was a year younger than Howard. And at 11, he was already beautiful and troubled—a brutal combination for any girl. Howard, by contrast, was taller, quieter, and beautiful in a lump-of-clay kind of way—he could be molded. The long frizzy locks trimmed or tamed, the acne treated, the quiet eyes revealed. These weren't the typical family friends.

I was sold. To be honest, until that moment, I'd never realized the power of inserting bits of description into a draft. Looking back now, I'm not entirely sure that my second version is that much better than the first, but back then I was dazzled by my own beautiful words—and I confess, I think I was also dazzled by just the memory of those beguiling brothers.

"Once a writer begins to see that revision makes writing dramatically better, that writer develops a disposition for revision, which relates not just to writing; it's a way of being in the world."

That day was a turning point for me. It was *that* easy? I write a draft, you show me a trick or two, and presto—my writing becomes intense and provocative? I think the reason this moment lingers, years later, is because that day I saw my writing improve before my very eyes.

I have a theory that revision may be addictive. That is, once a writer begins to see that revision makes writing dramatically better, that writer develops what I call *a disposition for revision*. That disposition relates not just to writing; it's a way of being in the world. It's a stance where no matter what you are doing—hiking, cooking, riding the subway—you think about, then try, ways to do that thing better.

This lesson on adding descriptive language while drafting aims in part to highlight the ways tiny writing actions, like adding descriptive language, may have big payoffs. But more than this, the lesson aims to give children a disposition for revision.

Adding Descriptive Language While Drafting

CONNECTION

Using the example of a famous author, explain that writers live in the visual world of their stories as they draft.

"Writers, I want you to picture the 'writing cabin' of Walter Dean Myers, the famous children's author and the National Ambassador for Young People's Literature. Above Walter's writing desk is a huge bulletin board. Tacked all over the bulletin board are photographs. If he's writing a book set in Harlem, there are lots of pictures of Harlem. If his characters are basketball-loving boys, there are pictures to match. These pictures are not decoration; they are part of his writing process because they surround him with the world his stories take place in."

❖ **Name the teaching point.**

"Today I want to teach you that writers live in the world of their stories and add tiny bits of description—of characters, setting, and objects—as they write. Sometimes they do that by writing a telling sentence, and then a showing sentence."

TEACHING

Tell your students that writers vividly imagine what the world of their stories looks like, and they capture those images in their writing. Ask students to study and discuss descriptive bits you've culled from fairy tales as examples.

"Writers, you may not be able to hang a huge bulletin board of photographs above your writing spots, but you can think like Walter Dean Myers as you write. You can *imagine* what the world your characters live in looks like, and you can think about the places in your stories where adding bits of description will help your readers see that world as clearly as you see it.

"To begin this work, I've copied a few lines from *The Real Princess* by Amy Ehrlich (1985) for us to study together. Let's read the lines and then try to figure out if there's a magic formula to adding descriptive details to our writing."

◆ COACHING

Walter Dean Myers spoke at a Teachers College Reading and Writing Project event in the summer of 2012 and taught us about his writing process. Because we are teachers, we listen as magnets, knowing that all the little bits of knowledge we can glean will become part of our own writing. Kids, too, can learn to live like magnets.

You'll find and use your favorite collections and versions of fairy tales throughout this unit. The lines used in this lesson were pulled from one of our favorite collections, The Random House Book of Fairy Tales *(1985). Substitute these lines with some of your favorites from your own collections if you wish.*

I read aloud the sentences that I had charted on the easel:

> A princess stood outside, but the storm had left her in a terrible state. Water streamed from her hair and her clothes; it ran in the toes of her shoes and out at the heels; but still she said she was a real princess.

"Hmm, . . ." I mused, marker in hand. "It kind of seems like this first sentence," I underlined it as I reread, "is telling us what's happening—there's a princess and she's been out in a storm." I read on and said, "But writers, look at this next part, now the author is showing us, describing for us, exactly what she looks like. I can totally picture her." I continued, "'Water streamed from her hair,'" I put my hands to my hair and pulled my hands down like streaming water, "and her clothes." My hands showed this too. "'It ran in the toes of her shoes and out at the heels,'" I said as I shook my very wet foot.

"Writers, I am not really sure this is a magic formula, but it appears that one way writers add descriptive detail is by writing a telling sentence and then adding a showing sentence. Here's another example that I've charted on the easel from *Jack and the Beanstalk* by Amy Ehrlich (1985). Check in with your partner; does this *telling* and then *showing* seem to be true?" I read,

> In the morning when Jack woke up, the room looked very strange. Shadows of leaves were on the walls and the sun did not shine through the window.

ACTIVE ENGAGEMENT

Ask students to try adding descriptions to their own writing while you circulate and prompt them to be specific.

After writers finished studying the lines from *Jack and the Beanstalk*, I said, "You know what I am thinking? You have to try some of this in your own writing! You may either reread and revise some of what you've already written or write on in your draft. Or both. Either way, you'll want to look for the places where you've told about a character, an object, or a place and add a sentence or two that *shows*."

After a moment, I said, "Come to a stopping place. Writers, I think we all want to hear some of the lines you wrote. Who can get us started?"

Andrew's hand popped up. "I can. Listen to how I described the main character in my fairy tale" (see Figure 16–1):

> Zander was a clever boy. He was so clever he could solve a Rubik's Cube with his eyes closed, one hand tied behind his back, hopping on one leg!

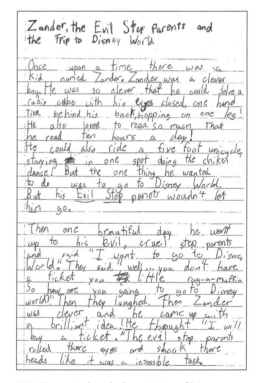

FIG. 16–1 Andrew's description of his character, Zander

Cora continued, "Here's how I described the magic swimsuit" (see Figure 16–2):

Breanna looked at the bathing suit with red fire on the sides and blue and black swirls.

"What a difference a little description makes!" I remarked. "Those lines really helped us picture the characters and objects in those stories."

LINK

Summarize recent new learning, and place it in the context of all narrative writing throughout students' writing lives.

"Writers, before you go off, let's take a moment to think about all of the ways we've been talking about that writers breathe life into their fairy tales. We just talked about adding descriptions that will invite readers into the visual world of the story, so I know that's fresh in your minds. Don't forget the work you've been doing with adding small actions—and focusing those small actions around an object. So as you work today, keep all of that new learning in mind. And writers . . . this kind of work is really important, not just in the fairy tales you're writing now, but in *any* kind of narrative writing that you do. Not just today, but *every day*, stretching out into the whole rest of your writing lives!"

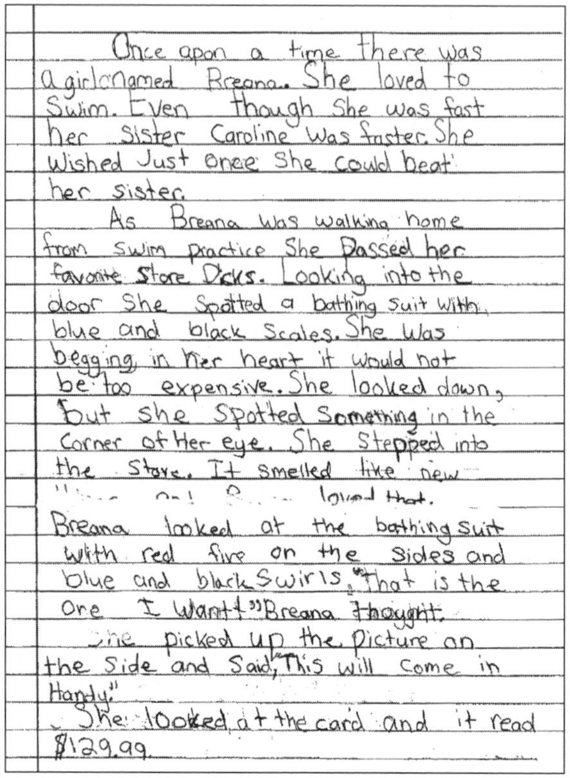

Once upon a time there was a girl named Breana. She loved to swim. Even though she was fast her sister Caroline was faster. She wished just once she could beat her sister.

As Breana was walking home from swim practice she passed her favorite store Dicks. Looking into the door she spotted a bathing suit with blue and black scales. She was begging in her heart it would not be too expensive. She looked down, but she spotted something in the corner of her eye. She stepped into the store. It smelled like new

Breana looked at the bathing suit with red fire on the sides and blue and black swirls, "That is the one I want!" Breana thought.

She picked up the picture on the side and said, "This will come in handy."

She looked at the card and it read $129.99.

FIG. 16–2   Cora's description of the magic swim suit

Tailoring Your Conferring along the Learning Progression

WHEN ANTICIPATING THE CONFERRING AND SMALL-GROUP WORK that you are apt to lead today—or any day—it is helpful to realize that in a sense, any particular minilesson always supports a point on a trajectory of learning. This means that there are always lessons on that same line of learning that come before the one you've just given, as well as lessons that come after. When you work with individuals and small groups, you try to figure out where learners stand so you can tailor your teaching to take them from where they are to where they can go.

This thinking informed my conference with Vicky. When I pulled my stool next to her writing spot, I said, as I am apt to do, "Tell me about your writing work." While Vicky talked about her writing work, I listened and scanned her draft. I noticed that she was already adding lines that described her setting into her draft. I guessed that she was ready to be taught a related lesson that might come a step or two further along the progression of the day's teaching point—that is, she was ready to dig a little deeper.

"Vicky," I said. "I so admire your willingness to have a go. When something is taught in this classroom, you always just dive right in and try it. I know that the new stuff you try doesn't always work and sometimes you end up taking things out or starting a completely new draft all over again, but the really crucial thing is that you do have a go. You listen, learn, and use what you learn as a matter of course, and not many kids do that. It is your secret strength and all your life, you are going to want to remember to do that.

"Are you ready for a tip?" Beaming, Vicky nodded. "Whenever I am taught something new as a writer, I play with the strategy a bit. Sometimes, if what I am learning feels hard, I try and make it a little simpler. And sometimes, if what I am learning feels easy, I think about ways to make it more sophisticated. I am guessing from just looking at your draft, and the way that you've added lines of description into your draft, that the notion of doing that feels kind of easy."

MID-WORKSHOP TEACHING
Envisioning Characters' Actions and Especially Reactions

"Writers, look up for a second. I want to remind you about a strategy you've been using for a long time now—probably since before you could even write words! It's an important one, and one that you'll be using throughout your lives as writers: Writers make movies in their minds to envision the world, the characters, and the action in their stories. It may be helpful, as you're envisioning, to act out the movie you're making in your mind. Acting out what you envision may help you discover new things about your characters.

"You might discover, for example, that your characters don't just act—they also *react*. As you are making movies in your minds and possibly acting them out, you might want to give this some thought—how do your characters *react* to what's happening around them? And how might you put those reactions into words to add to your stories?"

"Well . . ." Vicky hesitated. "Kind of."

"So let's look together at a place in your draft where you've added description and see if there's a way to make it better. Okay?"

Vicky showed me a spot in her draft where she'd described a table as "long and smooth." I showed Vicky a few ways she could ratchet up the ways in which she used description in her draft. I was able to do that because I had a sense of early, emergent work on this trajectory of description, and of advanced work on this trajectory. You need that sense as well. Following are some quick pointers—if you carry these with you, you'll be more ready to be responsive to each child's needs, no matter where they stand along the learning progression.

If it is new for a writer to add description, you might suggest that he or she be sure to insert the weather. Teachers across New York City have taught this to kindergarten and first-graders, and those little ones have taken to it like fish to water. Instead of writing, "I went to the park," they are writing, "One gray Saturday morning, I went to the park." Suddenly their writing sounds like literature!

As children become a bit more advanced, they can learn that the goal is not necessarily to add the actual weather, although in some personal narrative writing that makes sense, but instead to think what sort of weather would make sense for that part of the draft. If this is a story about a boy who felt alone, he might be sitting on a rock wall, staring up at the sky. What would the clouds be like that day? Gray, misty clouds, right? If the boy remembered, suddenly, that his all-time favorite cousin would arrive soon, what would happen to the sky? A beam of light would shine through, warming his face.

Very sophisticated writers can learn that the weather may be used to foreshadow upcoming parts of a story. When a crack of thunder is heard is the distance, this brings an ominous note into the story. Of course, the larger lesson is for children to learn that authors make choices for reasons. The reader of a story may ask, "I wonder why the author made this story take place just after the rain, when the saplings were springing to life?"

If your children are novices to adding description, you might help them to know that it is helpful to give each character his or her own defining feature. You'll see very young children do this when they draw accompanying pictures for their stories. They often begin by drawing a generic guy—man, woman, child, adult, none of that is decided yet. In the middle of making the picture, the child will announce, "It's my brother" and add the defining bushy hair.

Using Drafts to Notice and Name Evidence of Learning

Ask writers to look over their work with a partner to see the progress they've made. Highlight one example.

"Writers, you are improving tons. We don't have a video clip to study to see your progress, but you *do* have all of your drafts! Let's take these closing moments of workshop so that you can look across your drafts, and notice and name the things you're getting better at. In a couple of minutes I'm going to give you a moment to explain your growth with your partners."

After the students studied their drafts and shared with their partners, I highlighted one thing that a student had noticed about her growth.

"Writers. This is so great. I heard Maggie say that she's gotten much better at writing dialogue. All her characters used to sound the same. Now, the villain really sounds like a villain—'Curse you, Zebra, curse you!' and the mother really sounds like a mother—'It's not safe for my little ones to be alone.'" (See Figure 16–3.)

Set up writers to choose one of their drafts to revise, edit, and publish during the remainder of the unit.

"This is actually a great time to pause and celebrate your hard work, because tomorrow is a big day. You will begin revising the piece that you are going to publish at the end of this unit! Choose any of the three drafts you've worked on."

"You just spent a little time revisiting all three drafts, so they are fresh in your mind. Take a moment and consider which draft you'd like to begin revising tomorrow. This will be the piece you'll publish in a few days. Choose the piece you want to be remembered by as a fairy tale author! I bet your partner might be a good help as you make your decision. Turn, discuss, and decide!"

Children chatted excitedly with their partners. A few children couldn't decide and needed a bit more time. I leaned over a small group of writers and suggested, "Why don't you take tonight and think it over? Think it through tonight and come in tomorrow with your decision, ready to revise!"

> Then came the big, bad lion to the first zebra's house and said, "Let me in, little zebra, let me in."
>
> "Not by the stripes on my backy back back," the little zebra said.
>
> "Then I'll dig up your house!" And the lion did exactly that. But the zebra ran out and he heard his mothers voice say "Stick together." So he ran to the second zebra's house. When lion entered the first house, he found only a pile of straw on his head and roared, "Curse you zebra curse you!!"

FIG. 16–3 Maggie's draft with villainous dialogue

Revising the Magic

IN THIS SESSION, you'll teach students that writers revise their fairy tales and tether the magic in their stories to the heart of the story, the beginning, and/or the end of the story.

GETTING READY

✔ Drafts selected to revise and edit in Session 16 (see Connection)

✔ One student's story idea (see Active Engagement)

COMMON CORE STATE STANDARDS: W.3.3.a,d, W.3.5, W.3.10, W.4.3.a,e; RL.3.1, RL.3.2, RL.3.3, SL.3.1, L.3.3.a, L.4.3

TYPICALLY, THIS IS A TIME IN A UNIT when you will help children engage in significant revision. At the end of the previous session, children chose which draft to carry into this phase of the writing process. You could begin by reminding them of all that they already know about revising narratives. Some children might then revise their leads or endings, while others might revise the types of details and descriptions they've included. And then, you will presumably want to add one new way to revise, so they leave the session with an even larger repertoire of revision strategies to choose from.

In deciding upon the revision strategy to highlight, we thought about the essential components of a fairy tale, making sure we channeled students toward a significant element of

"Presto! That's a place in writing to include magic—in the heart of the story."

the genre. We decided to recommend you suggest students might revise by thinking about the role magic plays in their stories. Fairy tales are chock-full of magic—spells, talking animals, special powers.

Frankly, we chose magic because we hope its appeal lures children into revision and because we think magic in a story is very much a part of the heart of a story, part of the problem and the solution. This way, revising for magic makes a big splash in their writing!

There is no doubt that magic appeals to people. Seventeen million people visit Walt Disney's Magic Kingdom every year. It's consistently the number-one tourist destination in the world and has earned its title, "The Most Magical Place on Earth!" Millions of people flock through the Disney gates each year because the magic draws them. It's fun to believe in possibility. Or as Walt Disney famously said, "It's kind of fun to do the impossible."

We open the minilesson by acknowledging that adding magic will come naturally to your students, and most likely, magic will not be a new concept for them. You may have noticed, however, that as some students write magic into their stories, they go overboard, popping magical objects and events in willy-nilly with no regard for meaning. This session aims to harness children's natural enthusiasm for making magic, using it in a more controlled and effective way.

To help students revise the magic in their drafts, we did some research on magic in fairy tales. First, we teach that magic comes in many forms in fairy tales. There are magical characters who appear to help solve a big problem, like the fairy godmother in *Cinderella*. There are magical objects that either help save the day or ruin the day, like the poisonous apple in *Snow White*. There are even magical events that happen, like magic beans growing a magical vine into the sky in *Jack and the Beanstalk*. This session encourages children to revise with a sense of wonder, thinking how magic is involved in their original tales.

Second, we'll teach children *where* magic tends to occur in fairy tales. At first glance, magic seems to pop out of nowhere. But you'll teach children that magic usually arises to help (or hurt) the main character in some big way when the character needs it the most.

Moreover, problems crescendo in the heart of the story, so magic pops up there. Finding the heart of the story isn't new to children. In the *Crafting True Stories* unit, children learned to isolate and zoom in on the heart of the story, stretching it out bit by bit. You'll want to remind children that the heart of their story tends to include the main character facing and dealing with a big problem. And in fairy tales, magic may help that problem, or, at times, make the problem even a bit worse. Presto! That's a place in writing to include magic—in the heart of the story.

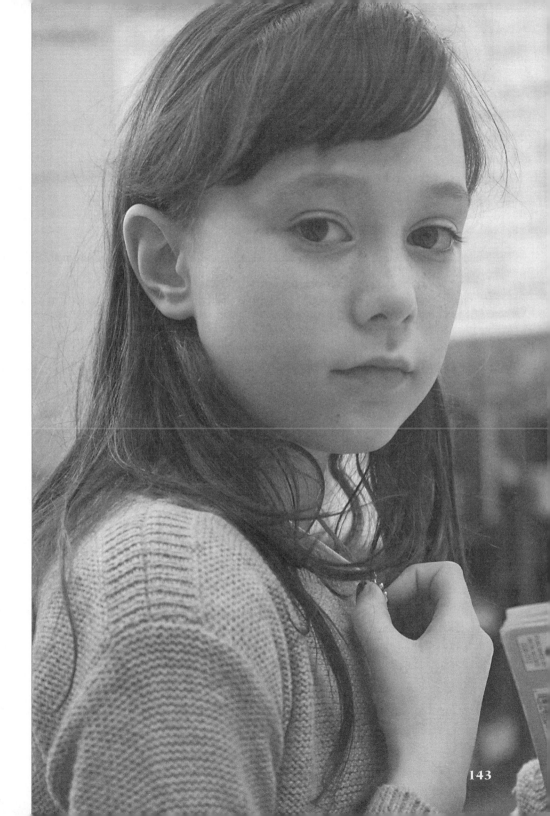

Revising the Magic

CONNECTION

Invite children to bring their favorite draft from the unit to the rug and gather for the minilesson.

"Writers, you made an important writing choice yesterday. You chose your favorite draft to revise and publish. It's time to bring it with you over to the rug—and writers, carry it like a treasure! It's a special piece of writing!" Children pulled out their choices from their folders and gathered at the rug, some tiptoeing while others carried their pieces like golden eggs.

Confess that studying fairy tales with your class has you eating and breathing fairy tale magic and wishing for some in your everyday life.

Once the children settled I said, "Writers, I have a confession to make: I can't stop reading fairy tales—yours and others! I read them after school, before bed, instead of washing the dishes! Last night when I looked up from reading and noticed how dirty my kitchen was, I wished a fairy godmother would wave her magic wand, say 'Bibbidi-bobbidi-boo,' and *poof*! My kitchen would be magically clean!"

I asked, "Have you ever wished for something like that to magically get done? Quickly turn and tell your partner: If you had magic, what problem would you fix? A misbehaving dog? Three strikes at the ball game?"

Students eagerly shared, "Winning the soccer game!" "Fixing my sprained ankle!" "Cleaning my room!"

Rally students to harness the magic of fairy tales in their own writing.

I regathered the class. "I've got good news. News you already know, actually: In the world of fairy tales, magic can do all this and more! Today you'll have a chance to revise your favorite pieces of writing from this unit, and one suggestion I have is that you might think about how to make the most of the magic in them. Most of your tales already include magic, sprinkled in some places and packed in others.

"I invite you to return to your writing with a close eye and pay attention to magic—or maybe just consider the possibility of magic. You are joining a club of fairy tale writers. And did you know fairy tale writers carefully consider the kind of magic they include and the best places to put it in their stories?"

Children have been writing up a storm over the past few weeks. Now, they are in the home stretch of the unit. As children hold the drafts of their future publications, set the tone for this final stage of writing—one of excitement and possibility.

Children love hearing about your life: dirty dishes. A perfect detail.

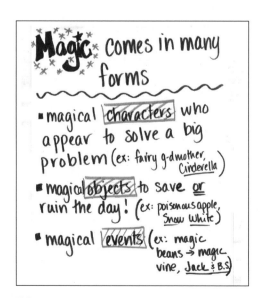

FIG. 17–1

❖ Name the teaching point.

"Today I want to teach you that one way writers revise their writing is to reread, looking especially at the role of magic in their stories. For a fairy tale to work, the magic can't be just sprinkled around willy-nilly, but needs to connect to the heart of the story. Magic usually pops up especially when the story's trouble pops up."

TEACHING

Set students up to notice that magical elements of fairy tales are meaningfully embedded in stories' hearts, either solving or contributing to problems.

"So, if you're revising today, this is something you might want to think about, to not just sprinkle magic in willy-nilly, but to think carefully about where to put it.

"Magic usually makes a big appearance in the hearts of stories: the places in stories where the trouble really gets going. Stories' hearts generally are focused around the main characters' problem. And in fairy tales, magic—in whatever form—may be a part of solving the problem or making it worse."

"Remember how in *Cinderella*, the fairy godmother comes just after the stepsisters and stepmother have left for the ball, when Cinderella is all alone? She's in serious trouble. That's the very moment when *poof*! The fairy godmother appears and her magic starts working on Cinderella's problem. Or how about in *Snow White*, when the evil queen finds Snow White at the dwarves' cottage and hands her that magic poisoned apple . . . that time the magic *creates* the trouble, right?"

Debrief, contextualizing what students have noticed in the mentor texts.

"Do you see how magic, whether it's a character, an object, or an event, is tied to the heart, to the problem, in each of these stories? It either makes the problem better . . . or worse. It doesn't just *poof!*, come out of nowhere. Characters are not just walking around with their pockets full of magic apples and wands and harps, meeting fairies and talking to animals every five minutes. The magic wouldn't be special or meaningful that way."

ACTIVE ENGAGEMENT

Using the work of a willing writer, rally the class to think of ways to include magic that is tied to the story's heart.

"Eliza has volunteered to help us practice a little with this. Some of you know this already, but in case you don't, her story is about a star soccer player named Liza who wants to win the championship game and another player intentionally injures her so that she can't play in the championship.

If you notice that your students need more support identifying and classifying magical elements of fairy tales, it is likely that a little brainstorming session will help, or perhaps a simple game in which you ask children to classify magical elements of familiar fairy tales. This will especially support those children in your class who may have had less cumulative experience with fairy tales.

As mentioned, magic may also appear in the opening and final scenes of fairy tales—anywhere, in fact. This minilesson focuses on linking magical elements to the heart of the story as a way to build on previous narrative work and to ensure that students are adding magical elements in meaningful ways. The share section of this session invites children to revise for the appearance of magic in opening or final scenes.

You may decide to focus on the more technical detail that some magic appears in fairy tales to make things better, and some magic appears to make things worse. You could ask students to think of examples of each kind of magic. But mentioning it in this subtle way is probably sufficient.

"So, where do you think the magic should come in this story? Remember, magic is really meaningful when it's connected to the heart of the story, to the main trouble. Of course Eliza will be deciding what kind of magic to include, and how the magic will affect the story—but if you want to brainstorm some ideas, feel free, right, Eliza?"

I listened in. Piper turned excitedly to her partner, "What about a magic pill? Like the magic beans in *Jack in the Beanstalk*, only instead of growing a beanstalk, they heal her leg."

Jackson nodded, "Or maybe there could be a magic soccer ball. . . . Well, I am not really sure how that would work." Jackson thought for a moment. "Oh! I know, what about magic shin guards? She puts them on and ta-da! she can play soccer."

"Cool!" said Piper.

Debrief, giving students some tips for how they might later do this work on their own, and rallying them to do the sometimes messy work of finding the story's heart.

"You might notice, if you decide to try this kind of revision work on your own, that it takes a lot of work to find the story's heart. You might spend a lot of time thinking about that, before you even start thinking about what kind of magic might be added, or how it might affect the character's trouble. It's worth it to take a bit of time to be really thoughtful about finding the heart, the most important part, the big trouble in your story—and *then* start thinking about how you can revise by adding meaningful magic."

LINK

Encourage writers to buckle down and get ready for the significant revision work that might take place today.

"I know that your stories are already full of magic, in one way or another. But today's idea is about revising for magic in expert ways! You know, you might also notice that adding new magic into the heart of your story might change it a lot—you'll probably be adding a *lot* of writing when you get to that part. Your story's heart might be just a line or two now—but at the end of revising how the magic goes, you might have expanded it into a whole page. If this happens with your writing, congratulations—you know that revising isn't always about making little changes—sometimes revision is about making *really big* changes to your writing."

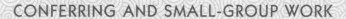
Teaching Students at Each End of the Spectrum

I T'S UNLIKELY THAT THE FAIRY TALES CHILDREN have been working on at this point will be lacking magic—magic is part of what makes this unit such an energizing one! But the conferences you have today will probably focus on helping students harness and make the most of that magic energy.

Typically speaking, you'll buzz around the room, noticing different levels of sophistication with incorporating magic into fairy tales. You'll want to keep your eye out for extremes—children who flood their writing with magic and go overboard; others who struggle with the decision of what kind of magic to include, let alone include it.

Have a couple of teaching moves tucked in your back pocket to teach children who struggle with incorporating magic. If you notice writers having a hard time deciding on what magic to include, you might try to lighten the pressure that builds over making the "right" decisions about what type of magic to create.

I gathered a few of these writers to the rug for a small-group lesson. Sensing the pressure these writers were putting on themselves, I began the lesson lightly. "Writers, one of the most magical books of our recent times is the Harry Potter series. Those books are filled to the brim with magic. The magic is so believable and compelling, it inspired millions of people to get lost in the pages of this magical tale. Millions of people! That's a lot of pressure, huh?" The already shy writers looked even shier with such an intimidating reference.

"The author, J. K. Rowling, was once asked how she found all her ideas for the magic she wrote. You know what she said? She said, 'It's important to remember that we all have magic inside us.'"

I repeated. "We all have magic inside us. We just have to find it. You ready to find the magic inside of you?" Children nodded. "Okay, one tip I want to teach you when you are trying the find the magic inside of you, the idea for the magic inside your fairy tales, is simple. Fairy tale magic doesn't need to be fancy. On the contrary, fairy tale magic

MID-WORKSHOP TEACHING
Using Mentor Texts to Revise for Magic

"Writers, look up for a moment. The work that many of you are doing today, revising with your eyes out for how and where to add meaningful magic into your stories, is not easy! Don't forget, you're not alone. Not only do you have each other's writing, you also know lots and lots of fairy tales by now—both classic versions and adaptations.

"If you are having a hard time figuring out what magic to include and how to tie it into your story's heart as you revise, don't struggle alone! Go to the classroom library, grab a text you love, and study how other authors have done it. If you're looking at a collection of fairy tales, you might even just skim the table of contents to remind yourself of what the stories are, what the magic is, and where in the story it happens. Or look more carefully at a particular tale and ask yourself how you might learn about writing in meaningful magic from that author.

"I'm guessing I'll see a few of you heading over to the fairy tale section of our library soon—that's great! Just remember to put the books back there when you've finished so others may study them as well. Remember all the different kinds of work writers of fairy tales can do to make their writing better. . . . You have so many choices!"

is usually something simple. Let's list classic fairy tale magic—beans, a pea, a mirror. You don't need to think of super-fancy magical objects like a string of pearls dipped in apricot nectar!"

I made a list of everyday simple objects with the small group of kids—pens, baseballs, a cellphone, a cat's whiskers. Then I said, "Remember, you have magic inside of you!

(continues)

Close your eyes. Let's play pretend. How might this object become magical in your stories? How might this magical object help or hurt the main character?"

Cora gave a thumbs up, then said, "Well, I've got this magical swimsuit. But that's it."

"Writers, let's think about Cora's story for a moment. She's included a magical object—a swimsuit. How could that object help or hurt the character?"

"Cora," asked Vicky, "What does your character want?"

"She wants to beat her sister in a swim race."

"Okay," said Gio, "So either the swimsuit makes her swim faster or her sister swim slower."

"What do you think, Cora?"

"That kind of makes sense," said Cora slowly. "I have to figure out how the swimsuit works."

"Exactly!"

The other extreme you may notice is that some children go so overboard with magic that it becomes almost unbelievable—a magical door has a magical godfather who guards it and his magical cane is the only way to fly! With this trend, you'll want to coach students to revise for restraint, picking or choosing one form of magic. For instance, you might teach how little bits of magic go a long way in fairy tales. Remind them that it's one magic mirror, one magic apple, two tiny magic beans. Choosing one form of magic and sticking to it is a way writers make their fairy tales imaginary yet believable.

For students who overuse magic, you could teach how writers introduce something magical in the beginning of the story and carry it through until the ending. For instance, in *Jack and the Beanstalk*, magic beans are introduced in the beginning of the story and impact the whole story. Or in *Princess and the Pea*, the pea is introduced quickly and is carried through the entire fairy tale. For children who want to write a ton about magic, teach them to write about magic in focused ways, perhaps introducing it in the beginning of the story and weaving it through the story. You could also teach how magic may be introduced earlier in the story as a way to foreshadow future events. For instance, in *Mufaro's Beautiful Daughters*, the magic snake appears early on, only to turn into the desired king.

Weaving Magic into Tales' Beginnings and Endings

After gathering your students, tell them that many authors weave magic throughout their tales, not just in the heart of the story.

"Writers, the magic you might use in your fairy tale may show up in the beginning, the middle, and the end of your tale.

"As you already know, fairy tale writers tie the magic really clearly into the story's heart. Now that many of you have revised to make sure the magic in your stories is connected to the heart, you might want to experiment with something else writers of fairy tales do: bring the magic into other places in the story—sort of weaving it throughout. Imagine tracing the magic all the way back to the opening scene of your fairy tale. How might the magic make its first appearance? Does it pop into the beginning scene and set up a problem, like the magic mirror in *Snow White*? Does it pop into the final scene and resolve a problem, like when the Beast turns into a prince in *Beauty and the Beast*?"

Encourage students to imagine how they might weave magic into their stories' beginnings or endings, and ask them to turn and story-tell to their partners.

"Think about your own fairy tale now. Think about how the magic in your story might pop up in the beginning or the end—and when you've got an idea, use your storytelling muscles to turn and tell your partner how it might go. Keep this in mind for writing time tomorrow—remember, you'll be celebrating these tales in just a few days, so you'll want to use every moment of writing time to write and revise like the wind!

> One day Liza was in her comfy wheelchair with pads looking depressed and thinking she would never be able to play soccer again because of the day Dahlia kicked her leg. She was thinking all about the bad things when ... POOF! A magic soccer fairy appeared. She had a soccer ball in her hand and a soccer uniform with purple and green stripes on it.

> The team ran onto the field. It was Dahlia's turn to go first. Dahlia, wearing a purple uniform with white with green stripes, dribbled down the field. Liza got the ball and passed to Maddie. Maddie passed it back to Liza. Liza dribbled twice, did a move around Dahlia and passed the ball back to Liza. Liza smacked the ball into the goal near the corner. The goalie dived for the ball and missed it by an inch. GOAL! "Thanks magic soccer fairy," thought Liza as her teammates lifted her into the air.

FIG. 17–2 Elizabeth's magical beginning and magical ending

Revising for Readers

IN THIS SESSION, you'll teach students that writers show their readers how to read a piece by varying the *pace* of the writing.

GETTING READY

✔ Excerpts from the class adaptation of *Cinderella* written on chart paper (see Teaching and Active Engagement)

✔ Sentence from a student's draft

✔ Post-it notes with ending punctuation marks written on them (see Mid-Workshop Teaching)

✔ *Prince Cinders* by Babette Cole (see Share)

W HEN I WAS LITTLE GIRL my favorite bedtime story was *Harry the Dirty Dog* by Gene Zion (1976). Night after night, my parents read me the story. I never tired of hearing about the white dog with black spots who did not like to bathe. I giggled with delight every time my father raised his voice to read the funny part when Harry buried the scrub brush in the backyard. I clutched my blanket tight when my mother lowered her voice and read the part where Harry ran away in search of adventure. I clutched tighter still when he returned home a black dog with white spots (because he'd gotten so dirty) and no one in the family recognized him. My parents read in a way that brought the story to life, lifting me out of my bed and into the story.

Part of what transported me so thoroughly into the world of the story was the *way* it was read to me—the cadence of my parents' voices, speeding up and getting louder during the exciting parts, slowing down and getting softer at the story's end. And how did they know how to pace the story as they read? Well, the story itself told them, of course.

In this session, you teach students to write stories that will be read in that same wonderful way. Specifically, you help writers experiment with varying the pace of a story—choosing some moments to slow down and some moments to speed up. Your third-grade writers won't master this practice; it's something that even adult writers continue to work on. In fact, prolific children's author Avi spoke to this very practice to an auditorium filled with writing teachers this past summer at Teachers College. During a discussion on writing, Avi shared, "Writers like me don't write *writing*. We write *reading*." You can help writers write *reading* by teaching them to become aware that one way to make a story sound good, and to be memorable, is to think about ways to cue readers into how to read the story well. Of course, working on the sounds of a story can't be separate from working on the meaning; this session, like the last, will remind writers that revision always requires a writer to think, "What's this story really about?" and to craft the text in a way that highlights the meaning.

COMMON CORE STATE STANDARDS: W.3.3.b, W.3.4, W.3.5, W.4.3.b,d; RFS.3.4, SL.3.1, SL.3.4, SL.3.6, L.3.1.a, L.3.2, L.3.3a, L.4.1.f, L.4.3.b

Revising for Readers

CONNECTION

Demonstrate one way in which writers leave clues that tell readers how their writing should sound.

"Writers, yesterday I was reading aloud *The Three Billy Goats Gruff* to Aidan and Max, two boys that live near me. And when I got to the '*Who's that tripping over my bridge*?' part, I made my voice deeper and louder. Aidan interrupted, 'Why'd you do that?' I looked confused, and he added. 'Why'd you make your voice funny?'

"'Oh!' I said. 'Well,' I looked at the page and thought for a moment. 'Because the author told me to,' and I showed Aidan and Max the page with its capital letters and the voice tag, 'roared.'

"Writers, this got me thinking about the power of writing, more specifically, the power of writers. I mean, think about it, I've never met Paul Galdone, I don't even know if he's alive! And yet, anyone and everyone who reads his book knows exactly how to be the troll because of how he wrote it. That's pretty amazing, when you think about it."

You might decide to set up today's minilesson by reading from The Three Billy Goats Gruff *directly as a way to illustrate how writers leave clues that indicate how their writing should sound.*

Ask students to think of other ways that writers leave clues for readers that tell them how a piece of writing should be read.

"When I write, I ask myself, 'How might I give people clues as to how to read this part?' Of course, you already know some ways to this. You know that when you write dialogue in all capital letters, like Paul Galdone, you tap your reader on the shoulder and say, 'make your voice deeper and louder in this part.' Are there other ways you show your reader how to read your writing? Turn and talk." I listened in. Not surprisingly, kids mostly talked about using ending punctuation to show their reader how to read their writing.

✤ Name the teaching point.

"Writers, today I want to teach you that writers show their readers how to read a piece by varying the *pace* of the writing—by altering whether a moment passes by quickly or slowly."

TEACHING

In the context of a shared text, demonstrate how writers help readers slow down and savor a moment by adding more words, sentences, and details.

"Let me show you what I mean. We've decided to revise our first *Cinderella* adaptation, right? So let's pluck a sentence from the draft and play with the pacing. First we'll try slowing the moment down. When you make decisions about pace, about how quickly or slowly you want a moment to pass as readers are reading, you are actually telling readers if this is a moment to be savored and studied or if it may be breezed through.

"But how? How to slow down or speed up a moment? Let's try revising a moment in our *Cinderella* adaptation to slow it down." On the easel, I'd written:

> Cinderella watched sadly as the invitation disappeared into the flames.

"Okay. Imagine you've got a remote control aiming right at this moment when Cinderella is watching the invitation burn. You know how you can use a remote to slow a movie way down? And when you do that, you see all kinds of details that you might have missed? Slow down this one moment with your remote and picture this with me. Everything is happening s-l-o-w-l-y. I see the invitation being tossed into the fire. I see the flames take some time to burn the invitation. I see Cinderella. One tear slides down her cheek as the invitation burns." I paused to think about how to write this on the page. "Maybe I would write that something like this. . . ." I picked up a marker and wrote on the chart paper:

> Cinderella watched sadly as the invitation landed in the fire. The edges started to burn first. A tear slid down Cinderella's cheek. The flames grew bigger and bigger as more of the invitation caught fire. Cinderella buried her face in her hands. Soon the invitation was a pile of ashes.

Debrief, asking students to notice how slowing down a moment leads to using more words and sentences to describe it.

"Writers, we just imagined we were using a remote to slow down that one moment in the *Cinderella* story and then to write the slowed-down version. Look at the difference between the original sentence and our slowed-down version. What are you noticing?"

> Cinderella watched sadly as the invitation disappeared into the flames.

> Cinderella watched sadly as the invitation landed in the fire. The edges started to burn first. A tear slid down Cinderella's cheek. The flames grew bigger and bigger as more of the invitation caught fire. Cinderella buried her face in her hands. Soon the invitation was a pile of ashes.

"There are more sentences," called Zander.

By this time in the year, students will be familiar with the concept of "showing not telling." This demonstration teaching builds from this, harnessing students' attention on the purposeful increase of words, sentences, and details (showing) with the intent to slow down the pace.

"And there are a lot more words, like maybe four times as many," said Maggie.

"I noticed that too, and I noticed that slowing the moment down helped us include more details than we used originally. When writers slow a moment down, they pack in more details. That tells readers to slow down as they read, to spend more time in that one moment." (See Figure 18–1.)

ACTIVE ENGAGEMENT

Rally students to practice speeding up a moment by taking out words or sentences.

"Let's try playing with the pace again, with a different moment from the same story. Except this time, instead of slowing down the moment, use your remote to speed it up! The way it's written now, Cinderella takes some time to notice the library as she walked into it. What if you wanted to speed this moment up so that readers get to the next part of the story, the part where she gives Donald the money and saves the library, more quickly—what would you do? Try it with your partner. What do you see as you speed this moment up with your remote? How would you write that on the page?"

> Cinderella entered the library. It was big and beautiful. And so empty it echoed. "Where are all the books?" Cinderella wondered aloud.

I listened in as the students talked and then regathered them. "Writers, I was listening in and I heard Charlie say something like, 'Cinderella rushed into the empty library and wondered where the books were.' Lots of you said something similar." I wrote Charlie's sentence below the example:

> Cinderella entered the library. It was big and beautiful. And so empty it echoed. "Where are all the books?" Cinderella wondered aloud.
>
> Cinderella rushed into the empty library and wondered where the books were.

Then I asked, "What do you notice about what happened to the writing when we tried speeding up the moment?"

"Fewer words!" Edwin called.

"It's just one sentence now," added Piper.

"I noticed that too," I agreed. When writers want a moment to speed by, they write it in fewer words and fewer sentences. They don't include as many details for readers to linger on. There's no right or wrong way here—you writers may decide for yourselves if you want readers to move really slowly or really quickly through a moment. What might you do if you are revising and you find a moment that you want to slow down?"

Students chimed in, "Add more sentences!" "Add details!" "Use more words!"

First time: Lainie started to practice and then CRAAACK! went the stick.

Slow time: Lainie walked into the garage. She took her hockey stick, Black Magic, and kissed it. She got into hockey position—legs apart, knees bent, two hands on the hockey stick—she shot. The puck went closer to the goal then all of a sudden CRAACK! went the hockey stick.

FIG. 18–1 Lainie's revised draft, playing with pacing

"And what might you do if you want readers to speed through a moment—how might you speed a moment up?"

They responded, "Take out words!" "Make it shorter!"

LINK

Encourage writers to be thoughtful about pace as they revise.

"Exactly. And part of your job as writers is to make decisions about the pace of each moment—how fast or slow you want it to go. When you're rereading your stories, if you find a moment that seems really important that you've just breezed right through, you might want to consider slowing it down, adding more sentences and more details. If you find a less important moment that passes really slowly as you read that you want to pass more quickly, you might want to consider speeding it up by taking out some words or sentences or details.

"There is so much work you could try now—you'll have to decide what to do that will most help your story. Use the charts in the room to remind you of things to try!"

Supporting Students Who Struggle with Creating Paragraphs

IT IS EASY IN ANY UNIT OF STUDY TO GET lost in the details, to lose sight of the big things you are teaching. For this reason, it's often helpful to remind yourself of the two or three big, important goals you have for any unit. In this unit, one central goal is helping students find structure in their writing. Writing in the footsteps of classic fairy tales helps young writers try on familiar story structures while also making them their own by writing adaptations. Mimicking fairy tale language supports young writers in learning more complex sentence structures. As you approach the end of this unit, you may notice students struggling with another aspect of structure—creating and routinely using paragraphs.

Young writers will most likely struggle in a variety of ways when structuring their writing using paragraphs. You may look out into the sea of writers as the unit's end approaches and notice a range of struggle around the routine (and accurate) use of paragraphs. During one of the final conferring and small-group sessions of the unit, you might look for the types of struggle groups of students are having regarding paragraphs. That way, you'll "brand" the types of paragraphical issues and address them in small bursts of small-group teaching as you circulate the room.

For instance, you might first notice the infamous "blob," where the entire piece is one amorphous section of writing. Or perhaps you notice the trend of students starting off with a strong use of paragraphs that dissipates as the draft continues. Or a pattern might emerge whereby students indicate time shifts with new paragraphs but lack the understanding that paragraphs occur when a new character speaks. Whatever the trend, enter the room with a handful of teaching tips for creating and sustaining paragraphs, such as

Writers create a new paragraph when . . .

- time changes: *The next day . . .*
- place changes: *Breana was walking home from swim practice . . .*
- a new character arrives: *Then the shark came in.*

MID-WORKSHOP TEACHING
Trying Out Punctuation

"Writers, at the beginning of the lesson, you told me that punctuation is another way you let your reader know how to read your piece. But did you know that some writers actually audition their punctuation marks?" Some kids looked a little puzzled. "Let me show you what I mean. I've written a sentence from Andrew's draft on the easel—*Zander showed his evil step-parents the ticket.* And, as you see, I've placed different ending punctuation marks on these Post-it notes."

I looked around the room. "Andrew, would you come up here and place one of these marks at the end of your sentence?" Andrew hustled to the front of the room and placed a question mark at the end. "Writers, let's read this out loud and Andrew, you decide if a question mark is the right punctuation mark for this sentence."

The class said, "Zander showed his evil step-parents the ticket?" Andrew shook his head.

"Try another one," I prompted. Andrew placed an ellipsis at the end of his sentence. The class said, "Zander showed his evil step-parents the ticket. . . ." Andrew shook his head again.

"Writers, Andrew knows how he wants his reader to read this sentence and he's going to continue to audition punctuation marks until he finds the right one. I suspect many of you will want to try this too."

- a new person speaks: *Jill replied, "That's fine with me!"*
- something important happens: *Poof! The pumpkin became a stagecoach.*

These helpful hints can provide young writers with the energy to improve their writing as they revise for structure.

Using Commas in a Series

Explain and give an example of a way commas give readers information about how to read a piece.

"Writers, it is so clear to me that you are taking Avi's words to heart. You are not writing *writing*, you are writing *reading*. That's why I must share one additional way that you may show your reader how to read your piece—using commas in a series." I pulled *Prince Cinders* from the basket of fairy tales and said, "Many of you are already doing this, but let me show you how Babette Cole does this and then you may check to see if there are places in your draft where you need to add commas because you've listed a series of items, actions, or even descriptions."

I opened the text to the first page, "Prince Cinders was not much of a prince." As I read this, I made my left hand flat, like a page, and with my right hand I made a "period" on the "page." I read on, "He was small, spotty, scruffy, and skinny." As I read each description in the series, I made a comma on my palm and ended with a period. "See how Babette Cole is using commas in a series to tell us how to read that part by separating each description with a comma? Try it with me." I reread the page and invited this kids to punctuate in the air on imaginary pages.

Rally students to try adding commas in a series in their own drafts.

"Now it's your turn. Look in your draft for the places where you've listed items, actions, or descriptions in a series of words. Make sure that you are adding commas to your list because this, too, tells your reader exactly how to read your piece. Not only will you do this now, you'll need to do this as a writer for the rest of your life."

Editing with an Eye Out for Broken Patterns

ear Teachers,

Today, there might be a buzz in the air. Drafts are most likely chock-full of revisions, evidence of rethinking that you and your students should be proud of! Children are probably sensing the end of the unit drawing near and are itching to celebrate their hard work with an audience of readers.

We honor and harness this energy to celebrate, and use it to create an authentic sense of purpose and drive to edit. One way to create purpose for editing is to make a real-life comparison. For instance, before having a friend over to play, you clean your room. Or before arriving for school picture day, you double-check your outfit to make sure things are just right. Before an important event, like publishing in a writing unit, it's important to pause, edit, and make sure you put your best foot forward.

You'll want to devote your final editing session to addressing issues most of your students seem to be struggling with. If your students need help with paragraphing or using quotation marks to offset dialogue, you'll want to start there.

One angle you might take when researching for trends is to look for breaks in patterns. That is to say, look for places students veer off the path in their writing. Perhaps they started out strongly, writing consistently in the past tense, but then with more and more dialogue, students fell out of writing in past tense and continued writing in present tense. Or perhaps students used paragraphs consistently in the beginning of their writing, but as they continued they got swept away and forgot to indent and format paragraphs. Just as it is important for you to notice when students break patterns of good writing, it's crucial for students to learn how to find the breaks in patterns, or inconsistencies, in their writing.

So today, you'll want to help writers find the pattern breaks in their writing. The session embraces the spirit that students know how to do a lot of things in their writing, grammatically and mechanically speaking; they might just struggle keeping it consistent across the scenes of their fairy tale. Essentially, the rallying cry of this session is to "Keep up the good work!"

COMMON CORE STATE STANDARDS: W.3.5, RL.3.2, SL.3.1, L.3.1.e, L.3.1, L.3.2

You'll want to teach students to find places in their writing where they veer off course and break a pattern of good writing. Specifically, writers might look for places in their writing where they become lax and drop the use of a writing move they know how to make. Then you'll want to teach them to find ways to put the writing back on track, using what they know about good writing.

MINILESSON

After children bring their rough drafts to the rug, you might draw their attention to a familiar nursery rhyme. You might alter this nursery rhyme to fall out of its rhyming pattern and encourage children to wonder what went wrong. You could say something like, "Hickory dickory dock, the mouse ran up the *plate*" or "Twinkle twinkle little star, how I wonder *where you live.*"

Children may respond by saying that the nursery rhyme doesn't sound right, or they may notice that it doesn't rhyme. You might draw their attention to the fact that a piece of writing goes off course when a pattern breaks—in this case, the broken pattern is the rhyme scheme. As they edit, writers look for lots of different patterns in their writing. You might suggest that students read their writing with an eye out for broken patterns, thinking about what they need to do to mend the breaks.

You might say something like, "Writers, today I want to teach you that writers try to carry good writing across a whole piece. Writers look back over rough drafts, noting the places where a pattern of good writing is broken. Then, they ask, 'How may I edit my writing to mend the broken pattern and fix the mess-ups, keeping the good writing going?'"

You might decide to distribute copies of a piece of demonstration writing that breaks common grammatical or mechanical patterns similar to students' inconsistencies. Only you will know what these patterns might be—you'll have studied your students' writing and made yourself a short list of common mistakes. You'll want to stock your demonstration piece with mistakes that are similar to the mistakes you notice students making. You could then demonstrate how to find a pattern break by rereading the first part of this piece of writing aloud, noticing a mistake—a broken pattern—and figuring out what to do to fix it.

You might set children up to read the next small section of the piece and work on noticing and correcting the pattern break with a partner. You might guide students to discuss *how they noticed* a pattern break with their partner, and *how they corrected it*. You'll then send students off to do this work in their own pieces, reminding themselves that all writers break patterns of good writing. The editing process is a built-in safety net that provides time to catch the places where they lose steam and fall out of a good pattern of writing.

CONFERRING AND SMALL-GROUP WORK

You might feel like a lifeguard during this session—scanning the room, keeping your eyes peeled for trouble. One common trend you may find as you circulate the classroom is that students might struggle with fixing a grammatical or mechanical pattern break. That is, students might find the place where they veer off course in their writing, but lack the strategies to put themselves back on track. If this is the case, you'll want to have a few fix-it strategies up your sleeves to coach students back on course. Fortunately, you'll have time prior to the lesson to identify the trends of your classroom and anticipate fix-it strategies. Following are a few common pattern breaks and strategies to help.

You might see students struggling with self-correcting a slip in tense. A young writer might realize that she started her fairy tale classically in the past tense, with *Once upon a time*, but after a few rounds of dialogue—which is typically in the present tense—she continued telling the story in present tense. In one instance, I gathered Jose and Gio together, as they were struggling with this issue and getting back on course. I sat between them and explained that writers make decisions about whether their story is *happening*, using verbs in the present tense, or whether it has *happened*, using verbs in the past tense. In the case of fairy tales, I continued, writers usually decide to write the story as if it already happened, using past tense. The important thing is to make sure that you are not breaking from the pattern. One way to do this is to create a T-chart with two columns, one for the present and past tense verbs you are using, and then to use the chart as a guide to make sure you are consistently using verbs in the past tense. I quickly sketched a T-chart on my clipboard and together we began pulling verbs from their drafts, figuring out the present and past tense for each verb.

Present Tense	Past Tense
Today my character . . .	In the past my character . . .
is	was
wants	wanted
loves	loved
names	named
says	said
sleeps	slept

You also might see students noticing an inconsistency with their use of quotation marks around dialogue. The sheer volume of dialogue could be enough to prevent a child from seamlessly reentering their piece and getting back on course. It might be overwhelming to start self-correcting if the piece has a high amount of dialogue or is filled with short bursts of dialogue with many different speakers. For example, as I walked past Cora's desk, I watched her editing pen hovering over a place in her writing that contained unquoted dialogue.

I sat alongside Cora and voiced over what I imagined her thinking. "It can be a little overwhelming, huh?" Cora nodded quietly. I continued. "By the way you're holding your editing pen, I can tell you're ready to swoop in and make some changes. But something's in the way. . . ." Cora picked up on the invitation to share. "I dunno where to start," she said.

"Ah, the case of the confusing dialogue, I see," I sympathized. "Here's one of my tricks. When I start to get overwhelmed by having so much dialogue to fix, I look for a few things. First, I find words like *said*, *asked*, or *answered*. Those words—dialogue tags—are signals to remind me where all my great dialogue lives in my writing. I can zoom in on those words, read the sentence before it and the sentence after it. That way, when I'm editing, I catch all the little places I may have forgotten quotation marks."

Cora and I went on to circle all the dialogue tags across the pages of her draft, creating a guide that would help her get started.

MID-WORKSHOP TEACHING

You may want to give students a final opportunity to make sure this piece carries as many good writing patterns as possible. You may let them know that pattern breaks are sometimes hard to catch on their own because they are so familiar with the piece of writing. Set them up to trade drafts with a writing partner to help each other find pattern breaks in each other's writing. You might ask them to even note patterns their partner carries throughout the piece; this action not only names the inconsistencies but also brings awareness to internalized or consistent grammatical or mechanical patterns.

SHARE

You may decide to have students reflect on the types of grammatical or mechanical patterns they tend to break in their writing and how to mend those patterns. That is, writers might reflect by writing, *I used to be the type of writer who broke the pattern of* _____. *But now I know how to mend that pattern by* _____. Bringing awareness to the inconsistencies of grammatical or mechanical patterns helps writers take ownership over their writing and the editing process.

Happy coaching,

Lucy, Maggie, Shana

Happily Ever After
A Fairy Tale Celebration

 ear Teachers,

Just as the first celebration of the year was a momentous occasion, the last celebration of the year is equally powerful! Your students have ended the year with a bang as they produced pages of writing, tackled multiple revisions, learned from a variety of mentor texts, and perhaps most importantly, studied how to tell and write a good story! As you step back to revel in your students' writing progress and accomplishments, it is important to recognize the fruits of your collective labor, not just from this unit of study, but from the entire year or writing. Today, indeed, is a milestone.

This session springs from the oral tradition of fairy tales, providing children with the opportunity to read their published fairy tales to others. Specifically, this session invites you to form storytelling circles, where a small group of four to six writers mixes with a small group of audience members, perhaps a younger class; a class of second-grade students would be perfect. This way, children get to lean on the rich storytelling and acting they used earlier in the unit and perform for a real audience, following the footsteps of fairy tales' storytelling history. Leading up to the celebration, you might also want to again show video excerpts of youth storytelling performances as a way to provide inspiration and a vision in which to model the storytelling circles. Children could watch a performance, taking note of performance tips they want to fold into their own storytelling performance.

You could recreate some of that fairy tale magic and transform your classroom into a fairy tale village for the day. Prior to the celebration, perhaps children chip in during recess and after school to paint a backdrop of a castle or village or deep, dark forest. Or children could draw some of their favorite characters from classic fairy tales, such as Little Red Riding Hood or the three little pigs, and hang them up around the room. You could invite children to bring in props that accompany their tales, such as a crown, a magic wand, and a shiny red apple, to use as they tell their stories. You might download a soundtrack to popular movie versions of fairy tales to have playing as children enter the room for the celebration.

COMMON CORE STATE STANDARDS: W.3.6, RFS.3.4, SL.3.1, SL.3.4, SL.3.6, SL.4.4, L.3.6

At this point in the year, your students will be familiar with the joyful ritual of writing celebrations. And, most likely, they'll be at the edge of their seats, excited to share their best fairy tales with a real audience. Adding a theatrical twist might be a way to add something extra special. The fairy tales unit is perfect for creating a magical, whimsical celebration that invites young writers to celebrate with a *Happily ever after!*

BEFORE THE CELEBRATION

The day before your celebration (or earlier, if you prefer), you might say something like, "Writers, our last author celebration is right around the corner. For this final writing celebration, we are going to make our room into a magical fairy tale land, and we're going to invite the second-graders to come listen as you share your fairy tales in storytelling circles! Just think, the second-graders are almost third-graders. You have an important job—you will be introducing them to the exciting world of fairy tale writing that they'll get to try next year!

You might continue, "During the celebration, we'll break up into small groups and form storytelling circles—small circles including both authors and audience members. You'll want to do some of your best storytelling tomorrow, using all that you learned about storytelling and acting earlier in this unit. So tonight, practice reading aloud your published fairy tale in your best storyteller's voice. It's almost like you're like actors preparing for a play; you want to rehearse your lines as much as possible tonight, so that you discover your best storytelling voice! Ask your families to listen to your story-tell, call a friend and practice storytelling on the phone, line up your stuffed animals and practice with them, or even record yourself storytelling and then listen or watch yourself!"

You'll want to set this up in the way that works best for you and your students. Some teachers prefer to give students time to practice storytelling and to prepare the room for the celebration during the several days leading up to the event. Others prefer to have students prepare at home. Do what makes the most sense for you and your students.

You'll want to have your students arranged in their storytelling circles before you begin the lesson so that they are ready when their guests arrive. You'll have budgeted a few minutes to set your students up for the celebration before inviting the audience in.

THE CELEBRATION

Before guests arrive, tell your students the "fairy tale" of their own journey as writers during this unit. You might say something like this: "Once upon a time, there were twenty-eight writers. The writers set off on a journey to become fairy tale writers. Their journey first led them to the land of their favorite tales. They followed in the footsteps of the familiar stories they've heard since they were small. These twenty-eight writers added their own twists to make these tales unique and new. They had written their first fairy tale adaptations! But their journey was not yet over. They continued on, in search of the tools and magic they needed to write their own original tales. Some days, the journey was smooth and joyful. Other days, there was trouble, and the journey was slow and challenging. On some days, writers struggled to find the perfect word to use. On other days, writers had to use every mental muscle they had to create the perfect ending, one that fit with the rest of the tale. The writers learned how to stitch scenes together with narration. They learned to tie characters' small actions to important objects. They learned to embed magic in the heart of the story. And in the end, the writers prevailed. The twenty-eight writers, each and every one of them, wrote and published an original fairy tale.

"And you know what happened in the end? They all continued to write—fairy tales and other stories—and they all lived happily ever after! But you know what they did before they lived happily ever after? They celebrated their writing!"

Remind students of the oral tradition of fairy tales and set up the celebration to follow in those footsteps, at this point. You might say something like, "Today, writers, we join an ancient club of writers. Fairy tales have existed for hundreds and hundreds of years across many cultures. You see, other cultures and countries have their own versions of some of our favorite fairy tales. *The Rough-Face Girl* by Rafe Martin (1998) is a *Cinderella* story told by the Algonquin Native Americans. *Yeh-Shen* by Ai-Ling Louie (1996) is a *Cinderella* story from China. Some of these tales are so ancient that they weren't written down—they stayed alive by being told out loud, passed down from generation to generation. So today, you are going to join that tradition and read aloud your fairy tales as a way to celebrate your hard work!"

At this point, you may decide to give students a moment to rehearse, reminding them of all they learned about storytelling and acting. You could say, "Authors, you are sitting in your storytelling circles and your audience is just about to come through those doors, into our magic fairy tale world! Let's get ready for our best performance yet and warm up our storytelling and acting muscles! Take a moment to practice reading the beginning of your fairy tale to a partner. Remember, play with your voice—should it be louder or softer as you read? What about gestures? Could you add hand or face gestures as you read?"

After a bit of rehearsal, you could stop students and prepare them for the arrival of the guests. Invite the younger class in and split them up among the storytelling circles. You might play fairy tale theme music, like the soundtrack to *Cinderella*, as the students find their spots.

When students settle, you could announce "Ladies and gentlemen! Royal kingdom! Loyal townsfolk! Let us begin our fairy tale celebration! Guests, you are an important part of our special fairy tale storytelling celebration. I'm sure we'll want to celebrate each author after they read. To keep the storytelling circle moving, I invite you to offer a quick, quiet cheer after each read. Let me teach you a few.

"First, there is the 'quiet raindrops' cheer." You could snap your fingers gently, inviting the children to try. "Next, the 'spirit fingers' cheer." Hold up both hands and wave your fingers. "Last, there's the 'round of applause.'" Clap your hands lightly, forming a circle in the air. "You may choose which cheer to offer each writer as a congratulations! And now . . . let the fairy tale celebration begin!"

AFTER THE CELEBRATION

After the audience has left, you could gather the class and say something like, "Wow! We turned our room into fairy tale land, didn't we? Not only have you transformed into excellent fairy tale writers, you have become stronger writers in general. The things you have learned about writing strong fairy tales are things you may carry with you as you write other stories throughout the rest of your lives! I could hear evidence of all of your hard work as writers—both in this unit and across this entire year—as you read. And now, authors, I'm wondering if you'd like to publish a collection. In the writing world, authors publish their writing together from time to time. Each author contributes a piece of writing to create a book full of stories, essays, excerpts, or poems—this is called an *anthology*. And creating an anthology of fairy tales into one big class collection feels like a perfect way to end the unit."

The way you gather the stories into an anthology is entirely up to you. You may want to alphabetize the stories, write up a table of contents, and ask students to create a cover. If you've got several willing cover designers, you might decide to make multiple copies. In fact, it's a good idea to make at least one backup copy as the audience of readers expands to other classroom libraries.

You might say to the chidren, "After a few days of keeping our collection all to ourselves, let's loan it to different classrooms. It will be a moving collection! Many people will get to read our writing. What a way to end the year, authors!"

If you've the inclination and the resources, you may even want to make a copy for each student to take home. They and their loved ones will undoubtedly treasure it.

Following are several examples of students' finished fairy tales. Enjoy!

Lucy, Shana, and Maggie

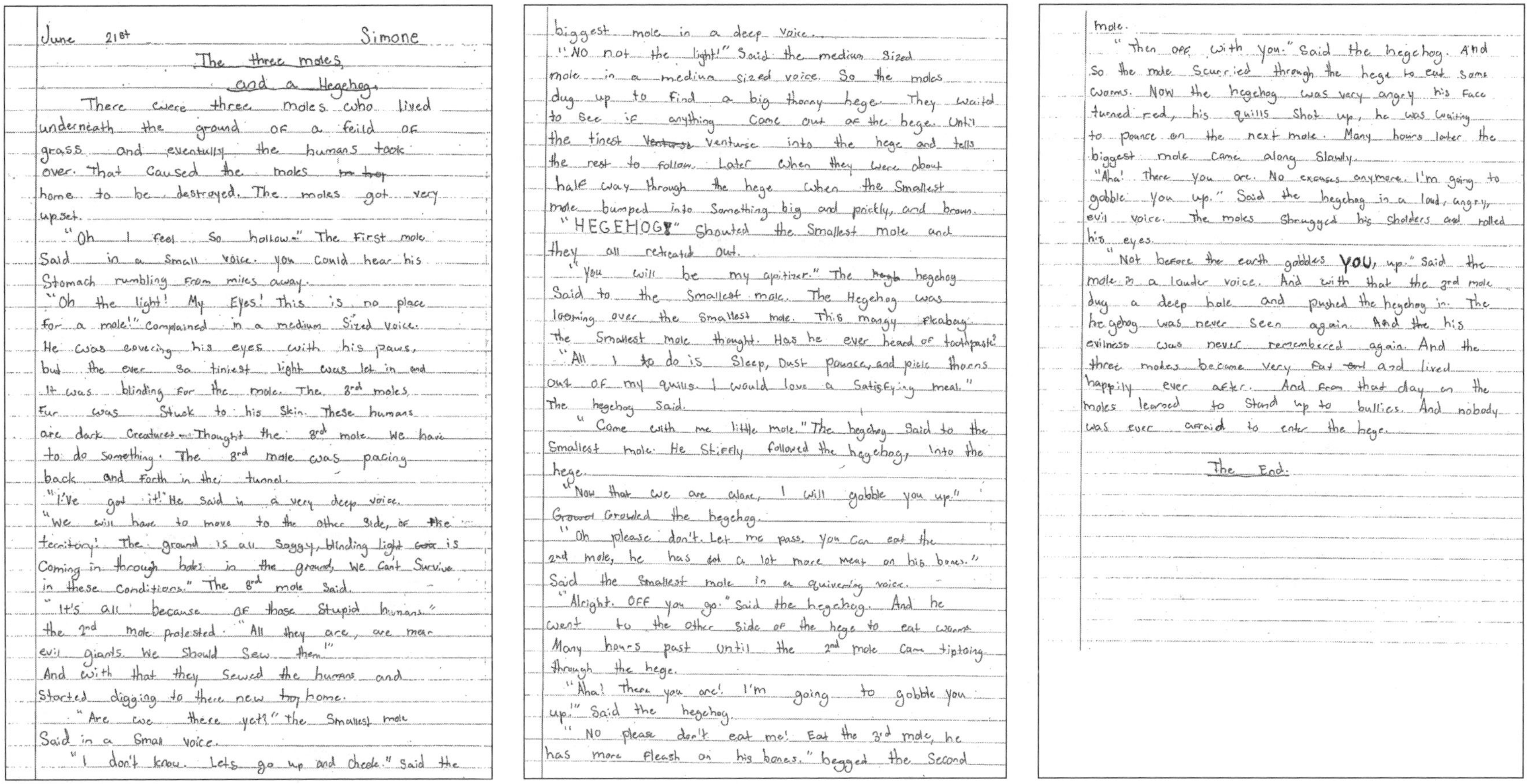

June 21st   Simone

The three moles
and a Hegehog.

There were three moles who lived underneath the ground of a feild of grass and eventually the humans took over. That caused the moles to top home to be destroyed. The moles got very upset.

"Oh I feel so hollow." The First mole said in a small voice. You could hear his stomach rumbling from miles away.

"Oh the light! My Eyes! This is no place for a mole." Complained in a medium sized voice. He was covering his eyes with his paws, but the ever so tiniest light was let in and it was blinding for the mole. The 3rd moles fur was stuck to his skin. These humans are dark creatures thought the 3rd mole. We have to do something. The 3rd mole was pacing back and forth in their tunnel.

"I've got it!" He said in a very deep voice. "We will have to move to the other side of the territory. The ground is all saggy, blinding light is coming in through holes in the ground. We can't survive in these conditions." The 3rd mole said.

"It's all because of those stupid humans." the 2nd mole protested "All they are, are mean evil giants. We should sew them."

And with that they sewed the humans and started digging to there new top home.

"Are we there yet?" the smallest mole said in a small voice.

"I don't know. Lets go up and check." said the

biggest mole in a deep voice.

"No not the light!" Said the medium sized mole in a medium sized voice. So the moles dug up to find a big thorny hege. They waited to see if anything come out of the hege. Until the tinest ventured venture into the hege and tells the rest to follow. Later when they were about half way through the hege when the smallest mole bumped into something big and prickly, and brown.

"HEGEHOG!" shouted the smallest mole and they all retreated out.

"You will be my apitizer." The hegh hegehog said to the smallest mole. The Hegehog was looming over the smallest mole. This maggy pleabag the smallest mole thought. Has he ever heard of toothpaste?

"All I to do is sleep, dust pounce, and pick thorns out of my quills. I would love a satisfying meal." The hegehog said.

"Come with me little mole." The hegehog said to the smallest mole. He stiffly followed the hegehog into the hege.

"Now that we are alone, I will gobble you up." Growed growled the hegehog.

"Oh please don't let me pass. You can eat the 2nd mole, he has got a lot more meat on his bones." Said the smallest mole in a quivering voice.

"Alright. Off you go." Said the hegehog. And he went to the other side of the hege to eat worms. Many hours past until the 2nd mole came tiptoing through the hege.

"Aha! There you are! I'm going to gobble you up!" Said the hegehog.

"No please don't eat me! Eat the 3rd mole, he has more fleash on his bones." begged the Second

mole.

"Then off with you." Said the hegehog. And so the mole scurried through the hege to eat some worms. Now the hegehog was very angry his face turned red, his quills shot up, he was waiting to pounce on the next mole. Many hours later the biggest mole came along slowly.

"Aha! There you are. No excuses anymore. I'm going to gobble you up." Said the hegehog in a loud, angry, evil voice. The moles shrugged his sholders and rolled his eyes.

"Not before the earth gobbles YOU, up." Said the mole in a louder voice. And with that the 3rd mole dug a deep hole and pushed the hegehog in. The hegehog was never seen again. And the his evilness was never remembered again. And the three moles became very fat and and lived happily ever after. And from that day on the moles learned to stand up to bullies. And nobody was ever afraid to enter the hege.

The End.

FIG. 20-1   Simone's final piece

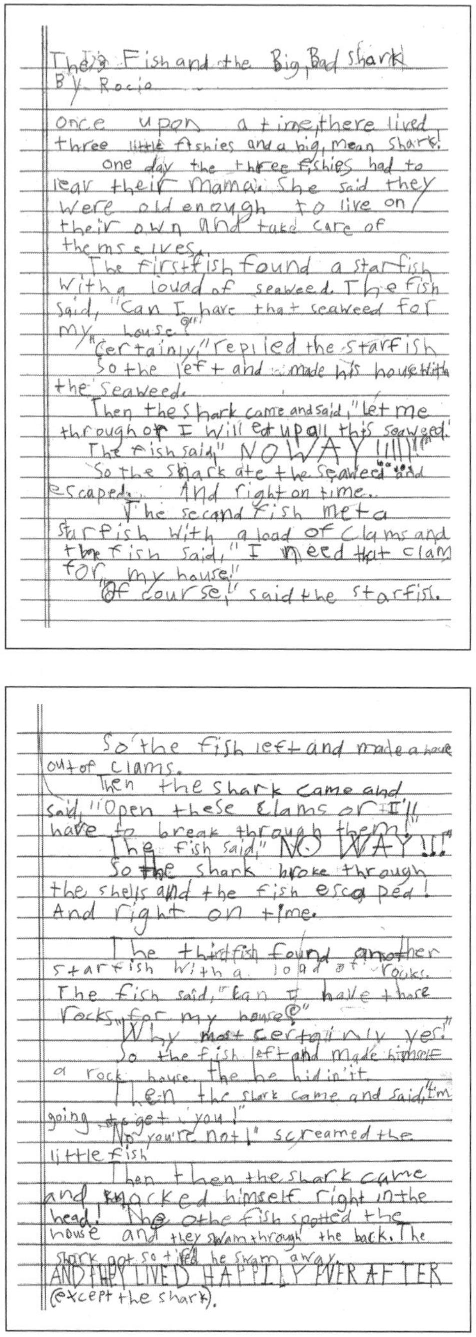

The Fish and the Big, Bad Shark

by Rocio

Once upon a time, there lived three little fishies and a big, mean shark!

One day the three fishies had to leave their mama. She said they were old enough to live on their own and take care of themselves.

The first fish found a starfish with a load of seaweed. The fish said, "Can I have that seaweed for my house?"

"Certainly," replied the starfish. So he left and made his house with the seaweed.

Then the shark came and said, "Let me through or I will eat up all this seaweed." The fish said, "NO WAY!!!!"

So the shark ate the seaweed and [the fish] escaped. And right on time.

The second fish met a starfish with a load of clams and the fish said, "I need that clam for my house."

"Of course," said the starfish.

So the fish left and made a house out of clams.

Then the shark came and said, "Open these clams or I'll have to break through them!"

The fish said, "NO WAY!!!"

So the shark broke through the shells and the fish escaped! And right on time.

The third fish found another starfish with a load of rocks. The fish said, "Can I have those rocks for my house?"

"Why most certainly yes!"

So the fish left and made himself a rock house. Then he hid in it.

Then the shark came and said, "I'm going to get you!"

"No you're not!" screamed the little fish.

Then the shark came and knocked himself right in the head! The other fish spotted the house and they swam through the back. The shark got so tired he swam away.

AND THEY LIVED HAPPILY EVER AFTER (except the shark).

FIG. 20–2   Rocio's final piece

Usher's New Outfit

by Zander

Once upon a time there was a big, white, fancy mansion. In the big, white, fancy mansion slept a singer named Usher. Usher loved clothes so much that his closet was bigger than his room! He could not get enough clothes.

One day Usher woke up and rolled off his king-sized bed in his pin striped, designer p.j.s. As he walked to his humongous closet he admired all the famous pictures of himself hanging on the walls. After he put on his outfit he walked to the mirror and thought, "Too dull, too bland, too boring." He tried on another outfit and thought, "Too dull, too bland, too boring." He tried on another outfit and thought, "I must wear something. This dull and boring outfit will have to do."

Usher really wanted something new and muttered out loud, "I must be cool. I must be hip. I need a new outfit." He picked up his blue cell phone, called his designer, and yelled, "I must be cool, I must be hip, I need a new outfit." The designer paused and in a scared voice said, "I'm sorry . . . we won't have the material for a . . . uh . . . a . . . month." Usher slammed the phone closed. "I must tell my public what I need. People put posters up on telephone poles all the time. I'll do that!" He thought as he raced off.

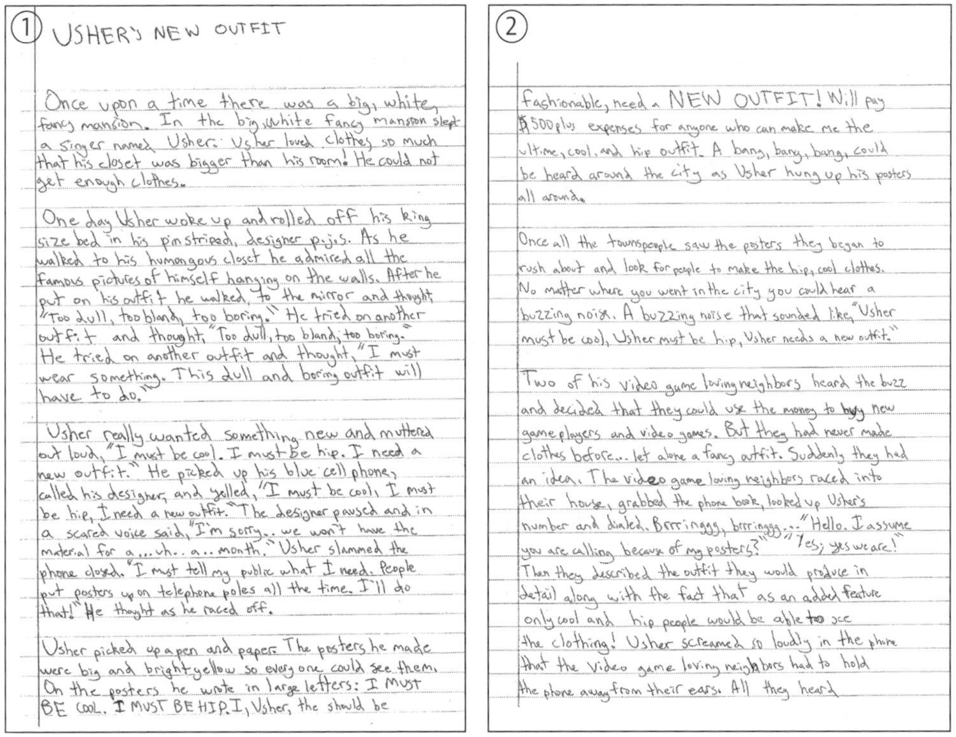

FIG. 20–3   Zander's final piece

Usher picked up a pen and paper. The posters he made were big and bright yellow so everyone could see them. On the posters he wrote in large letters; I MUST BE COOL. I MUST BE HIP. I, Usher, should be fashionable, need a NEW OUTFIT! Will pay $500 plus expenses for anyone who can make me the ultimate, cool and hip outfit. A bang, bang, bang could be heard around the city as Usher hung up his posters all around.

Once all the townspeople saw the posters they began to rush about and look for people to make the hip, cool clothes. No matter where you went in the city you could hear a buzzing noise. A buzzing noise that sounded like, "Usher must be cool, Usher must be hip, Usher needs a new outfit."

Two of his video game loving neighbors heard the buzz and decided that they could use the money to buy new game players and video games. But they had never made clothes before . . . let alone a fancy outfit. Suddenly they had an idea. The video game-loving neighbors raced in to their house, grabbed the phone book, looked up Usher's number and dialed. Brrringgg, brrringg. . . . "Hello. I assume you are calling because of my posters?" "Yes, yes we are!" Then they described the outfit they would produce in detail along with the fact that as an added feature only cool and hip people would be able to see the clothing! Usher screamed so loudly in the phone that the video game-loving neighbors had to hold the phone away from their ears. All they heard was Usher yelling, "I will be cool, I will be hip . . . I AM getting a new outfit!" The newly hired fake tailors think to themselves, "It was so easy to trick Usher into thinking we could actually make the clothes! Ha! And now he is going to fork over the $500 dollars!"

A day later Usher decides he must figure out how the work was going. He was way too excited. He decided to send his cool and awesome stage manager to check in on the clothes. The cool and awesome stage manager walked into the fake tailors' house. He saw them threading into nothingness. He was puzzled but being scared of not being cool and hip he pretended he could see the clothes. The fake tailors said, "Isn't this amazing!? I bet you'd want to have clothes as fine as these!?" In reply the stage manager said, "Well . . . duh! Yes, of course I would!" A little while later the stage manager said to Usher, "You've definitely hired magnificent tailors!" Usher asked, "Are they cool and hip?" "Yes, yes they are cool. Yes, yes they are hip!" said the stage manager.

In the next week or so Usher sent two of his cool and awesome stage crew members to see how the clothes were doing. They both returned with the same report. Yes the clothes were cool. Yes the clothes were hip. Then the person who went to see the clothes also told Usher the outfit could be picked up anytime Usher felt like it. Usher raced out the door, across the street, and into the home of the fake tailors.

When he ran into the room the first thing he saw were the tailors admiring an empty plastic bag. He thought, "Brilliant. I can't see them yet. This makes sense because I am not cool . . . not hip but once I have my new outfit I will be!" Once the outfit was in his hands he couldn't believe what an amazingly cool and hip outfit they had created. "Amazing, I am now the coolest, hippest person on earth!" Usher never even wore the clothes before the upcoming, big concert because he didn't want them to wrinkle. After all, the concert in Madison Square Garden was just two days away!

On the day of the performance Usher's nerves were so high that every time he looked in the mirror he saw himself wearing the coolest, hippest outfit of all time. Suddenly he heard his fans chanting, "Usher! Usher! Usher!" He decided it was time to go out on stage. As the crowd saw him the noise tripled in volume as they began to shout, "Wow. His clothes are so cool! His clothes are so hip!" Then out of nowhere a voice that was louder than the rest shouted, "Nice teddy bear boxers Usher!" The crowd became so silent all that could be heard was the chirping of two tiny crickets. To his complete shock Usher looked down and saw that he was in fact wearing nothing but his teddy bear boxers. The crowd realized it too! Now all that could be heard was laughter. Usher turned completely red and walked off stage feeling ashamed and embarrassed. The last thing he heard was the crowd demanding their money back.

Usher learned that day that wearing something dull and boring was better than wearing nothing at all.

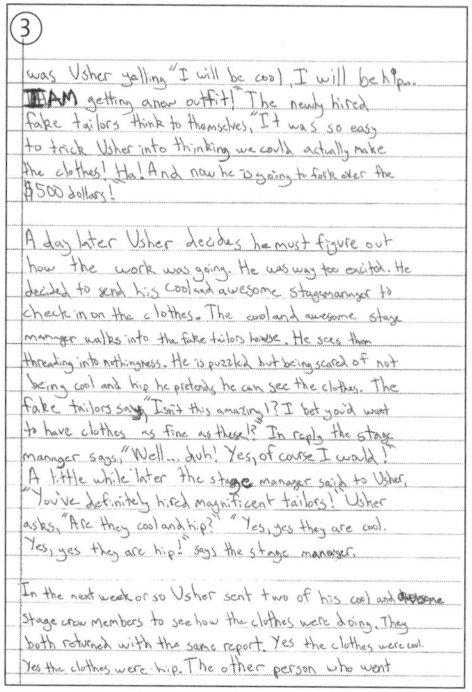

③

was Usher yelling "I will be cool, I will be hip... I AM getting a new outfit!" The newly hired fake tailors think to themselves, "It was so easy to trick Usher into thinking we could actually make the clothes! Ha! And now he is going to fork over the $500 dollars!

A day later Usher decides he must figure out how the work was going. He was way too excited. He decided to send his cool and awesome stagemanager to check in on the clothes. The cool and awesome stage manager walks into the fake tailors house. He sees them threading into nothingness. He is puzzled but being scared of not being cool and hip he pretends he can see the clothes. The fake tailors says, "Isn't this amazing!? I bet you'd want to have clothes as fine as these!?" In reply the stage manager says, "Well... duh! Yes, of course I would! A little while later the stage manager said to Usher, "You've definitely hired magnificent tailors!" Usher asks, "Are they cool and hip?" "Yes, yes they are cool. Yes, yes they are hip!" says the stage manager.

In the next week or so Usher sent two of his cool and awesome stage crew members to see how the clothes were doing. They both returned with the same report. Yes the clothes were cool. Yes the clothes were hip. The other person who went

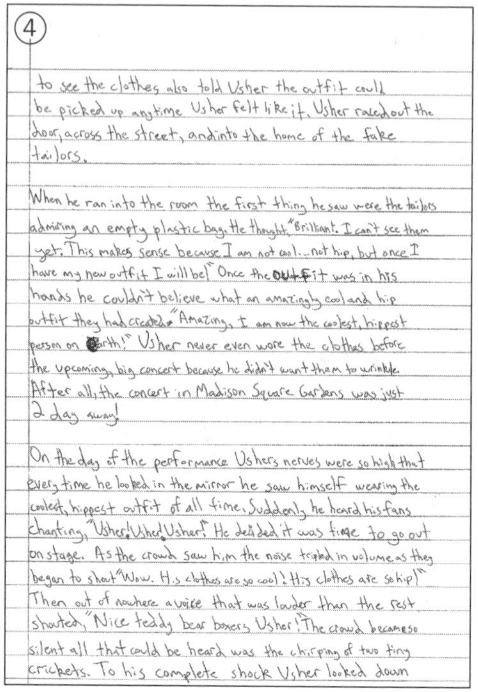

FIG. 20–3 (Continued)

④

to see the clothes also told Usher the outfit could be picked up anytime Usher felt like it. Usher raced out the door, across the street, and into the home of the fake tailors.

When he ran into the room the first thing he saw were the tailors admiring an empty plastic bag. He thought "Brilliant. I can't see them yet. This makes sense because I am not cool... not hip, but once I have my new outfit I will be!" Once the OUTFIT was in his hands he couldn't believe what an amazingly cool and hip outfit they had created. "Amazing, I am now the coolest, hippest person on earth!" Usher never even wore the clothes before the upcoming, big concert because he didn't want them to wrinkle. After all, the concert in Madison Square Gardens was just 2 days away!

On the day of the performance Ushers nerves were so high that every time he looked in the mirror he saw himself wearing the coolest, hippest outfit of all time. Suddenly, he heard his fans chanting, "Usher! Usher! Usher!" He decided it was time to go out on stage. As the crowd saw him the noise tripled in volume as they began to shout "Wow. His clothes are so cool! His clothes are so hip!" Then out of nowhere a voice that was louder than the rest shouted, "Nice teddy bear boxers Usher! The crowd became so silent all that could be heard was the chirping of two tiny crickets. To his complete shock Usher looked down

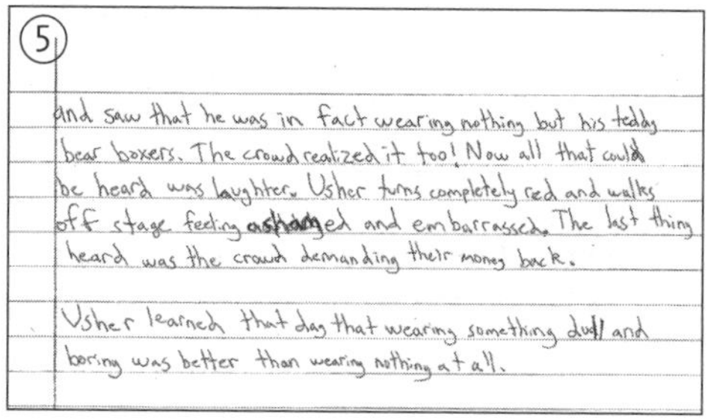

⑤

And saw that he was in fact wearing nothing but his teddy bear boxers. The crowd realized it too! Now all that could be heard was laughter. Usher turns completely red and walks off stage feeling ashamed and embarrassed. The last thing heard was the crowd demanding their money back.

Usher learned that day that wearing something dull and boring was better than wearing nothing at all.

Zander, the Evil Step Parents and the Trip to Disney World

Andrew

Once upon a time there was a kid named Zander. Zander was a clever boy. He was so clever that he could solve a rubix cube with his eyes closed, one hand tied behind his back, hopping on one leg! He also loved to read so much that he read ten hours a day! He could also ride a five-foot unicycle, staying in one spot doing the chicken dance! But the one thing he wanted to do was go to Disney World. But his <u>Evil</u> <u>Step</u> parents wouldn't let him go.

Then one beautiful day he went up to his evil, cruel step parents and said, "I want to go to Disney World." They said, "Well . . . you don't have a ticket you little ragamuffin. So how are you going to go to Disney World?" Then they laughed. Then Zander was clever and he came up with a brilliant idea! He thought "I will buy a ticket." The evil step parents rolled their eyes and shook their heads like it was an impossible task.

Zander walked out the door to the day care center where he saw a help wanted sign. In he went and said, "Can I please apply for the job?" Zander was excited when the owner said, "You got the job." For five days he worked and worked. At the end of his five days the owner was so impressed they paid him a ticket to go to Disney World.

Zander went back to his house and showed the ticket and said, "I got a ticket!" They said, "Well . . . you got a ticket but you don't have a way to get there you little ragamuffin. . . . so you can't go!" Zander didn't let this stop him but he's not 100% sure what to do. Then he went over to his friend's house who doesn't read well. So he asked, "Do you want help with your reading?" His friend said, "Yes please!" So then all day he taught his friend how to read. Then his friend's parents were so happy that they paid him their old car!

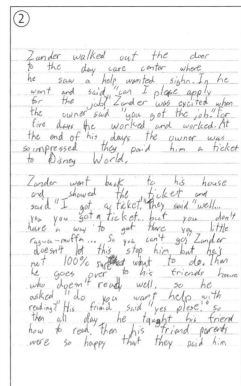

FIG. 20–4 Andrew's final piece

Zander goes back inside and shakes the keys. Jingle, Jingle, Jingle heard the Evil step parents. Zander said, "I've got a car!" The Evil step parents chins' hit the floor! "Well . . . you might have a ticket and a car but you don't have a chaperone and we are NOT going with you, you little ragamuffin!" Again, Zander remembered that he has a friend that wants to learn to ride a unicycle. He raced over to his friends house and asked while panting, "Do you want to learn to ride a unicycle?" His friend said, "Yes please!" All day Zander taught his friend how to ride a unicycle. His friend was so excited he said "Let's show my parents my learned hard skills!" He rode into the kitchen where his parents were making dinner. His parents immediately froze and said, "Thank you for teaching our son to ride a unicycle. Would you like to come to Disney World with us?" Zander excitedly said, "Yes, Yes, Yes!"

"Wait one minute," Zander said. "I need to go back and tell my parents." He ran home faster than ever and said, "I got a ticket, a car and a chaperone!" The evil step parents can't believe their ears. They said, "Well . . . you may have gotten a ticket and you may have gotten a car, and you may have gotten a chaperone . . . but, but, but. . . ." "You didn't get in my way," said Zander before they could say anything more. Then off Zander went to Disney World with his ticket, his car, and his friend.

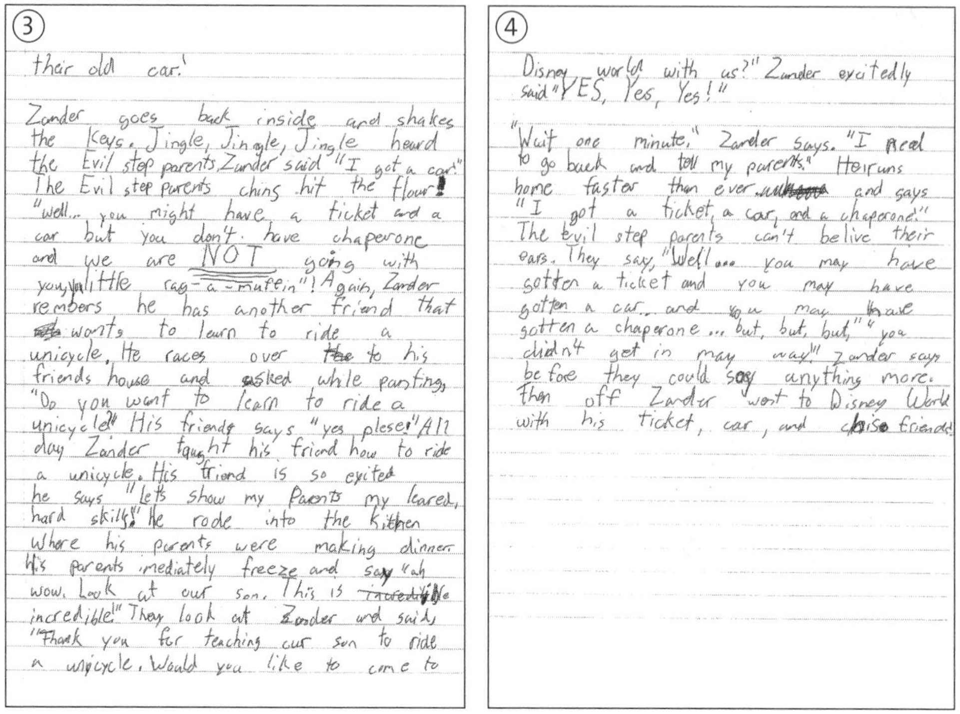

③

their old car!

Zander goes back inside and shakes the keys, Jingle, Jingle, Jingle heard the Evil step parents. Zander said "I got a car" The Evil step parents chins hit the floor! "Well.. you might have a ticket and a car but you don't have chaperone and we are NOT going with you, little rag-a-mufein"! Again, Zander rembers he has another friend that wonts to learn to ride a unicycle. He races over to his friends house and asked while panting, "Do you wont to learn to ride a unicycle" His friends says "yes plese!" All day Zander taught his friend how to ride a unicycle. His friend is so excited he says "Lets show my parents my leared, hard skills!" He rode into the kitchen where his parents were making dinner His parents mediately freeze and say "ah wow, Look at our son. This is incredible!" They look at Zander and said "Thank you for teaching our son to ride a unicycle. Would you like to come to

④

Disney world with us?" Zander excitedly said "YES, Yes, Yes!"

"Wait one minute," Zander says. "I need to go back and tell my parents." He runs home faster than ever and says "I got a ticket, a car, and a chaperone." The Evil step parents can't belive their ears. They say, "Well... you may have gotten a ticket and you may have gotten a chaperone... but, but, but," "you didn't get in may way!" Zander says before they could say anything more. Then off Zander went to Disney World with his ticket, car, and close friend!

FIG. 20-4   (Continued)

Breana and the Bathing Suit
Cora

Once upon a time there was a girl named Breana. She loved to swim. Even though she was fast her sister Caroline was faster. She wished just once she could beat her sister.

As Breana was walking home from swim practice she passed her favorite store Dick's. Looking into the door she spotted a bathing suit with a blue and black scales. She was begging in her heart that it would not be too expensive. She looked down, but she spotted something in the corner of her eye. She stepped into the store. It smelled like new things and Breana loved that. Breana looked at the bathing suit with red fire on the sides and blue and black swirls. "That is the one I want!" Breana thought.

She picked up the picture on the side and said, "This will come in handy!"

She looked at the card and it read $129.99. "Rats," Breana said, knowing her parents wouldn't get it for her!

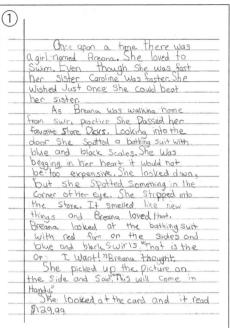

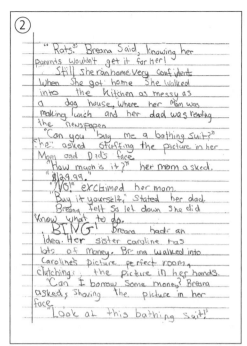

FIG. 20–5 Cora's final piece

Still she ran home very confident. When she got home she walked into the kitchen as messy as a doghouse, where her mom was making lunch and her dad was reading the newspaper.

"Can you buy me a bathing suit?" she asked stuffing the picture in her mom and dad's face.

"How much is it?" her mom asked.

"$129.99"

"No!" exclaimed her mom.

"Buy it yourself," stated her dad.

Breana felt so let down she did not know what to do.

BING! Breana had an idea. Her sister Caroline has lots of money. Breana walked into Caroline's picture perfect room, clutching the picture in her hands.

"Can I borrow some money?" Breana asked, shoving the picture in her face.

"Look at this bathing suit!" Breana said. Caroline gasped as she knew that was the magical bathing suit.

"Are you crazy? No!" shouted Caroline.

Breana was thinking, "I am never going to get that bathing suit!" Breana was feeling the world was not fair until . . .

Caroline said, "Work for it."

Later as Breana was sitting in a chair she had an idea: she could have a lemonade stand! She went downstairs and made lots of lemonade. Then Caroline walked in and Breana asked, "Could you put the sugar in the lemonade?"

"Sure," Caroline answered. But instead she put salt in. Finally Breana was outside.

A man said, "I will give you five dollars for a cup." The man took the cup and gave Breana five dollars. The man took a big gulp, "Deee-Gross!"

Breana gave the five dollars back. "What will I do?" and thought, I will never get the bathing suit.

Breana went for a walk and on the way saw a sign that said, "Sophie's Bakery Open—Hiring."

Breana said, "I want to do that," jumping up and down. She read the list, must be 11-18 years old, live three or less miles away and starts TOMORROW!

"I can do it," she thought out loud. She ran so fast she basically flew to the bakery.

Breana said, "I saw the sign, I want to do it."

"Okay," motioned Sophie, "Come right this way." Sophie walked into the kitchen and Breana followed.

"This is where you will work for now. You will be making cookies."

"Okay," Breana said. She went home and told her parents.

"Great," they said and Caroline smiled.

"Maybe I'll help a little bit," Caroline said mysteriously.

"Sure," Breana said too distracted to notice.

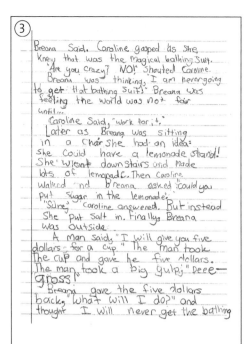

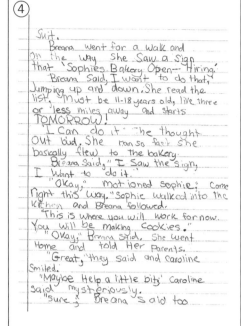

FIG. 20–5   (Continued)

"Time to go," Breana told Caroline, she was ready in a snap. When they got to the bakery they started right away. Caroline's job was to crack eggs, but instead of the eggs, she put in the shells. When Breana took the cookies to the tasters they yelled, "Disgusting! Gross! You are fired!"

Breana shuffled all the way home. Later she went to swim practice. When she got there she wished she had a bathing suit.

"Would you like to volunteer to help with the little kids?" asked her coach, "If you do a good job, I might give you a gift."

Breana accepted happily, "When should I come?"

"Tonight."

Breana could almost feel the magic on her skin.

Breana came prepared in her bathing suit ready to coach. Breana was nice to them, swam with them and did the strokes that they liked.

Breana's coach came and asked, "Can you come shopping? I know what you want."

Breana agreed. At the next practice Breanna was extra fast and smiled the whole time.

Well Caroline, she was not so happy . . .

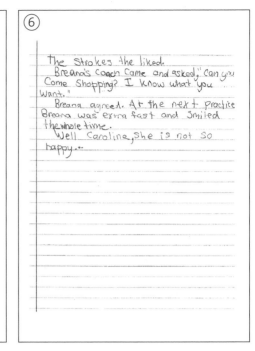

FIG. 20–5   (Continued)